W9-CBB-578

PRAISE FOR *THE LAST AGENT*

"The thriller equivalent of a *matryoshka* nesting doll: an outer layer of geopolitics; a deeper layer of intricate spycraft; and at its center, an unlikely CIA-FSB off-the-books alliance to save a brave Russian asset from the worst fate imaginable."

—Barry Eisler, *New York Times* bestselling author

"Dugoni supercharges his Charles Jenkins series with *The Last Agent*. Fast-paced and mesmerizing from start to finish, Dugoni flawlessly executes one of the best spy novels I've read in years. *The Last Agent* grabs you and doesn't let go—one twist and turn after another had me tearing through the pages."

—Steven Konkoly, *USA Today* bestselling author

PRAISE FOR *THE EIGHTH SISTER*

"*The Eighth Sister* is a great mix of spycraft and classic adventure, with a map of Moscow in hand."

—Martin Cruz Smith, international bestselling author

"Feels so fresh and authentic we could see the story breaking in the headlines tomorrow."

—Mark Sullivan, bestselling author of *Beneath a Scarlet Sky*

"Exhilarating . . . A tightly written, flawlessly executed espionage novel that takes the reader on a refreshingly unique, white-knuckle journey through the byzantine world of modern intelligence."

—Steven Konkoly, *USA Today* bestselling author

"A gripping thriller . . . [*The Eighth Sister*] is destined to be a classic in the genre, and Dugoni is arguably one of the best writers in the field right now."

—Associated Press

"With lean prose and spot-on local color, this plot-driven thriller pulses with tension and fraught escapes, the action capped by a courtroom drama as good as any from Grisham. A must-read for fans of legal thrillers and/or spy novels."

—*Library Journal* (starred review)

"Dugoni delivers an exceptionally gripping spy thriller that will keep readers on the edge of their seats."

—*Publishers Weekly* (starred review)

"[Dugoni] has outdone himself here, serving up a double-barrelled blast of action mixed with espionage in what's perhaps his most unputdownable thriller yet . . . Treason, moles, and plenty of misdirection . . . Robert Dugoni's *The Eighth Sister* is a high-stakes game between spies, and he doesn't take his foot off the gas pedal for a second."

—The Real Book Spy

"A marvelous read that begs for a sequel. There is more story to tell."

—*Missourian*

"*The Eighth Sister* is a taut thriller in the fine tradition of spy stories."

—Authorlink

"If you've eagerly devoured [Dugoni's] previous works for their cinematic pacing, tautly written thrills, and wonderfully developed characters, you're in for all of that and so much more with [*The Eighth Sister*]."

—Bookreporter

"The perfect pacing and brilliant intrigue of [*The Eighth Sister*] result in a page-turning, intelligent tale that will keep readers engaged until the very last page . . . The perfect combination of espionage, history, and quick-witted characters—a rare feat in the thriller genre."

—New York Journal of Books

"Dugoni's novel is, on all counts, a first-rate thriller!"

—Popular Culture Association

THE LAST AGENT

ALSO BY ROBERT DUGONI

The Extraordinary Life of Sam Hell

The 7th Canon

Damage Control

The Charles Jenkins Series

The Eighth Sister

The Tracy Crosswhite Series

My Sister's Grave

Her Final Breath

In the Clearing

The Trapped Girl

Close to Home

A Steep Price

A Cold Trail

The Academy (a short story)

Third Watch (a short story)

The David Sloane Series

The Jury Master

Wrongful Death

Bodily Harm

Murder One

The Conviction

Nonfiction

The Cyanide Canary (with Joseph Hilldorfer)

THE LAST AGENT

ROBERT DUGONI

THOMAS & MERCER

This is a work of fiction. Names, characters, organizations, places, events, and incidents are either products of the author's imagination or are used fictitiously. Any resemblance to actual persons, living or dead, or actual events is purely coincidental.

Published by Thomas & Mercer, Seattle

www.apub.com

ISBN-13: 9781542014984 (hardcover)
ISBN-10: 1542014980 (hardcover)

ISBN-13: 9781542014977 (paperback)
ISBN-10: 1542014972 (paperback)

Cover design by Kaitlin Kall

Printed in the United States of America

First edition

For my friend Martin Bantle
Martin passed away unexpectedly during the writing of this novel. He was just fifty-six years young. His death will always be a reminder that every day is a gift, one I will cherish. I will miss Martin's smile and his impish laugh, and the twinkling in his eyes that always made you think he held a powerful secret. I am grateful to his wife and to his children for New Year's 2019, when we all spent a wonderful evening together with friends and their families. When we left that night, my two grown children smiled at me and said, "That was a lot of fun. We should do that again." I wish we could, with Martin.
Making Martin a character in this book is a poor substitute for a husband, father, and friend, I know.
But I just didn't want to let him go.
And I know that while he didn't want to go, he didn't have a choice. But I also know that he's okay, and he's in a good place, watching over his family.

Prologue

Men rushed into her hospital room and yanked her from the bed without uttering a single word. They slid a black bag over her head and cuffed her wrists behind her back. Her stay in the hospital had come to an end, as she knew it eventually would, but she did not fear what next awaited her.

She no longer cared to live.

Ankle cuffs bit into her flesh, a link of chain between them. A stick jab to her ribs prodded her forward, and she shuffled, barefoot, the chain scraping the linoleum.

She had no idea how long she had spent in the hospital. No calendar told the month or the day of the year. No window revealed morning or night. No clock told the time. No newspapers, magazines, or books told her the news. Time had become meaningless.

The beeps and blips of the hospital machines and monitors had been the only sounds during her stay in isolation. No one spoke to her. Not the doctors. Not the nurses. They did not ask if she had discomfort, if she needed more pain medication. They didn't care—or had been ordered not to. No one came to interrogate or to threaten her.

That was about to change. She had existed in a fog, on the edge of pain, kept alive for one reason—to be interrogated.

Then she would be executed.

She would give them nothing.

A stick across her chest induced her to stop. A bell rang, this one the elevator. She stepped inside the car. It descended. Another bell. The stick prodded her forward.

Cold concrete scuffed the soles of her feet. The stick swat to the back of her legs instructed her to step up—like a trained circus elephant beaten into submission, another technique to make her feel no longer human.

She did so with difficulty, the chain too short. Two steps. She entered what she suspected to be a metal transport van. A stick to both legs, this time hard enough to induce her to sit. A bench. Her cuffed hands were fastened to the wall behind her, adding to the strain on her damaged shoulders, the pain exacerbated with every bounce and turn of the vehicle.

After a short ride, the van stopped. She knew her location. Moscow had long been her home. She knew it well.

A lock disengaged. The hinged door opened and she felt a cool breeze—the first fresh air since she'd awoken in the hospital bed. A guard freed her wrists from the wall, but they remained cuffed behind her back. Another stick tap instructed her to rise. She shuffled forward—the breeze now caressing her neck, the back of her hands, the tops of her feet.

A stick tap behind her right knee prodded her to step down. This time her bare foot did not touch solid ground and she fell, landing hard on her face and her shoulders. Despite excruciating pain, she withheld any moan of agony, any grunt of displeasure, any verbiage of hatred. She would not give them the satisfaction.

Hands gripped her elbows and yanked her to her feet. In pain, she moved forward, tasting the metallic tang of her own blood. Doors were opened and closed. Still no voices—complete isolation.

She smiled behind the mask. What did a condemned woman care if anyone spoke to her?

Another tap to the chest. She stopped. Another door opened. She stepped forward. The stick tapped her shoulders. She sat. A metal stool. Three legs. Easily toppled. A guard released her right hand, yanked both hands beneath the seat, then reapplied the handcuff to her wrist. Her feet were similarly immobilized, attached to the legs of the stool. She leaned forward, hunched like one of the monstrous gargoyles protruding from a church façade.

The door closed, leaving the buzz of an eerie and profound silence.

She waited, for what or whom she did not know. Or care.

Her shoulders, back, and knees burned from her fall and soon ached from her awkward posture atop the stool. Again, she lost track of time, whether she sat for minutes or hours.

"They say you have yet to speak."

A male voice. Soft-spoken. Deep and gruff—a smoker's voice. After months of silence even Russian sounded foreign. She did not react, did not respond. She had not heard a door open or close, or the shuffle of shoes on concrete. This man had been in the room. Watching her. Studying her. He would be her interrogator—calm at first, rational, perhaps even polite. That would change.

"They think, perhaps, it is brain damage from the accident." He audibly exhaled. Disbelieving. She smelled nicotine, not the acrid aroma of cheap Russian cigarettes, though she would have gladly smoked one. Sweeter, lighter, a high-end brand she could never have afforded.

"They don't know," he said.

Chair legs scraped concrete. Footsteps approached.

He pulled the hood from her head. The sudden and unexpected light blinded in its intensity. She closed her eyes, blinking back the pain.

The man came into focus. He leaned against the edge of a metal desk. Not particularly tall, but thick. Powerfully built. The fabric of his white dress shirt stretched across his chest and his arms. Gray hair closely cropped. Crow's-feet at the corners of his eyes. He had years under his belt. He looked at her from beneath a brow that extended well over dark, lifeless eyes. His jaw was scarred with crude stitch lines, another over his right eye, a third across the bridge of his nose, which looked to have been broken, perhaps more than once, and poorly fixed. So very Russian.

Tendrils of smoke swirled from the lit end of a cigarette held between his fingers, the smoke spiraling to an overhead cloud. She had never seen this man, not at the FSB offices—Russia's Federal Security Service—but from his practiced demeanor and his weathered appearance, she suspected he had once been KGB. Something.

He'd undone the top two buttons of his dress shirt and neatly folded back the cuffs of his sleeves, revealing thick fingers, meaty palms, forearms like woven ropes. A tie rested on the desk. Beside it, a red, rectangular brick. Odd.

"That is what I shall determine."

The first threat.

He took another drag and blew smoke ringlets into the stale air. Although more than half the cigarette remained, he dropped it. His eyes searched her face for a reaction; she had smoked three packs a day before the accident. Then he crushed the tip beneath the sole of his dress shoe.

He reached and picked up the brick as if weighing a gold bar. "Do you know what this is?"

She did not answer.

"It is fairly obvious, no? A brick, for certain. But not just a brick. No. A reminder. A reminder to always pay close attention. Pay close attention, or suffer the consequences. As a boy, I learned to pay attention."

It explained the scars, the kind left to heal on their own, and the ring finger of his right hand, bent to the left at the first knuckle.

"It took time," he said.

He set the brick back on the desk. "The question is: Are you paying attention?"

Close attention.

But she would not speak, not to this interrogator or to any other.

She would not prolong the inevitable, anxious to be with her brother and her family, those whom she had loved, and who went before her. She thought again of the biblical passage, of her mantra in the hospital.

You hold no power over me.

Though I walk through the valley of death, I will fear no evil.

I will lie down in green pastures.

And I will dwell in the house of the Lord forever.

The man gazed at her as if he could read her thoughts. "We shall see."

1

Freedom did not come the day a jury exonerated Charles Jenkins of espionage and federal judge Joseph B. Harden declared him "free to go." It did not come when the deadline for the government to appeal the jurors' decision passed. Though Jenkins was not physically incarcerated for the remainder of his life, and grateful for the jury's decision, his true freedom did not come until today, six months after the jury's verdict and Harden's proclamation. He returned home from his morning run, entered his office, and wrote the last check to the last security contractor hired by his former company, CJ Security.

His business had provided security to the discredited international investment firm LSR&C. That LSR&C had been a CIA proprietary and not a legitimate investment company, and that it had retained CJ Security under these false pretenses, did not matter. Jenkins had been lied to, defamed, shot at, and nearly imprisoned for life because of LSR&C's deception, but CJ Security's contractors and vendors had no part in any of that either. They had performed their services pursuant to a written contract, and they were entitled to be paid.

His attorney had recommended bankruptcy to get out from under the contractual obligations. Jenkins had rejected that advice. He would not right a wrong with another wrong. *Negotiate a payment schedule. I'll make it work,* he'd said.

And he had done so—not by accepting the six-figure book deal a publisher offered him to write of his escape from Russia and of his subsequent trial and acquittal of the espionage charge. He'd also refused to sell any of the acreage of his Camano Island farm.

He'd paid off his debts the old-fashioned way.

He'd worked his ass off.

He performed investigative services, served subpoenas, and did background checks on employment candidates for any business that would hire him. He made organic honey, lip balm, and hand cream from his beehives and sold those products at a store in Stanwood and online. He divided his pasture and boarded horses, and he cut and sold cords of firewood. He'd done what he needed to do to pay his debts and support his wife and two children.

Jenkins licked the back of an envelope and sealed the final payment to the final contractor. He stared at the address label, feeling a sense of accomplishment . . . but also betrayal—a bitter pill that left a taste more unpleasant than the envelope glue.

Let it go, he told himself.

He considered Max, his mottled pit bull asleep at his feet. "You ready to go outside, girl?"

Max instantly rose, her tail whipsawing the air. Jenkins had taken his early morning run without his trusted companion. Max was certainly willing—but she was also long in the tooth. Her joints would thank him for leaving her at home three of the five days he ran. In between, she gobbled glucosamine to ease her joint pain.

Fifteen minutes later, Jenkins had changed into his work coveralls and drunk a morning protein shake. He'd increased his workout regimen and started a plant-based diet that had cut another five pounds. He now carried 225 pounds on his six-foot-five frame—his weight on his military service records.

When he opened the back door, Max bolted outside, hurtling down the porch steps and across the lawn to bark at the boarded horses.

The two Appaloosas and the Arabian lifted their heads from their feed bags, twigs of hay protruding from their mouths, but they otherwise ignored the disruption of their meal. The paddocks had held up well since Jenkins had installed a hot wire across the top rail to dissuade the horses from using the posts to scratch their backsides.

He zipped his stained and well-worn Carhartt jacket against the winter chill and pulled his fur-lined work gloves and black skullcap from the pockets, slapping them against his coveralls to kill or displace spiders. Then he sat on the bench he'd made from a felled pine tree and slipped on his mud-caked boots. Max returned.

"Did you let those horses know you're still the boss?" Jenkins rubbed her face and scratched her head before he stepped down from the porch. The frozen grass crunched beneath his boots, and his breath marked the chilled air as he crossed the pasture to put his vegetable garden to bed. Alex, his wife, had spent a few hours earlier that month pulling weeds, which would ease his job this morning.

He retrieved what supplies he needed from his metal shed and rolled out black felt paper, staking the corners, then covered the felt with cardboard, which smothered the weeds but also released a sugar that would attract earthworms as it deteriorated.

As Jenkins turned on the water spigot to soak the cardboard, Max barked, though not at the horses. Jenkins didn't have neighbors, at least not nearby, and his friends rarely stopped by unannounced. Alex had taken Lizzie to day care and would work the morning teaching math in their son, CJ's, classroom.

Jenkins raised a hand to deflect the glare of sunlight streaming through the trees, and he watched a young man turn the corner of the house and start across the yard toward him. In a dark suit and a long black coat, with short blond hair, he looked like a Mormon missionary. His gait indicated he was eager and determined to change the world for the better.

"Easy, girl. Sit," Jenkins whispered when Max growled. "Let's be neighborly. Unless given reason not to be." Mormon missionaries traveled in pairs, and usually in neighborhoods where they could more widely spread their message. And while the Mormons were determined, this young man looked too cocksure, too composed to have come on religious business. He also looked too old for a mission. Jenkins hoped the man wasn't carrying a subpoena—or something more deadly. At present, all *he* had in hand was the gardening hose.

Max dutifully sat at Jenkins's side. The young man stopped when he stepped onto the soggy lawn and looked down at his polished black dress shoes. His determined expression became hesitant.

He looked up. "Are you Charles Jenkins?"

"What's this about?" Jenkins eyed the ground for a weapon.

"I'm hoping to speak with Charles Jenkins." The young man's voice rose in question. "Is he home?"

"I asked what this was about."

Max emitted a low growl, drawing the man's attention. "Russia," he said, redirecting his gaze to Jenkins. "It's about Russia."

2

Jenkins tilted his head, having difficulty hearing over the sound of a low-flying jet heading south to SeaTac Airport or Boeing Field. "Say that again?"

The young man stepped forward and raised his voice. "I said, 'It's about Russia.' The time you spent there."

"You don't have to yell, son. I'm not that old." Jenkins eyed the man's clothing and said, "You're dressed too nice to be a reporter, so I'm assuming you're not here to write a story. And I can't see a publisher sending an editor without calling first."

"I work for the agency," he said. "My name is Matt Lemore."

"You work for the CIA?" Jenkins asked. Maybe he *was* hard of hearing.

Lemore held up credentials. "You can verify my employment with the deputy director of Clandestine Services."

Jenkins had never heard of the department, though he understood the agency had recently undergone some restructuring. "What division?"

"Covert Action. Russia primarily."

"You're serious?"

"I can understand—"

"No. You can't." Jenkins chuckled at the agency's audacity. Then said, "Do you see the deputy director regularly?"

"Not regularly, but . . ."

"But you can deliver a message to him?"

"Her, actually. The deputy director of Clandestine Services is a woman. Regina Baity."

"You can deliver a message to Ms. Baity?"

"I can."

"Tell her to go—" Jenkins bit his tongue, for his deceased mother's sake. She'd always told him, *The f-word is a sign of a lack of intelligence.* "Tell her we don't have anything to talk about." He started up the lawn toward his house.

Lemore slid his identification inside his jacket and followed. "I understand why you'd be reluctant to speak to me."

"No, you don't."

"I read your file. And I followed the trial."

"I lived it."

"You have to understand—"

Jenkins stopped. A good five inches taller and probably thirty-five pounds heavier than Lemore, he leaned into the young officer's personal space. He kept his voice low. "Have to? Son, after I go to the post office and mail a check to a final creditor for a bill I incurred because of your employer, I don't *have to* do anything except die and pay taxes. Now turn your ass around and get off what still remains my property."

Jenkins started again for the back porch but sensed Lemore had not heeded his warning.

"I think we've gotten off on the wrong foot, Mr. Jenkins."

Jenkins shook his head, chuckling at the officer's understatement. He kept walking. "You think? Let me tell you something. There aren't enough feet in the entire agency to cover the wrongs that have been committed."

Lemore kept talking. "I'm authorized to pay all of your bills—"

"Little late for that." Jenkins reached the porch steps.

"Then I can reimburse you."

"Don't want it." Jenkins stepped across the porch to the back door.

Frustration entered Lemore's voice. "Then maybe I could just buy you a cup of coffee and apologize on the agency's behalf. It won't take long."

"It won't take any time at all, because the only coffee I'm going to drink I make, and that cup comes with no strings attached. Now, I'd suggest you head back to your car, drive to the airport, and fly on back to Langley."

Ordinarily Jenkins would have sat on the bench to remove his boots and his jacket so he wouldn't drag dirt into the house, but he was afraid of what he might do to Lemore if he stayed outside and listened to the agent's hubris much longer.

"Mr. Jenkins, you have a duty to at least hear me out . . ."

That was it. Jenkins lunged down the steps.

Lemore backpedaled, hands raised, alternately eyeing Max and Jenkins. "If you would just hear me out—"

"We're done talking." Jenkins grabbed Lemore by the lapels, intending to kick his butt back to his car.

Lemore drove his hands up through the gap between Jenkins's arms, stepped into him, and used his right forearm to push Jenkins backward while he swept his right leg. Jenkins landed hard on his back. The wet lawn squished upon impact. Lemore kept a lock on Jenkins's hand, bending it at the wrist, an angle intended to inflict just enough pain to keep Jenkins immobile.

Max barked and circled, but she did not charge.

"I'm sorry," Lemore said. "I didn't want to have to do that. If you would just—"

Jenkins wrapped his leg around Lemore's feet and bent the hand and arm that held his wrist. He thrust his free leg into Lemore's chest, flipping the young man off his feet and onto his back, then jumped to his feet, still holding Lemore's wrist. "And I didn't intend to do that either."

Lemore lay on the ground, face a beet red. "Okay. Okay," he managed. "I'll leave. I'll go."

Jenkins let go of the wrist and stepped away, his heavy breathing marking the cool air. He could feel water dampening his long johns beneath the coveralls, and his adrenaline pulsed in his veins.

Lemore slowly stood and brushed himself off, then backed away with his hands raised. "I apologize," he said. "I was just trying to do my job."

Jenkins stepped onto the porch and grabbed the doorknob.

"For what it's worth, we all know you got screwed," Lemore called out. "And we were all rooting for you. All the officers."

Jenkins stepped inside, slamming the door behind him. His anger spiked; he couldn't believe the agency that had allowed him to be tried for espionage now had the audacity to seek his help. To add injury to insult, he'd been physically embarrassed by a kid who couldn't weigh 170 pounds dripping wet.

As Jenkins paced, Lemore's final words rang in his ears. *We all know you got screwed.*

We. The agency's officers.

Jenkins shook his head, wondering what short straw Lemore had drawn to have landed the unenviable assignment of trying to talk to Jenkins.

I was just trying to do my job.

Jenkins stopped pacing. "Shit."

He moved quickly to the front door, leaving bits of dried mud and wet bootprints on the hardwood floor. Outside, a car engine revved. Jenkins pulled open the door and stepped onto the front porch as Lemore spit gravel down the driveway, the car disappearing behind the trees.

3

Showered and shaved, Jenkins drove to nearby Stanwood, slipping on sunglasses to combat the brilliant winter sunshine. He made his way to the post office and mailed the final payment, then, since he was close to Stanwood Middle School, he called to see if Alex had finished tutoring.

"I hoped to convince a pretty lady to have a late breakfast or early lunch at the Island Café."

"Which pretty lady did you have in mind?" Alex asked.

"I don't know. I thought maybe you'd give me a few introductions?"

"Fat chance, lover boy." Alex sounded like she was walking. "I'd love to join you, but I have to pick up Lizzie from day care and take her to see Dr. Joe."

Lizzie, now a year old, had been fussy and waking up in the middle of the night. "How is she?"

"I assume it's another earache." He heard Alex's car chirp, and the door open and shut. "How are you enjoying your day off?" she asked.

"Working." He stared at the sunlight glistening on the muddy waters of the Stillaguamish River separating Stanwood from Camano Island. "I finally put the garden to bed." He contemplated bringing up Matt Lemore but decided to wait before discussing that subject. Alex sounded like she was in a rush.

"Well, at least get out and enjoy some of this sunshine."

"I hope to," he said. "I'll pick up CJ."

"How long are you planning on being at the diner?" Sarcasm leaked into her voice.

"Long enough to save you the trip," he said.

Jenkins drove the short distance to the café. Back in New Jersey, where he'd grown up, they would have called the establishment in the one-story stucco building a diner. The red tile floor was well-worn, as were the Formica tables, banquet chairs, and green vinyl booths. The café never changed—not the décor, not the menu, not the owner, who was also the cook, and not the waitress or the patrons, though a few regulars had died. Even after his very public trial, this was one place where no one gave Jenkins a second look.

The morning crowd had departed. Jenkins greeted a few stragglers sitting on bar stools at the counter sipping coffee from porcelain mugs, then he grabbed a copy of the *Seattle Times* from an empty table and made his way to a booth beneath red-and-white-checked bunting adorning a window. He sat, and the waitress, Maureen Harlan, filled his mug with coffee.

"What are you having?" She gazed out the window.

"Two eggs, sunny-side up. Fruit instead of hash browns. Hold the bacon and the toast."

"The Countryman, extra bacon. Hash browns, extra crispy. Wheat toast?"

Jenkins smiled. "Sounds good to me."

"And a doggie bag?"

"Max would be most appreciative."

"Picked up some of your lip balm the other day. Stuff really works."

"I'd never cheat the person responsible for serving my meals."

"Smart man," she said, departing.

Jenkins flipped open the newspaper. A headline caught his attention. An American citizen claiming to have traveled to Moscow for a wedding had been detained by the Kremlin and charged with spying. After weeks of saber rattling, the man had been released from Moscow's infamous Lefortovo Prison.

About to turn the page, Jenkins sensed someone hovering over his table. Maureen was fast when the restaurant was hopping, but not this fast. He lowered the paper. Matt Lemore wore a sheepish grin, his hands raised. "I promised to buy you a cup of coffee," he said.

Jenkins folded the paper and nodded to the other side of the vinyl booth. Lemore sat and picked up one of the laminated menus from a rack on the table. "What's good around here?" he asked.

"Coffee," Jenkins said, and he sipped from the mug.

Maureen returned with a pot and topped off Jenkins's mug. "I'll have . . ." Lemore began, flipping the laminated menu, but Maureen turned and walked from the table as if she hadn't heard him.

"She doesn't know you," Jenkins said.

"She only serves people she knows?" Lemore smiled through his nervousness.

"Or likes." Jenkins sipped his coffee.

Lemore slid the menu back into the rack.

Jenkins set down his mug. "That move you made at the farm, what was it?"

"The wrist takedown? Sorry about that."

"What was it?"

"Judo mostly, a technique called *osoto-gari*, with some Krav Maga," Lemore said. The latter term referred to the tactical training techniques of the Israel Defense Forces. Jenkins had employed Krav Maga on the countermove to take down Lemore, though in his day it had been called *Tang Soo Do*.

Lemore was not a desk jockey.

"Paramilitary training. Where? Harvey Point?" Jenkins asked, meaning North Carolina.

"Camp Peary," Lemore said, referring to a covert CIA facility known as "the Farm."

"Where were you assigned?"

"Mostly Russia and Eastern Europe. More recently I've been sitting at a desk in Langley. I'm newly married. My wife is expecting our first child. We thought it best if I stayed closer to home."

"Congratulations."

"Thanks."

"So your spy days are at an end?"

Lemore nodded. "For now. As are my wife's."

Many officers married other CIA officers—Jenkins included. Officers understood why their spouses could not come home and share the details of their day, and why they could leave on a moment's notice and return without a word as to where they had been.

"And how did you get this plum assignment?"

Lemore tapped on the newspaper. "I was running *him*."

Jenkins reconsidered the article on the inside page. "You were his case officer?"

"Well, yes, though we use different terminology now."

"How old are you?"

"Forty-two." Lemore looked like a college kid.

"How many years do you have in?"

"Sixteen. I entered after college and four years in the marines."

"You served?"

"I wanted to fight for my country."

"Did you?"

"Two tours in Iraq."

"How'd you get to the agency? Let me guess. You wanted to serve your country again."

"No. I needed a job."

Jenkins chuckled. "Why Russia and the Eastern Bloc countries?"

"That was my area of study in college. The Bolshevik revolution, the rise of communism and the Soviet Union, and the economic collapse and ultimate breakup."

"Not if Mr. Putin gets his way."

"Russia today is a lot like the Soviet Union used to be," Lemore said, not sounding impressed.

"You're telling me?"

"Sorry. I just meant there's a lot of bluster they're not always capable of backing up."

"Are you Russian?"

"My mother's family is Russian. Lemore is French."

"A ty govorish' po russki?"

"Da."

"The country interested you?"

Lemore smiled. "That and I couldn't do math worth a shit, so accounting was out . . ."

Maureen returned with Jenkins's meal. Lemore kept his eyes down and his hands folded. He looked like a penitent in a catechism class.

"Hey," Maureen said. Lemore looked up. "You going to eat?"

"Ah, yeah. I'll—"

"Have what he's having?" Maureen said.

Lemore's eyes shifted to the platter of food. "Sure. What's he having?"

She flipped over and filled Lemore's coffee mug before departing.

"She must like you," Jenkins said. "That's as much hospitality as you're going to get." He picked up one of his bacon slices and took a bite. "How'd your guy get caught?" Jenkins tapped the newspaper article.

"He was supposed to get caught."

Interesting. "Why?"

"You recall Olga Ivashutin?"

"The Russian attorney accused of playing a part in the meeting with Donald Trump's election staff during the 2016 campaign."

"We couldn't hold her, and we'd gotten everything out of her that we were going to get. We wanted the Russians to think they had us over a barrel and that we'd release her only because they had one of ours."

"You wanted them to believe they had the upper hand and forced yours. You did study Russian culture."

Lemore smiled. Then he said, "There was another reason for him to get caught. It's why I'm here."

Jenkins set down his mug. "I'm all ears."

"We've been seeking to confirm a months-long rumor about Lefortovo Prison. I figured the easiest way to do so was to get someone in who we knew we could get out again."

"What's the rumor?"

"Could I ask you a few questions?"

Jenkins cut into his eggs and took a forkful mixed with the hash browns. "You can ask."

"When you were in Russia, how did you get out?"

"I came across the Black Sea on a Turkish fishing boat and eventually made my way to Çeşme, then paid my way across the Aegean Sea to Chios."

"I meant how did you get out of Moscow to the Black Sea?"

"An agent. A Russian woman. It's a long story."

"Paulina Ponomayova?"

Jenkins set down his fork, sensing something coming. He'd initially gone into Russia after his former case officer, Carl Emerson, told him that seven unrelated Russian women known as "the seven sisters" had been targeted by Russia's secret police. The women had served for decades as American moles privy to highly classified information. Three had been exposed and executed. Emerson told Jenkins the hunter was known as "the eighth sister" and asked Jenkins to determine that person's identity. But everything Emerson had told Jenkins had been a lie.

Emerson himself had exposed the three sisters in exchange for millions of dollars. Paulina Ponomayova had been working not for Russia's secret police but for the CIA, trying to identify the CIA leak. When Jenkins learned of Emerson's betrayal, he'd barely escaped Russia alive, and only with Ponomayova's significant sacrifice. Once back home, things got worse. When Jenkins alerted US authorities to Emerson's betrayal, Jenkins had been accused and tried for espionage. Only his lawyer's brilliance and a judge with brass balls had kept him from a life in prison.

"Do you know what happened to her?" Lemore asked.

"She died." Jenkins sipped his coffee and set down the mug. The subject matter remained raw and painful.

"You saw her die?" Lemore asked.

Jenkins recalled his and Ponomayova's final moment in the rundown beach house in Vishnevka, Paulina stepping out the back door to a car they had stashed. She intended to create a diversion to give him time to flee. The diversion had worked. "No."

Lemore sat back, clearly disappointed.

"Why are you asking? What was the rumor about Lefortovo?"

"That a highly placed asset was brought to Lefortovo and was being interrogated there—a female asset believed to have information on a clandestine US mission of a long-standing nature."

Jenkins shoved his plate to the side, no longer hungry. "When? When did you first get word?"

"Several months after you returned to the States."

His optimism vanished. "It has to be someone else then."

Lemore spoke over him. "The woman had been in a military hospital in Moscow under heavy security for months. She'd had some sort of car accident and was in the intensive care unit for several months before being transferred to Lefortovo."

Jenkins gave that some thought. "The Russians went to extremes to keep this person alive."

"Which means the asset had to have been highly placed, and that the FSB was concerned about what she had already divulged and what more she might know."

Jenkins tapped the newspaper on the table. "What did your asset tell you? What did he learn inside the prison?"

"He said the Russians were being cautious, and paranoid, more than usual. Prison guards usually talk for the right price. Not this time."

"You don't know her identity."

"No. I thought you might be able to help."

Jenkins shook his head. He couldn't.

But he knew someone who could.

4

With Alex on Lizzie duty, Jenkins picked up CJ after his soccer practice at the middle school. Perhaps the only positive outcome from the trial had been the tutor they'd hired to ensure CJ wouldn't fall behind in his classwork. The tutor had played professional soccer. CJ's grades and his game both improved dramatically.

"Good practice?" Jenkins asked.

His son slid into the passenger seat in his uniform and soccer cleats. He slung his backpack into the back seat and buckled his seat belt. "It's been a little boring. Nobody is able to stop me."

Jenkins suppressed a smile, recognizing a fatherly opportunity. "Well, I hope you haven't said anything like that to any of your teammates."

"No, I didn't say anything." CJ turned on the radio. A middle schooler, he'd begun to pick up the social norms, like an interest in music. He'd also developed body odor, and they'd been working on getting him to use deodorant. Based on the smell, it remained a work in progress.

"Can we stop at Burger King?" CJ asked.

"Mom's cooking," Jenkins said.

He pulled onto the highway, heading across the bridge toward home. The conversation he'd had with Matt Lemore remained fresh. Jenkins had assumed Paulina Ponomayova had driven the car as far as she could and, when caught, that she had bit down on a cyanide tablet. This had triggered the Baptist sermons he'd endured as a youth.

Greater love has no man than this, that a man lay down his life for his friends.

John 15:13.

Letting Paulina leave the beach house in Vishnevka, knowing the sacrifice she intended to make, had been the hardest thing Jenkins had ever done.

I'm not quitting, Charlie. You have to understand that if you survive, if you get back, then I have done my job. You must get back and stop whoever is leaking the information on the seven sisters, before others die.

They'll kill you, Anna.

Paulina, she'd said. *My name is Paulina Ponomayova.*

Now Lemore was telling him she might still be alive.

"Dad?"

Jenkins shook his thoughts. "What's that?"

"Can I go to William's after practice on Saturday? He invited me over."

"Let's check with your mom and make sure you don't have any other commitments."

CJ looked at him the way his son had when Jenkins had been on trial. Uncertain and concerned. "Are you okay, Dad?"

"Yeah, sure. I'm fine."

"Really?"

Jenkins smiled. "I just have a couple of things on my mind."

After the acquittal, Jenkins had done his best to be present at home, to help CJ overcome his fear that his father would again be taken away. Still, it had been months before he regained the boy's trust.

When they arrived at home, Jenkins helped CJ with his homework and participated in the dinner discussion, struggling to stay engaged so his mind didn't drift back to the Russian beach house, and to Paulina. He was not always successful.

Do not be sad for me, Charlie. This is a day I have anticipated, and for which I have long prepared. I am at peace with my God, and I am anxious to see my brother dance the ballet in the greatest ballroom in all eternity. Give me this gift. Give me this opportunity to know that I have harmed them one last time.

Paulina had been as tough and determined as any KGB or CIA officer Jenkins had ever known. She'd made dying sound honorable and heroic. Now Jenkins struggled with the possibility that she had not died, and the consequences if she had not. Lefortovo was notorious. The Russians would slowly and painfully squeeze every ounce of information from her.

Then, they would execute her.

"I'll finish the dishes if you take care of Lizzie," Alex said.

Jenkins smiled and cleared plates.

"You okay?" Alex asked.

"Yeah. No worries."

Nights at home had returned to routine. Jenkins and Alex took turns putting CJ and Lizzie to bed. CJ still asked to have a book read to him, though he was more than capable of reading the books on his own. As Alex liked to say, *There are moments he doesn't want us around, and moments when he just wants to be a little boy. Cherish those.*

Jenkins changed Lizzie's diaper and put her in her crib, cautiously handing her the bottle of water, which she had recently become prone to throwing in protest; Alex had read that formula would rot Lizzie's new teeth and gums. But tonight, Lizzie stuffed the nipple in her mouth, sucking contentedly.

"Elizabeth Paulina Jenkins," Jenkins whispered, rubbing his daughter's curly black hair. They had named Lizzie after his mother—and the woman whose sacrifice allowed Jenkins to stand at the crib this night.

"Good night, baby. Daddy loves you," he said.

Jenkins went downstairs to the family room. Alex would be another half hour reading to CJ. He made a fire, smelling the sap from the pine and dogwood logs. When the fire lit, the wood crackled and popped. He sat on the brown leather couch but made no move to turn on the television and channel surf. He thought again of that final conversation with Paulina, and her desire to reunite with her brother, who killed himself when his dream of dancing for the Bolshoi was taken from him.

I will tell them that for decades my brother did them more harm than they could ever have imagined doing to him, or to me. And they will have to live with the knowledge that revenge has eluded them, once again.

Maybe not.

The thought sickened him.

Alex descended the staircase. "Thank you for waiting," she said.

"What's that?" he said.

"Are we going to watch another episode of *The Marvelous Mrs. Maisel*? I assumed you waited for me."

"I did," he said.

She gave him an unconvincing grin. "No *SportsCenter* while waiting? That's not like you."

"I had a visitor today," he said.

She paused, no longer smiling. "Everything all right?" She sat on the couch beside him, and Jenkins filled her in on his meeting with Lemore.

"I hope you told him to go to hell."

"I did. He didn't give up so easily."

"What do you mean?"

"He showed up again at the Island Café. You recall the recent news story about the man who went to Russia for a wedding and ended up arrested for espionage?"

"Vaguely."

"This guy, Matt Lemore, told me he was running him. Lemore also said they intended for the man to get caught."

"Why?"

Jenkins explained what Lemore had told him. "Lemore said the agency wanted the Russians to believe they had the upper hand, that they forced the exchange."

"So they wouldn't dig deeper into why the man had been so easy to arrest?" Alex asked.

"Lemore said the goal was for the officer to get sent to Lefortovo Prison to confirm a persistent rumor that a high-level CIA asset was being held there."

Alex studied his face, reading his eyes. She, too, had once been a CIA officer, though in analytical operations. "A high-level asset you met in Russia?" she asked.

"Paulina."

Alex looked stunned. "You said she died."

"I thought she did. She told me she had a cyanide capsule, and when she could no longer lead them away, she would take it."

Alex blew out a breath, then sucked in another. She stood, wrapping her arms around herself as if suddenly chilled. She walked to the fireplace, facing the mantel and its framed photographs. "What evidence is there that she's still alive?"

"Nothing solid. It's thin, but we both know that human intelligence often is."

"It could be anyone."

"Apparently not. The rumors started shortly after I returned home from Russia, so the timing is right. And the asset was said to have been in a car accident and believed to have information on a clandestine US mission of a long-standing nature."

She turned. "The seven sisters."

Jenkins nodded.

"You don't have any way to confirm it."

"I don't," he said, his tone giving him away.

"But Viktor Federov would," she said. "That's what you're thinking, isn't it?"

"Federov would know if Paulina lived," he said.

Federov had been the FSB officer who had chased Jenkins from Moscow to the Black Sea and across it into Turkey. When Jenkins escaped, the FSB had fired Federov. Rather than harbor any bitterness toward Jenkins, Federov instead told Jenkins he considered them to be kindred spirits.

"Can you reach him?" Alex asked.

Jenkins shook his head. "While I waited for CJ to finish soccer practice, I looked back through cell phone records. His calls to me were too far back, and I suspect the number was either encrypted or from a burner phone he has long since discarded. He has no further reason to get in touch with me."

"Then you have no way to find him." Alex clearly wanted to end the discussion.

Jenkins gave her an uncomfortable smile. "There might be a way."

"You think you can find him? How?" she asked.

"The Swiss bank account."

The last time Federov had called, he informed Jenkins that he had hunted down Carl Emerson and located the money Russia had paid Emerson to disclose the names of three of the seven sisters. Federov had killed Emerson and split the money sixty-forty, providing Jenkins with the Swiss bank account that contained Jenkins's share, though Jenkins had never touched it and now likely never would. Some weeks after the account was opened, he learned the Russian government had frozen it.

"The bank is the Union Bank of Switzerland in Moscow. The account is frozen, but I have the account number. If I went into that bank and made a deposit, then told them I needed to update my signature card, I could learn the name of the Russian banker who opened my account."

"What good would that do?"

"Odds are that the same banker opened Federov's account on the same day and at the same time, though Federov would have used an alias. If I find the banker, I can find the alias."

"There's no guarantee that banker would tell you the name."

Jenkins gave Alex a tired smile. "I know from chasing the KGB that if you are an established Russian banker in Moscow, you're purchasable, have a handler in the government, or have already done nefarious transactions for oligarchs and organized crime figures. Giving me the name on an account for a price would be nothing. Lemore could then run credit card and debit card records, and I could find Federov."

"That's crazy, Charlie. They could send an asset to look for Federov. You don't have to go. You owe them nothing."

"You're right—I don't owe the agency anything . . ."

She sat on the coffee table in front of him. "Paulina made her own choice, Charlie. If she is alive—and that is a big 'if'—it is not because of anything you did or didn't do."

"She was willing to lay down her life for me, Alex. I never would have seen you or CJ again. Never would have met Lizzie."

"You don't know that."

"I'm the only one who can get the account identification card and determine the name on the other account set up at the same time."

"Bullshit." She stood. "The agency could send in a Moscow asset and do exactly what you explained, someone who could pose as you. Federov likely set up both accounts electronically."

"I agree, but if the asset gets the information, then what? Federov won't speak to just anyone, not about this. He'll be guarded. If it gets out that Federov killed Emerson and stole the money, he's a dead man. Like it or not, I'm the only one he'll trust, and I'm the only one who can blackmail him."

"The asset can threaten to expose him."

"And Federov will expose the asset to the FSB, as well as his intentions to find out if Paulina is still alive. If she is, the FSB will move her and bury her, and we'll miss any opportunity to get her out."

"Get her out? Get her out of where?"

"Lefortovo," Jenkins said. "Russia."

"Are you out of your mind? Do you know what that would take? Even *if* it is her. Besides, *if* she was in a hospital for months and is now in Lefortovo, you have no idea what kind of physical or mental condition she's in."

"I have to take this a step at a time. First, determine if she's alive and if she's in Lefortovo. If she is, Lemore and I will come up with a plan to get her out."

She shook her head. "Are you even hearing yourself? You're going to trust an agency that was about to let you go to prison for life?"

"Not entirely, no."

"Then who? Who are you going to trust to help you do this, Charlie?"

"Federov."

She looked at him like he was crazy. "A colonel in the FSB?"

"A disgruntled former colonel in the FSB."

"The man who hunted you across three countries."

"His agency and country screwed him."

"He isn't trustworthy, Charlie. He could have set up that account to trap you. Maybe that's why he didn't use an alias."

"He didn't use an alias because he expected me to empty the account as soon as it opened. It was frozen weeks later. I had time to move the money and close the account. I chose not to do that. It's blood money."

"Regardless, this could all be a trap. The FSB could have spread a false rumor that Paulina is alive to lure you back to Moscow. Putin is arrogant, persistent, and vindictive. Look at the lengths to which he's gone to kill those who spy on Russia."

"I don't think Federov did this to trap me. He never would have given me the four million dollars in the first place."

"Putin was KGB. Federov was and may still be an FSB officer," Alex said. "And, he profited from having killed Carl Emerson. What, are you going to tell me that he's now some kind of a Boy Scout?"

"Mom?" CJ stood halfway down the stairs, dressed in his pajamas. "Why are you mad at Dad?"

"It's okay, CJ," Jenkins said. "We were just having an adult conversation. Go on back to bed."

Concern and fear etched CJ's face, as it had the prior spring and summer. "Are you in trouble again, Dad?"

"No, CJ. I'm not in any trouble. Everything is fine. Go on back to bed. I'll be up in a minute to kiss you good night."

But CJ did not go up the stairs. He stood resolute, tears streaming down his cheeks. "If everything is fine, why is Mom crying?"

5

The following morning Jenkins drove his son to school, and even this small change in routine did not go unnoticed.

"Why isn't Mom driving me?" CJ asked.

"I thought it would give us the chance to talk, in case you have more questions."

CJ shook his head.

"I know you're scared, CJ. After what we all went through, you have a right to be scared. But I promise you no one is threatening to put me in jail."

"Then what were you and Mom fighting about?"

"It wasn't a fight . . . I have a friend, a good friend, who may be in trouble and need my help."

"What kind of trouble?"

"I can't really say, CJ, but if my friend needs help, you'd want me to help, wouldn't you?"

CJ thought for a moment, his chest rising and falling. "I guess so. If it was a really good friend."

"It is . . . a really good friend."

They arrived at the school drop-off. Rather than bolting out of the car as usual, CJ leaned across and hugged Charlie, then pushed out the door and ran up the breezeway. Jenkins fought back tears until a car behind him tapped its horn, and he drove from the drop-off zone.

He returned to the Island Café to wait for Matt Lemore. Jenkins and Alex had agreed that he would get more information, which they would then discuss before he made a decision. He'd called the young officer at 5:00 a.m., fully expecting to wake him, but Lemore, who was on East Coast time, had been working out at an Anytime Fitness.

The café was significantly more crowded and significantly noisier this early in the morning, but Jenkins managed to slip into a booth as four construction workers gathered their hard hats and gloves and departed. The busboy cleared the table, and Maureen filled his coffee mug, not bothering to greet him; she was hopping busy. Jenkins sipped his coffee and pretended to consider the menu. Despite the usual rich aromas coming from the café's kitchen—bacon and the sausage gravy spooned over biscuits—Jenkins didn't have much of an appetite. He peeked out the bottom half of the window. A light fog had rolled in from Skagit Bay, dimming the streetlamps. Across the street a blue Ford parallel parked at the curb. Matt Lemore stepped out.

White puffs escaped Lemore's mouth and nostrils as he waited for a car to pass, then he jogged across the street and stepped inside the café. He wore blue jeans, white tennis shoes, and a black down jacket that made him look even younger than the previous day. Spotting Jenkins, he crossed to the booth and slid onto the bench seat across the table. He blew into his hands, and his cheeks glowed red from the cold. "Have you been here awhile?" he asked over the clatter of silverware and plates, as well as voices in conversation.

"Just got here."

Maureen dropped off an order at the table beside them, picked up a pot of coffee, and approached. She flipped over Lemore's mug. He put a hand over the rim. "Decaf?"

Her eyebrows knitted together, then raised in a challenge. Lemore removed his hand. She filled the mug before moving on to the next table. "Thank you," he said, calling after her.

"You're learning. Slowly," Jenkins said.

Lemore ripped open two sugar packs and stirred in the granules. Someone from the counter called out an order. The cash register rang.

"I think I have a way to find Viktor Federov," Jenkins said.

Lemore sipped from his cup and placed the mug on the table, cradling it to warm his hands. "Yeah?" he said.

Jenkins nodded. "Maybe. Federov won't speak to just anyone. I do think he'll speak to me."

"Okay. If you can find him, we can provide a secure number to call—"

"He won't trust just anyone sent to find him. And he won't trust a number provided to him by the CIA. He's aware of my trial for espionage, and he sees the two of us as kindred spirits—each screwed by our agencies."

Lemore sat back against the green vinyl. "Then, what are you proposing?"

"I'm proposing the only thing that might work. I go. I find him."

"Go back into Russia?" Lemore asked with an uncertain smile.

Jenkins nodded.

Lemore chuckled, apparently thinking it a joke. The chuckle faded and the smile disappeared when he realized it wasn't. He crumpled the empty sugar packs and set them on the table. "You're serious?"

"I'm serious." Jenkins sipped his coffee.

"Even if we got you in . . . It would set off all kinds of bells and whistles, and cameras all over Moscow. You're not exactly inconspicuous, especially over there. The black population in Russia is less than one percent. Your light skin helps, but only to an extent."

"Yeah, well, I don't plan on living there," Jenkins said. "And I have a way in . . . maybe. What I'll need is a way out. For two."

Lemore's brow pinched in confusion. "Two?"

"I don't come out without her . . . If it's her."

Lemore's mouth opened but he spoke no words. He sipped his coffee, letting a few seconds pass. Finally, he said, "My job is only to confirm the asset."

"You've run missions before?"

"Of course." He sat forward. "But this would require approval at a very high level. And by approval, I mean even if we were given the green light, they won't acknowledge the mission. Relations with Russia are sensitive right now. The agency is not going to publicly do anything that could be linked to an international incident."

"I understand. How good is your intel that an asset exists at Lefortovo, that this isn't some lure by the Russians to get us to make a mistake?"

"We're reasonably certain—"

"Don't give me agency speak." Jenkins stared at Lemore. "I want to know how certain you are."

Lemore looked over his shoulder and lowered his voice. "As I said yesterday, we have HUMINT confirming that an asset was kept as a patient at the intensive care unit of the Hospital for War Veterans in Moscow." HUMINT stood for human intelligence.

"When did that patient arrive at the hospital?"

"Undetermined."

"Best estimate."

"Intel started sending reports late January."

Jenkins counted the days in his head as Lemore continued. He had returned to Russia—the second time—during the second week of January and spent approximately five days trying to get out of the country and another four to five days getting to Chios, Greece, before getting home.

"What about hospital records?"

Lemore shook his head. "The patient was never admitted, never given a name. Not even a John Doe."

"You're sure it's a woman?"

"Reasonably, though the patient's sex was also not documented. Intel said the hospital security was intense. The patient was kept isolated in a secure ward with FSB occasionally showing up dressed as doctors, nurses, and civilians."

"How long was the patient in the hospital?"

"Approximately four months."

"And then moved to Lefortovo?"

"Without any written records of discharge and no record of admittance at Lefortovo. The prisoner is being kept in an isolated prison block under secure measures with limited access."

And inadequate medical attention, Jenkins knew, *based upon recent findings by the European Court of Human Rights.*

"What we're being told is the asset refuses to speak," Lemore said.

That sounded like Paulina. Tough as nails.

"How do you plan to get Federov to help you?" Lemore asked.

"There will need to be a financial incentive. He won't do it for ideological reasons, and he isn't going to be happy with me after I tell him what has happened to the money he did have."

"I'm not sure I can get money—"

"Federov doesn't need money . . . not yet anyway." Jenkins told Lemore about the money Federov stole from Carl Emerson and split with him. When Jenkins checked his Swiss bank account balance that morning, it confirmed that Federov had deposited $4 million into the account on October twelfth the prior year, which meant he'd stolen roughly $10 million. "I need to steal that money so Federov has an incentive to get it back," Jenkins said, and he had a plan to make that happen. If he could get Federov's alias, he'd have Lemore's computer gurus steal the money in Federov's account also.

"To get access to my account I'm going to need to make a deposit, seed money, which will require the bank to unfreeze the account. When it does, I'm going to need technological support to steal it."

"What if they won't unfreeze the account?"

"You've studied Russia. Have you ever known a Russian bank to refuse money?" The question was rhetorical. "When the account is unfrozen, I need someone to hack the bank and quickly drain the money from my account. When I get the alias Federov used on his account, I'll need someone to drain it as well, and transfer the money to a place where Federov and the Russians can't get it back," Jenkins said.

"I can get some people started on figuring out the technology side. If it can be done."

"After we move the money from the two accounts, you keep the new account numbers until I have Paulina—*if* it is Paulina. When I tell you, you release the four million to Federov. When Paulina and I are back on American soil, you release the six million. That way, Federov will be less inclined to double-cross me."

"Less inclined?"

"If he sees an opportunity to make more money . . ."

Lemore smiled. "Then this is a go. We're going to do this?"

"You check with whoever you need to check with and get back to me, especially about the technological side, if it can be done. I have someone much more difficult to convince. One more thing," Jenkins said. "You've heard the saying 'fool me once'?"

"Shame on you," Lemore said.

"Fool me twice . . ."

"Shame on me."

"I have two children and a wife. Fool me twice and I'll make you, and anyone else responsible, regret it."

6

After putting CJ and Lizzie to bed, Jenkins and Alex wrapped themselves in warm clothing and blankets and went into the backyard to speak in private. On the concrete patio was a firepit surrounded by Adirondack chairs. Alex sat and placed the baby monitor in her lap so she could hear if Lizzie cried out.

Jenkins lit the fire and sat beside her. They sipped from Yeti tumblers with decaffeinated coffee and a shot of Bailey's Irish Cream, and they looked to the darkened pasture. Jenkins could see the shadows of the three horses and occasionally hear them snort and snicker. The flickering flames crackled and popped and sent sparks dancing into the star-laced sky. The subject on both their minds soon came to the forefront.

"Have you made a decision?" Alex asked.

"I promised I wouldn't make a decision without you."

"Were you being polite? Or do you mean it?"

He turned his head, considering her. "I mean it," he said. "If you tell me no, I won't go."

She looked to the flames as if for an answer. "I'm conflicted. I'm sure you are as well."

He nodded. "Very."

"We have two children to think of, Charlie."

"I know."

"Your responsibility is to them."

"And to you. My first responsibility is to you and to the children. I realize that, more now than ever before."

"At the same time, if it wasn't for Paulina . . . you wouldn't be here right now."

He reached over and held her gloved hand. "I've had similar thoughts," he said. "I know Paulina would tell me not to come for her. In Russia she told me she was prepared to die for her brother. I doubt that has changed. I've also considered what you said, about what type of condition she'll even be in, if it's even her, whether she's even mentally capable of understanding who I am, or is physically capable of getting out."

"They wouldn't have kept her alive if she wasn't mentally capable."

It was a good point.

"What did Lemore say? Does Paulina even know the identities of the remaining four sisters? I assume that is the agency's primary concern."

"Lemore didn't say. Carl Emerson did say the names of the seven were known only at the highest levels within the agency."

"Yes, but let's not forget that Emerson was a liar," Alex said. "The agency would need someone in Russia to communicate with the sisters, wouldn't it?"

"Seems logical."

Alex sighed and let go of his hand. A breeze blew across the farm, fanning the flames and sending sparks flittering higher into the sky. "I don't know, Charlie. Maybe I'm just jaded after everything that has happened, but I don't trust the agency to do right by you. I'm afraid this could be some sort of a trap."

"After I talked to Lemore at the Island Café, I called an old friend, someone I worked with and trusted in Mexico City. He called a friend still working at Langley, who confirmed Lemore works in Clandestine Services and focuses on Russia and the Eastern European countries, and that he'd been an officer in the same arena. All of which comports with what he told me."

"That helps, unless this whole thing is a setup and Lemore is as much a pawn as you."

"For what purpose?"

She shook her head. "I'm being paranoid. But I have the right."

"Tell me why. Let's talk it through."

She sighed. Jenkins could see that something else weighed on her. "Assume this highly placed asset is real, and the Russians have this person in Lefortovo, and the agency here wants him or her back."

"Okay."

"What if Russia has already agreed to an exchange? And what if Russia really wants . . ." She turned her gaze to him. "You?"

Jenkins hadn't thought of that possibility.

"Tell me I'm wrong, Charlie."

"The Russians could have sent someone here to poison me, like the Russian spies in London. Putin thinks it enhances, not disparages, the FSB's reputation. They could have arranged a traffic accident, a cardiac episode, a fatal mugging, any number of things they've been known to do. They haven't."

"Not yet," she said. "But you took away the best chance Putin had to find the remaining four sisters when you exposed Emerson. And remember, Russia doesn't know Federov killed Emerson. They think the US did it."

"If Paulina could be Putin's best last chance to learn the identities of those remaining," Jenkins said, "why would he exchange her for me?"

Alex shrugged. "He might already be convinced she can't identify any of the other sisters and is looking to get something for nothing. I don't know. I'm not saying this is how it is, Charlie; I'm saying this is how it could be."

Coyotes barked and yipped, then howled from deep in the forest. The sound had become more rare as Camano Island developed and once-wooded land became cul-de-sacs with houses. The horses snorted, whinnied, and pawed the ground. They feared the coyotes, though they were big enough to stomp them. But that wasn't Jenkins's initial thought. What immediately came to mind was that the pack sounded like a woman wailing in pain.

"I can't leave her in that prison. If it's her."

"I know," Alex said. "But promise me that if it is her, and if you try and fail, that you won't let that cloud your judgment. That you won't do something stupid."

"My judgment isn't clouded anymore, Alex. You and the kids focused it. If I find Federov and he tells me Paulina is dead, I'll get out. And if it's her and I can't get her out, I won't do anything stupid." He took hold of her hand once more. "That's a promise."

"When do you meet again with this Matt Lemore?" Alex asked.

"Tomorrow morning, at the diner."

"Tomorrow's Saturday," she said. "Have him come to the house for dinner."

"With the kids here?" he said.

"Exactly."

7

Saturday evening, at six o'clock sharp, there was a crisp rap of knuckles on the front door, which caused Max to bark, which caused Lizzie to cry, which annoyed CJ, who was trying to watch television, which caused Alex to reprimand their son—which caused Jenkins to liken parenting to dominoes falling into one another. As Alex tended to Lizzie, Jenkins silenced Max and answered the front door. Matt Lemore held a box of ice cream bars and a bouquet of flowers. Except for the casual clothing, he looked like a high school senior picking up his prom date.

"For the kids." He handed Jenkins the ice cream bars.

"They'll be delighted," Jenkins said. "As will my wife. Tulips are one of her favorite flowers."

Lemore nodded. "The woman at the flower shop in town recommended them."

Jenkins smiled. "Good intel. I've bought a few dozen over the years to dig myself out of some deep graves. Come on in."

Alex came down the hall as Jenkins shut the door and Lemore stepped inside. A little over five foot ten, she nearly matched Lemore in height. She wore comfortable blue jeans and an old, white V-neck T-shirt. "Mr. Lemore," she said, extending a hand.

"Matt, please." He handed her the flowers. "These are for you."

"You didn't need to bring anything."

He chuckled. "My mother would beg to differ."

"Tulips." She looked at Jenkins with a raised eyebrow. "My favorite. I'll put them in water." She started down the hall to the kitchen. "I hope you like lasagna."

"I do. Very much," he said, following her into the kitchen.

Lizzie had fresh tears on her cheeks as her stubby fingers struggled to corral Cheerios and navigate the tiny circles to her mouth. Her other hand bashed the tray with her water bottle. "This is Lizzie," Alex said. "Do you have children?"

"No. Not yet. My wife and I are expecting."

"Congratulations," Alex said. "We're the poster parents for raising children past your forties."

"I might actually be a national symbol," Jenkins said. "Can I get you a beer?"

"Sure, love one."

Alex led Lemore through the kitchen into the family room. CJ sat on the couch, watching TV. "CJ?" Alex said. "Can you turn off the television and introduce yourself to Mr. Lemore?"

CJ did so. He shook Lemore's hand as Charlie had taught him, looking him in the eye. "It's nice to meet you, Mr. Lemore."

"Nice to meet you, CJ."

"Do you and my dad work together?"

Lemore looked to Alex, uncertain how to respond. "Maybe," Alex said. "We'll see."

Charlie entered the room carrying three Coronas, each with a wedge of lime in the stem. He handed one to Lemore and one to Alex. "Cheers." They touched the necks of the bottles.

"Make yourself at home," Alex said. "Dinner will be ready in a few minutes."

She handed Lemore plates and glasses, and he and CJ set the kitchen table under Lizzie's watchful gaze. Jenkins knew Alex was more intent on Lemore seeing the full extent of Jenkins's family responsibilities than on impressing him.

Jenkins sat at the head of the table. Lemore sat to his right, next to CJ. Alex sat at the other end of the table, within reach of Lizzie's high chair. Jenkins picked up his fork, but Alex said, "Can we say a prayer?"

Though raised Baptist, Jenkins lost his religion when he served in Vietnam and hadn't rediscovered his faith. Alex, Catholic, wanted their children to be raised with a faith, and Jenkins capitulated. They clasped hands, forming a circle. Jenkins noted that Lemore bowed his head.

"Dear Lord, bless this family, and bless our guest, Matt Lemore," Alex said. "You are the way, the truth, and the light. Let your light shine down upon all of us present so that we can be truthful." Jenkins tried not to flinch or otherwise react. "Anyone else?" Alex said.

CJ spoke. "And thank you for helping us win our game today, and thank you for the three goals I scored today."

Jenkins caught his son peeking out from the corner of his eye at Lemore. "And teach us all to share in your humility," Jenkins said.

At that moment, Lizzie hurled her bottle onto the table with a loud thud. "That's Lizzie's way of saying, 'I'm hungry,'" Alex said, retrieving it.

"I don't blame her. It smells wonderful," Lemore said.

They ate lasagna, salad, and garlic bread with a bottle of Chianti. The conversation flowed easily, and Lemore seemed comfortable in the chaos. If the young agent was putting on an act, withholding information, or lying to them, Jenkins could not detect it. Lemore told them he and his wife lived in Virginia, not far from Langley. They'd married later in his life, travel and work commitments having made it difficult to date with any consistency. He also had played soccer at the University of Virginia. It comported with the information Jenkins had learned from his contact.

"What position?" CJ asked.

"Center fullback," Lemore said.

"Stopper," CJ said.

Lemore speared his salad. "I had a coach who believed that if the other team didn't score, we had a better chance to win. It worked too," Lemore said. "My senior year we made the quarterfinals of the NCAA tournament."

"Did you play professionally?" CJ asked.

"No. I really wasn't good enough, and I wanted to serve my country. I enlisted in the Marine Corps."

"I'm going to play professionally," CJ said.

"CJ," Jenkins said in a tone intended to convey a message to his son.

"I mean, that's what I want to do . . . If I work hard enough and I'm good enough." CJ looked to Jenkins for approval.

Jenkins gave him a nod.

"I like your confidence," Lemore said.

Following dinner, after they'd cleared the table, Alex let Lemore give CJ and Lizzie an ice cream bar each. CJ took his into the family room to watch television.

"Don't get it on the couch or the remote," she called after him. Lizzie was a different story. She'd make a mess, adding to the lasagna all over her hands and face. Alex turned to Lemore. "Can I get you coffee, Matt?"

"Decaffeinated?"

"No problem."

Lemore smiled. "You're a lot easier than the waitress at the diner. I asked for decaffeinated the other morning and thought she was going to pour it in my lap."

"Maureen takes a while to warm up to people," Jenkins said.

"A decade or two," Alex said. "Instant okay?"

"Fine."

Alex handed Lemore cream and sugar, and sat again while waiting for the kettle to boil. Lizzie was making a mess of her ice cream and loving every minute of it.

"I'm not going to insult you," Alex said. "I think you understand what this night was about."

Lemore nodded. "I do," he said. "Charlie is a husband and a father. He has a lot to lose."

Jenkins nodded but remained silent. This was Alex's conversation.

"We all have a lot to lose. We almost lost him once. Charlie's dedicated. He can be loyal to a fault. Lizzie's middle name is Paulina."

Lemore sat back from the table. "I didn't know that."

She nodded. "Charlie wanted to remember Paulina's sacrifice. You understand why I'm concerned about you coming here and telling him that she might be alive."

"I do," Lemore said. "And I wish there was something I could say that would alleviate your anxiety and your worry, but since I know you were also an officer, I won't insult your intelligence. And since I can see what you've created here, how special it is, I won't insult you by saying I understand."

"Just tell me you'll be there if he needs help this time," she said. "Tell me that you won't abandon him."

"I won't abandon him." Lemore looked to Jenkins. "I won't abandon you. You have my word. And not because I've met both of you, and CJ and Lizzie, though that's a serious concern. I won't abandon you because I was a case officer. I was in the field on my own." He looked to Alex. "I told Charlie we all knew of the trial, and we were all rooting for him."

"He said that. Not sure it means much," Alex said.

"It does to me," Lemore said, sounding sincere. Again he looked to Jenkins. "You're one of us. What happened to you could have happened to any of us. I won't forget that. And I won't abandon you. That's my word."

The kettle on the stove whistled, at first a low hum that grew in volume and pitch. Charlie turned to the kettle, but the sound reminded him of the night he'd had tea in Paulina's apartment, and the sound he and Alex had heard the other night, of the coyotes howling.

The sound of a woman in pain.

8

A week after his dinner with Matt Lemore, an unshaven and bleary-eyed Charles Jenkins stepped off a Turkish Airlines flight at the new airport in Istanbul. He'd slept little of the eighteen hours of flight time, spending nearly all of it practicing his Russian.

Given the recent conflict between Turkey and the United States, Jenkins flew under a British passport provided by Lemore. After clearing a crowded customs line and locating his checked bag, Jenkins stepped outside into the night. The temperature had dropped into the thirties, but the cold invigorated him after breathing recycled airplane air. Jenkins hailed a taxi at the curb and climbed into a well-worn back seat that held the aroma of Turkish cigarettes, which reminded him of the smell of rum.

"Rumeli Kavaği," he told the driver, providing a street address.

The driver turned and looked at Jenkins as if he'd misspoken. "Rumeli Kavaği?"

"Ne kadar tutar?" Jenkins asked. *How much will it cost?*

They negotiated a price, and the driver turned off the meter and pulled from the curb. Jenkins leaned his head against the window, hoping to sleep on the long drive.

He awoke as the taxi wound its way through the hills above the Bosphorus strait. The lights in the homes and the hotels glistened on the sloped hillside and clustered in cluttered marinas at the darkened water's edge. Further out in the strait, tankers had set anchor and turned on lights, looking like dozens of islands.

The driver slowed and Jenkins searched for an address on the homes, not finding one.

The driver stopped the taxi. *"İşte,"* he said. *Here.*

"İşte?" Jenkins asked.

"Evet. Bir yerde." Yes. Somewhere.

Jenkins hoped the man was right. He thanked him and exited the cab with his bag. He approached a home with a light shining on the pink stucco siding. Somewhere down the block a dog barked; several more joined in. Jenkins stepped down concrete steps and pushed open a wrought-iron gate that swung into a center courtyard with a squeal. He crossed to the door. To his right, a plate-glass slider revealed lights on inside the house, but he saw no one. He knocked, unsure what to expect, whether he'd be welcome, or if this was even the right home. When no one answered, he knocked again.

A woman, middle-aged and heavyset, pulled open the door. She had graying hair tied back in a bun. *"Evet?" Yes?*

"Esma," he said, recalling the name of Demir Kaplan's boat that had provided Jenkins safe passage across the Black Sea. The Turkish captain had told Jenkins he'd named the boat for his wife. *"I am with you, Esma, even when I am at sea."*

The woman's brow wrinkled, and she considered Jenkins with an inquisitive but distrusting gaze.

"Demir? Demir Kaplan?" Jenkins said.

"Kimsin?" Who are you?

A word Jenkins had learned on his last visit to Turkey. As he was about to answer, Demir's baritone voice called out, deep and rough from cigarettes. The words were spoken too quickly for Jenkins to understand.

Esma turned, about to speak, when the door was pulled open, revealing the stocky man with the unkempt salt-and-pepper beard. Demir Kaplan's eyes widened in recognition and, likely, some concern.

"Mr. Jenkins." He sounded as if he didn't believe his eyes.

—

Jenkins sat at a round table near a small kitchen with Demir and his two sons, Yusuf and Emir, who worked the fishing boat with their father. The sons, in their late forties, had come to the home quickly after receiving their father's phone calls. Jenkins recalled Yusuf telling him that his father had purchased three homes on the same street, all a short distance from one another. The brothers had hugged Jenkins as if greeting a lost relative and started asking him a slew of questions. Esma, however, had cut them off and told them to sit, which they dutifully obeyed.

Esma remained cold toward Jenkins, but that did not stop her from the Turkish custom of providing the guest with massive amounts of food and drink. She set down a serving tray with a teapot and four tulip-shaped glasses, followed by a second tray with dark bread, cheeses, figs, and vegetables. Esma's gaze lingered on Jenkins before she departed the room.

Demir poured the tea, bright red and with a fruity aroma. His two sons added multiple cubes of rock sugar. Emir, the older of the two brothers, commented on Jenkins's beard, which was salt-and-pepper like Demir's. Jenkins hoped the beard might help him to better fit in. He couldn't hide his size, but with the light color of his skin, the beard changed his facial features and, he hoped, made him look more Middle Eastern.

Demir raised his glass. *"Sağliğiniza!" To your health!*

The tea had a sweet taste.

"We were uncertain you made it home," Yusuf said, "until we read of your trial." Yusuf had transported Jenkins from the *Esma* to the Bosphorus strait on an inflatable, successfully outmaneuvering a Russian Coast Guard vessel. He then drove him to the bus terminal in Taksim.

"The Russians followed me into Greece, but I was able to elude them," Jenkins said. "I hope they didn't give you much trouble."

"As I said on the boat," Demir replied. "They wanted you very badly. They came to my home. One was . . . persuasive." Jenkins knew Demir spoke of Federov, and he wondered again whether he could trust the former FSB officer, even with so much money at stake.

"We had to tell them you'd taken a bus from Taksim to Çeşme," Yusuf said. "We were glad to hear that you made it home safely, though not so much about the trial."

"Why have you come back?" Demir asked, cutting to the chase.

Jenkins had contemplated how much to tell Demir, who as a young man had a career in the Turkish Navy, including its special forces, before he took over his father's fishing boat. With the decrease in fish and income, Demir had supplemented his earnings by smuggling items and people into and out of the various countries surrounding the Black Sea, including Russia, for which he had no lost love.

"I need to get back into Russia," Jenkins said.

Demir's eyes widened. He sat back from the table, shaking his head.

"Can it be done?" Jenkins asked.

"Our president has made nice with the Russians for now," Demir said, "but the tensions remain high between Russia and Ukraine. The Russian Coast Guard and navy have become much more diligent."

"I have money. Whatever the cost."

Demir shook his head. "A man cannot value money so much as to lose his family. My Esma, after the visit from the Russians, begged me to quit. It is not about money when one can die, Mr. Jenkins."

"I know," he said. "And I don't want to create more conflict for you. I wouldn't have come to you if I had another way." When no one responded, Jenkins said, "You asked why I came back. I will tell you."

The cups clanked against the silver tray as Emir and Yusuf set them down.

"It is to save someone who saved me. She is in trouble."

Demir's chest rose and fell, a deep breath. He looked to his two sons, who had remained quiet throughout the discussion, their eyes fixed on their father.

Yusuf broke the silence. "Would it be damaging to Mr. Putin?"

"If I can save this person, it would be very damaging."

Yusuf looked expectantly to his father, but the family patriarch raised his hands and said, "Revenge is never a good reason to act. My sons and I will talk. I will give you my word tomorrow. Do you have a place to stay?"

"I can get a hotel."

"It is best to leave the faintest footprint. The Russians now know me and what I do. Though I have remained quiet these past months, it is possible I am still being watched. You will sleep here tonight."

They made a bed for Jenkins in the basement—a mattress on the concrete floor with sheets and blankets. Esma did not warm to Jenkins, and he did not blame her. Federov must have scared her, and now Jenkins was asking her husband to again take his boat back into the bear's jaws. Seeing Esma's pain and her worry gave Jenkins a greater appreciation for how Alex felt, and he deduced it was easier to empathize with loved ones than to acknowledge one's own fears.

Jenkins knew the risk of again engaging the Turkish captain, but he wanted to get into Russia in a manner familiar to him, without agency help, in case, as Alex had speculated, he was being set up. He'd told Lemore that communication would be minimal and provided only on a need-to-know basis until he was in Russia.

In the basement, Jenkins pulled out the encrypted phone. He and Lemore both knew there was no such thing as a safely encrypted cell phone and had agreed to a code. Paulina would be referred to as a painting, Russia as the owner, Lefortovo as the art gallery, and Federov as the art dealer.

He sent Lemore a text.

Transportation being discussed to meet owner of painting.

He contemplated calling Alex but decided it best not to provide her with each update, not to make her predisposed to hearing from him—which would only exacerbate her worry when he didn't, or couldn't, call.

He set the phone on the bedcovers and looked out a narrow rectangular window, high up the stucco wall. Through it, beams of moonlight streamed, the blue-gray the only light in the room.

9

The following morning, Jenkins awoke to bright sunshine, and the light revealed the window to be covered with grime. He checked his watch and calculated that he'd slept nearly twelve hours, another reminder that he was no longer young. He dressed and walked upstairs into a quiet house. Demir sat at the table, speaking with his two sons. It looked almost as if they'd never left their places from the prior evening.

"We thought maybe you were going to sleep all day," Yusuf said.

"I feel like I did," Jenkins said. "I'm a little groggy."

"Sit down. Have some breakfast," Demir said. "The tea will help to wake you."

Along with tea, Esma again served a mountain of food—plates of rye bread, several cheeses, honey, and jam. On another plate she placed tomatoes, cucumbers, and hard-boiled eggs. Demir poured the red tea into Jenkins's glass, and Yusuf handed him the cubes of sugar. This time Jenkins added two and stirred to break up the rocks.

"We have discussed your proposal," Demir said.

Jenkins set down his spoon. His eyes searched the three men but found no indication of an answer.

"I was glad to hear that your return has good intentions. For this, God will bless you." Demir looked to his sons, then to Jenkins. "We have decided to take you back to Russia. But it will be expensive."

"As you said, money is not an issue in these circumstances," Jenkins said, relieved.

"The extra money is not for me, but for another vessel. I will need help keeping the Russian Coast Guard occupied. We cannot be confronted."

"A diversion," Jenkins said.

Demir nodded. "Today I am making phone calls to see if anyone is willing."

"Assuming someone is, when would we leave?"

"Tonight. There is a storm brewing. The waters will be rough, but hopefully that means fewer Russian patrol boats."

"How big a storm?" Jenkins asked.

"Big enough to deter them, but we have fished in worse weather. If I am successful finding a . . . diversion, we leave at dusk. Dress warmly. It will be very cold."

At dusk, having found another boat to serve as a diversion, Demir took no chances of Jenkins being seen leaving the house. Jenkins sat low in the back of the family's windowless van, and when they reached the marina dock, Yusuf wheeled over a basket. Jenkins tumbled inside and Yusuf covered him with blankets and fishing supplies. As Emir and Yusuf wheeled the basket down the dock to the *Esma*, they bantered with other fishermen.

When alerted, Jenkins climbed from the basket into the pilothouse. With deft precision that defied the haphazard mooring of the other ships, Demir and his sons guided the trawler through the marina maze into the Bosphorus strait. Jenkins stood inside the pilothouse, warmed by the air from a space heater and struggling to get his sea legs while watching the lights on the moored tankers drift past. He didn't know

Demir's plan for getting him back into Russia; he'd left the details to the old fisherman and smuggler.

"The fishermen say the possibility of bad weather remains," Demir said, replacing the microphone in the clip of the radio mounted over his head. "We will have to be careful. If the storm strengthens, we will have to turn back."

They passed beneath the enormous white suspension bridge spanning the two landmasses. The last time Jenkins had done so, the bridge had represented the entrance to the Bosphorus strait and, symbolically at least, Jenkins's escape from Russia. Not this night.

Jenkins held out his hand and was pleased it remained steady. The last time he'd been in Russia he'd developed a tremor, what he thought could be the start of Parkinson's, but which a doctor said had been caused by situational anxiety and stress.

When he looked up, he noted Demir watching him from his position at the wheel. "The weather is good for now," Demir said. "You can lie down if you like."

"I'll keep you company, if that is okay."

Demir nodded. "It is okay."

Yusuf and Emir spelled their father at the wheel. In between, they drank tea and played cribbage. Waves soon began to crash over the bow, and the boat shook and shuddered from the impact.

"The weather will get worse," Demir said from behind the wheel. "It is coming from the northeast."

"That is Mother Russia trying to blow you back to America," Emir said, looking up from the cribbage table at Jenkins with a mischievous smile.

"Can we make it?" Jenkins said.

"We have fished in worse weather," Emir said, trying again to summon a fisherman's bravado.

"It may present a challenge getting you to shore, however," Demir said. He barked at his sons. "We are entering Russian waters. No more games."

His sons stored the cribbage board in a cabinet and locked the doors shut, then went about ensuring everything was lashed down or stowed.

"We must be diligent," Demir said. "Unlike before, there is no fog in which to hide."

A short time later, the radar screen emitted a persistent beeping. Demir studied it.

"Is it the Russian Coast Guard?" Jenkins asked, walking to the machine.

"I do not yet know. At present the boat does not appear to be marking us." Demir picked up the radio speaker and adjusted the dial, presumably to a frequency not monitored by the Russians. He spoke Turkish, then lowered the microphone. It clicked, followed by a male voice. Demir spoke again, then clipped the mic overhead.

"I think we have company," Demir said.

Jenkins watched the green blip on the screen. After a moment, he noticed a second blip, this one running parallel with the *Esma*, shadowing it.

"Ahmet," Demir said. Their diversion.

The second boat maintained a parallel course, then veered off, forming a Y as it moved toward, rather than away from, the larger blip, which Demir speculated to be a Russian Coast Guard vessel.

"We will know soon enough if it is Russian," Demir said.

"Can the Russians catch him?" Jenkins asked.

"Unlikely. Ahmet is skilled, and his boat is fast and designed for this type of weather. The question is not if they will catch Ahmet's boat. It is whether they will follow it. We will need time to get you to shore."

Jenkins watched the radar. The Y became more pronounced, now a V as Ahmet's boat widened the distance from the *Esma* but shortened the distance to the larger blip. The radio clicked. Demir answered it.

"Evet?"

This time the male voice sounded more animated. Demir listened, then swung his boat to the left, in the opposite direction. "It is Russian Coast Guard," he said to Jenkins. "A Rubin-class vessel. Maybe your friend Captain Popov has come back again. Let us hope not."

"Can Ahmet outrun it?"

"Not forever, but enough to get back into Turkish waters, if it follows. With the recent accord between our two presidents, Russia will avoid an international incident and be satisfied it has chased Ahmet away. Yusuf," Demir called out. *"Şişme hazirlayin." Prepare the inflatable.*

"This will not be easy, Mr. Jenkins. The waves are considerably larger than I would like. Put on survival suits. Both of you."

Minutes later, Yusuf and Jenkins had put on the thick red-and-black suits, leaving the hoods off for now. The waves increased in size, fueled by a strong wind blowing whitecaps across the water's surface. Yusuf hooked a winch to the apex of cables attached to the four sides of the Zodiac inflatable, and Demir's plan became clearer.

Jenkins followed Yusuf back inside the pilothouse.

"The Zodiac is prepared," Yusuf said to his father.

Out the pilothouse windows, Jenkins could see spotted lights and the dark shadow of mountains rising seemingly from the water. The waves intensified, crashing over the bow of the boat and causing it to pitch.

"I will get you as close to shore as is safe, but I must be careful. There are many unseen rocks. Go," Demir said to his son. "We are almost in position."

Yusuf handed Jenkins a dry bag with a tether and a Velcro strap he could attach to his ankle or wrist. "Put what you can in here. You will have to leave the rest."

Jenkins opened his duffel and stuffed what clothes he could into the dry bag. He pulled out several passports, various other pieces of identification, the encrypted cell phone from Lemore, and rubles and dollars but did not put them in the dry bag. He sealed those inside a plastic bag he shoved inside his dry suit, against his chest.

"We go," Yusuf said.

Jenkins followed the two sons outside, mimicking their movements. He pulled up the hood of his survival suit. The spray from waves hit his face, and the water was as he recalled—numbingly cold. The two sons fought to steady the inflatable as they lowered it, the winch whining. Demir slowed the boat, which increased the impact of the waves and the resulting pitch. Several times Jenkins nearly lost his footing, but he remained upright.

"Go," Emir yelled from the pilothouse door over the howling wind. He looked to be repeating his father's instructions, motioning with his hands that they needed to get into the inflatable.

"We cannot slow any further in this weather. We will be like a cork in a storm. Get in," Yusuf shouted at Jenkins. But that was easier said than done. The inflatable banged against the side of the *Esma,* then swung four to five feet away. Jenkins held the cable and timed the swaying. When the inflatable swung inward, he jumped, falling into the boat with his dry bag.

"Try to center your weight," Yusuf yelled to him.

Jenkins remembered his position from their earlier escape and got on hands and knees in the center of the boat. He gripped the holds on the two pontoons with his gloved hands. Yusuf jumped in behind him, and Emir lowered the winch.

"Hang on, Mr. Jenkins," Yusuf called out. "We are going to have to do this the old-fashioned way."

Without further warning, the boat dropped from the hook and hit the water with a thud and a violent jolt that nearly caused Jenkins to lose his grip on the handholds. Yusuf, who had already started the engine, steered the inflatable sharply to the right, away from the *Esma* so it didn't pinball against the ship's side.

The inflatable rose and fell on the wave crests, water splashing onto both men. With each rise Jenkins felt as though the boat would get caught in the wind, like a kite, and tumble across the whitecaps. Each time the inflatable rose, he could hear the engine whine as the prop came out of the water. With each spray he tasted salt, and he was glad he'd grown the beard, which protected his face.

"I am going to try to get behind those rocks," Yusuf shouted. "It might help to calm the waves."

Water crashed into and over a jetty of rocks. Jenkins gripped the holds. His arms strained from the torque and pressure as he struggled to keep his center of gravity as low as possible. His face and hands soon grew numb. The wind and crashing waves slowed their progress.

"Hang on," Yusuf yelled. He cut the bow of the boat sharply to the right and gunned the engine. For a moment they were sideways in the surf, and Jenkins thought for sure they would capsize, but Yusuf quickly corrected. They hit a wave and the inflatable shot into the air, landing with a violent bounce that yanked the hold from Jenkins's grip. He fell sideways into the pontoon. The inflatable pitched again, this time to the right, and, before Jenkins could grip the hold once more, he fell overboard into the water.

10

The stinging cold water felt like a slap across his face, but Jenkins resisted the urge to gasp, which would cause him to suck liquid into his lungs. Immersed in darkness, he held his breath until he shot to the surface, gasping as he bobbed, as Yusuf had said, like a cork in the ocean. He looked for the inflatable but didn't see it. Another wave loomed over him. He held his breath and tried to descend, but the suit made him buoyant, and the wave crashed on top of him and drove him under. Another lifted him and shoved him forward, toward the rock jetty. Jenkins curled into a ball as he pitched under the crest and slammed into the rocks, bringing a sharp pain to his rib cage. He shot to the surface and again looked for but did not see the inflatable. Probably for the best. The rocks would destroy it.

On his own, Jenkins turned and searched for the shore. He kicked and swung his arms, but the suit made movement difficult, as did the pain to his ribs. The tethered dry bag dragged behind his right arm. Another wave drove Jenkins under. He reached for the Velcro strap on his wrist and wrenched it free, letting it go. When he popped to the surface, he kicked with the waves and the wind.

After several minutes, the mountains appeared closer. Progress.

He lowered his head and kicked with everything he had. Another wave hit him, forcing him under. This time his knees struck the rocky stones. He popped up, realizing the waves would pound him against the bottom. His right side, where he'd struck the rocks, already burned in pain. He could not afford a serious injury.

He tucked into a ball as a wave lifted him and shoved him, tumbling forward. He breached the surface, took a breath, and tucked again. This time he unfurled his legs, pushing off the pebbled bottom with his feet and springing ahead. He fell, went under, but managed to get to his feet, eventually crawling from the sea on hands and knees, gagging and gasping for air.

After he'd caught his breath, Jenkins looked back to the sea. A white light furiously flashed—Demir seeking to determine if Jenkins and Yusuf were alive. He stood with difficulty, legs weak, his side painful. A second light flashed. Yusuf on the inflatable. Jenkins felt for the nipple on the shoulder of his suit and pulled it. The light activated, flashing. After a few seconds, the two lights at sea extinguished, he hoped voluntarily.

Each breath brought pain to Jenkins's side where he'd struck the rocks. He hoped his ribs were not broken, or badly bruised. He coughed and the pain radiated down his side. Again, he bent over, but this time he vomited seawater, retching for several minutes and feeling the cold settle in, the whipping wind chilling him.

Jenkins considered his location. Nothing looked familiar. A white foam filled the shoreline and blew along the stones and pebbles. He walked down the beach, struggling to see, hearing only the howling wind. He was uncertain of where he had entered these same waters nearly a year ago, if he was even close. If he could not find the safe house, it would be a very long night. He looked for anything remotely familiar. Nothing was.

Another few minutes and he'd run out of beach. The tide met where the hillside extended into the water. Jenkins stepped calf-deep, wiggled his feet into the rocky bottom to better anchor them, and looked around the landmass. He saw the glow of streetlights, a trail that led to a gap, perhaps the path he had once taken. Maybe. Thirty feet of turbulent water, of unknown depth, stood between him and the rest of the beach.

He contemplated whether he could climb the hillside looming above him, but the darkness made it difficult to see any path.

He looked again to the sea. His only option.

Jenkins took a deep breath, then another, fighting the pain in his side, trying to steel himself. He walked into deeper water, up to his calves, then his knees. Offshore, a series of large rocks acted as a break against the crashing waves. He stepped carefully, sure of each step before taking another. The water rushed in and sucked out.

Then it deepened. Jenkins became less stable and struggled to keep his balance.

Halfway across.

He stumbled, nearly fell, but remained upright and climbed around the landmass and walked up onto the beach on the other side. After a moment to regain his breath, he moved toward the streetlights, reaching a gap. Relief washed over him. He recognized it. He climbed the path to the deserted street. With the wind whistling and his body feeling the cold more acutely, he'd need to quickly get warm.

The windows of the houses—mostly vacation homes, according to Paulina—were dark. He cut along the side of the second house on his left and crossed the backyard to a vacant lot. He followed the waist-high stone fence to the fourth house in and climbed over the fence into the backyard. The rusted clothesline still whined as it spun in the wind. One of the windowpanes in the back door remained broken where an FSB officer had hit it with his elbow. Jenkins put his ear to the remaining glass panes, listening for any sounds—voices, a television or radio.

He reached into the opening, unlocked the door, and stepped inside. The house still smelled of must and stale air. He walked past the lime-green counter and stepped into the living room. No one. He confirmed that the rest of the house remained unoccupied. Hungry and thirsty, he went to the kitchen and checked the fridge. Empty. He checked each cabinet. Also bare. The water faucet produced no water. He stepped into the room off the kitchen, the one that had held the crate containing scuba gear. The crate had been removed. The Russians had emptied the house. Jenkins was amazed they hadn't burned it to the ground.

In the living room, he unzipped and removed his survival suit. The cold air chilled him, raising goose bumps on his arms. He wished he could light a fire, but even if he had the materials to do so, he knew it would be a mistake. He searched the house for blankets, towels, anything. He found nothing. Tonight would be uncomfortable.

He retrieved the plastic bag and turned on the encrypted phone. It still worked. He pulled up his shirt and checked his side with the phone light but did not see any cuts or bruises, not yet anyway. He touched the skin with the tips of his fingers. It was tender, but he did not think he had cracked any ribs.

He sent Matt Lemore another encrypted message.

Have met with painting owner.

Jenkins set the phone on the floor, lay on the couch, and pulled the survival suit over his body. Exhausted, he closed his eyes, hoping sleep would come, if only for a few hours.

11

Three days after his inauspicious arrival in Vishnevka, Charles Jenkins drove a rented Range Rover into a parking garage beneath an office building in downtown Moscow. The weather had cooperated on his long drive into the city the prior day, when he'd performed a dry run of what he intended for today, if everything went according to plan.

An arctic blast brought clear skies and sunshine, but also bitter cold, dropping the temperature to just five degrees Fahrenheit. He noted the heating and ventilation van remained parked on the first floor near an exit. According to a worker he'd spoken to, the van would be there all week. He parked on the second level near an exit door and stepped from the SUV, feeling a twinge of pain in his side. He'd wrapped his torso with an elastic bandage, but his ribs remained sore.

He slipped on a wool coat over the dark-gray suit he'd bought at a high-end department store, paying exorbitantly for expedited tailoring, along with a fitted shirt, tie, black dress shoes, and socks. Jenkins knew Russian men dressed as well as their salaries allowed, and he needed to impress upon the Union Bank of Switzerland that he did very well.

He walked into the salmon-colored mid-rise on Paveletskaya Ploshchad, across the Moskva River from the Kremlin, at 11:40 a.m., as planned, and crossed a lobby buzzing with people to the bank's glass-door entrance. Up until this point, he had managed to remain anonymous. That was about to change.

He sent a text message to alert Lemore.

Entering freezer.

He typed a second message, but did not yet send it.

Inside the bank he approached the young, and hopefully inexperienced, male teller he'd picked out the prior day. The teller greeted Jenkins with a warm smile. He looked fifteen, with peach fuzz above his lip.

"Dobroye utro," Jenkins said. *Good morning.* He had rehearsed this interaction in the bathroom mirror of the Vishnevka beach house until confident. "I wish to make a deposit," he said, speaking Russian.

"S udovol'stviyem," the bank teller replied. *With pleasure.* "I will need a photo identification."

Jenkins put his Russian passport on the counter. The young man studied the photograph and looked up at Jenkins. *"Mne nravitsya boroda,"* he said. *I like the beard.*

"S ney litsu zimoy tepleye," Jenkins said, returning the smile. *It helps keep my face warm in the winter.*

The young man rubbed at his peach fuzz. *"Ne vsem tak povezlo." Some of us are not so fortunate.* He smiled and clicked his keyboard, his eyes shifting between the passport and his computer screen. He studied the account, and though he didn't overtly show it, a subtle eye blink indicated he was impressed with the balance. Then he grimaced, no doubt noting the account had been frozen. "You said a deposit, correct?"

"Da," Jenkins said.

"One moment, please."

The teller stepped away and spoke to a middle-aged woman, who looked over at Jenkins, then walked to the computer screen, studying it. She smiled at Jenkins. "Your account has been frozen," she said.

"Yes, I am aware. My initial deposit was substantial. I hope to resolve the matter with my personal banker later today." He didn't elaborate or try to overexplain.

"You wish to make another deposit?" she asked.

"I do," he said.

Another smile. "How much do you wish to deposit, Mr. Jenkins?"

"One million, six hundred fifty thousand rubles," Jenkins said, which was roughly twenty-five thousand American dollars. He placed a check, drawn on the account of a CIA proprietary, on the counter.

The woman considered the check, then typed. She nodded to the teller to finish the transaction, smiled warmly at Jenkins, and departed. When the teller looked to the computer screen, Jenkins hit the "Send" button on the encrypted phone.

The cold freeze has lifted, but likely not for long.

So far, so good.

After another minute, the teller handed Jenkins a receipt for his deposit. *"Spasibo."*

"Oh," Jenkins said, subtly hitting the stopwatch button on his wristwatch. *"Ya pereyehal. Mne nuzhno obnovit' informatsiyu na kartochke s obraztsom podpisi, poka ya zdes'." I've moved. I'd better update the information on my signature card while I'm here.*

"Certainly. Let me get your card," the teller said. A minute later the young man came out from behind the counter, keys in hand. "If you'll follow me."

Jenkins did. He checked his phone.

Confirming freeze lifted. Freezer emptied.

The teller led Jenkins into a small private room much like the room with safe deposit boxes used at banks in the United States.

"Take your time," the young man said.

Jenkins smiled. *"Spasibo."*

He would do no such thing.

—

Georgiy Tokareva sat at his computer terminal in the basement of the main Lubyanka building nursing a hangover. The basement had once been the notorious KGB prison, where spies, political dissidents, and various other enemies of the Soviet state had been imprisoned and interrogated. It had been renovated after the fall of communism and converted to a staff cafeteria, plus some limited office space. Tokareva and his cubicle mates joked that the food had not improved much.

Tokareva, an analyst, was grateful just to have a cubicle. Lubyanka had become more crowded as perestroika faded and the government returned to its days of paranoia and distrust. The Kremlin kept hiring additional FSB officers, and those officers needed work space. Tokareva and half a dozen of his mates were moved from the second floor to the basement, what they referred to as "the Siberian gulag," though never out loud. It was a spin on an old Soviet joke.

"What's the tallest building in Moscow?"

"Answer: Lubyanka. You can see Siberia from its basement."

Not that Tokareva minded his exile. Just twenty-four years old, and a recent graduate of Moscow State University with a degree in computational mathematics and cybernetics, he was essentially his own boss. Their supervisor remained on the second floor and rarely, if ever, ventured to the basement. Proof, his fellow analysts said, that the man would never lower himself to their level. Ha!

"S glaz doloy, iz serdtsa von!" his cubicle mates said. *Out of sight, out of mind!*

Tokareva and the other analysts came and went as they pleased. This morning, Tokareva arrived hungover after a late night. One of his fellow analysts had clocked him in and logged on to his computer terminal to ensure Tokareva received full pay. He, of course, returned the favor when needed.

Tokareva sipped coffee and rubbed his temples. He'd taken two ibuprofen, but it had yet to put a dent in his headache.

"I think you have a headache because she was beating you about the head with her fake tits." Arkhip Bocharov stood at Tokareva's cubicle, his ribbing adding to Tokareva's headache. Bocharov shook his head from side to side as if being beaten. "You should have seen this woman," he said to the others. "She had melons the size of basketballs and just as firm."

She'd also been in her midfifties and wore enough makeup to put a clown to shame. Tokareva had flirted with her until Bocharov departed, then excused himself to use the bathroom and slipped out the back door. He went to another bar, where he drank alone.

At present, Tokareva texted a woman he'd met in a Moscow bar two nights ago. He wanted to grab a drink, hoping it could lead to something more, possibly dinner, and perhaps a trip back to what had been his grandfather's apartment, which his parents had inherited and Tokareva gladly occupied. The fourth-floor apartment in Moscow's Arbat District had sweeping views of the Bolshoy Kamenny Bridge over the Moskva River, and across it to the armory and the Cathedral of the Annunciation.

"Yesli u vas ne poluchitsya zdes' perepikhnut'sya," Bocharov had once said upon taking in the view, *"vam nichego ne ostanetsya, krome kak zaveshchat' svoy chlen nauke." If you can't get laid here, you might as well just donate your dick to science now.*

Tokareva hit "Send" just as Bocharov plucked the phone from his hand and read aloud to their fellow exiles Tokareva's prior text messages and the woman's responses.

Dinner and drinks?

"With a cute little smiley face," Bocharov said, stepping around the cubicle as Tokareva stood to advance. "How touching. Ooh, listen to this response."

Who is this?

They all laughed. "You must have made quite an impression, Georgiy."

"Give it back," Tokareva said.

Bocharov laughed. "She loves you, Georgiy boy."

Bocharov and the others made catcalls. He held the phone high over his head. Tokareva, just five foot six, was unable to grab it from his taller colleague. "You keep dating women in bars, and you are going to have a full calendar . . . of doctor's appointments," Bocharov said, and he tossed the phone into the air. Tokareva missed it and the phone hit the carpet with a dull thud.

"You're as good at catching your phone as you are women."

As he was about to sling a retort, Tokareva's computer pinged. It pinged a second time.

"Maybe that's your girlfriend with the big melons. She forgot her dentures in your apartment."

Tokareva went into his cubicle and typed on the keyboard, reading the message. His adrenaline spiked. "Shit." He dropped into his chair and quickly typed. "There is movement on one of the flagged accounts."

"What?" Bocharov stepped into Tokareva's cubicle and studied his computer screen.

"One of the flagged bank accounts has just been accessed," Tokareva said. "At UBS."

"A Swiss account," Bocharov said, peering more closely.

"Of course it's a Swiss account, you idiot. It's a Swiss bank."

"A withdrawal? Did they close the account?"

"No." Tokareva sat back. "A deposit."

"A deposit? On a frozen account?"

"One million, six hundred fifty thousand rubles."

Bocharov leaned over his shoulder. "Who is the officer on the case?"

Tokareva's fingers again flew across the keyboard. He read the name of the FSB officer in charge of the monitored account. "Simon Alekseyov."

"Then you better get this to his attention."

"No kidding?" Tokareva stood and pushed past Bocharov. "Get out of my way, you shit ass."

12

Charles Jenkins checked his stopwatch as he crossed from the private room to the bank teller who had initially helped him. Just under six minutes had passed since he made the deposit. He and Lemore were convinced it would trigger an alert at the FSB. Once it did, Lubyanka was roughly eight minutes by car from the bank, though Moscow traffic could be notoriously unpredictable, especially during the lunch hour, another reason Jenkins had chosen this particular time for the transaction. Jenkins figured he had fifteen minutes, maximum, to finish and get out of the building.

A woman stood at the teller's window talking to the young man, but otherwise she did not look to be conducting further business. Young and attractive, she was way out of the teller's league, but her smile and wide eyes clearly indicated she was enjoying the tease. Jenkins checked his watch. Seven minutes. He didn't have time for this.

He cleared his throat, loud and brusque enough to cause the woman to turn from the counter. When she realized his noise had been intentional, she made a face as if to say: *How rude!* Jenkins, in turn, stared at the woman and arched his eyebrows as if to say: *Take your little amusement ride someplace else. I have business to transact.*

She gathered her things and stepped away. At a safe distance, she turned and flipped him the bird. Jenkins smiled. *"Khoroshego dnya."* *Have a good day.*

The young teller looked sheepish as Jenkins stepped to the counter. "I'm sorry to have kept you waiting, Mr. Jenkins." He looked to the signature card. "You are finished?"

Jenkins handed back the card. "Not quite. I wish to speak to Dimitri Koskovich, please." Koskovich had been the name of the banker on Jenkins's signature card.

The young man looked perplexed. "Is there a problem? Perhaps I can help you."

"Thank you for the offer. Is Mr. Koskovich here?"

The young man looked at the large clock on the wall behind Jenkins. "Let me check." The teller picked up the phone and punched in a number. A moment later he lowered his voice and turned his head, speaking into the receiver. *"Spasibo."* The young teller hung up and redirected his attention to Jenkins. "I'm terribly sorry, but Mr. Koskovich just left for lunch." The young man's eyes shifted to a tall man with gray hair heading toward the bank doors.

"Spasibo." Jenkins moved toward Koskovich, who pulled gloves from the pocket of his long wool coat just before he stepped through the bank's glass doors into the building lobby. Jenkins hurried to the doors but had to stop when a woman with a child in a stroller struggled to enter. He pulled one door open for the woman, then stepped behind the stroller and hurried across the lobby, dodging people leaving for lunch. Koskovich stepped through the revolving door leading to the outside. Jenkins ignored the revolving door and pushed open a glass door next to it. The cold air hit him instantly.

Koskovich, at the bottom of the steps, had opened the back door of a cab, about to lower himself inside.

"Mr. Koskovich?" Jenkins called out, hurrying to the curb.

Koskovich turned at the sound of his name. His facial expression clearly said, *Do I know you?*

"I'm sorry," Jenkins said, speaking Russian as he reached the cab. "I know you are on your way to lunch. I need a minute of your time."

"For what purpose?"

"I need the name on a signature card."

"Have one of the tellers help you," Koskovich said, dismissive. He lowered himself into the cab. Jenkins grabbed the cab door by the edge.

"I'm afraid this is a delicate matter on an account that you opened. Two accounts actually."

"I am a vice president," Koskovich said, pulling on the door. Jenkins refused to release it. "A teller can assist you. Now if you don't mind, I have an engagement."

"I do mind," Jenkins said. "And if you wish to keep your position as vice president, you will tell your engagement you are going to be late."

Koskovich did not immediately protest or express outrage, which indicated a learned demeanor—he'd been previously purchased, or he had performed nefarious transactions.

Jenkins had him.

Koskovich now struggled to determine whether Jenkins was referring to one of those transactions and, more importantly, if Jenkins worked for the federal authorities. He gave Jenkins a smug smile that fooled no one.

"And who might you be?"

"I might be the guy for whom you opened one of the accounts," Jenkins said, switching to English.

That got Koskovich's attention.

The cabdriver turned around, irritated. He made hand gestures to the pair. *"Ey! My ukhodim ili kak? Primi resheniye." Hey! Are we leaving or what? Make up your mind.*

Jenkins ignored him, continuing to hold the door open. "I am not looking to create any trouble for you, Mr. Koskovich. In fact, I believe this information can be financially rewarding to both of us."

The cabdriver sought an answer. Koskovich told him to keep his pants on. "How rewarding?" he said to Jenkins, also speaking English, perhaps so the cabdriver did not understand.

"Five thousand American dollars for five minutes of work."

Koskovich exited the cab and swung the door shut. "I think I can help you, Mr.—"

"Jenkins," he said, sensing a ridiculous James Bond moment. "Charles Jenkins."

—

Tokareva stepped from the elevator and hurried down the parquet floors. The department secretary told him that Alekseyov was attending a mandatory meeting in the conference room and could not be disturbed. The alert on the bank account, however, said otherwise.

Tokareva moved past empty cubicles to the tall wooden door leading to the conference room. He paused just outside it to catch his breath and straighten his appearance, then pushed in the door. Half a dozen men and one woman sat at a long rectangular table reading from packets. At the head of the room, beside a projected computer screen displaying graphs and numbers, stood Dmitry Sokalov, the deputy director for counterintelligence. Tokareva froze. Had he known Sokalov was conducting the meeting, he never would have interrupted. Everyone in the room turned and stared, as if Tokareva had two heads.

"I am sorry to disturb," he said, finding his voice. "I am Georgiy Tokareva. I have an urgent alert for Simon Alekseyov."

At the mention of the name, all eyes shifted to a young, blond officer seated in the middle of the table who had turned his head to the analyst.

"Can it not wait?" Sokalov asked from the front of the room, his stomach protruding over the belt of his pants and straining the buttons of his shirt.

Tokareva cleared his throat. "It cannot." He quickly added, "I apologize for interrupting."

Sokalov motioned to Alekseyov to leave the room, and Alekseyov picked up his packet and hurried from his seat, reaching the end of the table as Sokalov resumed speaking. Alekseyov grabbed Tokareva by the elbow and hustled him out the door. "Tell me what is so vital that you would interrupt a meeting with the deputy director?"

"We received an alert on a flagged bank account. It says to provide immediate notice of any activity . . . day or night. You are the assigned agent."

"A bank account?" Alekseyov asked.

"A Swiss bank account. The assigned agent was originally Viktor Federov."

"Federov? What is the name on the bank account?" Alekseyov asked.

"Charles Jenkins," Tokareva said.

Alekseyov momentarily froze. Then he said, "What is the nature of the alert? Has he withdrawn funds and closed the account?"

"No," Tokareva said. "He could not do so. The account was frozen."

"What then?"

"He deposited one million, six hundred fifty thousand rubles."

"Deposited?"

"Yes."

"From where?"

"I'm sorry?"

"From where did he make the deposit? Could you track his location?"

"The deposit was not done electronically." He handed Alekseyov the printout of the alert.

"He made the deposit in person?" Alekseyov said, looking up from the printout.

"It would seem so," Tokareva said.

Alekseyov scanned the pages. "When?"

"Minutes ago," Tokareva said.

Alekseyov pushed the papers at Tokareva, speaking as he hurried down the hall. "Notify Moscow police. Tell them to block every entrance and exit to and from the bank, and any parking structure associated with it."

"But I am just—"

"Do it, quickly."

Alekseyov turned and ran. The soles of his leather shoes slapped the parquet floor. Inside his cubicle he picked up his desk phone as he grabbed his winter coat from the rack in the corner. "This is Simon Alekseyov. I need a pool car immediately. Have it brought out front at once." He hung up the phone and reached into his desk drawer for his MP-443 Grach, fitting it into the holster at his hip. He started from the cubicle, but another thought stopped him. He picked up his desk phone again and called a number he had not called in months.

The deep, sullen voice answered on the first ring. "Volkov."

"Charles Jenkins is back in Moscow," Alekseyov said.

Jenkins followed Koskovich back inside the bank as his stopwatch sped past nine minutes. Koskovich led Jenkins to a door at the back of the bank, pulled a key on a chain attached to his belt, and unlocked the door. He stepped inside a modest office with utilitarian furniture, tossed his coat over the handrail of one of two chairs, and stepped around his desk to his computer terminal. Floor-to-ceiling windows looked out at a parking lot. An interior door led to a bathroom with a small window.

"Tell me what it is you want." Koskovich dropped all pretenses and spoke English.

"An account was opened in my name on October twelfth of last year. You opened that account. Your name is on my signature card. A second account was opened on the same date at the same time. I want to know the name of the person on the second account."

"For what purpose?" Koskovich asked.

"For this purpose." Jenkins removed $5,000 and put the stack on Koskovich's desk. Koskovich moved to take it but Jenkins leaned his knuckles on the bills.

Koskovich looked up, meeting Jenkins's gaze, clearly trying to determine if there was more money to be had. "If you ask for more money," Jenkins said, "I'll alert the FSB—"

"I highly doubt—"

"I suspect you do not wish to have the names of the parties for whom you have served as a private banker made public knowledge. Moscow is very cold in the winter for the unemployed."

Koskovich pulled back his hand and looked to the computer screen. "What is the name on your account?"

"My name." Jenkins placed his Russian passport on the desk so Koskovich could read it. He did not release his grip. Koskovich typed in Jenkins's name and studied the screen.

"I recall this," he said, which was logical given the amount Federov had deposited in each account. "Once I opened your account, the money was electronically transferred. Everything was handled electronically."

"I need the name on the second account you opened that day."

"Your account has been flagged," Koskovich said.

"I'm aware. So, if you would speed up the process, I think we would both like to get this done quickly."

Koskovich typed. He put a hand on the computer mouse, clicking and moving the cursor. Jenkins snuck a look at his watch. Ten minutes and forty-two seconds. He stepped around the desk, trying to read Koskovich's computer, but saw only an assortment of numbers and Cyrillic letters. Koskovich typed again. Jenkins heard a commotion coming from inside the bank. He checked his watch as he went to the door and cracked it open. Two Moscow policemen had entered. One approached the tellers. The other remained at the doors.

Jenkins shut the door. He'd run out of time.

"Here!" Koskovich said.

Jenkins locked the door and hurried to the desk. "You have a name?"

"Vasilyev, Sergei Vladimirovich," Koskovich said. He looked to the door with a smug smile. "Though I'm not sure it will do you much good."

"Put the money in a drawer so it is safe."

Koskovich took the money from the desk and put it in the bottom drawer, using a key to open and close it.

"You will have to tell them what I have asked of you," Jenkins said.

"Yes," he said.

"You will also have to tell them that I forced you to provide the information."

"Of course."

"And that I physically assaulted you."

"Yes. Wait . . . What?"

Jenkins delivered a straight jab, hitting Koskovich in the face and knocking him over his chair. His head banged against the wall and he lay unconscious. Jenkins pulled the retractable key chain from Koskovich's belt and clipped it to his own belt as he walked to the office door. He took a breath before he stepped from the office, closing the door and locking a deadbolt. He walked with confidence toward the police officer stationed just to the left of the glass doors, resisting the urge to turn his head to determine if the young bank teller was watching him.

The officer gave Jenkins a stern stare and raised a hand like a traffic cop.

Jenkins waved it away. *"Ya Dimitri Koskovich, vitse-prezident banka. Ob'yasnite mne, chto proiskhodit." I am Dimitri Koskovich. I am the bank vice president. Tell me what is going on.*

"Nikogo ne vypuskat'," the guard said. *No one is to leave.*

"Kto vam dal pravo?" On whose authority?

"Federal'naya sluzhba bezopasnosti." The Federal Security Service.

Jenkins nodded, continuing to speak Russian as he pulled out the key chain. "Do you wish for me to lock the doors until the FSB arrives? It would ensure compliance and keep customers out."

The officer turned to the glass doors. "Do as you like."

Jenkins walked to the doors. He had no idea which of the three keys on the chain opened and locked the bank's front doors.

Behind him, a voice called out. *"Izvinite." Excuse me.*

The bank teller.

In his peripheral vision, Jenkins watched the police officer step away from the doors. Jenkins inserted the first key. The lock didn't turn.

"Chto vy khoteli?" What is it you want? the officer asked the teller.

Jenkins inserted the second key. It turned.

"That man at the door."

"What about him?"

"What is he doing?"

"What does it look like he's doing? He's locking the door."

"Why?"

"Why not?"

"Why would he have a key?" the teller asked.

Pause. "He is the vice president."

"No. He is not."

Jenkins stepped out the glass door and pulled it shut. He tried not to look but saw the two police officers turn their heads toward him. He assumed, since it was a bank, that the doors would be at least shatter resistant, but he didn't intend to hang around to find out. He inserted the key and turned the lock, deadbolting the doors. The officers sprinted toward him, but Jenkins turned and folded into the lunch-crowd lobby as the doors rattled behind him.

13

Simon Alekseyov stepped out from the passenger seat as soon as Arkady Volkov pulled the black Škoda Octavia to a stop behind several Moscow police cars parked in the plaza of the salmon-colored building. Volkov had been Viktor Federov's partner for years, until Charles Jenkins put Volkov in the hospital and Alekseyov took his place. Alekseyov and Federov had chased Jenkins across the Black Sea and into Turkey and Greece. Alekseyov presumed Volkov had a working knowledge of Jenkins, which is why he wanted him along.

Alekseyov hurried around the front of the vehicle and flashed his FSB credentials at several officers braced against the cold. Additional officers stood inside the lobby peering through a glass-door entrance to the bank. Good. They had locked the bank down, as instructed.

"We have a bit of a problem," the ranking officer said after Alekseyov introduced himself. "Someone has locked the door and taken the key."

"I instructed them to lock down the bank," Alekseyov said.

The officer shook his head. "Yes, but the person who locked the door was not a bank employee. He locked the doors from the outside."

"What?" Alekseyov stepped up and rattled the doors. "Open them," he said to the officer.

"We are trying. There is another key inside the bank, but they are having trouble locating it, and the bank officer is presently indisposed."

Alekseyov swore and stepped back. "And the person who locked the door?"

"Fled," the officer said.

"They've been locked inside," Alekseyov said to Volkov, who had joined them. Volkov still had a red scar along a crease in his forehead that extended down the side of his face, earned from his prior confrontation with Charles Jenkins. Alekseyov turned back to the officer. "How long have they been locked inside?"

"Five minutes, perhaps," the officer said.

"Go to the garage," Alekseyov said to Volkov. "Ensure they have shut the gate and that no car leaves."

Volkov crossed the lobby and pushed back outside.

Inside the bank, a woman quickly approached, key in hand. She inserted the key and turned the lock, pulling the door open. Alekseyov stepped inside. "Who is in charge?"

A man stepped forward holding a towel to his face. He had blood on his chin and his white shirt. He looked somewhat startled and perhaps dazed. "I am," he said.

"And who are you?"

"I am Dimitri Koskovich, vice president of this branch."

Alekseyov held up a photograph of Jenkins used in the prior investigation.

"Is this the man who came into the bank today?"

Koskovich glanced at the photograph as if it hurt his eyes to do so. "Yes, but he has a beard. He assaulted me in my office and took the keys."

Alekseyov was not interested in the explanation. "Describe the beard."

"Black and white. A beard."

"Was it thick, thin? Groomed, ungroomed?"

"It was thin. Groomed."

"Where is the teller who accepted the deposit?"

"Here." A young man in a cheap suit raised his hand.

Alekseyov showed him the photograph. "You helped this man make a deposit?"

"Yes. One million, six hundred fifty thousand rubles."

Alekseyov now understood why the account had been unfrozen. "Was that the extent of the transaction?"

"No. He also asked to review the information on his signature card."

"Did he change the information on his signature card?"

"No. But he asked to speak to the person who opened his account."

"And who was that?"

The young man pointed. "Dimitri Koskovich."

Alekseyov walked back to Koskovich, who was wiping at the blood on his shirt with the towel. "You opened Mr. Jenkins's account?"

Koskovich looked up. "I was a bank teller at the time. Everything was done electronically."

"When?"

"October twelfth of last year."

"What did Mr. Jenkins want from you when he came in today?"

"Of me? Nothing." Koskovich looked and sounded uncertain. Alekseyov wasn't buying it.

"Why did he ask for you? Why did he assault you?"

"He wanted the name on a second account I opened at the same time. It is strictly against bank policy to reveal such information, but he hit me and forced me to provide it."

"He forced you? How?"

Koskovich hesitated. "I believe he had a gun."

"Did you see it?"

"Well, no . . . But he said he had a gun."

Unlikely. During their prior chase across Turkey and Greece, Jenkins never used a gun. "Did you give him the name on the second account?"

"As I said, it is against bank policy, but he—"

"Just answer the question," Alekseyov said, growing impatient. "Did you give him the name?"

"I had no choice. I could lose my—"

"What was the name?"

"I am not supposed to divulge—"

Alekseyov stepped forward, inches from Koskovich's face, keeping his tone stern but his volume low. "If you wish to keep your job, you will answer my questions. I know full well that many oligarchs and Bratva use this bank, and I have no doubt they have made it worth your while to ensure their names and their money are undetectable. I also highly doubt that Mr. Jenkins had a gun. I would suspect that rubles, not threats, would be the more likely incentive to loosen your tongue. Tell me the name on the second account, or you will find yourself part of a criminal investigation. Do I make myself clear?"

No pretenses now.

The FSB knew Jenkins was back in Moscow.

He stepped around the rented Range Rover and got behind the wheel. He didn't know how much time he had, but he knew the Range Rover was out of the question. The parking structure had cameras that would identify the car and license plate, and it would be easily recognized on surface streets. He pulled from the parking space and punched the gas, tires squealing as he made a sharp turn up the ramp to the first level. He stopped beside the heating and ventilation van at the back of the floor. The workers had left promptly at noon for lunch, as they had the prior day. What Jenkins cared about was the service van, which blocked the garage cameras. A short reprieve, no doubt, but he'd take what he could get. He grabbed a duffel bag with a change of clothes from the back seat, then removed the rental car papers from the glove box. He tossed the car keys on the car floor, hit the manual lock, and shut the driver's door. Time to move. He flipped up the collar on his coat and slipped on a black knit cap, pulling it low on his head as he hurried to the exit.

Significant commotion remained outside the bank, with more Moscow police vehicles and police officers arriving, as well as unmarked cars with bar lights atop their roofs and in back windows. Despite the cold, a crowd milled on the sidewalk, likely believing there had been a bank robbery. Jenkins dropped the car rental papers in a trash bin and checked his watch as he walked away from the garage. At the street corner he took a right and watched a bus pull to the bus stop precisely on time. He knocked on the door, which the driver kept shut against the cold. The doors pulled open and Jenkins stepped on board, keeping his head down and displaying the pass he had also picked up the prior day.

The bus departed almost immediately after Jenkins boarded. He found a seat at the back, removed the encrypted cell phone, and sent Matt Lemore another message.

Art dealer's name is Sergei Vladimirovich Vasilyev. Need address.

Jenkins slid the phone inside his jacket pocket, sat back, and took a deep breath. The bus made several stops along the busy Third Ring Road. On the fourth stop, Jenkins exited through the back door. The beltway remained congested with Moscow's lunch commute, but this stop was closest to an exit. He hailed a Moscow taxi and slipped into the back seat.

"Aeroport Sheremet'yevo," he said.

Alekseyov stood beside the Range Rover. Fingerprint technicians had been dispatched, but that was a mere formality. A security camera had captured the SUV with Charles Jenkins behind the wheel. Additional cameras showed Jenkins driving the Range Rover up the ramp. The vehicle, however, had never exited the garage, never even approached the kiosk at the top of the ramp. Alekseyov and Volkov walked the ramp and eventually found the car parked behind a heating and ventilation service van that had blocked the camera on that floor. The workers, speaking over the sound of the heating units, had never seen the car or the person driving it. They found it on return from their lunch break and discovered the doors locked.

Charles Jenkins was buying himself time, and succeeding. But for what purpose? The bank teller said the frozen account contained more than $4 million, but Volkov expressed skepticism when Alekseyov suggested that money had been the purpose for Jenkins's return to Moscow.

Alekseyov called the phone number for the rental car company identified on the sticker on the back window and determined the car had been rented to a man named Ruslan Scherbakov, who fit Charles Jenkins's physical description. The company described him as being of Middle Eastern descent. Alekseyov called Lubyanka and provided the name, not that he thought Jenkins would use "Scherbakov" again.

He looked to Volkov, who hadn't uttered more than a few words since the two men got inside the car and sped to the bank. He wondered how Viktor Federov and Volkov had worked together so many years. Volkov's silence would have unnerved Alekseyov. "Why else would Mr. Jenkins come back to Moscow, Arkady? Why else if not for the money?"

Volkov did not answer.

It was like talking to himself. "You drive," Alekseyov said. "I have phone calls to make."

Back at Lubyanka, a secretary approached Alekseyov and Volkov as soon as they stepped from the elevator. She directed them to a conference room on the third floor. Uncertain what awaited them, Alekseyov looked to Volkov, but the man only shrugged.

When Alekseyov pushed open the door, he was surprised to find half a dozen analysts working telephones and computer screens, including Georgiy Tokareva, who had initially interrupted the deputy director. A barrel-chested man stood over Tokareva, who feverishly typed on a keyboard. Alekseyov did not know the barrel-chested man, but as he stepped toward him, he heard Volkov utter a name under his breath.

"Adam Efimov."

Before Alekseyov could ask Volkov for clarification, he heard Tokareva say, "Both accounts were emptied electronically. More than four million from Mr. Jenkins's account and nearly six million in Sergei Vasilyev's account."

"Can you trace where the money was sent?" the man asked.

"I am trying, but whoever emptied the accounts was sophisticated. There are many firewalls and false trails."

"Determine where the money went and whether it can be diverted or frozen. Also determine, if you can, from where the diversion took place, from what country."

The man turned, noticing Alekseyov and Volkov. He didn't bother to greet them, stepping past them and motioning them to follow him from the conference room. They walked into an adjacent, unoccupied office. He shut the door.

"Who are you?" Alekseyov asked.

The man raised a hand. "I have been asked by the deputy director to take over this investigation."

"Take over?" Alekseyov said.

"I assume you are Simon Alekseyov and you are Arkady Volkov?"

"I did not receive this news," Alekseyov said.

"I just told you," Efimov said. "Please, feel free to speak to the deputy director, but do so on your own time. I understand Mr. Jenkins was previously involved in a highly sensitive CIA operation." When Alekseyov did not immediately answer, the man said sternly, "Is that correct?"

"Yes, the seven sisters," Alekseyov said.

"Listen carefully, both of you. The director does not want it revealed that Mr. Jenkins exposed a highly placed source within the CIA. He is concerned it could jeopardize other ongoing operations. He also does not want the specter of international embarrassment."

"Embarrassment?" Alekseyov asked.

"What would you call allowing a cadre of Russian women acting as American agents to spy under our noses for decades?" Efimov did not wait for an answer, his question apparently rhetorical. "This matter will be handled with the utmost sensitivity and discretion. It is no longer an official FSB investigation. Is that understood?"

"Not an FSB—"

"Is it understood?"

"Yes," Alekseyov said.

"Good. Local police will be utilized to the extent possible and told only that Mr. Jenkins is a common criminal guilty of crimes in Moscow. Any public information will come only from the deputy director's office. You are to reveal nothing. Is that also understood?"

Alekseyov had not anticipated this, and though he was confused, a sense of relief washed over him. He did not want to be the lead officer. Not now. Similar instructions had been in place during Viktor Federov's prior attempt to capture Charles Jenkins, and Federov had paid the price for his failure. Alekseyov did not want to become the FSB's next scapegoat. "If it is no longer an FSB investigation, why am I involved?" he asked.

"We have work to do." Efimov ignored the question and pulled open the door. Alekseyov looked to Volkov, but the man remained expressionless.

Efimov led them back into the conference room and approached the analyst Tokareva, who remained seated at a computer terminal. "Pull up the footage of Mr. Jenkins leaving the garage," Efimov said.

Alekseyov knew that in 2016 Moscow had installed thousands of Italian Videotec cameras throughout the city, ostensibly to monitor traffic and traffic accidents, but the cameras also allowed Moscow police, the FSB, and other interested government agencies to conduct surveillance throughout the city.

Efimov pointed at the screen with a thick finger. "This is camera footage on Paveletskaya Ploshchad just after Mr. Jenkins left the bank and presumably went to his car," he said. Alekseyov watched Jenkins ascend from the stairwell. "Stop the footage. Confirm his identity," Efimov said. It was not a question for Alekseyov or Volkov. Moscow had also installed 174,000 closed-circuit, facial-recognition cameras throughout the city, one of the largest and most expensive systems in the world.

Tokareva's computer screen indicated a match with a previous photograph of Charles Jenkins.

Alekseyov said, "He has grown a beard since he last came to Moscow—"

"And he is black," Efimov said, "which is far more descriptive."

"Yes." Alekseyov rushed to add, "I gave instructions to close the garage. Mr. Jenkins abandoned his rental behind—"

"Run the tape," Efimov instructed Tokareva. They watched Jenkins walk from the bank building and turn the corner at the end of the street. Tokareva typed on his keyboard and brought up different camera footage. "We picked him up walking southwest on Valovaya Street to this bus stop," Efimov said.

Jenkins boarded the bus just before it departed.

"He timed the bus," Efimov said to Alekseyov. "He never had any intention of taking the car. He parked it behind the van because it blocked camera coverage in the garage. Shutting the garage was, therefore, superfluous. Mr. Jenkins is buying precious minutes, and we are already behind. Pull up the bus route," he said to Tokareva.

Sweat dripped down Tokareva's forehead. He pulled up a map of Moscow that included a red line depicting the designated bus path.

"It crosses Krymsky Most Bridge over the Moskva River, then follows the Third Ring Road around the city. A loop," Efimov said, "which means he had no intention of staying on it for long. It was intended to be disinformation. I want every camera in that area searching for that bus."

"We can analyze camera coverage—" Alekseyov started.

Efimov spoke over him. "Yes, while we all grow old and Mr. Jenkins gets further away. Moscow police have been instructed to find and to detain the bus as well as the bus driver for questioning. Now, do either of you know why Mr. Jenkins returned to Moscow?"

"It appears he came to obtain more than ten million dollars held in two Swiss bank accounts," Alekseyov said.

"Why would he come back to Moscow to do this?" Efimov asked.

"We froze the account opened in his name after we learned of it," Alekseyov said. "He returned, it appears, to make a deposit. When the account was unfrozen to deposit the funds, someone emptied it electronically."

"I understand it was two accounts. Who is Sergei Vasilyev?"

"We do not know."

"Find out."

Across the room, an officer held up a cell phone and called to Efimov. "Moscow police," the officer said.

Efimov took the phone and listened for a moment, then asked, "Does he recall how long Mr. Jenkins was on the bus? Press him. See if you can jar his memory."

Efimov handed back the phone, speaking to Alekseyov and Volkov. "The bus driver does not recall where Mr. Jenkins got off the bus." He raised his voice. "Do we have camera coverage yet?" No one answered.

"That bus route is one of the busiest in Moscow at this time of day," Alekseyov said.

"Precisely why Mr. Jenkins chose it," Efimov said.

Another voice called to Efimov, this time a woman. She turned the monitor of her computer to face the three men, revealing a British passport depicting Charles Jenkins with a salt-and-pepper beard and the name Scott A. Powell.

Efimov raised his voice, speaking to the entire room. "Check all the airlines and train stations for any reservations existing under the names Scott A. Powell or Ruslan Scherbakov." He turned to Alekseyov. "Alert the border service. Ensure they have updated photographs of Mr. Jenkins with and without the beard." To another analyst he said, "I want to know if any credit cards or debit cards associated with either of those names have been used in the last three hours."

"And what of Sergei Vasilyev?" Alekseyov said.

The woman seated at one of the computer terminals called out. "A credit card in the name of Scott A. Powell was used within the past thirty minutes to make an airline reservation on British Airways flight 235, leaving Sheremetyevo Airport at 1:35 this afternoon."

Efimov considered his wristwatch. "Alert the airport police. Tell them that if they must detain the plane, they have the deputy director's authority to do so."

"It's too easy," Volkov said softly, just before another analyst called out.

"I have located an airline reservation for a Scott A. Powell on Turkish Airlines flight TK3234, leaving Vnukovo Airport at 2:09 p.m."

"Airline reservation for Ruslan Scherbakov leaving Domodedovo Airport on Emirates flight EK7875 at 1:53 p.m. today," a third analyst said.

Several more analysts called out names and details of additional reservations.

Volkov shot Alekseyov a glance out of the corner of his eye.

"Pull up a map of Moscow," Efimov said to Tokareva. The analyst did so. Efimov pointed with a pen as he spoke. "Moscow is serviced by ten airports. Three have international airlines. Sheremetyevo, Vnukovo, and Domodedovo. Mr. Jenkins stepped on the bus as a diversion. It does not service any of those airports. Domodedovo is the farthest away . . . forty-five kilometers. Sheremetyevo and Vnukovo are about thirty kilometers and can be reached by high-speed train or by taxi. Of the two airports, Vnukovo services mostly domestic flights, which does Mr. Jenkins no good. Belorussky railway station provides nonstop services to Sheremetyevo and is close to the bus line. That is likely where he exited the bus."

Tokareva shouted animatedly, "I have camera footage of Mr. Jenkins exiting the bus."

Efimov hurried to the terminal. "He's in the back of a taxi. Follow the taxi as far as you can."

Efimov gave orders to get film footage of the Belorussky railway station during the past hour, and to have police sent to the two nearest airports. Then he turned and spoke to Alekseyov and Volkov. "We will travel to Sheremetyevo."

"We?" Alekseyov said.

"This is your case file, is it not?" Efimov said, moving to the door without waiting for an answer.

Alekseyov sat in the passenger seat doing Efimov's bidding as Volkov drove. He struggled at first to get around and through the heavy Moscow traffic, but made good time once outside the city limits.

Alekseyov made calls to the airport police, who confirmed a Scott A. Powell had checked in for flight 235 and boarded that plane to Heathrow. Upon Efimov's orders, Alekseyov instructed that the plane be detained at the gate under the pretense that it awaited connecting passengers. Airport police asked Alekseyov if he wanted them to deplane Scott Powell and hold him at the airport security office, and he relayed the question to Efimov.

"Tell them not to do anything until we arrive. With Jenkins on the plane, he is in—what do the Americans call it . . ."

"A crucible," Volkov said, surprising Alekseyov with a verbal response.

"Yes, a crucible. He has nowhere to go," Efimov said.

Alekseyov relayed Efimov's orders and disconnected the call.

"It looks as if Mr. Jenkins's day of reckoning is at hand," Efimov said.

Neither Alekseyov nor Volkov responded.

"You've been quiet, Arkady," Efimov said from the back seat. "You *are* quiet. I thought you would perceive this as good news given what transpired before . . . No?"

"Mr. Jenkins did what he had to do," Volkov said without emotion.

Efimov chuckled. "I wonder if Federov would be as . . . gracious as you. Losing Mr. Jenkins cost him his job."

"One does not lose what one never possessed," Volkov said, again displaying no emotion. "The FSB needed a scapegoat to save face. Viktor was the easy choice."

"Maybe so," Efimov said. "At least with you in the hospital."

Alekseyov glanced at Volkov, but if the man was offended by the insult, he gave no indication.

Volkov parked at the curb outside Sheremetyevo Terminal F. Efimov instructed Alekseyov to flash his badge at an overzealous police officer on parking duty while he and Volkov hurried inside the international terminal. Alekseyov rushed to catch up, wondering again what Efimov had meant when he said, *This is your case file, is it not?*

They encountered a handful of airport police, including a woman. She extended a hand to Alekseyov, who introduced himself. Alekseyov noted that Efimov did not introduce himself or provide any credentials.

"I am Captain Regina Izmailova. We spoke on the telephone," the officer said to Alekseyov. "Mr. Powell remains on the plane, as instructed. The passengers have been told the plane has been delayed while it awaits connecting passengers from Frankfurt."

"And you have allowed no one to leave?" Alekseyov asked.

"The doors have been closed since we spoke."

Alekseyov eyed three fit-looking men dressed in jeans, tennis shoes, and windbreakers. They carried identical backpacks. "These are plain-clothed officers?" Alekseyov asked.

"Also as instructed," Izmailova said.

They didn't exactly look inconspicuous, but Alekseyov concluded they were better than officers in uniform. With cell phones recording every perceived injustice, removing a black American from a flight could become the face of Russian discrimination. Beyond that, once posted on the Internet, the footage would alert the American intelligence community that Russia had arrested Jenkins, which would cause the telephones in the Kremlin to buzz.

"Take us to the gate," Efimov said to the woman.

They climbed into two electric carts and sped down the terminal, honking the horn at unsuspecting travelers. At the gate Efimov spoke to the plain-clothed officers. "Remove Mr. Powell from his seat with as little disruption as possible."

Izmailova stepped forward. "If I may? We have a plan that takes into account your concerns." Izmailova turned to a woman dressed in a flight attendant's uniform. "This is Officer Pokrovskaya. She will tell Mr. Powell that he has been upgraded to business class, as he requested. Once he is brought forward, she will close the drapes behind him, and the three officers will enter the plane. I believe Mr. Powell will see the futility of a struggle."

"But if not," Efimov said, turning again to the three male officers, "you are authorized to remove him by any means necessary. Cover his head before he is brought through the gate into the terminal. Are there any questions?"

No one spoke.

"Get it done," Efimov said.

When the gate door opened, the four officers moved down the ramp. Alekseyov looked to Volkov, but his placid expression revealed no thoughts.

Efimov also noted this. "Relax, Arkady. This time it will be Mr. Jenkins who is quite surprised."

Less than five minutes later, the door to the gate opened and the plain-clothed officers escorted Charles Jenkins from the plane, a hood covering his head, his arms zip-tied behind his back. He wore the same suit he'd worn in the photos Alekseyov had collected of Jenkins departing the bank parking structure earlier that day. The officers quickly moved Jenkins to the electric cart, putting him in the middle seat between them and shoving him forward so he was not in view of airline commuters.

At the security center they hustled Jenkins from the cart into a room. Efimov stepped in after Jenkins, followed by Alekseyov and Volkov. The officers seated Jenkins in a chair at a table.

"Remove the hood," Efimov said to one of the plain-clothed officers.

"What the bloody hell is going on here?" the black man said in a clipped British accent. "I demand to speak to the British embassy."

Efimov tapped the table for several seconds. He looked to be chewing nails, and not enjoying the taste. Then he stood, turned, and departed the room without a word.

Alekseyov turned to Volkov. The longtime FSB officer looked to be suppressing a grin, though Alekseyov could not be certain; he'd never seen Volkov smile.

14

Forest surrounded the Rozhdestveno Estate and M'Istral Hotel and Spa, situated on Istra Lake, which Jenkins had noted on a map pulled up on his phone. A single two-lane road provided access to and from the hotel. If the FSB had checked credit card transactions, as Matt Lemore had done, and if they had sent officers to the M'Istral Hotel, Jenkins might already be too late. The FSB did not yet know Viktor Federov and Sergei Vasilyev were one and the same, and Jenkins needed to protect that secret for his plan to succeed.

Jenkins figured he had two things working in his favor. First, when his name popped up at the bank, the FSB, embarrassed once by his actions, would be overly aggressive in pursuing him and therefore devote much of their resources to the airports, as Jenkins had intended. They wouldn't recognize their mistake until they physically obtained the black British MI6 agent Lemore had secured. Jenkins hoped the delay would allow enough time for him to get to the hotel to find Sergei Vasilyev and for them to leave before the FSB changed its focus.

Second, according to the credit card transactions, Vasilyev—Federov—planned to enjoy several days at the hotel and spa. Jenkins hoped the FSB would conclude, as he had, that Vasilyev appeared in no hurry to go anywhere, while Jenkins looked to be fleeing the country. But there was no guarantee. Jenkins, trying to think two moves ahead, contemplated how he and Federov—assuming Federov cooperated, and that was a big assumption—might leave the spa if the FSB closed the access road. He knew from his past interaction with Federov that the former FSB agent was divorced and not close to his ex-wife. Therefore, she was not his likely massage partner for the couple's massage Vasilyev had booked. He also doubted that Federov, bitter from his first marriage, had remarried in the past year. That meant the person Federov checked into the hotel with had, at the very least, a different last name, which could be useful.

After pulling over the car he'd rented at the airport, Jenkins changed from his suit into warm clothes and boots he kept in the duffel bag. Then he drove until stopping at a wrought-iron gate to the hotel. No roadblocks. At least not yet.

A young security guard reluctantly stepped from his booth into the cold. He did not look happy. His breath preceded him as he approached Jenkins's car. Jenkins lowered his window partway and advised that he was meeting his friend, a guest, Sergei Vasilyev. The guard, looking less than interested, checked a list on a clipboard.

"A kak tebya zovut?" And what is your name?

"Volkov, Arkady Otochestovich," Jenkins said. He slowly and deliberately spelled the name, but the guard cut him off, anxious to return to his warm shack. He pressed a button attached to his belt to activate the gate and waved Jenkins through.

Jenkins drove over red pavers, sprinkled with a dusting of snow, that weaved through manicured landscaping to a center island. The building entrance stood three stories tall, with a columned porte cochere. Above it, a large Russian flag—white, blue, and red horizontal stripes—fluttered in a light breeze. Behind the entrance rose an eight-story, pale-yellow hotel capped by a white cupola.

Jenkins handed the valet parking attendant the keys to the rented car and walked inside the circular lobby of polished marble and mahogany wood. An enormous crystal chandelier hung over an elaborate flower arrangement, and live music emanated from a piano played by a tuxedo-clad man. Federov looked to be enjoying his retirement.

Jenkins approached the counter and smiled at the young woman. He spoke Russian. "Good afternoon. I am to meet your guest Sergei Vasilyev. Would you be so kind as to tell me his room number?"

The young woman typed on the computer screen. "Yes, Mr. . . . ?"

"Volkov. Arkady Volkov." Jenkins hoped the name of Federov's long-time FSB partner would pique his curiosity rather than scare him, though Jenkins did not expect the woman to give him the number of Federov's room. Still, it couldn't hurt to ask.

"I'm afraid hotel policy does not allow me to give out guest room numbers, and he is not answering the phone in his suite."

"I understand. He and his companion have arrived, though?"

The woman nodded. "Yes, he has arrived, Mr. Volkov."

"Hmm . . . ," Jenkins said. "I have not been able to reach his cell phone for the past half hour, which is not like him." Jenkins checked his watch. "I'm worried we will miss our meeting."

"Another moment, please." The woman typed, then studied the computer. "I see the problem. Mr. Vasilyev has scheduled a couple's massage this afternoon. Cell phones are not allowed in the spa center."

"Ah," Jenkins said. "That is a relief. I'll walk the grounds a bit and wait so as not to disturb his massage. This cold weather can be hard on the joints, and he has been working long hours as of late."

Jenkins reached across the marble counter and handed the woman a folded note, one thousand Russian rubles, roughly fifteen dollars. *"Spasibo."*

The woman looked to a door to her right before stuffing the money in her vest pocket.

Jenkins followed posted signs directing him to the spa center, a separate building just a short walk out the back of the hotel. Inside the building he passed a pristine pool with potted palms and poolside lounge chairs situated beneath a peaked glass atrium. A young child's voice echoed as he launched himself from the side, splashing into the pool. His mother ignored him, reading a magazine.

Jenkins stepped through glass doors and approached another young woman behind the counter. He informed her that he had just arrived after a long drive and was hoping she had an opening for a massage. The woman checked her computer terminal and advised that she would have an opening in roughly fifteen minutes.

"Actually, my wife would like to join me. She's in the room making telephone calls. I understand there's a designated room for a couple's massage?"

"There is. The doors are marked. It will be door number three."

The woman handed Jenkins plush towels and invited him to change in an adjoining locker room. "I'll let my wife know," he said. "If you could be so kind as to direct her to the correct room when she arrives?"

The woman said it would be her pleasure.

Jenkins took the towels into the locker room, set them on a bench, and stepped out a door on the other side into a short, carpeted hall. Soft instrumental music played from overhead speakers, mood music to soothe and relax the guests. Jenkins hoped that was the case, because Viktor Federov had a big surprise coming.

As he approached the door marked with a "3," a man and a woman exited the room, closing the door behind them. They wore uniforms similar to the woman at the counter—khaki pants and yellow shirts with the spa logo above the right breast. The masseuses. Jenkins waited for them to depart the hall, then he slowly pushed open the door, revealing a room with see-through yellow curtains pulled closed across floor-to-ceiling windows. Snow-sprinkled lawn sloped to a pier extending into a glass-calm lake. A man and a woman occupied the two massage tables; the woman lay on the table to his left, the man to his right. Both looked to be asleep.

Jenkins approached the man. A pale-red sheet covered his lower half. His upper half glistened with what was likely oil. Jenkins picked up a towel and walked to the side of the table, getting a look at the man's face. Federov. Sound asleep.

Jenkins gripped Federov's shoulders and lowered his mouth to Federov's ear. "Since you could not come to the United States, I decided to come to you," he said.

Federov's eye opened and angled to look at Jenkins. Well-trained, the former FSB officer did not startle, sit up quickly, or lash out, knocking things over. Federov lifted his shoulders when Jenkins eased his grip. "Unless you wish the woman to know your true name, I would suggest discretion," Jenkins whispered. "But I would also suggest expediency. The FSB is likely not far behind me."

Efimov had no idea whether the man they'd removed from the airplane was a CIA officer or MI6. Given his physical resemblance to Charles Jenkins, including his clothes, it seemed unlikely to have been a coincidence. Not that he had time to care. He had a singular purpose—find Charles Jenkins. That Efimov had grown up in Saint Petersburg with both Vladimir Putin and Dmitry Sokalov was largely the reason he had secured his current position. After the FSB had formally released the prisoner, the president had made it clear that, childhood friendships aside, he expected results, not excuses, if Efimov wished to retain his position. Putin had remained in a foul mood since Efimov had been unable to get any information out of Paulina Ponomayova, and the president did not like to be disappointed more than once.

Efimov was certain Ponomayova had no information to give. If she did, he would have retrieved it. He remained convinced Ponomayova was either brain damaged from the car accident that led to her months-long hospitalization, or she had far less information than the FSB, and the president, had initially given her credit for. Efimov had always been particularly effective in his interrogations, and he refused to believe Ponomayova was his first failure.

In the interests of time, and not wanting to create another possible incident depicting Russia's perceived mistreatment of people of color—which would reflect badly on the administration—and predicting that the British man would have no information of value, Efimov had him released with apologies, and he turned his attention elsewhere.

"What other leads do we have on Mr. Jenkins's whereabouts?" Efimov asked Alekseyov from the back seat of the car as Volkov drove from the airport.

"We have alerted the border patrol and provided the office with Jenkins's recent picture as well as his known aliases."

"He can change his appearance, and he has already demonstrated he has many aliases. He will not use the same name twice," Efimov said. "I asked what other leads we have."

Alekseyov flipped through pages of a spiral notepad, reading, then said, "When Mr. Jenkins went into the bank, he asked the vice president about a second account, one belonging to a Sergei Vasilyev."

"Call Lubyanka. Determine if they have learned anything more about Jenkins or this Vasilyev."

Minutes later, Alekseyov disconnected a cell phone call to Lubyanka. "They have identified credit card traffic for a Sergei Vladimirovich Vasilyev."

"Do you have an address?"

"A pochtomat in a railway station in the Cheryomushki District," Alekseyov said, referring to a machine with lockers where packages and mail could be left.

Volkov turned his head to Alekseyov.

"Something you wish to say, Arkady?" Efimov asked.

"No," Volkov said.

"What were the most recent credit card charges?" Efimov asked.

"Yesterday morning at 7:42 a.m., a charge was made at the M'Istral Hotel and Spa in Rozhdestveno."

"Did they get a photograph—a driver's license?"

"They have not found one."

Strange, Efimov thought.

He checked his watch. "Call the hotel. Find out if Vasilyev remains a guest. If so, alert the local police. Provide them with the most recent photographs of Charles Jenkins. Tell them to establish a blockade outside the hotel, and to have every car entering or leaving stopped and searched."

—

Jenkins allowed Federov to swing his legs over the table and sit up. The Russian looked stunned. As Federov tied a towel around his waist, he looked over his shoulder at the woman. She stirred but turned her head away from them. Federov quickly slipped on his robe and slippers, then he nodded for Jenkins to follow him out of the room.

They got just a few steps when the woman spoke.

"Kuda vy?" Where are you going? The woman had lifted herself from the table, looking back at them. She sat up, the sheet slipping to her waist, and made no effort to cover herself.

Federov approached her table, speaking softly, as if to soothe a child. "I'm afraid something has come up," he said. "Business I must immediately attend to and cannot avoid."

He looked back at Jenkins, who motioned with his head to the exit.

"I am sorry," Federov said. "We need to move quickly now."

"No my tol'ko chto prishli," she said. *But we just got here.*

"I will make it up to you," Federov said. "Come. Now we must go."

The woman stood up. She looked like a pouting teenager as she slid on a plush robe and tied it closed, then stepped into slippers.

Federov led her by the arm to the hallway, Jenkins following. If the woman was curious about him, she didn't ask. They walked from the spa across the pool deck. The young mother and her son were now seated on adjacent lounge chairs. The trio hurried the short distance to the hotel, and Federov summoned an elevator. When the car reached the ground floor and the doors opened, a man and a woman stepped off wearing matching hotel robes. Once they were in the elevator and the doors shut, Federov turned to Jenkins.

"What are you doing here?" he said in English.

Jenkins looked to the woman.

"She does not speak English," Federov said.

"Looking for you," Jenkins said.

"Why?" Federov looked genuinely perplexed and concerned.

"I need to ask you some questions."

The elevator stopped and a hotel employee in uniform stepped on. He smiled and wished them all a good day. The elevator proceeded to the top floor in silence. The man departed. Jenkins followed Federov and the woman to double doors at the end of the hall. Federov used a card key from the pocket of his robe and stepped inside a plush suite with marble floors, cream-colored furniture, and flat-screen televisions.

"Khvatay svoi veshchi, bystro," Federov said to the woman. *Grab your things, quickly.*

She moved slowly into the bedroom and removed a suitcase from the closet, shoving clothes into it—a lot of lingerie. She and Federov had not intended to leave the room often or for long.

"How did you find me?" Federov asked, grabbing clothes from the closet.

"You're not going to be happy with me, I'm afraid," Jenkins said.

"How?" Federov asked again. He'd stopped packing.

"I'll tell you, but I think you better get dressed while I do. I'm not sure how much time we have."

"What? Why?"

"Because, as I said, the FSB will not be far behind me."

"What did you do?" Federov asked, now sounding more concerned.

"I made a deposit to my account at the Union Bank of Switzerland, obtained my signature card, and bribed the banker who opened the account to give me the name on the second account opened at the same time. Sergei Vasilyev?"

"What?" Federov looked angry. "Why would you do that?"

"I told you. I needed to find you."

"They put a trace on your account. The FSB would have been alerted."

"They were, trust me. They came to the bank. If they have my name, we have to assume they now have yours, or at least the name Sergei Vasilyev. It wasn't difficult getting a trace on your credit card, which is why I don't think we have a lot of time. If I could find you, we have to assume the FSB can as well."

"Shit!" Federov turned to the woman. *"Bystreye, bystreye! My dolzhny idti." Hurry, hurry! We must go.*

He quickly removed the towel and put on underpants, a T-shirt, and long pants. "Is this the thanks I get for giving you four million dollars?"

"Yeah, about that. When the bank unfroze my account so I could make a deposit, the money was removed electronically."

"From your account." Federov had stopped buttoning his pants.

"Both accounts."

"You emptied *my* account?"

Jenkins pointed to the belt buckle. "We don't have a lot of time. Ask questions while you get dressed."

"Why would you empty my account?"

"If I hadn't emptied both accounts, the FSB would have frozen yours. I had to get the money out when I could." This, Jenkins reasoned, was as good an answer as any to keep Federov from going ballistic.

"Where is my money, Mr. Jenkins?"

"Safe," Jenkins said. He pointed. "You're going to need shoes."

Federov sat on the bed, putting on socks. "Where?" he said, voice rising.

"You're going to have to trust me, Viktor."

"Trust you? You stole my money."

"Yeah, but in fairness, you stole it first. And I didn't really steal it. It's all still there. Just in a different place. We'll have plenty of time to talk logistics when we get out of here. Do you have shoes?"

Federov got up from the bed, swearing. He slipped his feet into boots, zipping them up the side.

"I admit that it does look like I ruined a very promising weekend, and for that I'm sorry," Jenkins said.

Federov pulled open one of the mahogany cabinets and slipped a sweater over his head, then grabbed a long black leather jacket. "Do you have a car?"

"I do, but there's only one road into this place for miles, and if the FSB are smart, they'll set up a roadblock at the gate and stop everyone who leaves."

"How do you propose that we get out of here?" Federov asked.

Jenkins looked to the woman. "Can I assume you haven't remarried?"

"What? No. Of course not. She is whore."

"Can you trust her?"

"She is a prostitute, Mr. Jenkins. I can pay her. That's as far as her trust goes."

"Well, since I emptied our accounts and ruined your weekend, it seems right that I pay her."

Federov let out a deep breath. He rubbed a hand on his forehead. "If I lose my money or you expose me, I will kill you."

"Time's wasting, Viktor. I'd save the threats for later."

15

Efimov lowered the window in the back seat of the Mercedes as an officer exited one of two police cars parked on the road leading to the gated entrance of the M'Istral Hotel and Spa. The officer approached the driver's-side window.

"How long ago did you arrive on duty?" Efimov asked.

"About half an hour ago," the police officer said.

"Has anyone left the spa since your arrival?"

"Not since we arrived, no," the officer said.

"Any arrivals?"

"Yes, but none matching the picture provided."

Efimov motioned for Volkov to drive to the security shack positioned at the gated entrance. The guard did not depart his booth, and Volkov held up his credentials. The gate swung open.

As Volkov accelerated, Efimov said, "Wait." Volkov stopped. "Go back."

Volkov reversed. The guard, looking confused, pulled open the door to his shack but again made no effort to get out. Efimov pushed open the back door of the Mercedes and stormed out. He grabbed the surprised guard by his collar and yanked him from his stool and the warmth of his booth, toppling the stool and tossing the young man onto the ground. The guard's hat went sailing across the snow-covered ground.

Efimov grabbed the young man by his jacket lapels and lifted him to his feet. "Is it not your job to check everyone who enters these hotel grounds?" Efimov elevated the guard so that he stood on his toes.

"Yes," the guard said, voice cracking.

Efimov dragged the man to the car and snapped his fingers in the driver's-side window. Volkov handed him a photograph of Charles Jenkins. Efimov held it up to the guard's face. "Have you seen this man today? And I hope for your sake that you have."

"*Da.* He arrived about half an hour ago," the guard stammered. "Maybe less."

"Did he say he was meeting someone?"

"Da."

"Who?"

"I don't know. I . . . I need my checklist."

Efimov shoved him toward the guard booth. The guard stumbled, fell to a knee, then stood and retrieved a clipboard, quickly flipping the pages as he returned.

"Sergei Vasilyev. He said he was a friend of Sergei Vasilyev."

Efimov said, "Did he tell you his name?"

"Name?"

"Yes. What name did he give you?"

"I don't recall."

"You didn't write it down?"

"No. I . . . Wait. It was . . . Volkov. He said his name was Volkov."

Efimov glanced at Volkov, who had turned his head to the guard at the mention of his name but otherwise provided no reaction. "Arkady Volkov?" Efimov asked.

"Yes. Arkady Volkov. That was the name."

"Do not allow any car to leave the hotel grounds without the police stopping it. Is that understood?"

"Yes."

"Retrieve your hat. If you are going to do a job, then do it well, or do not do it at all. Do you understand?"

The guard nodded.

Efimov returned to the back seat. "Drive," he instructed Volkov. He folded the picture of Charles Jenkins and slipped it into his coat pocket as they drove up the cobblestone entry. "Why would Mr. Jenkins use your name, Arkady?"

Volkov shrugged. "This I do not know."

"Why not just make up a name?"

Neither Volkov nor Alekseyov answered.

Volkov parked beneath the porte cochere and dealt with the valet while Efimov and Alekseyov hurried up the steps and crossed the marbled lobby to the reception desk. At Efimov's instruction, Alekseyov flashed his identification to the young woman behind the counter. Efimov pulled out the picture of Jenkins from his coat pocket and unfolded it. "Have you seen this man today?"

"Yes," the woman said. "He said he had a business meeting with a guest and had been unable to reach him on his cell phone."

"Was the guest Sergei Vasilyev?"

"Mr. Vasilyev was having a massage."

"Where is the spa?"

"It is out back." Efimov started from the counter when the woman again spoke. "But they are no longer there. They took the elevator perhaps twenty minutes ago."

"What is Sergei Vasilyev's room number?"

"I cannot give out that kind of information."

Efimov was in no mood. "Do you have a superior?" he asked.

"I'm sorry?"

He slapped the counter with the palm of his hand, making the woman jump back. "A superior . . . Do you have a supervisor, someone in a position of authority? I don't care who, just get them out here now."

Flustered, the woman departed through the door behind the counter. Volkov entered the hotel and crossed to the reception desk. Efimov checked his watch. If the woman's sense of time had been accurate, they were now just twenty minutes behind Jenkins. The young woman did not return, but a middle-aged man slipped on his coat and wiped the corner of his mouth with a napkin as he came through the door.

"Can I help you?" the man asked.

Alekseyov again flashed his identification, which caught the man's attention.

"Provide the room number for your guest Sergei Vasilyev," Efimov said.

"Yes, no problem." The man typed on the computer. "Mr. Vasilyev is in the suite. It is on the top floor of the hotel."

"Take us. Bring a key."

—

Jenkins followed Federov and the woman into the hallway, where soft music filtered down from speakers in the ceiling, and directed them past the elevators to a door beneath an exit sign. He pushed it open, listening for a moment before they quickly shuffled down the steps. When they reached the ground floor, Jenkins again paused before he pushed the door open. He peered out at the lobby.

Jenkins saw Simon Alekseyov, Arkady Volkov, and a third man standing at the marble reception counter and quickly retreated.

"Shit," Federov said, having also seen the men. "What did you do, Mr. Jenkins? What the hell did you do?"

—

After imparting his instructions to Ruslana, the young prostitute, Jenkins pushed the door open just a few inches. He watched the three men step into the elevator with a hotel employee, a middle-aged man. When the elevator doors shut he nodded to Ruslana. "You remember what to do?" he asked in Russian.

She rolled her eyes. *"Ladno." No problem.* She walked to the building's front entrance, dragging her suitcase behind her. Federov and Jenkins walked in the opposite direction, down a hall leading to an exit at the back of the hotel. Jenkins pushed open the glass door, and the cold air stung his uncovered hands and face. The temperature felt ten degrees colder than when he had arrived.

"Who is the third man with Alekseyov and Volkov?" Jenkins asked.

"Now is not the time," Federov said. He removed a knit cap from his pocket and pulled it down over his ears, then slipped on gloves. Jenkins also put on a knit cap, but he'd left his gloves in the rental car.

"The FSB will utilize local police as much as possible," Federov said, "to avoid an international incident. Local police will not have the same vested interest, and we can hope that the cold will further deter their curiosity."

Hopefully it would be enough for Ruslana to get through a blockade. Jenkins had paid her five hundred American dollars and promised to pay her another fifteen hundred dollars when they met at the car. If the police asked for registration, the name on the rental agreement would be meaningless, another alias. Jenkins had instructed Ruslana to advise that the car was registered to a boyfriend and, if pushed, to intimate he was cheating on his wife with her.

"What do you know of this area?" Federov asked Jenkins as they walked toward the trees.

"Only what I was able to determine from Google Earth."

"Shit," Federov said again.

"I'm kidding, Viktor. Relax."

"Relax?"

Jenkins and Federov walked past a large chessboard set up on the outside pavers, following a path between patches of lawn covered in snow. The path led to the lake.

"We hike along the water's edge several hundred yards, then cut through that stand of trees." Jenkins pointed. "It leads to Rozhdestveno, where, hopefully, Ruslana will be waiting."

"Yes, we can hope," Federov said. "Because if we must walk back to Moscow, in this weather, you will freeze to death. If I don't kill you first."

Volkov continued to ponder why Jenkins would use his name, of all names, to enter the hotel. It made little sense, especially since this man, Vasilyev, had enough money to rent the penthouse of the hotel. Volkov knew no one with that kind of money.

The hotel manager opened the penthouse door and quickly stepped back. Efimov, his gun in front of him, pushed on the door and slid into the room, sweeping the pistol left to right. Alekseyov, also armed, moved in the opposite direction. Volkov had also removed his weapon, but only to be the good soldier. From past experience, he didn't believe they would find Charles Jenkins or Sergei Vasilyev, whoever he was, inside the room. Efimov had underestimated Jenkins at the airport and again here at the hotel.

Volkov stepped into a bedroom, where Efimov was considering an unmade bed. The sheets revealed what looked to have been quite a romp. Volkov opened closets and checked dresser drawers. He found neither clothes nor luggage.

Moments later Alekseyov entered the room. *"Nichego." Nothing.*

"They have left," Efimov said. "Call the front gate."

Volkov walked out of the bedroom and approached the floor-to-ceiling plate-glass windows in the living room. Whoever Vasilyev was, he had significant money to spend on the plushest suite at the hotel. During the day, the windows likely provided sweeping views of the Istrinskoye Reservoir and of the tiny farming towns nearby. At present, the fading winter dusk made it difficult to see anything but the sporadic twinkling of distant lights.

Movement on the footpath below him caught Volkov's attention. Two people walked toward the water, which seemed odd given the cold temperature. They were not running, but they seemed to be walking with a purpose. Volkov stepped closer to the window. The taller of the two turned his head and took a quick glance back at the hotel, as if to determine whether they were being followed. He did this just as he stepped beneath one of the lamps lining the path. It was only an instant, but Volkov did not need any longer to recognize the man he had confronted in the Metropol Hotel bathroom in Moscow. He'd gotten a close-up look at Charles Jenkins, one he would never forget.

He was about to call out to Efimov when something familiar about the second man drew Volkov's attention. Something in the man's gait, his long black leather coat, the hunch of his shoulders, the black knit skullcap pulled low on his head.

Viktor Federov.

And just as quickly as Volkov recognized his former partner, he understood why Charles Jenkins had chosen to use his name at the hotel's gated entrance, a name that would be unfamiliar to Sergei Vasilyev but certainly familiar to Viktor Federov.

Viktor was Sergei Vasilyev.

Volkov looked over his shoulder. He heard Alekseyov and Efimov speaking inside the bedroom. Alekseyov relayed information from the front gate to Efimov. A handful of cars had left the hotel grounds, but they'd been checked thoroughly, and the registration and license plate numbers recorded. No one named Sergei Vasilyev and no one resembling Charles Jenkins had departed.

Volkov quickly considered why Jenkins would have emptied Vasilyev's bank account, and how Federov would have obtained so much money. He briefly considered whether Federov could have been a double agent—he'd certainly expressed more than once that his ex-wife and his daughters were bleeding him dry—but Volkov dismissed that thought almost as quickly. If Federov had been a double agent, there would have been no reason for Jenkins to empty his bank account. Jenkins certainly didn't need the money, not after withdrawing $4 million from his own account.

He had to have emptied the accounts to gain some sort of leverage over Federov.

But for what purpose?

"They have to be somewhere on the hotel grounds." Alekseyov slipped his cell phone into his coat pocket as he and Efimov exited the bedroom.

"What are you looking at?" Alekseyov asked.

The two men disappeared into the tree line. Volkov turned from the windows. "The view," he said.

Alekseyov gave him a quizzical stare and stepped to the darkened windows. He glanced over his shoulder to the front door, speaking under his breath. "We have no time for the view, Arkady. The guards are adamant that no one named Sergei Vasilyev and no one who looks like Charles Jenkins have left the grounds. Efimov will not tolerate it if we lose Jenkins again."

"I told you, Simon. We cannot lose what we have never possessed."

"Tell that to Efimov. He will cook your balls for dinner, and mine."

Efimov stepped back into the room. "What are you doing? We must move quickly."

Volkov spoke. "In Moscow, Mr. Jenkins went inside another guest's room to make it appear as though he had left before we arrived. He may be doing so again."

Efimov considered this for a moment, then turned to the hotel manager, who remained outside, a good distance down the hall. "You will take us room to room."

"But the guests—"

"You will take us room to room," Efimov said again. This time the manager did not argue.

At the door Volkov said, "Perhaps I should speak to the front desk and to the spa and get a description of Sergei Vasilyev, since we apparently have no photograph. It would be good to have, no?"

Efimov nodded. "Meet us in the lobby when you are done."

Volkov glanced back again at the window before exiting the suite.

16

Ruslana was good to her word, or at least good to the dollars Jenkins had promised to pay her. He and Federov found her smoking a cigarette behind the wheel of the rental car on a side street in the small town of Rozhdestveno. She had the car running and the heater and radio on, and gave them a decidedly disinterested expression when Jenkins knocked on the driver's-side window.

"Kakiye-to problemy?" Federov asked as she opened the car door. Smoke poured out. *Any problems?*

"Nyet, vsyo normal'no." No, everything is fine. Ruslana stepped from the car still looking disgruntled. She tilted back her head and blew smoke into the night sky, then flicked the burning embers of her cigarette down the dirt-and-gravel street. She held out her hand to Jenkins.

"Oni obyskali mashinu?" Federov asked. *Did they search the car?*

Ruslana shrugged and gave Federov a thin smile. *"Mashina ikh, pohozhe, ne zainteresovala." They did not seem to be interested in the car.*

"Oni poprosili dogovor arendy?" Did they ask for the rental agreement?

Another headshake. *"Nyet."*

Federov looked to Jenkins. "She said they—"

"Did not check the rental agreement," Jenkins said. "But they likely wrote down the license plate. I want to get rid of the car as quickly as possible."

"Yes, but for now it is all we have, and we need to depart, quickly," Federov said.

Jenkins handed Ruslana the remainder of her payment, which she pocketed before sliding into the back seat. She leaned her head against the headrest and closed her eyes. Federov climbed into the passenger seat. Jenkins slid behind the wheel. He put his palms to the warm air coming from the car vents and flexed his fingers to restore the flow of blood to his hands.

Jenkins cracked his window to ease the smell of cigarettes. He drove back roads, concerned about additional checkpoints.

Once they reached the main route to Moscow, Federov spoke English. "I think it is time you told me why you have come back to Russia, Mr. Jenkins. Can I assume it was not to retrieve the money in *your* bank account?"

"You can assume that," Jenkins said. "But first, who is the third man?"

"Adam Efimov. The Brick," Federov said.

"The Brick?"

"Everyone who knows him knows his nickname."

"You worked with him?"

"No. Efimov grew up in Saint Petersburg with Vladimir Putin and the deputy director of the FSB, Dmitry Sokalov. He, too, was KGB, and one of Putin's closest allies. He moved up the ranks quickly, but his temper caused problems and kept him from being promoted to higher positions within the FSB. It is said that Efimov is brought in when the FSB does not wish to be connected to an investigation."

"He's off the books," Jenkins said.

"This is term I do not understand. Efimov now does the bidding of the president and the deputy director, but you will find no record of it or of him."

"He's a ghost," Jenkins said.

Federov shrugged. "He's no ghost. He's quite real."

Jenkins decided not to define the term for Federov. "Why is he called The Brick?"

"As the story goes, his father was a bricklayer in Saint Petersburg and Efimov his reluctant apprentice. He spent much of his youth catching or throwing bricks to his father high on the scaffolding, and he has the scars and the muscular build to prove it. His hands and forearms are said to be as hard as concrete. It is also said that he kept a brick in his office as both a reminder and a warning to those who worked for him—a reminder of his nickname and a warning to never take your eyes from the goal. I have heard stories of agents who had that brick tossed in their faces for failure to pay attention, or to achieve expected results."

"So, you're saying he's a psychopath," Jenkins said.

"He's practical, pragmatic, and relentless. If he is involved, it is bad news for you. He is singularly focused."

"And a psychopath."

"This is no joke, Mr. Jenkins. If Efimov is involved, you are of the highest priority."

"We already suspected that."

"Yes, but it is also an indication that the FSB's focus has changed."

"How?"

"My job was to capture you. Efimov is ordinarily sent to kill."

"I'm flattered," Jenkins said, though another chill ran through him, this time unrelated to the temperature. "If he and Putin and the deputy director are friends, why is he off the books?"

"These are unsubstantiated rumors," Federov said. "But rumors I believe. Apparently one of the bricks did considerable damage to the son of a prominent Russian politician—a politician who also had connections, his more powerful than Efimov's at the time. Efimov disappeared, but obviously not completely. Now, tell me why you have been so foolish to return."

"I need information and I had no way of getting in touch with you."

"It must be very important, this information, for you to take this kind of risk," Federov said.

"If you're angling for a bigger payout, forget it. You'll get what I took. I've made arrangements for you to get back your six million dollars—"

"I already had six million—"

"As well as the four million dollars in my account."

Federov stopped talking.

"That's ten million dollars, Viktor. Four million will be released when I get what I want. The rest will be released when I get back to the United States." As with his negotiations with Ruslana, Jenkins knew to never open with his best offer, and to hold back a future payment until he had reached safety. "Do we have a deal?"

"You are offering me just four million dollars. I had six before you went into the bank. And that was before I knew Efimov was involved. For this you are asking me to take a pay cut."

"You'll get six million more when I'm out of the country."

"*If* you get out of the country. Efimov will have much to say about that. I stand to lose two million dollars."

"And you stand to gain four million. That's the deal I'm offering. This is not a negotiation."

Federov shrugged. "Again, there is no guarantee. Besides, how do I know that I can trust you?"

"The same way I knew I could trust you, Viktor. Blind faith."

"I am not a religious man."

"Neither am I. But from where I sit, you could get nothing. That's a lot to lose, especially given how you're apparently spending it."

"And from where I sit, I could call the FSB as a Russian patriot and you would spend the rest of your life in Lefortovo. If you were so lucky."

"Maybe, but that wouldn't change the fact that you would once again be penniless, Viktor, and probably still out of a job."

"One never knows Russian gratitude. I may be reinstated. I may even get a bonus."

"You think so? When I give them proof you killed their best double agent, Carl Emerson? The man who was providing the names of the seven sisters?" Jenkins glanced over at Federov, who was no longer smiling. "Besides, do you think the Russian government would give you a ten-million-dollar bonus?" Jenkins nodded to Ruslana in the back seat. "Take a good look at her, Viktor, because you won't be able to afford her again."

Federov smiled. "I like you, Mr. Jenkins. I like the way you think."

Jenkins didn't believe him, not for a moment. "Does that mean we have a deal?"

"One exception. If things do not go as planned, and my involvement is more than . . . how do you say it . . . either of us anticipated, you will make it worth my while, yes?"

"You'll want more money?"

"You Americans always play your cards close to your chest. I know there is more money. I want only to know that you will authorize it, if circumstances dictate it to be so."

"Agreed," Jenkins said, "though I'm not saying there is more money."

"Nor did you deny it." Federov stuck out his hand. "As you do in your country." The two men shook hands, not that Jenkins put much stock in it.

"Tell me. What is it that is so important you have risked so much to ask me?" Federov asked.

"I want to know if Paulina Ponomayova is still alive, and if she is, where she is being kept. Tell me what happened that night in Vishnevka."

Federov hit the accelerator and slammed into the car's back bumper. The Hyundai swerved, but the driver corrected. Federov steered to his right and tapped the rear bumper, a move favored by police. The Hyundai spun. This time the driver could not correct. The car slid across the centerline and the adjacent lane before it slammed into a tree trunk, coming to a violent and certain stop.

Federov hit his brakes and spun a U-turn, stopping ten meters back from the car. He considered the windows, looking for any movement inside the car. Seeing none, he removed his gun and stepped out, using the car door as a shield. He took aim at the back window.

"Vyidite iz mashiny, ruki za golovu!" Get out of the car with your hands on top of your head!

There was no response. Smoke rose from the shattered engine.

Federov repeated the order.

Again, he got no response.

He rose up from behind the door and shuffled forward, finger on the trigger, muzzle aimed at the car. He moved deliberately, cautiously, to the driver's side and used his left hand to yank on the door handle. It opened with a metallic crunching noise. The woman, Ponomayova, lay draped over the steering wheel. Federov looked across the car to the passenger seat, then to the back seat of the car. He did not see Jenkins. Infuriated, Federov grabbed Ponomayova by the neck and yanked her backward. Blood streamed down her face from a cut on her forehead.

"Gde on?" *he shouted.* "Gde on?" Where is he?

Ponomayova's eyes cleared momentarily and she smiled, her teeth red from the blood. "Ty opozdal. On davno ushol," *she said, voice a whisper.* You're too late. He is long gone.

Federov stuck the barrel of the gun to her temple. "Tell me where he is. Where did he go?"

She spit up more blood. "So very Russian of you to threaten to kill a dying woman," she said, speaking through clenched teeth.

"Where is he?"

She smiled, this time purposeful. Federov saw the white capsule wedged between her teeth.

"For Ivan. May those of you who killed him rot—"

—

The story Federov told Jenkins sounded a lot like the Paulina he had come to know—tough as nails and defiant. She had little to lose or fear; all of her family was deceased.

A wet snow splattered the windshield, and Jenkins turned on the wipers to clear the glass, the rubber blades occasionally shrieking. "So she's dead?" he asked Federov.

Federov shook his head. "It would be better for her . . . and for you, if she *were* dead. But no. She did not die that night."

Jenkins's pulse quickened. His mouth went dry. "Tell me what happened."

—

Federov reacted before Ponomayova finished her sentence. He slapped her hard across the face. The white capsule, likely cyanide, dislodged and fell somewhere into the dark recesses of the car. Whether that would be enough to keep her alive, Federov did not know; her injuries looked to be significant. She'd passed out from the blow, slumped over the steering wheel, blood trickling from the corner of her mouth. Federov put a hand to her carotid artery. Her pulse was faint but still present.

He removed his cell phone and called Timur Matveyev, the Vishnevka chief of police. "This is Federov. I am roughly three kilometers east on M27. Send an ambulance and one of your patrol cars immediately."

—

"You didn't stay?" Jenkins asked.

"If you recall, it was you I was after, not her."

"But she was alive when you left her."

"Yes. As I said. Her pulse was weak and her injuries significant, but she remained alive."

"Do you know what happened to her after you left her?"

"Only what I heard after I was dismissed. Of this I have no personal knowledge."

"What did you hear?"

"She was flown by helicopter to a hospital in Sochi, then to a trauma center in Moscow."

"A military hospital?"

Federov stared at Jenkins, clearly wondering how he knew that bit of information. "They had the expertise to keep her alive."

"What else did you hear?" Jenkins asked.

"Nothing. After your escape, I was dismissed. I put my experience to other interests."

"Did you hear anything else about Ponomayova?"

"No."

"If she lived, where would she be now?"

"If she lived? If she lived, she would be in Lefortovo," Federov said. "And let me warn you, Mr. Jenkins, even if she survived the car crash, there is no guarantee she has survived Lefortovo, and she would soon wish that she did not. Russian interrogation techniques are designed to break the subject physically and mentally. Once accomplished, Ms. Ponomayova would have been shot as a traitor."

"How do I find out if she is in Lefortovo and if she is still alive?"

"You do not."

"How would you find out?"

Federov chuckled. "I have no interest in finding out."

"You have a ten-million-dollar interest," Jenkins said.

Federov exhaled. He tilted his head left, then right, stretching his neck as if it were stiff from stress. He brushed at lint on his sweater, and Jenkins recalled the movement from his prior encounter. Federov's tell. Everyone had a tell. He waited. Federov eventually spoke. "I may have access to individuals who might advise me. But it is likely that Ms. Ponomayova's existence and location has been kept . . . what you Americans like to call 'top secret.' Only those at the highest levels could confirm this type of information. And I do not have such access. Nor would I risk asking, not with Efimov involved."

Jenkins ignored everything except what he wanted Federov to do. "So you might be able to find out."

Federov laughed. "You do not listen. It would be very dangerous."

"But for a price?"

"Everything has a price, Mr. Jenkins. The question is the cost. But let me ask you a question. What good would it do you to know this information?"

"If she's alive, I'm going to get her out."

Federov laughed, a deep and full chuckle that awoke or annoyed Ruslana, who groaned and whined in the back seat. When Jenkins did not laugh, Federov leaned across the gap between the two seats. "Have you gone crazy, Mr. Jenkins? Did that trial scramble your brain? You think you are going to get Ponomayova out of Lefortovo? This I wish to know. Tell me. How?"

"Not Lefortovo. Out of Moscow. Out of Russia."

Again, Federov laughed. "You might as well release my money now, because I will never see the rest. This is a suicide mission you are undertaking. You understand that, no?"

"My coming for the eighth sister was supposed to be a suicide mission, Viktor. But it didn't work out that way."

"Let me ask you another question. Why are you here? Surely it is not some ideological reason motivating you. And you never struck me as a man motivated by money. So why come back?"

Jenkins shrugged. "She saved my life."

Federov gave this a moment of thought. "You feel obligated."

Jenkins didn't respond.

"You do this out of some loyalty? Duty? Honor? . . . Guilt?"

"I do it because it's the right thing, Viktor. Because of Paulina I got to see my wife and son again. I was home for my daughter's birth. You have two daughters. Perhaps you can appreciate that."

"I can appreciate it," Federov said. After a moment of silence, the windshield wipers again shrieked. Federov stared out at the darkened road. Then he said, "But be careful, Mr. Jenkins. There are millions of forgotten young men buried in the ground who gave their lives for duty and honor, and their families have nothing to show for it but a gravestone. Some don't even have that."

17

Efimov stood at the window on the third floor of the main Lubyanka building smoking a cigarette and drinking Scotch. He stared down at Lubyanka Square, illuminated under bright streetlamps, and the lingering remains of Moscow traffic. This view, or one just like it—perhaps in the office down the hall, the office of the deputy director—should have been his. He had earned it—not through political ass kicking, but through decades of hard work.

His years in the KGB with Vladimir and Dmitry had resulted in much success, like their childhood in Saint Petersburg—though it would always be Leningrad to Efimov. Vladimir had been the smartest of the three, certainly; Efimov always knew his friend would go on to do great things. Efimov had no such illusions about himself. He'd been the brawn, Vladimir's enforcer. Dmitry was a parasite, one who would go only as far as Vladimir could take him.

Efimov understood his place and his role. He'd learned both from his father.

He'd never had the chance to succeed in school, to develop his intellect and to earn the degrees that would elevate him to positions of prestige. His father had removed him from classes after his primary education. He'd told Efimov that further schooling was a waste of time, that Efimov did not have the brains to amount to anything academic; that it would be better for him to learn a trade.

Efimov had hated the work from the moment he caught his first brick at eight years of age, and he hated it more with each summer that his father conscripted him, until the work became his life. During his first years, his father forced him to carry bricks up to him on the scaffolding, sometimes several stories. He asked his father why they didn't fashion pulleys and use a crate to pull the bricks up, but his father told him no man learned anything doing things the easy way.

"You will carry the bricks, which will motivate you to get stronger, so that you can toss them up to me. Then you will understand."

Efimov did get stronger, much stronger, until he could toss the bricks to his father at any height, and catch them. When he demonstrated this, his father told him, "Now you don't need the pulley and the basket."

Efimov had never understood the lesson his father tried to impart. He never understood why doing things the more efficient way was not the better way. But he also did not have the time to find out. Whenever his mind wandered in search of such answers or to his friends, who spent the warm summer months hiking and swimming and enjoying the weather before Leningrad's brutal winters, his father regained Efimov's attention by tossing a brick in his face. Efimov had the jagged scars of abuse to show for it: across his forehead and the bridge of his nose, on his chin, and the backs of his hands. His father refused to take Efimov to the hospital. He did not want to waste time that could otherwise be spent working.

"Besides," he would say, "you will get nowhere with that face. You have my grandfather's brow and his jaw. The scars are an improvement."

But his father had been wrong. Efimov's face would take him places. After his father fell from the scaffolding in a drunken stupor and, thankfully, died, Efimov reunited with Vladimir and Dmitry, though at a level far below theirs. He did not have the education for advancement within the KGB, but he had the face and the brawn, and soon the reputation.

His father had been right about one thing.

Fear was the best motivator.

Those who worked for him paid attention to the goal, or they suffered the consequences.

But Russia had changed. The KGB was no more, and Efimov had difficulty finding his place within the FSB and other successor organizations. While Vladimir's and Dmitry's political careers advanced, Efimov's career stagnated. Then it collapsed. And not even Vladimir's rise to the presidency had been able to fully resurrect it.

Dmitry threw him bones, at Vladimir's suggestion, for old times' sake, for the friendships they had made as boys on the streets of Leningrad. But those bones now came with the same warning his father had once imposed.

Get the job done, or suffer the consequences.

Efimov turned from the view and joined Alekseyov and Volkov in his barren office. The walls of the room contained no photographs. The desk and shelves were bare. Efimov's jacket and tie hung over the back of the desk chair where he had placed them. His cuff links rested on the desk. He'd rolled his shirt cuffs to his elbows.

Efimov poured another drink and carried the glass to a cream-colored leather chair. He didn't bother to ask Alekseyov or Volkov to join him. This was not a celebration. Far from it.

He sat and lit another cigarette, inhaling the nicotine deeply, then motioned to the two chairs across the desk. Alekseyov and Volkov dutifully sat.

Alekseyov tried not to look or sound uncomfortable or concerned, though Efimov knew he was both. He'd seen it often in those who worked for him, the young officer's wandering eye contact and rigid posture, the anxious way his left leg shook. Volkov, on the other hand, looked as he always looked, imperturbable, as if nothing said or done would have any impact on him. Perhaps he no longer cared for the

FSB. Many old KGB agents felt the same. If that was the case, Efimov admired him for it.

But he'd still sacrifice him in an instant, were this matter to fail.

They discussed in detail what had transpired at the airport and at the M'Istral Hotel, where they had searched every room and every closet without success.

"Mr. Jenkins's counterintelligence skills are very good," Alekseyov said.

"I have read Viktor Federov's prior reports," Efimov responded. He had not been impressed. He believed Federov's reports had been more to cover his own ass. It hadn't worked. He sipped his drink, sucked in more nicotine, and blew smoke across the desk. "What more do we know?"

Alekseyov clearly had not been expecting the question. Perhaps he'd expected Efimov to yell and scream and lose his temper, then tell them what to do. But Efimov had learned how to modulate his responses for maximum effect. Besides, to scream and yell defeated the purpose of this late-night meeting. The purpose wasn't to intimidate them to a point of paralysis. It was to motivate them to think, to act, to succeed. Another lesson from his father.

"Sir?" Alekseyov asked, sounding as uncertain as he looked.

"Where do we go from here?"

Alekseyov stared at Efimov, mouth agape, as if uncertain whether Efimov's question was serious. "I . . ."

"This is your investigation, Simon."

Efimov's words found their mark, as he knew they would. Alekseyov looked like he'd been stabbed with a dagger. His Adam's apple bobbed and the knee continued to shake. Consequences for one's failures were also a strong motivator. "My investigation?"

"Is it not?"

Efimov could see the ramifications crystallizing in the young agent's mind. This was *his* investigation. Efimov worked in the shadows. He did not exist. Volkov was old, and largely unmotivated. It would be

Alekseyov's ass on the line, at least publicly, should they fail. In private Efimov would bear the brunt of the president's anger, and the likely consequences. But Alekseyov and Volkov did not need to know that.

Alekseyov said, "We provided the description Arkady obtained of Sergei Vasilyev from the hotel employees to our analysts to narrow the pool of potential candidates, but so far we have not had much success."

"And they have still not found a driver's license or identification card?"

"No. In fact, although Vasilyev used a credit card to make the reservation at the spa and for the massage, he paid the bill in advance, in cash."

Alekseyov looked to Volkov for some confirmation and affirmance, but the old officer provided none. Perhaps he, too, understood the consequences should this assignment fail. So close to retirement, he likely did not want to be out front, taking the first bullet.

Volkov sighed as if bored. The act was so brazen and out of character it was as if he had jumped onto Efimov's desk and pissed. Efimov shifted his attention from Alekseyov to the older officer. "You have something more to add, Arkady?"

"I think it is a waste of time," Volkov said.

Alekseyov cringed.

Efimov suppressed a smile. He respected the old officer's balls. He'd read his file, which was much like Efimov's—a limited education but not a limited intellect. The strength he'd earned working in the fields as a young man had been put to good use. Efimov had read of Volkov's interrogation techniques and admired the reputation he, too, had cultivated. "Do you, Arkady? Tell me why."

"Because I believe it is more likely that Sergei Vasilyev is a double agent, working for the CIA, and that the name was deliberately chosen because it is so common. It would also explain the lack of any Russian identification and his use of cash."

Alekseyov sat looking stunned by the analysis—a further indication that while Volkov did not say much, what he said was insightful. Efimov's father would have described Volkov as a heavy boulder at the top of a hill, hard to get going, but once pushed he quickly picked up speed.

Efimov leaned back, studying both men. His chair creaked. "And so, what then do you propose to do at this point?"

"I propose that we determine why Mr. Jenkins has returned to Russia, given the significant risk for him to have done so. If we determine why Mr. Jenkins has returned, perhaps we will determine where he is most likely to be next."

"And do you have any thoughts on why Mr. Jenkins has returned?"

"No," Volkov said, without elaboration or apology.

Efimov stared at him but did not see any indication Volkov was being insolent. After a few moments his gaze shifted back to Alekseyov. "Do you?" he asked.

"But I do not believe it was to retrieve money," Volkov said before Alekseyov had the chance to speak, no doubt saving the young officer the embarrassment of admitting that he had no idea why Jenkins had returned to Moscow.

"No?" Efimov asked.

"No."

"Why then?"

"This I do not yet know, but Simon brought up a brilliant idea, someone who may know why Jenkins has returned. Someone who knows him better than anyone sitting in this room."

Efimov and Volkov looked to Alekseyov, but the young officer continued to look stumped. Then the answer came to him, like a thunderclap on a clear day, unexpected and sudden.

"Viktor Federov," Alekseyov blurted, trying to not look or sound surprised.

Efimov knew he was both.

—

After driving Ruslana to a high-end apartment building, Jenkins was directed by Federov to the Cheryomushki District, southwest of the Kremlin—what Jenkins considered to be downtown Moscow, though Federov explained that Moscow did not have a "downtown." He didn't even understand the term. He said the government had buildings throughout the twelve administrative *okrugs* that comprised Moscow, and those *okrugs*, or regions, were each divided into multiple districts that housed Moscow's twelve million inhabitants.

Federov also explained that the Cheryomushki District was at one time named for the former Soviet dictator Leonid Brezhnev, and it had been synonymous with cheap Soviet-style apartments—what Jenkins likened to housing projects in the United States. Most of those buildings had been demolished during Putin's never-ending reign and replaced with modern apartment buildings. Federov had purchased his apartment in one of the buildings following his divorce.

"Turn here," Federov directed.

Jenkins descended a driveway to a gate beneath a multistory building. Federov handed him a card key that Jenkins pressed to a pad, and the gate rolled back. Just before midnight, the garage was full of cars but, thankfully, no people.

Federov directed Jenkins to a parking space and got out of the vehicle. "Wait here. There is a camera in the elevator lobby."

Federov used his card key to activate a lock on a metal door. Seconds later he gestured to Jenkins. When Jenkins stepped into the lobby, Federov said, "The building cameras are outdated and easily manipulated."

Jenkins noticed a detached wire dangling from the back of the camera. "What about a guard?"

Federov smirked. "Most likely asleep at the front desk. The camera will be this way until I fix it."

Federov used his card key to activate the elevator and again to activate the keypad to gain access to the eighth floor. Moments later Jenkins waited as Federov stepped from the elevator and scanned the hallway, then nodded for Jenkins to follow. They slipped inside apartment 8B.

Federov placed his key in a basket on a small table just inside the door and hung his coat on one of several pegs. Jenkins did the same. Federov turned on a radio, a classical station.

"The walls are solid, but keep your voice down."

Jenkins walked down a narrow hall into a surprisingly spacious, and clean, living room. The furniture was modest but spotless, despite being white. Throw rugs covered much of the tile floor. The living room and a bachelor-style kitchen were separated by a counter. Federov removed two glasses from a cabinet and a bottle of Johnnie Walker Black. He held it up. Jenkins nodded.

The apartment was not what Jenkins had expected—sparkling white, from the countertops to the walls and cabinets, in contrast to brightly colored paintings. The interior looked like it had been cleaned for a showing. Jenkins walked to the mantel above the fireplace and considered framed photographs of two young women, likely Federov's daughters. One of the daughters appeared to be married with two children. Jenkins did not see a picture of Federov's former wife, which didn't surprise him. He walked to a sliding glass door that opened onto a small balcony with a table and chair. Late at night, the view was minimal. Streetlamps illuminated a tree-lined street with cars parked along both curbs.

"Not bad, Viktor," Jenkins said when Federov joined him and handed him a glass.

"My wife got the family apartment." Federov held up his glass. "I would offer a salute, but I think in these circumstances it might not be for the best to tempt fate."

Jenkins sipped his Scotch. It burned at the back of his throat.

Federov retreated to one of two white club chairs. Jenkins took a seat on the couch and set his drink on a glass coffee table. Federov opened a drawer on a side table between the two chairs and flipped Jenkins a coaster. He slipped a second coaster beneath his drink. Federov was fussy. Perhaps it was the reason he had never remarried. Jenkins would not have guessed it, but it also reminded him that most Russians did not have much, but what they had they protected.

"Tell me what you know, Mr. Jenkins."

Jenkins remained distrustful of Federov. He wasn't going to disclose much of what Lemore had told him. He paraphrased and summarized instead of giving details.

"Why did you suspect the asset to be Ponomayova?"

"As I said, the timing was right, and American intelligence confirmed the prisoner at Lefortovo to be female and mid-to-late forties." Jenkins wasn't about to discuss the American arrested as a spy and sent to Lefortovo who made this determination.

"If Ponomayova is being held under such tight security and secrecy, then it is not likely she will be used to bargain for a Russian asset in the United States. Mr. Putin despises traitors. It can be assumed she was kept alive to extract what information she possesses. What does she know of the remaining four sisters?"

Jenkins shook his head. He didn't know and he wouldn't tell Federov if he did. "She told me she didn't know their identity. She said her involvement was to find the person who had leaked the identities of three of the seven to the FSB."

"She herself does not know these women?"

"No."

"That is too bad. President Putin wants that information very badly. When he is convinced Ponomayova has nothing to offer, she will be shot as a traitor."

"I suspected as much."

"I see only one possibility. You allow yourself to be caught and hope you are taken to Lefortovo as a political prisoner to be traded for a Russian asset. This, I think, is no good for many reasons."

"I can think of one," Jenkins said with sarcasm.

"There is no guarantee you would be taken to Lefortovo, and if Ponomayova is being held under tight security, it would be unlikely you would see her. Second, Mr. Putin is said to have been embarrassed by my inability to capture you, and by the subsequent loss of a high-level intelligence asset within the CIA. It is unlikely he would seek to trade you or even acknowledge you were being held captive. Efimov's involvement supports this."

"Any other options?" Jenkins asked.

"To get her out of Lefortovo? I can think of none. I believe this, too, is what you Americans call a 'pipe dream,' no?"

"Maybe," Jenkins said.

"Let me ask, Mr. Jenkins. Why come to me with this problem?"

"I told you, I needed to confirm whether Paulina was still alive, and I figured you were one of the last to see her."

"Yes, so now you know. What made you think I would not give you up, and thereby regain favor with the FSB?"

"Three things."

"Three? I am impressed." Federov sat back, drink in hand. "Please. Tell me."

"First, I have your money, which you went to some lengths to get, so it means a lot to you. Second, I'm offering you nearly twice as much if I'm successful. Third, I know that you killed Carl Emerson, which, as you have said, upset Mr. Putin."

"And I would say that *you* killed Mr. Emerson."

"Yes, but then that wouldn't explain the mysterious existence of Sergei Vasilyev or his bank account with nearly six million dollars, would it?"

Federov studied him. "It appears that we are both going over the barrel, no?"

Jenkins ignored Federov's bastardization of the American expression. "I respect you, Viktor. I respected your counterintelligence skills and your determination. I also believe your government screwed you, as mine screwed me. But make no mistake. I don't trust you any more than you trust me, and, if forced to do so, I will burn you."

"Then at least we both know where we stand," Federov said.

Something buzzed. Jenkins looked to the kitchen counter. Federov's cell phone illuminated. Federov looked to Jenkins, then to the phone, clearly not expecting a call at this late hour. He considered his watch as he walked over and picked it up.

"The FSB." His voice dropped and he turned to Jenkins, clearly upset.

"You're sure?"

"Of course I'm sure. I spent twenty years of my life there. The number is impressed in my brain."

"Answer it," Jenkins said.

Federov paused.

"Answer it, Viktor, as if you have nothing to hide."

Federov answered the phone, took a moment, then moaned as if he'd been asleep. *"Allo?"* He listened.

Federov blanched, his face becoming almost the color of the apartment walls. Jenkins had never seen Federov respond in such a way.

"Da." Federov's gaze shot to Jenkins, panic in his eyes. He spoke Russian. "Tomorrow? Yes, I can be there. What is the purpose of this meeting, if I may ask? No. No, I will say nothing. Yes . . ."

Federov slowly lowered the phone.

"Who was it?"

"Efimov."

Jenkins felt a twinge of anxiety—this was unexpected. "What did he want?"

"He has summoned me to Lubyanka tomorrow morning. I fear, Mr. Jenkins, that I am already, how did you say it? Burned?"

Jenkins gave the matter some thought, then shook his head. "I don't think so."

"No?" Federov sounded incredulous. "Adam Efimov does not call a former agent in the middle of the night and request a meeting to reinstate him, of this I am quite certain."

Jenkins returned to the plate-glass door and slid it open. He stepped onto the balcony and looked down at the street.

Federov stepped out behind him. "What are you looking for?"

"What do you see on the street, Viktor?"

Federov gave him a quizzical stare. "I see nothing. I see parked cars, trees."

"Exactly. If you were burned, Efimov would not have summoned you by phone and given you the chance to escape. If you were burned, this building would be surrounded by dozens of Moscow police and FSB officers."

The color gradually returned to Federov's face.

"Did Efimov tell you the purpose of the meeting?"

"No. Only that I was to report to Lubyanka at 9:00 a.m."

"He wants me."

"Of course he wants you."

"That's not what I mean. He summoned you because you were the officer who hunted me the first time. The meeting is probably to determine what you learned about me, my tendencies, potential contacts, why I might have returned. He may want to know if you have heard of Sergei Vasilyev. We need to discuss how to use this to our advantage."

Federov went to the counter and poured himself another drink. "I hope, for my sake, that you are right, Mr. Jenkins. Otherwise, perhaps I will be the one put inside Lefortovo. And if that happens"—he raised his glass—*"Bozhe, pomogi nam oboim."*

God help us both.

18

The following morning, Federov returned to a once familiar routine. He departed his apartment dressed in a suit and tie and a warm topcoat. Stepping out the front door of his building, he pulled on fur-lined leather gloves and his black knit skullcap, fitting the cap low on his head—a winter outfit he had worn often. He stepped onto the Kaluzhsko-Rizhskaya line of the Moscow Metro, transferred to the red line, and departed that train at Lubyanka station beneath Lubyanka Square, a commute he had taken almost daily during his years at the FSB.

He ascended the escalators to street level. This morning, beneath a heavy cloud layer, he stared at the building that had once been his home, or should have been, given the number of hours he had spent there. The main Lubyanka building looked pale orange, rust-colored trim delineating each of its floors, windows, and the clock centered atop the structure.

Up until this moment Federov had moved on autopilot.

No longer.

He took a deep breath and crossed to the building entrance. When he stepped inside, he approached turnstiles and realized he no longer carried the fob with the randomly generated access code that accorded him entry. He greeted one of two security guards seated behind a marble reception counter and told him his purpose inside the building. The guard picked up the phone, checked a log of numbers, and punched one in. He hung up and handed Federov a ridiculous-looking clip-on badge identifying him as a visitor and advised that someone would be down to escort him into the building.

For a once senior FSB officer, this was a humiliating return. The badge might just as well have said "Fired" or "Dismissed." He wondered if it was purposeful.

Federov shoved his gloves and hat in the pockets of his topcoat, then slid it from his shoulders. He straightened his nub-short hair, a nervous reflex, and otherwise worked to get his nerves under control. He hoped Mr. Jenkins's assessment of the situation was correct. If not, this could be the last time Federov was escorted into the building. In the days of the KGB, he would have been locked in a cell in the infamous basement prison, tortured for information, then forgotten. With that prison no longer operating, Federov would most likely be taken to nearby Lefortovo. Before leaving his apartment, he had sent text messages to his two daughters advising that he had been summoned to Lubyanka for a meeting. He said he hoped the meeting would lead to his reinstatement.

He didn't.

He sent the text messages because he could think of no one else who cared enough, should anything happen to him, and he was not even certain his daughters met that criteria. Rightfully so, perhaps. Frequent travel and long hours in this very building had made him mostly absent from their lives—his wife's life as well. Their marriage had been loveless, at least between the two of them. They each had affairs, more than one. Federov had spared his daughters this knowledge, and when a court judicially terminated his marriage because of an "irretrievable breakdown," his daughters lived with their mother in the family apartment. Federov saw his daughters once a week and every other weekend until they left for their tertiary education. Then he saw them less.

He'd paid for Renata's private acting lessons, a hopeless cause, and for Tiana's computer science courses, a degree she had used before marriage and children. They had intermittent contact during those years, mostly because Federov served as their bank. Upon completion of that financial commitment, their contact became less frequent—cards and phone calls on birthdays and holidays. They were busy with their own lives now.

They had learned by example.

"Colonel Federov?" A young, attractive woman greeted him in the marbled entrance. The woman had Slavic features and a figure that had been either a gift from God or hard-earned in a gym. Federov caught himself before his eyes roamed and possibly offended the young woman.

"I will escort you into the building."

"Spasibo," Federov said with a slight bow.

They stepped from the elevator to the third floor. Federov knew from experience that the deputy director for counterintelligence sat in the corner office at the end of the hall, and he thought, for a moment, that was their destination. However, the woman stopped one door short, knocking before pushing the door open. "May I offer you coffee or a glass of water?" she asked.

"Thank you, no."

Federov stepped into a Spartan office. Efimov stood behind a large desk, watching his approach, though his eyes diverted, for an instant, to the young woman.

Efimov looked every bit the thug as reputed, with Neanderthal features and the stocky build of a man who'd worked labor much of his life. It was an odd contrast to his crisp white shirt—which looked heavily starched, but which Federov quickly realized was stretched tight across the man's upper torso—and gold cuff links and a blue tie, crisply knotted.

Efimov appeared serene, which also did not comport with his reputation.

Federov reached across the expansive desk to shake the man's hand. As he did, he noticed a red brick in the out-box, the only item, other than a computer screen, on the otherwise pristine desktop.

The two men shook hands, Efimov's grip living up to his rumored strength.

"Please, have a seat," Efimov said in a deep, quiet voice.

Federov draped his coat across the second chair and sat. Efimov got straight to the matter at hand. "I'm sure you are wondering why I have called you here today."

"It was unexpected," Federov said, offering a thin smile.

"I have reviewed your employment file, Colonel Federov. You had a stellar work history."

"Thank you—"

"Up until your final assignment."

Federov smiled, tight-lipped. "Charles Jenkins," he said. "A formidable adversary."

"Yes. That was noted in your reports." Efimov stared for a moment, as if to ensure Federov knew Efimov didn't agree, or perhaps didn't care. He did know that. "That is actually why I asked you here this morning."

"Is it?" Federov said, trying not to sound concerned.

"Yes." Efimov sat back, the leather of his chair crackling. He looked to be eyeing Federov, as if evaluating an opponent for the placement of a lethal blow. Federov hoped that was not the case. "Something has come up, and we believe you may be of assistance."

"I am always willing to be of assistance to my country," Federov said.

Efimov looked mildly amused. "It seems your nemesis has returned to Russia."

"I had many nemeses when I served."

"Perhaps. But this is the one responsible for your dismissal."

Federov squinted, trying to appear confused, but also evaluating whether the man was being sincere or probing for information, attempting to trip him up or determine how much Federov knew. "Charles Jenkins has returned to Russia?"

"So it seems."

"Excuse me for saying so, but that seems an unlikely scenario."

Efimov rested his elbows on the chair arms and folded his hands together, his index fingers tapping against one another. "Why would you say that?"

"Because Mr. Jenkins went to great lengths to get out of Russia and managed to do so only by the skin of his teeth."

"And yet we have visual confirmation he has returned."

Efimov pivoted a computer screen, and Federov leaned forward to watch a video. Charles Jenkins entered what appeared to be a bank, dressed in a suit and tie, and approached a teller.

"Do you recognize that man to be Charles Jenkins?" Efimov asked.

"He has a beard, but yes, I recognize him. Where was the film obtained?"

Efimov pulled the screen back. "A camera inside the UBS branch in Moscow."

"Huh?" Federov said. "What was his purpose for being there?"

Efimov explained Jenkins's apparent purpose inside the bank.

Federov listened as if hearing it for the first time. Then he asked, "For clarification, the account was in Mr. Jenkins's name?"

"Yes."

"And he supplied the teller identification using his real name?"

"Yes."

Federov pondered this, or at least hoped he looked to be doing so. Then he said, "Mr. Jenkins's counterintelligence skills are such that he should have expected the account to be frozen, and that Lubyanka would be notified of any activity."

"That would seem to be the logical deduction. Unfortunately, he fled the bank before officers arrived. But let me ask . . . As someone who pursued Mr. Jenkins, do *you* have any suspicions about what would bring him back to Russia?"

Federov scowled. "The obvious deduction would be that Mr. Jenkins came back because it was the only way to open a frozen bank account . . . but . . ."

"But . . ."

"Such a supposition raises a number of other questions I'm sure you have already considered."

"Such as?" Efimov asked. "I summoned you for your opinion."

"Well . . . Where did Mr. Jenkins obtain the funds in that Moscow account?"

"Unknown."

"I think we must assume the funds came from the CIA, but then, why would they use an account that could be so easily frozen? Why use his name, which again would be easily recognizable? In addition, Mr. Jenkins did not strike me as a man motivated by money."

"Arkady Volkov said the same thing."

"Did he? May I ask how much was in the account?"

"More than four million American dollars."

Federov feigned surprise and hoped he had succeeded. "Perhaps I spoke too quickly then." He smiled. "You said Mr. Jenkins fled the bank. Has he fled Russia?"

Efimov discussed their unsuccessful chase of Jenkins to the airport and to the M'Istral Hotel and Spa, and introduced Vasilyev and his stolen money.

"But you've apprehended this man, Vasilyev?" Federov asked.

"As yet, no."

"But he appears to be a key factor in Mr. Jenkins's return to Russia," Federov said, beginning to see an opportunity to lead the conversation toward what he and Jenkins had discussed the prior evening.

"That would seem to be the case."

"A double agent perhaps. Someone to provide Mr. Jenkins with information and financial resources and perhaps a way out of the country after he had succeeded in taking the money in the two accounts."

"Perhaps," Efimov agreed.

"And the money in this second account was also frozen?"

"It was not."

Again, Federov paused to give this due regard. "I don't understand. I thought perhaps Mr. Jenkins's return was to unfreeze both accounts and flee with the money, but if the second account was not frozen, then . . ."

"A conundrum."

"Yes, but not unlike Mr. Jenkins. The man was a paradox."

"In what way?"

"He served as a young CIA officer in Mexico City but left abruptly and lived in isolation for decades, or at least appeared to. The fact that he remained highly skilled in counterintelligence dictates against that conclusion."

"Perhaps he never actually left the CIA's service."

Federov understood now what Jenkins had meant when he called Efimov a ghost. He suspected Jenkins was also a ghost. "I considered that possibility also—a disgruntled former officer willing to sell secrets—but that, too, was a ruse. His real purpose was to identify and kill the person disclosing information on a cadre of American moles: Russian women referred to as the seven sisters."

Efimov did not respond.

Federov shook his head. "I wish I could be of more help."

Efimov nodded. "As do I." He stared at Federov, who was uncertain what to do. After some time Federov stood and reached for his coat. Then he paused.

"Something else?" Efimov asked.

"I'm not certain. But . . . Perhaps there is someone who knows of this Sergei Vasilyev, and perhaps also the reason Mr. Jenkins has returned." Federov shook his head. "If she is alive."

"She?" Efimov said.

This was the $10 million moment, and Federov was about to put everything on the line. "Mr. Jenkins evaded our attempts to capture him at Vishnevka largely due to a Russian woman. A spy. Paulina Ponomayova."

"I read your report."

"Then you know that she led us away from the safe house in Vishnevka to allow Jenkins to escape. She crashed her car."

"You said '*If* she is alive.'"

"She intended to take her own life. I succeeded in preventing that, but perhaps only prolonging the inevitable. She was in bad shape from the car accident. I understood she was taken to the Hospital for War Veterans here in Moscow, but I was then dismissed. I'm afraid I do not know whether she survived. If she did . . . Well, she spent many hours with Mr. Jenkins and seems a logical choice for interrogation—that is, I would interrogate her thoroughly. If I still worked here."

Efimov responded with a thin smile. "I can assure you that Ponomayova knows nothing."

"You've interrogated her?" Federov said, not anticipating this answer.

"The doctors speculate that Ponomayova suffered brain damage in the car accident, and that appears to be so."

Federov had not considered this possibility. If Efimov had interrogated Ponomayova and she had not spoken, there was a good chance she *had* suffered brain damage. If this were true, everything to this point was for naught. He went for broke, suspecting Efimov was arrogant and would not appreciate a challenge to his abilities. He might just want to prove Federov wrong.

"If I may be so bold," Federov said, "perhaps you employed the wrong techniques."

Efimov did not physically react, but his grin waned. The blood vessel on the side of his head pulsed. "You think you could do better?"

"Not better," Federov said, allowing the man to save face. "Differently. I suspect I know something you did not have the benefit of knowing."

"And what would that be?"

"Ms. Ponomayova's weakness."

Efimov smirked and looked to the window before reengaging Federov. "And what would that be?"

"Charles Jenkins," Federov said.

19

Charles Jenkins bundled himself in a warm coat, knit cap, and gloves, and exited Federov's apartment building through the garage, where the camera in the elevator lobby remained broken, as Federov had predicted. Jenkins took the Metro train south to Bitsevsky Park, keeping a watch on those on the line to determine if anyone exited at his same stop. The park covered eighteen square kilometers, making it nearly six times larger than Central Park, an easy place for Jenkins to get lost, if he was followed. He was not.

In the clear morning, Jenkins walked a trail toward a stand of trees. A dusting of snow covered the ground, and the temperature had dropped to a bitter cold, which he hoped would discourage others from the trails and thereby make anyone present conspicuous. Two hardy women jogged past him wearing leggings, long-sleeve shirts, and earmuffs, their breaths trailing them like steam engines. Otherwise, as Jenkins had correctly predicted, the trail was deserted. He called Matt Lemore on the encrypted cell phone, the call routed through France, the prefix for Paris's third arrondissement—Marais, home of France's Picasso Museum.

"Hello," Lemore said.

"It's me," Jenkins said.

"I was concerned when I didn't hear from you. You have news?" Lemore asked.

"I made contact with the art dealer, and I've confirmed the painting remains in the owner's possession," he said, again using the agreed subterfuge of Ponomayova as "the painting," Federov "the art dealer," and Russia as "the owner."

"Where is the painting at present?"

"I am attempting to obtain further confirmation, but it appears the painting is located in the art gallery as we originally suspected."

Lemore paused. "Can it be purchased?"

"There appear to be many obstacles that would make purchase unlikely. The owner considers the painting to be of great value and has gone to extremes to protect it."

"Any chance the painting will be moved in the near future?"

Jenkins entered the woods. The trees blocked the sun, and he walked in the shadows, feeling the temperature further drop. "That appears unlikely."

"Would the owner take an exchange of some sort, perhaps?"

"I am told by the art dealer that the owner highly values the painting and has a sentimental attachment that exceeds a monetary value, making an exchange unlikely. There was, however, an interesting development this morning. The art dealer has been summoned to speak to the owner."

Lemore did not immediately comment. After a pause he said, "Did the dealer provide any indication on the likely subject of his discussion with the owner?"

"Not as of yet, though I'm hoping to speak to the dealer tonight."

"If the dealer is detained beyond an acceptable period of time, do not wait to speak to him. Abandon the purchase."

"Understood."

"You have other paintings here at home," Lemore said, off script. "And they are far more valuable."

"I will be in further contact soon." Jenkins disconnected the call.

—

After shutting the door to Efimov's office behind him, Federov released a long sigh. Beneath his suit coat, his shirt clung to his skin, like he had worn it into a shower, but at least he wasn't being sent to a gulag—not yet anyway. Beyond that good fortune, he might very well have crafted a challenge that would allow him to speak with Ponomayova—if Efimov took the bait. He had not yet done so, but that was also not unlike the man's reputation. Though Federov suspected Efimov had a large ego and would be reluctant to admit that Federov, or anyone else, could extract information from Ponomayova when he himself had failed, he might also want to prove his point. Efimov's failure would be a black stain on his reputation, a stain he might seek to minimize with evidence that others had similarly failed. He might also be right. Ponomayova might be brain damaged—if not before the interrogation then certainly after it.

But Efimov's reputation was also of a man who acted deliberately—unless his temper got the better of him.

Federov did not know which Efimov he would get—if Efimov would give him the chance to interrogate Ponomayova. But investigations required a first step before a second, and a first step was one step closer to a $10 million payout, likely more. Federov also knew Jenkins had not opened with his best offer. Federov would have done the same.

Federov, however, was not going to put that cart before the horse. Things would not be so simple, not with Efimov involved. He would have his scarred hands in every detail. That would complicate things, especially if Efimov did not trust Federov, and Efimov, it was said, did not trust anyone.

Federov exhaled another long breath and summoned the elevator car. When the elevator doors on the far left pulled open, he moved to step inside and nearly bumped into Arkady Volkov.

Federov stopped, surprised by the encounter. "Arkady?"

Volkov, always a bull leading with his horns, didn't immediately see his longtime partner. He looked up, hesitating, as if also trying to reconcile Federov's appearance at Lubyanka, which was certainly unexpected.

"Viktor."

Federov stepped back. "Are you getting off?"

Again, Volkov paused. He glanced down the hall, then said, "No. No, I am riding to the ground floor for some fresh air."

"Fresh and cold," Federov said. "I will ride with you and enjoy the chance to catch up." The doors closed and the elevator descended. "How have you been? You have recovered?"

Federov had visited Volkov many times in a Moscow hospital bed after Volkov's confrontation with Charles Jenkins. He had brought meals to the waiting room, consoled Volkov's wife, and played chess with his partner to help him pass the time and to recover his mental acumen. He'd brought Volkov reading material, mostly magazines with crossword puzzles, as well as the newspaper. Volkov had never admitted to reading a book in his life.

"I am back at work," Volkov said, always a man of few words. These sounded somber.

"You don't sound happy."

"Times are different now, Viktor."

Volkov and Federov had come from different eras. Volkov had started with the KGB during a time when the Russian government employed nearly two-thirds of Russia's workers. He had received a modest income, but also an apartment and a garden plot. He had little to no chance of being promoted or of improving his living situation, and thus had no incentive to try to do so. Federov had come to the FSB well after the fall of communism. The pay still stunk, but a chance to improve one's situation through hard work and ingenuity existed. Success was rewarded, if one did not get oneself fired.

"And you, Viktor? Why are you here?"

The two men exited to the lobby. "One of my old cases," he said. "Our case, actually."

"Charles Jenkins?"

Federov studied Volkov. He had a strange sense his former partner knew the reason for his visit, but then Volkov had always struck him as a man who knew more than his persistent silence revealed. "You are aware of this?"

"I am aware that Mr. Jenkins has returned," Volkov said. They pushed through the turnstile into the lobby. "I spent a late night with Simon Alekseyov in Adam Efimov's office. Simon is the lead officer on the file."

Federov gave some thought as to what that meant. Efimov was clearly in charge, but no doubt it would be Alekseyov's head that rolled if he failed.

"So you have met with him, then?" Volkov asked.

"Efimov? Yes, just now."

"Efimov has taken over the investigation," Volkov said. "At least in principle." They discussed what had transpired to that point, then Volkov asked, "And did the director mention that Mr. Jenkins also removed funds from a second account?"

"He did. Sergei Vasilyev, I believe was the name. Efimov wanted to know if we had encountered him in our prior dealings with Mr. Jenkins."

"What did you tell him?" Volkov asked.

Federov shrugged. "I told him I did not recall the name. Do you?"

"I recall little from that time, Viktor."

Federov smiled. He needed to change subjects. "Of course. But you are well again, yes?"

"As well as can be expected for an old officer. I think my time here is coming to an end. The millennials make me expendable."

"The millennials do not have your experience, Arkady."

"This no longer appears to be valued," Volkov said.

"What would you do?"

Volkov gave a blank stare.

"I, too, did not know life outside of Lubyanka, Arkady. Perhaps you will have more time to plan than I had when you decide to retire. I am finding it is good to be kept busy." Federov extended a hand. *"Nadeyus', my eshche uvidimsya." I hope to see you again.*

Volkov shook hands, seemed about to say something, then appeared to reconsider and, as he had done so often during their nine years working together, remained silent.

Jenkins returned to Federov's building just before noon. He looked up to Federov's balcony. The chair faced the apartment rather than the street—a sign agreed upon to indicate Federov was inside and it was safe to come up. Jenkins surveyed the building and the tree-lined street for an additional five minutes. He did not detect any surveillance.

He took the same path to the eighth floor and used Federov's spare key to enter the apartment.

"You're not on your way to a Russian gulag, so I assume the meeting went well?" Jenkins asked, disrobing from his winter gear and hanging it on the peg.

Federov had sweat rings beneath both armpits. "'Well' is not the word I would choose, but no, I am not in a gulag."

Jenkins entered the living room and sat. Federov provided him with details of the meeting. "I told Efimov I did not have any knowledge as to why you would return to Moscow, but as we discussed, I suggested there may be someone who has such information."

Jenkins sat forward, elbows on his knees. He admired Federov's moxie, or his desire to receive millions more in cash. It didn't matter.

They agreed that the suggestion might just get Federov into Lefortovo to talk to Paulina, which was one step closer to Jenkins getting her out.

"Before you get too excited . . . or optimistic, you need to know that Efimov interrogated Ponomayova, many times apparently, and she did not speak."

Jenkins smiled. "She's a lot tougher than she looks."

Federov shook his head. "You are giving her far too much credit, and Efimov far too little. There is a reason he was chosen for the interrogation, Mr. Jenkins. Efimov was considered the best of the best, or worst of the worst. He has had blood on his hands . . . many times. If he did not extract information from Ponomayova, it may be because she has none to give, or because she suffered some brain injury in the car accident and is not able to do so."

"Did you challenge him?"

"I did. I advised Efimov that you and Ms. Ponomayova spent long hours in the car driving to Vishnevka. I told him that something changed in your . . . how do you say, dynamics—to what end I did not know—but that Ponomayova had been willing to give her life so that you could get out of Russia. I told him that you were her weakness."

"What was his response?"

"He studied me. Adam Efimov is detailed in his thinking. He will take time to digest what information I provided before he makes his decision, and not just because he has a large ego and will not believe I can do better. I can tell you, however, that the fact that Ponomayova was willing to die to save you increased his interest and curiosity. Be assured he will tell this to the deputy director, and the deputy director will advise the president. It will tweak their interest as well, maybe enough for them to tell Efimov to give me a chance to interrogate her. Understand, however, that security will be very tight."

"But he may let you speak to her?"

"This I do not know." Jenkins heard the beeping of a truck backing up outside the apartment. Federov continued, "Then again, he may use someone else." Federov wore a wry smile.

"But you don't think so."

"I told him I had studied Ponomayova's profile and yours, and that she will remember me as the person who hunted you. She will, therefore, believe me when I tell her that you were unsuccessful in your escape from Russia, that you, too, occupy a cell in Lefortovo, and that the information she provides may very well save your life. This she will not believe coming from anyone else."

Jenkins smiled. "It's brilliant, Viktor. You baited him."

"We shall see, Mr. Jenkins, if this is enough to bait Efimov, and if Ms. Ponomayova feels as strongly about you as you do about her."

"Can you get her out of Lefortovo to speak with her?"

Federov raised a hand. "Do not be rash, Mr. Jenkins. These things take time. You Americans are too impatient. It is your consumerism. You want everything now. This minute. You must learn Russian patience. We must take the first step before we take the second." He shrugged. "What more can be done?"

"Patience is one thing. Time is another. And I don't have a lot of the latter, and that goes for Paulina as well. You said so yourself."

"Yes. This is true." Federov looked to be caught in a thought. "Something else," he said. "On my way out of Lubyanka I ran into Arkady Volkov, my former partner."

"I recall him," Jenkins said. "The statue."

"Do not interpret silence to be a lack of intellect; Arkady is quiet, but that is because he believes one learns more from listening than speaking. He is also intuitive, which is my concern."

"Why?"

"His silence makes him a hard man to know, but he said some things . . . things that seemed to have a purpose."

"About what?"

"About you. About this case. I think Arkady might be the reason Efimov summoned me to his office."

"What did Volkov say?"

"It was not so much what he said, but that he said anything at all. Arkady has a way he looks at you . . ."

"Looks at you?"

"In Russia, especially in Arkady's time, you learned to be careful with your words. One never knew who was listening. Facial expressions conveyed much."

"So how did he look at you?"

"He looked at me as if we would be seeing one another again."

"You're friends."

"No." Federov shook his head. "No. We were partners, but never really friends."

"Do you think he can be trusted?"

"Arkady told me he is nearing retirement. Retirement on a government pension is not much. When one nears retirement in Russia, one contemplates more closely how one is to survive, ways to make money, such as ingratiating oneself with those in power."

"Efimov."

Federov nodded. "So, no, I would say Arkady cannot be trusted, any more than either of us trusts one another."

"I'd hoped we were getting past that, Viktor."

Federov smiled but did not otherwise respond.

"Do you think Volkov has figured out you are Sergei Vasilyev? Did you ever discuss Carl Emerson's money with Volkov?"

"No. No discussions. By then Arkady was in a Russian hospital, by your hand."

"He could have been probing to determine what you know about me and my return."

"Probing?"

"Questioning you."

"Possibly."

Jenkins sat back. It was a problem, but not the immediate one. "Let's talk about Paulina, what you might say to her, if you get the chance to talk to her."

"Yes, let's talk about that. And let's also talk about how much more it is going to cost you."

20

For the next several days, Jenkins remained almost exclusively inside Federov's apartment, rarely venturing outside. He imagined it was a bit like how Anne Frank and her relatives had existed, living in fear of being discovered, in a few rooms in an attic—keeping one's voice down, moving only as necessary during the day, and worrying that at any moment someone would kick in the door and arrest him.

Efimov had not called, and with each passing hour it seemed less likely he would, and that perhaps their best chance to possibly get Ponomayova out was slipping away. To keep from going stir-crazy, Jenkins and Federov played chess; Jenkins had learned the game at a young age from his grandfather, and at one time considered himself a good player, but he had not played in many years, and the rust showed. Federov beat him handily. By the end of the second day, however, Jenkins had remembered much of what his grandfather taught him, and the games became much more competitive, or so he thought. Federov suggested they play for money. The amount was nominal, five hundred rubles a game. Jenkins soon realized Federov had been toying with him—giving Jenkins a false sense of hope to win his money. The Russian was highly competitive. He liked to win. Jenkins filed that away, along with something else he'd learned.

Never to fully trust Federov.

At night, Jenkins walked outside to break the monotony and to call home. The brisk weather helped to clear his thoughts, and the walk alone provided time to think. He talked to Alex and to CJ and listened to Lizzie yelling gibberish in the background. The calls were short, and he and Alex did their best to get in as much as they could, without saying anything of import. Jenkins missed them all and wondered often if this had been the right choice. He also called Matt Lemore, providing him with updates, but until Federov was given permission to talk to Paulina and determine her physical and mental status, Lemore's hands were also tied.

Federov grocery-shopped, mostly for prepared meals. His cooking stunk. And though Jenkins and Federov spent long hours together, Jenkins thought of Federov the way his father, who'd suffered two heart attacks, had thought of death. *We're acquainted, but we ain't friends.*

Jenkins reminded himself often that Federov had $10 million at stake, and that the price would undoubtedly increase if Federov successfully convinced Efimov to let him interview Paulina at Lubyanka, or some other place outside of Lefortovo.

On the third night, as Jenkins sat on the couch reading, Federov's cell phone rang. He looked to Jenkins. "FSB," he said. Answering, he listened intently. Then he said, "I will be there. *Da.* If she knows anything, I will—" He disconnected, but clearly the caller had cut him off. He looked again to Jenkins, exhaling a held breath. "Be careful what it is that you wish for. That is the saying?"

"Something like that," Jenkins said.

"Tomorrow I go to Lefortovo. *Ya nadeyus', radi nas oboikh, chto eto ne bilet v odin konets.*" *I hope, for both our sakes, it is not a one-way ticket.*

—

Lefortovo Prison, built close to the Kremlin, had a long, violent history since it opened in 1883. Federov, a history buff, knew the prison had housed political prisoners dating back to the Bolshevik revolution, and that those prisoners had been systematically executed after years of torture to coerce them to confess their "crimes." A similar "Great Terror" occurred during Joseph Stalin's reign. Prison conditions reported by those few who had been allowed to tour the facility were said to have remained markedly consistent with those barbarous times.

He also knew from half a dozen occasions speaking to prisoners within Lefortovo that Ponomayova would be subjected to isolation, inconsistent exposure to total darkness and bright lights, insufficient food and blankets, constant surveillance, and controlled access to bathrooms and to cold showers. The worst, however, was not the physical mistreatment, but the psychological impact of those conditions on all but the mentally strongest prisoners.

Upon his arrival at the prison, Federov filled out enough paperwork to kill a small forest, then passed through metal detectors and locked portals, despite his presence at the prison having been approved by Dmitry Sokalov. Once these rituals were completed, he was escorted through cell blocks with brown carpeting, the presence of which, he deduced, dampened sound. With each step he descended into the prison, he became more anxious, wondering if his permission to interrogate Ponomayova was just a ruse, if the FSB was onto him, and if he was about to be thrown into a cell, interrogated, and tortured.

A second guard opened a door to a windowless, poorly lit room with a small metal table and chair and a footstool, beneath a single overhead light. The guard told Federov to wait.

"Where would I go?" Federov asked, trying to lighten the atmosphere.

The guard did not respond—or smile.

The room was stifling hot and smelled of perspiration. Federov pulled out the chair, the legs making a hellacious screeching noise against the concrete, unbuttoned his suit jacket, and sat. He looked to the right corner of the ceiling, to a camera with a red light. When he moved, the light turned green. He opened his briefcase, which had also been searched, and took out the folder on Paulina Ponomayova he had read so many times he had nearly memorized it. The file had been added to since Federov last possessed it. It described Ponomayova's serious injuries from the car crash and her time at Lefortovo. It also described Efimov's efforts to extract information. Despite her injuries, which Efimov had exploited, and despite other trusted techniques, Ponomayova had not spoken.

Remarkable, Federov thought. He had heard of hardened foreign agents breaking down and crying like children inside Lefortovo. On a page of his report, Efimov had written:

> *Despite my employing proven techniques, Ponomayova has refused to speak or to identify any of the women in the photographs shown to her to be members of the seven sisters. She has no family or relatives to be used as leverage, and seemingly no fear of dying. Her attitude could best be described as recalcitrant, but that intimates acting or speaking with an intent, and the prisoner displays none. She either has been mentally compromised due to injuries sustained in the car accident or she is projecting that to be the case. I believe it to be the former. I have yet to encounter a prisoner this mentally strong and do not believe her to be the first. She has not uttered a single word.*

Federov set the file to one side of the table. It confirmed what he had suspected. Efimov had never failed to get what he wanted, and he did not believe anyone else could do better. He expected Federov to fail, thereby absolving his own failure.

Minutes passed before the guard again opened the door and escorted a woman into the room—her hands cuffed to a belly chain. A second chain descended from her wrists to ankle cuffs, rattling and scraping the concrete floor. The woman had her head lowered, but from what Federov could see, and from what he could recall, she looked nothing like the bloodied woman collapsed over the steering wheel of the car in Vishnevka. Her hair had been shaved and she looked as small and frail as a terminally ill child. She wore black-framed glasses too big for her face, and the sleeves and pant legs of her blue jumpsuit had each been rolled multiple times. She also walked with a pronounced limp.

The guards sat her on the footstool and locked her chain to a ring cemented to the floor, then retreated to the corners of the room where, Federov realized, they would not be filmed.

Federov's eyes shifted to the camera. The red light had again turned green.

He stared at the top of the woman's bowed head and deliberately tapped his pen on the table. The noise had no effect on her. Her gaze remained fixed on the ground.

"You are Paulina Ponomayova?" he said.

The woman did not respond, not verbally and not physically.

Federov flipped open the cover of the file and pulled a black-and-white photograph from a clip on the inside cover, studying the picture Ponomayova had used on her FSB identification card. She had been an attractive, middle-aged woman with light-brown hair and sharp features.

Deliberately, he slid the photograph across the table where she could see it.

"Are you Paulina Ponomayova?" he asked again, his voice even and soft.

Again, she did not respond.

One of the guards stepped from the corner of the room, but Federov caught his gaze and gave him a slow, subtle headshake. The guard retreated. A good sign. Federov was respected as an FSB officer.

"I am Colonel Viktor Federov, Ms. Ponomayova. Do you remember me?"

No response.

"I chased you and Charles Jenkins across Russia to Vishnevka. We were acquainted when you crashed your car into a tree while attempting to flee."

No response.

"I did, however, manage to save your life."

Nothing.

"You were creating a diversion intended to allow Charles Jenkins to escape by boat to Turkey, were you not?"

Nothing.

"You failed."

Not even an eyeblink.

"We apprehended Mr. Jenkins at the safe house in Vishnevka. He has been a political prisoner here in Lefortovo since that day. His country denies any knowledge of his being in Moscow and has made no overtures seeking his return. At first, we believed this was indicative of a low-level officer. Now we are not so certain. Like you, Mr. Jenkins was recalcitrant, but in time he saw the wisdom of speaking to us. He told us that he came to Russia to determine the identity of the individual supplying us with the names of the seven sisters, so that individual could be terminated. In this, he failed. Our contact has since provided us with the names of the remaining four sisters and they, too, are now prisoners here in Lefortovo."

Again, nothing.

"We do not believe there is anything more to be obtained from Mr. Jenkins. He has no value to us. We wish only that you confirm what he has already disclosed to be the truth. If you will do so, we will return him to the United States, to his family . . . to his wife and to his son."

Federov paused, keenly aware of the camera lens in the corner of the room. He perspired beneath his shirt, and the stagnant air became difficult to breathe.

He was about to continue, when . . . subtly, slowly, Ponomayova raised her gaze, meeting his.

Federov saw an opportunity for a breakthrough. "If you do not assist us, Mr. Jenkins will remain here in Lefortovo and will never again see his wife or his son."

Ponomayova's gaze searched Federov's face, as he and Jenkins had hoped. He shifted his eyes, for just a brief moment, to the camera in the corner of the room, to impart that they were being filmed. "Do you understand what I am saying to you?"

She stared at him, and Federov hoped she had picked up on the subtlety of his question. He had left out the fact that Jenkins had told Ponomayova in Vishnevka that his wife had been pregnant, and Ponomayova had predicted they would have a girl, a fact of particular import to her valiant attempt to get him home.

Federov saw something in Ponomayova's eyes. Was it an acknowledgment? He was about to speak when Ponomayova uttered her first word since arriving at Lefortovo, which gave Federov a success Efimov had never achieved.

"Da," she said softly.

21

Federov returned to his apartment shortly after nightfall and went immediately to the cabinet in the kitchen, removing the Scotch and pouring himself a drink. He spent much of the next hour advising Jenkins of what had happened when he'd attempted to speak to Ponomayova, a six-hour grind that had elicited only the one-word response, giving him a leg up on Efimov and proving that Ponomayova had not suffered brain damage.

Federov poured himself a second Scotch and held the glass up to Jenkins. Jenkins declined. Federov took the glass to the living room and sat. "I believe she was trying to determine why I had not mentioned your wife's pregnancy or subsequent birth. As with Arkady, it was less what she said and more the look on her face. I told you, in Russia a facial expression can convey more than a thousand words. I looked to the camera in the corner of her room to let her know we were being filmed."

"And that was when she told you she understood."

"Yes."

"That's a start."

"Yes, but I fear it will not go far with Efimov. He will not easily concede that someone can do what he could not."

"You already have," Jenkins said.

"Which is why he will be ever more vigilant," Federov said.

"What was his response when you told him?" Jenkins asked.

"Little. But he cared. He cared because he will have to tell the deputy director and the president that I succeeded where he failed. But a one-word answer is not going to buy me much more time with Ponomayova—I can also tell you that. And if I cannot get her to respond to my questions, then I am of no use to Efimov. He will dismiss me and go in another direction."

Throughout the remainder of the evening, Jenkins thought back to his conversations with Paulina, the things he'd told her, things only she would know, and what she had told him, hoping that if Federov fed them to her, it would gain her trust and she would talk, giving him and Lemore time to finalize plans.

"The FSB understands I came here to identify the person exposing the seven sisters, does it not?" Jenkins asked as they ate dinner.

"That was our understanding."

"And you said Efimov's interrogation was primarily because the FSB believed Paulina knew the identity of the remaining four of the seven."

"Efimov told me this himself."

"He showed her photographs?"

"It is in his report."

Jenkins paced an area behind the couch, near the fireplace. "Okay, so what if you brought in those same mug shots of women for Paulina to consider—"

"I don't see—"

"And in that stack, you handed her a photograph of me holding my baby girl." Jenkins pulled his wallet from his pocket and removed a picture of him holding Lizzie.

"Again, not likely. My briefcase and all my materials are searched before I am allowed into the room and when I depart. And again, anything I produce in the interview would be seen by the camera."

Jenkins continued brainstorming, thinking out loud and hoping something good developed. "Is there any portion of the room not within the camera's coverage?"

"The back of the room, but her guards remain there throughout the interrogation."

"Can you get rid of them?"

"Not likely. What are you proposing?"

"Some way to get the picture in front of her, to prove that I am not in Lefortovo, and to confirm that you intended to get her a message from me."

Federov waved him off. "This is not possible. Not with the camera. I am not a magician."

Jenkins stopped pacing, struck by another memory from his youth. "You wore your suit?"

"What?"

"A suit. You wore a suit."

"You saw me. Yes, I wore my suit."

"Did they search you?"

"I told you. They searched—"

"No. Did they search your body, your clothes, your pockets?"

"I passed through a metal detector."

"But did they physically search you?"

"Not physically, no."

"Sit down."

"What?"

"Sit down at the table." Federov took his drink to the table and sat. "Where is the camera in relation to where Paulina is seated?"

Federov pointed. "Behind her. In the corner of the ceiling, the right corner from my perspective on the other side of the table."

"Over her left shoulder." Jenkins considered this and gestured to the right side of the table. "So this area of the table would be blocked by her shoulder."

Federov frowned. "Even if it is blocked by her shoulder, there is the guard in each corner."

"And how attentive are the guards?"

Federov shrugged. “I did not pay close attention to them.”

“The trick,” Jenkins said, “is to make a photograph appear and disappear from the stack of photographs you bring in.”

Federov shook his head. “Appear and disappear . . . What does this mean?”

“Do you have a deck of cards?”

“A what?”

“Cards. Do you have a deck of cards?”

“You wish to play a game?”

“No. I wish to show you something.”

Federov exhaled and pushed back his chair. “You Americans are crazy.”

He rummaged through several drawers in the kitchen and returned with a deck of cards, handing them to Jenkins. “Here.”

“You’ve heard the expression that the hand is quicker than the eye?”

“No. I have not heard this.”

Jenkins took out the deck of cards, which were different than cards in the United States—fewer in number and of a different design. The differences were not important. He shuffled the deck using just his right hand. “When I was a boy, my grandfather showed me magic tricks to amuse me. He was an amateur magician. Loved Harry Houdini, René Lavand, and Bill Malone.”

“Houdini I have heard of. The others I have not. What is your point?”

With the same hand shuffling the deck, Jenkins made a card appear faceup. Just as suddenly, he made it disappear and replaced it with a different card. “The point is that he taught me, just like he taught me chess.”

“Yes, but you stink at chess,” Federov said.

Jenkins set the deck down and picked out seven cards. “Imagine these seven cards are seven photographs of women who could be, or are suspected to include, one or more of the remaining original seven sisters. The first thing you need to do is replace one of these pictures with the picture of me holding Lizzie. Are you left- or right-handed?”

"Right hand."

"You'll hold the deck in your left hand, like this." Jenkins demonstrated, holding the top edge with his index finger and the bottom edge with his thumb. "You're going to bend your ring finger so it is behind, and in contact with, the top card of the deck. Like this. You see?"

"Yes, I see this, but—"

"Just keep watching. You can gesture to Paulina using your right hand, like this. It will draw the guards' attention, if they are watching, to that hand. Meanwhile, this bent finger will slide the top card off the deck, like this." Jenkins demonstrated in slow motion. "You then pinch it behind your hand between your ring and middle finger, seemingly making it disappear. When you bring your hands together, you slip the hidden card into your right hand, again cupping it using your ring and small finger."

"I am not following this," Federov said.

"Watch. I will do this at regular speed."

Jenkins performed the trick with Federov seated directly in front of him. Federov flinched when Jenkins showed him the card in his right hand. Jenkins did it again. Again, the expression on Federov's face indicated he did not see Jenkins slide the top card and put it in his right hand.

"Yes, but . . ."

"Now you create a diversion with the seven cards like this. The guards' eyes will go to the cards. You could even drop them on the table. When you do, the right hand exchanges the card you removed with the photograph of me holding Lizzie, which you will have in your pants pocket or in your belt at the small of your back." Jenkins performed the trick a second and then a third time.

"When you bring your hands together to pick up the cards, you place the new photograph on the bottom. Like this. You said Paulina had her head down?"

"Yes."

"So you lean forward as if to put the photographs under her gaze, then fan them out." Jenkins moved his hand across the table, right to left. "She sees the picture of me and Lizzie closest to her right shoulder, which obscures the camera's lens, and she knows I am not imprisoned at Lefortovo and that I am trying to communicate with her through you. You then gather the cards back into a stack, putting my photograph on top." Jenkins lifted the cards into his right hand.

"And to get rid of the picture of you and your daughter before I leave the room, I do the same thing?" Federov said.

"Exactly. Watch. Let's say the six of spades is my picture." He stuck it in his pants pocket. "I have seven cards in my hand. I'll even show them to you." He did the diversion and quickly fanned the cards in front of Federov. Seven cards, including the ten of clubs, appeared on the table.

"Now to get rid of it." He repeated the process and handed the cards to Federov. Federov put them on the table and spread them out. The ten of clubs had vanished. Jenkins pulled it from his pants pocket and tossed it on the table.

"You want me to learn some card trick?"

"Not just any card trick, Viktor. That's a six-million-dollar trick." Jenkins smiled.

Federov did not. After a moment he said, "How can I do this?"

"Practice."

"Yes, but—"

"I'm going to make some phone calls and make sure the agency leaks that Sergei Vasilyev is a double agent handling the remaining four of the original seven sisters."

"Fine," Federov said. "But tell me, how long did it take you to learn this trick, Mr. Jenkins?"

Months, Jenkins thought. Months before he could fool people. "A couple of days, maybe a week of intense practice," he said.

But only if the guards were not paying attention.

22

Efimov granted Federov further interviews. In the interim he purchased a camera like the one at Lefortovo and installed it in the corner of his kitchen ceiling. He used his briefcase to get a rough measurement of the height of the table at the prison, purchased a used table and modified it accordingly, then put it the same distance from the camera as the metal table at Lefortovo. Jenkins sat so that his left shoulder blocked the camera's view of the corner of the table, though Ponomayova would be significantly shorter and not nearly as wide.

As the week progressed, Federov's continued interviews of Ponomayova took on multiple purposes. The first was to convince whoever watched the tape, Efimov certainly, that Federov was a skilled interrogator making progress. Efimov remained skeptical in their debriefings, and Federov was hoping to further challenge him by asking to show Ponomayova the photographs of the women.

Federov's second purpose was to further convince Ponomayova that he and Jenkins were working together and that Federov could be trusted. Each session Federov would drop into the conversation something only Jenkins and Ponomayova would know, what Ponomayova had told him about her brother's suicide at the Bolshoi, his reason for having done so, and what Jenkins had told her about his unexpected anxiety and claustrophobia. Ponomayova, however, remained guarded, and Federov knew she was not convinced the information had not been pried from Jenkins in a cell at Lefortovo. He needed something more. The picture of Jenkins in America with his newly born little girl would likely convince her, but Federov was not ready, despite hours of practice each night with the cards.

The third goal, Federov knew, could very well be the most crucial. He needed to establish a hierarchy with the guards, and he had been plying them with packs of quality cigarettes to gain their trust and, more importantly, to establish the psychology that he was a colonel with the FSB, a ranking officer who had power and prestige, and whose orders were to be followed, when given, without question.

Finally, with each visit, Federov carefully considered his surroundings, and he provided Jenkins with details that the American could pass along and discuss with his CIA contact, though Federov remained unconvinced they would ever get Ponomayova out of Lefortovo.

Unlike Jenkins, who had big hands and long fingers, Federov's hands were small and his fingers thick. It limited his ability to slide the top card from the deck. If he couldn't do that, he couldn't do the trick.

"My grandfather said some magicians put a resin on the back of their finger to help them grip the card," Jenkins said one night. "A Band-Aid also works."

They used the bandage and applied a bit of resin. Federov improved exponentially and for the first time began to believe he could perform the trick undetected. Just as his confidence increased, however, Efimov summoned him to Lubyanka.

After Federov had taken a seat in the barren office, Efimov came around the desk, bracing his arms on the edge and leaning back, just a foot from Federov—a form of intimidation. The brick remained close at hand. Another intimidation technique.

"What success have you had with Ms. Ponomayova since her first response?" he asked.

Federov was certain Efimov was asking a question to which he already knew the answer, but he played the game. “Limited, but I believe I am very close to a breakthrough.”

“I think you’re being too generous, Colonel. I’ve watched the tapes. I would say you have had no further success.”

Federov delivered a dig of his own. “These things take time, as you well know.” He folded his legs. “I have been employing various techniques to try to further gain the witness’s confidence.”

Efimov grew red in the face, and the vein in his head pulsed. His brow furrowed and his voice became terse. “I am not interested in the witness’s confidence. I am interested in what she knows. She has offered nothing of import, as I confirmed.” Efimov picked up the brick, as if to weigh it. Federov did his best to ignore it. It wasn’t easy. He had an image of the brick flying toward his face, too quickly for him to raise his hands.

“Perhaps if I were to show her photographs of women suspected to be some of the remaining members of the seven sisters.”

Efimov did not immediately answer, and Federov suspected that was because the FSB did not have a strong grasp on any suspected women. Instead, he asked, “You believe you would have more success than I had?”

“What is there to lose?”

“Time. We are well behind Charles Jenkins.”

“You have no information he has yet fled.”

Efimov smiled. “Did you expect him to personally notify the border patrol? Your purpose in interrogating Ponomayova was to determine what she knows of Charles Jenkins, his purpose for his return. I am convinced she knows nothing. I am ending your interrogation before we waste any more time.” He rounded the desk to return to his chair, which gave Federov precious seconds to think.

“I think I would have better success if the two guards were not present in the room, and of course the camera is a further hindrance to gaining her trust. She knows she is being filmed." Federov asked for something he knew Efimov would never allow, but which might make him amenable to what Federov actually sought. "She can go nowhere inside that room, certainly not with her chain bolted to the floor. And I am unconcerned for my well-being; have the guards wait outside."

"That is against prison policy."

"If I am to gain her confidence—"

Efimov slammed the brick onto the desk, a dull thud. His voice rose in volume, and spittle flew from his lips with each hard syllable. "Your job is to extract information about Charles Jenkins, why he has returned and where he is, not to . . . gain her confidence or her trust, Colonel. As I said, your interrogation has failed, as I knew it would. Leave."

A dozen retorts flashed through Federov's mind, but he resisted the urge to verbalize them. The brick, if meant to scare, had failed, instead provoking defiance and bitterness at being treated like a cadet by the agency to which Federov had given and lost so much of his life. "That is, of course, your prerogative." He stood. "*If* you believe you can find someone who would be more successful." Federov let that thought linger, though not for long. He needed to move to the alternate plan he and Jenkins had discussed. "But may I say that I believe we are taking the wrong approach with this prisoner."

Efimov did nothing for several seconds. Then he released the brick and rubbed the dust from his hands. He sat, no doubt fully contemplating the ramifications of Federov's failure, one that would also be his failure—and from what Federov had learned in these meetings, Efimov did not have a viable alternative. He was clearly under pressure to find Charles Jenkins, and he was no closer to doing so.

After a full minute of silence, Efimov chose the lesser of what had to be two bitter choices and asked Federov to explain why he believed Efimov had taken the wrong approach. "How so?" he asked.

"I don't believe Ponomayova will give up anything on Charles Jenkins or the remaining four sisters."

"Then what—"

"She may, however, be willing to provide information on Sergei Vasilyev."

Efimov stared at Federov for several seconds, then gave a vague hand gesture for Federov to continue.

"Carl Emerson was the CIA officer who supplied the identities of three of the seven sisters, and he was paid well to do so."

"Too much, in my opinion," Efimov said.

"Perhaps, but the information was of import to the president."

Efimov again waved away the comment. "Water under the bridge."

"Bank accounts in the names of Charles Jenkins and Sergei Vasilyev were opened at the same time, in the same Moscow bank. Why?"

"You have a theory?"

Trickles of sweat ran down his sides, but Federov kept his voice even. "I do. Mr. Emerson could not very well bring home ten million dollars, or have it deposited in a US bank. So, he had it deposited here, in Moscow, but in a bank with secrecy laws to protect him. A Swiss bank."

"What are you suggesting?"

"I am suggesting that Mr. Emerson would have acted in a manner intended to implicate those trying to implicate him. It would be a way to control them. To control Charles Jenkins."

"Meaning what?"

"Mr. Jenkins would have no reason to open a bank account in his own name in Moscow. Surely, he would have contemplated that the account would be frozen. No. I believe Mr. Emerson opened the bank account in the name of Charles Jenkins as part of his plan to have Mr. Jenkins tried for espionage. A Swiss bank account containing four million dollars at a bank in Moscow would certainly be strong evidence

Mr. Jenkins was being well compensated for information he provided. That he was guilty of espionage."

"Mr. Jenkins was not convicted," Efimov said.

"He was not. And once freed, Mr. Jenkins knew of Mr. Emerson's deceit and of the account's existence."

"You believe he killed Carl Emerson to gain access to the accounts?"

"No. I believe he killed Carl Emerson because Emerson betrayed him and his country. But access to the bank accounts would certainly assist a man on the verge of bankruptcy."

"And Vasilyev?"

"I wonder whether, perhaps, there is a deeper relationship there than we have considered." Federov found the courage to pace. His own form of intimidation.

"Such as?"

"Emerson ran counterintelligence against the KGB in Mexico City in the 1970s. He was Mr. Jenkins's station chief. This is about the time we first learned of the seven sisters, I believe. And Mr. Putin made finding them a priority while he worked for the KGB."

Efimov shook his head. "I'm not following you."

"I believe the man using the name Sergei Vasilyev likely served the KGB in Mexico City, where he first became acquainted with Carl Emerson."

"You believe he was KGB?"

"I believe it is a distinct possibility. And so one must ask, what if Mr. Emerson did not obtain the names of three of the seven sisters from someone within his own government? What if we have been wrong in making this assumption? What if the information came from someone within the KGB?"

"Who?"

"Sergei Vasilyev." Federov spread his hands as if it were obvious. "Tell me, why would Carl Emerson pay anyone sixty percent of what the FSB paid him?"

"You believe Vasilyev is the source of Emerson's information?"

"I believe Vasilyev is the alias of the person who provided the information. At least the facts—the two bank accounts and the lack of any identification on Vasilyev—certainly indicate this to be a possibility."

"Why would a KGB officer give Mr. Emerson *any* money if he knew the names of the seven sisters?"

"Because Vasilyev needed Emerson. He couldn't very well provide the information himself and seek to profit from doing his job. He knew what the information was worth, especially when Mr. Putin became president. He needed Emerson, someone he was acquainted with, someone who could make it look like the information was coming from a mole in the United States seeking to be richly compensated."

Efimov displayed no emotion, but he also didn't interrupt.

"The ten million dollars gets paid to Emerson, and Emerson pays Vasilyev—the actual source of the information. Jenkins extracts this information from Emerson before he kills him, then comes to Moscow to steal the money in both accounts."

Efimov stretched his neck from side to side. Then he asked, "Why? You said Mr. Jenkins is not motivated by money."

"I don't believe he is. So clearly taking the money was to gain leverage over Vasilyev for some other purpose."

Efimov's bland expression indicated he hadn't rejected the scenario outright.

"We know that Jenkins and Ponomayova were working in concert. Why?" Federov asked. "What joined them together? What did they both want?"

"To find the source of the leak," Efimov said.

"And if they learned the leak wasn't Emerson, but someone Emerson was working with . . . Someone who provided Emerson with the identities of three of the seven sisters in exchange for a lot of money . . ."

Efimov rocked in his chair, the creaking spring the only sound in the room. He kept his gaze on Federov, as if looking through him.

Federov did not speak. He did not want to oversell the idea. Better for Efimov to figure it out on his own. If Federov's theory was correct, then by finding Vasilyev, Efimov might not only find Jenkins, but a possible source who knew the identities of the remaining four sisters.

After nearly a minute, Efimov leaned forward and replaced the brick in the box on the desk, setting it down gently. He wiped at the dust on the desktop. "You have tomorrow to find out if this is true. If you do not make progress . . . whatever your theory, I will make alternative arrangements."

"I will need photographs of men who worked for the KGB in Mexico City during the time that Carl Emerson was the CIA's station chief there."

"Do what you need to do. But understand. This will be your last chance."

—

Charles Jenkins could tell the moment Viktor Federov entered his apartment that something was wrong.

"What happened?"

Federov crossed the room to the cabinet and pulled out a glass, but not the Scotch. From the freezer he removed a bottle of vodka. "I was summoned to Efimov's office following my continued interrogation of Ponomayova. He wants to replace me."

"Did you offer the alternative reason we discussed?"

Federov unscrewed the cap, poured himself a considerable shot, and downed it. "Yes. Of course."

"And?"

"And then I said bullshit. I said a lot of bullshit."

"What was his response?"

Federov told Jenkins the details of his conversation.

"In return, Efimov has given me one more day. If I don't get any information out of Ponomayova tomorrow, then I will be replaced."

"Then you've got to do the card trick tomorrow. You've got to let her know—"

"I am not prepared," Federov said. He slapped the glass on the counter.

"I've watched the film. The switch is almost undetectable."

Federov stood at the counter shaking his head. "I am not prepared, Mr. Jenkins. One slip and it is the end for me, and I won't have to go far to find a cell."

"We don't have a choice," Jenkins said.

"You don't have a choice," Federov shot back. "I can do whatever the fuck I want, and don't tell me about the millions of dollars of mine that you control. A man in Lefortovo has no need of money. Nor does a man in Novodevichy," he said, referring to the famous Moscow cemetery.

Jenkins sat in silence. He'd suspected this day might come, and he'd thought it through, what might motivate a man like Federov. Turned out, Federov had already let him know.

In the kitchen he found a pen and a piece of paper. He wrote on it. Then he handed the paper to Federov.

"What is this?" Federov asked.

"It's your money," Jenkins said. "All of it. Six million dollars."

Federov stared at him with untrusting eyes. "This is a trick."

Jenkins returned to the living room and sat. "No trick."

"Why would you do this?" Federov asked, skeptical.

"Because it's yours."

"And what of Ponomayova?"

"I don't know. Maybe there's another asset. I'm going to have to start over."

Again, Federov studied him. "I don't believe you. This is a ploy. This is a number to some . . . I don't know what. I enter it and I get arrested."

"You can confirm it in about five seconds on the Internet."

Federov stared, as if trying to solve some complex game.

"It's an account at a bank in Switzerland," Jenkins said. "The password is 'Dostoevsky.' Your favorite writer."

Federov flipped open his laptop on his kitchen counter. He again looked to Jenkins, letting several seconds pass. When Jenkins remained silent, Federov typed on the laptop's keyboard, then again considered Jenkins as the site loaded. He typed again and waited, presumably having entered the account number Jenkins had written on the slip of paper.

Another beat. He typed in the password.

Federov's eyes widened.

"You can transfer the money anywhere you like," Jenkins said. "Then you're done. You can go wherever you wish."

Federov studied Jenkins.

"But I don't think you will," Jenkins said.

Federov closed his laptop. "No?"

"No." Easy now. He heard his grandfather's calm voice teaching him to fish. *Set the hook first. Then reel him in.*

Federov smiled and scoffed. "You wish to offer me more money. I told you, a dead man cannot spend—"

"No. No more money. Just yours. Six million dollars."

"You don't think I will transfer it."

"No. I don't. Not yet, anyway."

Federov pondered this, as if contemplating whether he wanted to ask the next question or to hear the answer. His curiosity got the better of him. "Why not?"

"Because you haven't won yet."

For once, Federov did not respond. Jenkins had found his pressure point. He'd set the hook.

"Money is not what motivates you, regardless of what bullshit you tell me and everyone else."

Federov stepped toward him. "Really?" was all he could muster, and it wasn't very convincing.

"Really," Jenkins said.

Federov sat on the couch, crossing his legs, one arm draped over the back of the pillows. He picked at imaginary lint on his suit pants. "Please. Tell me what motivates me?"

Reel. Slow and steady. Keep pressure on the line. When he runs, let him run.

"I already told you. Winning. You don't like to lose. Not even a friendly chess game. It isn't about the money. It's about winning. It's about beating me. It's about beating the FSB, Efimov. That's why you're still here, in Moscow, though you have enough money to live anywhere in the world."

"I have two daughters, grandchildren."

"Who you never see and who never make the effort to see you. You have no wife. No girlfriend. No job. You have nothing keeping you here except the fact that the FSB beat you . . . and you want a second chance."

"Moscow is my home, Mr. Jenkins."

"Is it? Your parents are gone. You're divorced. You haven't remarried. You live in a sterile apartment with almost no personal touches to make it a home. You took a prostitute with you to the M'Istral Hotel—someone you could pay to have a good time. What exactly is keeping you here, Viktor?"

Federov didn't answer.

Now boat him.

"They made you a scapegoat, after all the years you gave them. After everything you gave up. Your job cost you your marriage, your daughters, maybe your grandchildren." Jenkins paused. Federov did not respond. "Go ahead, Viktor. Tell me I'm wrong."

Federov continued to pick at imaginary lint.

"You tell me," Jenkins said. "Where are you going to get another chance to kick the FSB in the nuts the way it kicked you?" An offer that had surely influenced Federov's decision from the start.

Federov kept his eyes on Jenkins but leaned forward to pick up the deck of cards from the coffee table. He shuffled them with one hand, as Jenkins had taught him, showed Jenkins the top card, the ace of spades, then buried it. His right hand theatrically shot to the side, a distraction. He flashed the top card again. The ten of clubs.

Then he reached behind him and produced a card. He tossed it on the glass tabletop, where it landed faceup.

The ace of spades.

23

Federov stepped through the metal detector and waited for his briefcase on the conveyor belt. When it reached the other side, a guard removed it. Still young, still naïve, and still malleable, Dementi Mordvinov opened the briefcase, giving the interior a cursory glance. He removed the stack of photographs inside and slid off the paper clip, tossing it in a wastebasket at his feet.

Federov retrieved the photographs and his case, and he and Mordvinov walked down the corridor together. "Another day in this shithole, Colonel Federov?" Mordvinov said under his breath. "This is my job; I have to be here. How did you get such a plum assignment?"

They stepped into an elevator and descended several floors. "I made a crass comment about the deputy director's niece," Federov said. "A real good-looking piece of ass with a flirtatious smile and a body to make the heavens sing."

"No?" Mordvinov said, eyes wide. "You are bullshitting me."

Federov shrugged.

When the doors opened, they walked the pitted, concrete hallway illuminated beneath fluorescent lights in round metal cages. The hallway held the damp odor of mildew. Federov reached into the pocket of his coat and produced a pack of smokes, as had become his routine. The young guard glanced over his shoulder before taking the pack and sliding it into the breast pocket of his uniform. "My wife thanks you. She can't stand to smoke the Belomorkanal anymore. I've spoiled her."

"I hope she's been appreciative," Federov said.

The guard grinned like a prepubescent youth. "I've taken more turns among the cabbages this week than I have in a year."

Federov laughed.

Mordvinov nodded to the door at the end of the hall, the room where Federov had been interrogating Ponomayova. "This bitch going to say anything today?"

"One can only hope," Federov said. "I'm getting sick of staring at her face, but I am following orders of the deputy director and, I am told, he is following orders of the president."

The young guard stopped in midstride. "Putin?" He looked and sounded both impressed and concerned.

Federov shrugged as if this were no big deal. "Just means a sharper ax will swing if I am unsuccessful."

"Maybe she would prefer a different kind of persuasion. The face may not be so good, but the body is not bad, a little skinny. If she puts some meat on the bones . . . Here she comes now."

A guard Federov did not recognize led Ponomayova down a narrow side hall, an arm on her bicep. The chain connected to her wrist cuffs dangled between her legs and dragged on the floor. At the moment, however, Federov's focus was on the guard. He was older, with a hardened appearance—the way some of the other guards looked after years working in Lefortovo. Over time, the suppression of emotion and the acceptance of inhumane treatment wore on them, at least those who were not sociopaths or psychopaths. The guards compensated by becoming robotic and strictly adhering to rules and regulations to justify the treatment.

This guard walked too quickly, a deliberate act that caused Ponomayova to stumble on the links of her chain, nearly causing her to trip and fall to the ground. This was not a good development. Federov had spent much of his time acclimating the guards to his orders and to his position of authority. He needed the guards to think of him as a superior officer, someone whose orders were to be followed without question.

"I have not met this guard before," Federov said to Mordvinov.

Mordvinov turned his head, whispering. "Ravil Galkin. He's been out. Disciplinary charges. He's a jackass."

Ponomayova wore the long-sleeve, navy-blue jumpsuit. Mordvinov unlocked the door and motioned for Federov to enter the cell. Federov stepped inside the now familiar concrete room and glanced at the camera mounted in the corner. The light changed from red to green. He stepped behind the table and slid back the chair, setting his briefcase on the ground before sitting. He folded his hands on the metal surface as the older guard, Galkin, shoved Ponomayova to the footstool. She lost her balance and fell to a knee but was able to right herself.

Galkin clipped the chain to the ring in the floor, with just enough slack for Ponomayova to sit upright, then he retreated to the corner beneath the camera. Mordvinov took his position in the alternate corner, both staring straight ahead, at nothing.

Ponomayova's gaze remained fixed on the tabletop. Federov reached down and pulled his briefcase onto his lap. The locks clicked in the otherwise silent room. He opened the briefcase and pulled out a folder, setting it on the table before returning the case to the floor. He compulsively straightened the file to align with the table edges, then flipped open the file cover. He removed the black-and-white photographs of former KGB agents assigned to Mexico City, all now deceased or in their late seventies and eighties. Each man wore a dark suit, white shirt, and thin tie.

Federov set the photographs aside and commenced his inquiry, hoping to further dull the new guard's attentiveness. After forty-five minutes Federov lifted the stack, holding them as Jenkins had taught him, as he had practiced.

Jenkins said the trick was all about deception and misdirection, two words that described what had been Federov's chosen profession for more than two decades. He told himself this time would be no different than the dozens of times he had practiced in his kitchen. His nerves made it abundantly clear that was not the case. Still, he could not allow the guards to see any crack in his well-honed demeanor.

"Ms. Ponomayova," he said, keeping his voice low and deliberately precise. "I'm going to show you seven photographs. I want you to consider them carefully. Then I am going to ask you questions about each one."

Paulina did not respond. She did not raise her gaze.

Federov pushed back his chair and stood. About to place the photographs faceup on the table, he noticed Galkin advance. The guard stuck out his hand.

Federov fought to remain calm, to appear even a bit annoyed. He stared at the hand as if it were distasteful, then slowly raised his gaze to Galkin's face. "What do you want?"

Galkin motioned with his fingers for the photographs.

"My briefcase was checked upon my entering the building," Federov said. "Go back to your post and do not interfere again with my interrogation."

Galkin did not rescind his hand. "It is protocol if you intend to hand the witness the photographs."

Federov knew better than to back down, that this was his chance to establish a chain of command with Galkin. "Protocol for you. Not for me. I am a colonel in the Federal Security Service, and you are interfering with my interrogation. Now step back." The two men glared at one another. Time to let Galkin save face, or at least believe he had. "And I don't intend to hand the photographs to the prisoner, only to have her look at them."

Galkin stared for another moment, glanced down at Ponomayova shackled to the floor, and retreated to his corner as if he'd won.

Federov held the photographs in his left hand and returned to his interrogation.

"As I was saying, Ms. Ponomayova." He made a gesture with his right hand while bending his left index finger, the one with the bandage, placing it against the back of the bottom card. Blow this one move, and he would be looking at Galkin through a small slit in a metal door. Deftly, he slid the card from the pile and flipped it behind his right hand, cupping it.

"I am going to show you seven photographs." He gestured with his left hand as he slipped his right hand into his pocket and exchanged the photograph for the one of Jenkins. Using only his right hand, he flipped the top card over onto the table, as he'd practiced, directing everyone's attention to the first photograph while he cupped the picture of Jenkins behind his hand. "Do you recognize this man?"

Ponomayova shook her head.

Federov brought his hands together and flipped the photograph of Jenkins to the bottom of the deck. Federov had practiced with seven photographs in his apartment and decided to keep that same familiar number. Slowly, methodically, he placed the second photograph on the table followed by the third, fourth, fifth, and sixth, each time pausing to ask, "Do you know this man? Have you ever seen his face before?"

Each time, Ponomayova shook her head.

He set the Jenkins photograph faceup in the corner of the table blocked by Ponomayova's shoulder.

"And this man, do you know this man?"

Charles Jenkins stared up from the table. He held his daughter in his arms. The word "Paulina" was scrawled in black ink across the baby's blanket.

"Look carefully," Federov said. "Is there anything about him that you recognize?"

Ponomayova did not move, but a tear slid from the corner of her eye along the edge of her nose and dropped onto the ground.

Federov noticed Galkin stepping forward, tilting his head as if to determine if Ponomayova was indeed crying. He quickly gathered the photographs. The picture of Charles Jenkins was now on top of the deck. "We are going to try this again, Ms. Ponomayova." Federov bent his left ring finger and flicked the photograph of Jenkins from the top, deftly cupping it on the back side of his hand. "But before we do, I want to ask if you have ever heard the name Sergei Vasilyev." While speaking, Federov moved his hand to slip the picture of Charles Jenkins into his back pocket, but his nerves, and Galkin's unexpected attentiveness, caused him to miss his mark. The photograph fluttered to the floor behind a table leg.

Charles Jenkins stared up at him from the ground.

Galkin stepped toward the table, as if to retrieve the photograph.

"Yes," Ponomayova said in a bold voice. "I have heard that name before."

Galkin stopped his advance, turned, and considered Ponomayova. From the look on his face they were perhaps the first words he'd heard Ponomayova speak at Lefortovo. Federov pulled the seventh photograph from his back pocket and placed it on top of the pile while he bent and retrieved the picture of Jenkins.

"Tell me where you have heard that name," he said, straightening.

"Let me see the photographs again," Ponomayova said.

Federov cupped the photograph of Jenkins behind his left hand. This time when he leaned to put the first picture on the table, he slipped the Jenkins photograph into his back pocket. Galkin took another step forward, intently watching the table as Federov set down all seven photographs.

"The third one," Ponomayova said. "He looks familiar."

24

Jenkins listened as Federov told him everything that had happened. Federov was spent from the stress of the interrogation, the almost failed card trick, and his debriefing by Efimov, but he was also amped on an adrenaline high, like a marathoner at the finish line. It confirmed for Jenkins what he already knew. Viktor Federov liked nothing more than to win, and he had won, for now.

"Something I've been meaning to tell you," he said. "Ponomayova walks with a noticeable limp. I don't know what you intend, but it will make her easily identifiable."

"I'll make a note of it," Jenkins said. He had not told Federov of the multiple conversations he and Lemore had had about ways to get Ponomayova out of Lefortovo. The basic idea had come to Jenkins one night while sleeping. He'd awoken and called Lemore immediately to discuss its potential, and what might be needed.

"What did Efimov say when you briefed him?" he asked Federov.

"Little. He said only that I should continue the interrogation, but that if I did not quickly obtain more information, he would end it."

Jenkins smiled.

"Do not look so happy, Mr. Jenkins. Efimov did not say I could question Ponomayova outside of Lefortovo. In fact, her willingness to talk to me inside the prison makes that a moot point. You still have the same problem. How to get her out? And that will be much more difficult than gaining her trust. Efimov is not a patient man, especially when he has been made to look bad."

Jenkins pulled out an envelope and removed a square patch that looked like a Band-Aid.

"What is that?" Federov asked.

"Applied to Ponomayova's skin, it will induce symptoms of a heart attack."

"I don't . . . ," Federov started, then stopped and looked from the packet to Jenkins.

"You don't have to get Efimov's permission to get her out of Lefortovo," Jenkins said. "Now that she's talking, she's valuable. Everyone will want to keep her alive, at all costs."

"This is true," Federov said, though he did not sound convinced. "But Lefortovo prisoners are taken to the military hospital in Moscow, and she will be under security as tight as Lefortovo. Maybe more so."

"She would be if she were taken to a military hospital," Jenkins said. "But we're not going to give them that chance."

Two days later, Federov returned to Lefortovo and went through the same routine. Mordvinov and Galkin were again assigned to his interrogation, and Galkin seemed, at least, more respectful of Federov's position. Federov continued to question Ponomayova about the KGB agents in Mexico City and was impressed by her ability to make things up on the fly.

This did little, however, to calm his nerves. Once he applied the drug patch to Ponomayova's skin there would be no going back. He'd either get out of Lefortovo and flee Russia, with $10 million, or he'd be in a cell in this very prison for the rest of his life, however long that might be.

He laid the photographs on the table, then glanced up at the light, as if it distracted him.

"Are you certain you can see well enough? The light is poor."

Federov moved as if to allow better illumination on the table and again looked up at the light. "This glare is a problem. Perhaps we can move the table." He pivoted his body to block Mordvinov's view and slid his right hand beneath the fabric of Ponomayova's prison jumpsuit, where he applied the drug patch to her skin. She did not react to his touch.

"Nothing is to be moved," Galkin said, taking a step forward, but retreating when Federov glared at him.

The pecking order had been established.

Federov resumed his questioning of Ponomayova for another twenty minutes, watching her carefully. In the middle of an answer, her body slumped forward then jerked back, as if she were falling asleep. Her breathing became labored.

"Are you all right?" Federov asked to draw the guards' attention to the prisoner. "Ms. Ponomayova?"

Her head again fell back, then to the side, and her eyes rolled up just before she fell forward. Her forehead struck the edge of the table with a dull thud and she pitched to the side, onto the floor.

Federov rushed to her and put a hand on her carotid artery. "Her pulse is weak." He lifted her head and used his thumbs to raise her eyelids. "Her pupils are dilated and she is not breathing." He turned to Mordvinov. "Call for the doctor, now."

The young guard moved quickly and without question to the door.

Still kneeling beside Ponomayova, Federov turned to Galkin. "Unlock her chains."

"It is against regulation," Galkin said, though he no longer looked sure of himself.

"We need to start chest compressions. She is dying," Federov said, for now remaining firm but calm. "Unlock the chains."

Galkin shook his head. "It is against—"

Federov stood and stepped into Galkin's personal space, getting an inch from the guard's face and using every bit of hubris he had learned during twenty years at the FSB. He exaggerated his authority to further intimidate the guard. "I am here at the direction of the deputy director for counterintelligence. His orders come from President Vladimir Putin. I am making progress interrogating this woman. If she dies before I can question her further about this photograph and this man, you will have interfered with a decades-old investigation of personal interest to the president. And if that happens, I swear I will see you fired."

Galkin stuttered. "The rules state . . ."

Federov shouted over him. "I don't give a good Goddamn what the rules state. If my orders are good enough for me, they are good enough for you. You can talk about your Goddamn rules in the unemployment line. Unlock her chains!"

Galkin looked to the door. Voices and footsteps echoed down the hallway.

"Unlock them!" Federov shouted.

Galkin dropped to a knee and unlocked the chain from the ring in the floor.

"Take off her cuffs. Now. Do it."

Again, Galkin hesitated, but only for an instant before he complied.

Federov laid Ponomayova on her back. As he did, he reached beneath the fabric of her uniform and pulled off the patch. Her breathing was almost undetectable. Her chest did not appear to rise or fall. This was a complication Jenkins had said he could not completely predict. He said the drug patch, sufentanil, acted as an anesthetic and caused respiratory depression, a slow heart rate, and low blood pressure. The proper dosage depended on the weight of the patient, her physical health, and any other drugs already in her system. Neither Federov nor

Jenkins could make those predictions with any degree of certainty. They knew only that Ponomayova was in a severely weakened physical state, first from her injuries and then from her imprisonment.

Federov bent and put his ear close to Ponomayova's mouth, listening to her shallow breath. He thought of the irony—if he and Jenkins had come this far and risked this much to get Ponomayova out of Lefortovo, only to kill her in the process.

Mordvinov slammed into the doorjamb upon his return. A man introduced himself as the prison doctor as he entered and dropped to a knee. "What happened?"

"I was questioning her when she fell unconscious. She isn't breathing."

"She's barely breathing," the doctor corrected. He grabbed her wrist. "And her pulse is weak."

"This prisoner is my responsibility; it is imperative that she survive." Federov spoke in his most authoritative voice. "We must get her to a hospital, immediately."

"That is not your decision—"

"It *is* my decision," Federov said, allowing anger to inch into his tone. "I would not be here if it were not of the highest import, and if my orders did not come from the highest authorities. Get her on a gurney and move her—quickly."

Two men wheeled a gurney to just outside the door. Federov and the doctor lifted Ponomayova from the floor and placed her on it.

"Go," Federov said.

The wheels hummed down the hallway to the elevator. Federov stepped in beside the gurney and the car ascended. When the doors parted, they hurried along additional hallways, turning left and right before pushing the gurney into the prison infirmary.

Federov checked his phone. He had reception. He hit "Send," the encrypted number preprogrammed, then entered a room with limited medical equipment. The doctor pressed a stethoscope to Ponomayova's chest.

Mordvinov entered the room. "An ambulance is at the front gate."

"Move her. Quickly," Federov said to the men who had brought the gurney.

"I am not finished—" the doctor started.

"We do not have time to wait until you are finished." Federov again motioned for the men to move Ponomayova. The doctor stepped back. They pushed the gurney along additional hallways and through a door leading to an exterior courtyard with a ten-foot stone fence and razor wire.

The cold air chilled him, and Federov realized the extent to which he was perspiring.

A metal gate rumbled open and an ambulance drove into the courtyard. When it stopped, a man in a dark-blue uniform with a cap pulled low on his brow stepped down from the driver's seat, holding a clipboard. He handed the forms to Mordvinov and hurried to the gurney.

Federov looked to the windshield. Charles Jenkins slid from the passenger seat to the back of the ambulance, out of view. They had agreed they could not risk having Jenkins photographed in the courtyard. His skin color and size would make him too memorable, maybe even recognizable.

This was it. They would either get out or both be caught. His anxiety spiked.

The prison doctor spoke to the driver as he accompanied the gurney to the back of the ambulance, Federov following. The driver pulled open the doors. Inside, Jenkins busied himself with equipment. The legs of the gurney collapsed as the men slid it into the ambulance. The doctor and Federov climbed in, followed by Galkin.

Another unexpected confrontation. Federov glared at him. "Get out."

"The prisoner is to be accompanied by guards to the hospital," Galkin said.

"My prisoner," Federov said. "My responsibility. I will accompany her. Get out."

"We are losing her," Jenkins said, speaking Russian. The blue cap covered much of his face. "Her pulse is weakening."

The doctor spoke to Galkin. "Get out."

Galkin reluctantly stepped out, stumbling and nearly falling off the back of the ambulance. The driver slammed the doors shut and, a moment later, pulled himself up behind the wheel. He made a U-turn and drove out the gate with two blasts of the horn.

Federov felt a sense of relief, but he knew it would be short-lived. Getting Ponomayova out of Lefortovo was the biggest and most challenging hurdle, but far from the last.

Inside the ambulance, the doctor issued instructions to Jenkins while checking Ponomayova's vital signs. Jenkins pulled open one of the drawers and removed a syringe.

"What is that?" the doctor asked, looking and sounding perplexed.

Jenkins pulled the stopper from the tip of the needle and squirted out a small amount of the fluid.

"What are you giving her?" the doctor asked again.

Federov grabbed the doctor's arms from behind, pinning them to his sides, and Jenkins plunged the needle into the man's neck, depressing the plunger of midazolam, a central nervous system depressant. The doctor slumped forward and Federov pushed him to the side. He would be out long enough for them to hopefully get away, but otherwise unharmed.

Jenkins lowered his ear to Ponomayova's mouth. "She's barely breathing." From his pocket he removed a nasal spray and squirted naloxone into each of Ponomayova's nostrils to revive her.

She did not react.

"Come on. Come on." Jenkins grabbed the back of her neck and lifted her head, speaking to her. "Paulina? Paulina?" He checked her pulse.

"What can be done?" Federov asked.

"I don't know."

"Can you give her more?"

"I don't know," Jenkins said.

25

Mordvinov watched Galkin stumble awkwardly from the back of the ambulance but manage to keep his balance. The driver slammed the doors shut with a dull thud. Moments later, the ambulance departed the prison with two blasts of its horn, causing crows in the surrounding trees to take flight, black arrowheads against the gray Moscow sky.

Mordvinov turned his head to suppress a smile. It was good to see someone put the arrogant prick in his place.

"Let the shift commander know what has transpired so he can order Moscow police to meet the ambulance at the hospital and remain with the prisoner—if she lives," Galkin said. "If he asks why we did not accompany the prisoner, tell him we followed orders of the FSB. I don't plan to get fired because of that asshole. I'll get started on the paperwork."

Mordvinov had no problem telling their shift commander what had happened. In fact, he relished the chance to impress upon Artem Lavrov that he could think independently and adapt to an emergency without hesitation. He had no desire to suffer the same career fate as Galkin.

Mordvinov made his way to Lavrov's office inside the prison administration building. Glass windows, two inches thick and reinforced with mesh, provided a view into the hall and allowed natural light in. Mordvinov greeted Lavrov's assistant and advised that he had an urgent matter to discuss with the shift commander. After a brief call, the secretary motioned for Mordvinov to enter an inner door.

Lavrov sat behind a desk cluttered with paper. On the wall hung a large green chalkboard with a permanent grid—the board once used to record the names of each guard on duty and the hours of their shifts. Computers had rendered it obsolete. Winter light filtered through windows that provided a view across the street to a three-story brick apartment building above a retail pharmacy with a hideous orange façade. Whether it was the poor light or poor health, Lavrov looked sickly pale. His stomach hung over the waistline of his pants, and he squinted behind glasses as if having difficulty seeing Mordvinov.

"I thought you were on duty for the interrogation of Ponomayova," Lavrov said. "Has it ended already?" He glanced up at a large clock hanging on the wall above the chalkboard.

"Ponomayova suffered a heart attack during the interrogation. Upon the FSB officer's orders, she is being taken by ambulance to the veterans hospital. Galkin is starting the paperwork, but I wanted you to know, in case—"

Lavrov stood, speaking over the end of Mordvinov's sentence. "Why was I not immediately notified? Ponomayova is a high-security prisoner."

"It happened quickly," Mordvinov said. "There was little time—"

Lavrov stepped out from behind his desk. "Alert the Moscow police. Advise them of the situation."

"Galkin is doing so."

"Tell them to post officers at the emergency room entrance and, if the prisoner survives, outside her hospital room. Send orders that only hospital staff and authorized personnel are to be admitted to her room. No exceptions. Credentials are to be checked."

Mordvinov started from the room as Lavrov's desk phone rang. The shift commander picked up the receiver. *"Da."* Lavrov called out to Mordvinov, who had opened the office door, about to step out. Lavrov covered the speaker with his hand. "You said Ponomayova was taken by ambulance?"

"Yes. Just minutes ago."

"Then why is the guard at the front gate calling to ask about an ambulance seeking to enter?"

—

Within minutes of receiving the phone call from Lefortovo, Efimov sat in the back seat as Volkov weaved through Moscow traffic to the prison. He issued orders to Alekseyov to notify Moscow police of the ambulance and to tell the analysts at Lubyanka's task-force center to find it.

Efimov now knew the purpose for Jenkins's return to Moscow, and for Federov's suggestion that he interrogate Ponomayova. Federov had issued Efimov a challenge, and Efimov had fallen for the trick. A victory perhaps, but it would be short-lived. Efimov would find them, and Federov would personally experience Efimov's interrogation techniques.

"Guards at Lefortovo describe the ambulance as white with red stripes and a blue light bar on the roof. It has the number 103 on the side panels," Alekseyov said, describing the vehicle to the analysts at Lubyanka.

"They will abandon the ambulance as soon as possible, if not already." Efimov spoke from the back seat, his mind racing. "Tell Moscow police to search side streets, parking garages, and alleys—any place where the ambulance could be abandoned. Tell the analysts to focus on traffic footage of every street leaving Lefortovo within the last twenty minutes. Tell them to find that ambulance and to alert Moscow police."

Efimov had also ordered roadblocks on every major road out of Moscow and instructed that the border patrol be provided the most recent photographs of Jenkins, Ponomayova, and Federov—who would be treated as guilty until proven innocent—as well as the paramedic from the ambulance.

Volkov drove through the prison gate into the courtyard. Efimov exited the back seat before the car had come to a complete stop. He wore no winter coat, hat, or gloves despite the falling snow. A guard inside the building escorted him past security to the shift commander's office. Efimov had instructed Alekseyov to speak to Artem Lavrov and to order Lavrov to secure footage taken of Federov's interrogation of Ponomayova the prior day and that morning, as well as footage of the ambulance in the prison yard.

Lavrov greeted them, but Efimov did not have the time or the desire. He stepped past the man's outstretched hand to the computer monitor on the desk. "Clear this office of everyone but the two prison guards in the interrogation room with Federov and Ponomayova . . . and the doctor who treated her."

"The doctor accompanied Ponomayova in the ambulance," Lavrov said.

"Have one of your men provide his name and a photograph." He turned and spoke to Alekseyov. "Treat the doctor also as complicit until proven otherwise."

Lavrov said, "I assure—"

"You assure nothing. Your prisoner has escaped, and you and your guards will be held accountable. Now clear this office!"

Lavrov issued orders clearing the office, leaving a young guard who introduced himself as Dementi Mordvinov. An older, heavyset officer with pockmarked skin similarly introduced himself as Ravil Galkin. "Why did you not accompany the prisoner in the ambulance?" Efimov asked.

"The FSB officer ordered us not to," Galkin said. "He said the prisoner was his responsibility, that he was acting upon the orders of the deputy director for counterintelligence and the president, and that I was interfering with his investigation."

Efimov looked to Alekseyov and Volkov. He had his answer. Federov was complicit.

"Play the footage of Federov's interrogation of Ponomayova yesterday afternoon," Efimov said to Lavrov. Lavrov leaned across Efimov and struck several keys on the keyboard. While the footage played, Efimov spoke to the younger of the two guards. "Tell me what happened."

"Colonel Federov was interrogating the prisoner when she slumped forward, suddenly unconscious," Mordvinov said.

"Was she unconscious?"

"She did not appear to be breathing."

"Did you check her pulse, her vital signs, anything?"

"No. Colonel Federov did so and said it was a heart attack. He ordered me to summon the doctor immediately. I left the interrogation room to do so."

Efimov looked to the second guard. "Did you check the prisoner's vital signs?"

"She was alive, but her pulse was weak and her breathing minimal," Galkin said.

"You confirmed this yourself?"

Galkin paused. A lie. "I—"

Efimov turned his attention back to Mordvinov. "Had Ponomayova complained of any chest pain before she collapsed?"

"No."

He looked to Galkin. "Did Federov instruct you to call an ambulance?"

"No," Galkin said.

"You do not know how it arrived?"

"It arrived through the front gate," Galkin said.

Idiot. He returned his attention to Mordvinov. "Did you summon the ambulance?"

"No."

Efimov looked to Galkin. "You remained in the room. What did Federov tell you to do?"

"He ordered me to unlock the prisoner from the floor bolt and to remove her shackles."

"And you did this?"

"I protested. I told Colonel—"

"I do not care what you told him," Efimov said, rising from behind the desk. "Did you do it?"

"Yes."

Efimov swore. Ponomayova was no longer restrained, making it far easier for her to flee.

"Stop the tape." Efimov directed his attention to the screen. "Go back ten seconds."

Lavrov did so.

"Stop." Efimov hit "Play." On the tape, Federov stood from his seat behind the table, movement that had caught Efimov's initial attention. Federov looked to have photographs in his hand. "What is he doing?"

"He is about to show the prisoner photographs," Mordvinov said, pausing the tape.

"Photographs of what?"

"Men who worked for the KGB in Mexico City," Mordvinov said. "Ponomayova identified one of them."

Efimov hit "Play," listening as Federov continued his interrogation, surprised that Ponomayova was speaking without seeming reluctant. A further trick. He hit "Stop" and reversed the tape when a card fell from Federov's hands and fluttered to the ground.

Ponomayova spoke in a bold voice. *"Yes. I have heard that name before."*

Efimov rewound the tape and again hit "Play," peering closely at the computer screen. The photographs had been a diversion, he was sure of it, but from what? So, too, had been Ponomayova's affirmation that she recognized one of the men in the photographs. She had spoken to redirect the guard's attention away from the fallen photograph and to give Federov time to retrieve it. Efimov hit "Play." This time the tape proceeded slowly, frame by frame. Federov gestured with his right hand. Efimov hit "Stop." "Look at his finger," he said.

"I don't see . . . ," Alekseyov said. Then, "It has a bandage."

"Watch closely."

The men in the room leaned forward, watching the tape progress frame by frame. Efimov hit "Stop." "Did you see?"

"It looks as though he slid the top photograph from the others," Alekseyov said.

Efimov hit "Play" and they watched a card flutter to the floor, but Galkin stepped forward, blocking the camera's lens. *"The third one,"* Ponomayova said. *"He looks familiar."*

Efimov glared at Galkin, who retreated a few steps. Efimov turned his attention back to the screen. What had Federov been up to? In Efimov's office Federov had suggested that Sergei Vasilyev might have been a former KGB officer who had served in Mexico City. Efimov watched the tape for another minute, then said, "Show me the tape of this morning's interrogation."

Again, Lavrov complied. The tape ran for several minutes. Efimov hit "Fast Forward" and watched Ponomayova's head slump forward, roll back, and fall to her shoulder. She pitched forward, striking her forehead on the table. He slowed the tape.

"Are you all right?" Federov asked. *"Ms. Ponomayova?"*

Efimov watched the aftermath, Federov issuing orders, Galkin's tepid challenge. Then he said, "Show me the film of the ambulance arriving in the prison grounds." He slid back the desk chair to give Lavrov space. Lavrov opened a second window, pulled up the video taken of the prison courtyard, and hit "Play." The ambulance drove in and a paramedic stepped out. He was roughly the same height as the doctor and the two prison guards. Charles Jenkins was six feet five inches. "You said there were two paramedics?" Efimov asked Mordvinov.

"Yes. One never left the back of the ambulance."

"Describe him."

"He wore the same uniform and hat."

"Was he black?"

"I don't know."

Still smoldering over the guard unlocking Ponomayova from her chains and blocking the view of the camera, Efimov looked to Galkin. He struggled against an urge to strike him. "Did you see him?"

"Not well."

"Was he black?"

"He might have been."

"Was he black?"

"I don't . . ."

"You don't know?"

"Not for certain."

Efimov moved toward the door while speaking to Alekseyov. "Have the tapes delivered to Lubyanka. Tell the analysts to break them down frame by frame." At the door he turned back to Lavrov and pointed to Galkin. "Fire this man. Immediately. Or I will have you replaced."

26

The ambulance driver, a CIA asset in Moscow secured by Lemore, drove into an underground parking garage beneath a private building near Komsomolskaya Square. The parking kiosk was unmanned, as expected—every move to this point choreographed. The driver pressed a fob to a plate to raise the gate, then drove down the ramp to one of the lower floors, tires squealing on the slick concrete. He parked in a designated space for the disabled between two cement pillars at the back of the garage floor. The overhead light had been broken, and though the garage was equipped with security cameras, the camera on that floor had also been disconnected.

As Jenkins continued to work to revive Paulina, he could hear the man stripping the bar of lights from the roof, then peeling off the red striping, the red cross, and the blue universal medical signs on the back panels. When he had finished, the vehicle would be a plain white van. The driver opened the passenger door and tossed everything on the floor, then went to work removing and replacing the license plates. When he'd finished, he opened the back doors of the van.

"Why haven't you changed?" he asked Federov and Jenkins in English but with a strong Russian accent. "We need to move."

"She's not coming to." Jenkins looked to Paulina, who remained unconscious on the stretcher. The doctor lay unconscious on the floor, hands zip-tied behind his back, a rag shoved in his mouth.

The driver checked his wristwatch. He removed his blue jumpsuit as he spoke. "Your train will leave Leningradsky station precisely at 1:15. Moscow trains are punctual. We have timed this to the very minute. We have a head start on the FSB, but they will make up time quickly. You need to move."

Underneath the jumpsuit the driver wore nondescript clothing—boots and jeans. He pulled on a black leather jacket and a knit skullcap and shoved black leather gloves into his coat pocket. Then he peeled off the beard and threw it and the glasses into the back of the van.

"Go," Jenkins said. "Your job here is done."

The man again checked his watch. He handed Jenkins train tickets. "Remember. The train will leave on time. Not a minute after 1:15. Misinformation is being spread. Everything is timed to give you the best chance to get through the station and to the train. You must be on it."

"I understand," Jenkins said.

The man lit a cigarette, then shut the van doors.

Jenkins looked to Federov. "You go also."

Federov had peeled off his suit and threw the clothes on top of the doctor. He wore jeans, boots, and a blue down jacket over a second coat. He would abandon the down jacket at some point. He went to work putting on a mustache, which he checked in a mirror, then fit glasses onto the bridge of his nose and pulled a black Adidas baseball cap low on his brow. Disguise complete, he opened the back door and stepped from the van. "I wish you luck, Mr. Jenkins."

"I'll wire the rest of your money into the account when I'm stateside."

Federov smiled. "I would argue with you, but a deal is a deal, no? I have four million reasons to hope you are successful. *Udachi.*" *Good luck.* He slammed the doors shut.

Jenkins checked his watch, then put a finger to Paulina's carotid artery. Her pulse had grown stronger, a good sign, he hoped. He leaned close. Her breathing remained steady. He didn't know whether to give her more naloxone; whether it could harm or even kill her.

Outside the van, he heard the sound of tires squealing and wondered if it was FSB coming for them. Yes, he had a head start, but as the driver had said, it would not be for long. Federov said the FSB had access to traffic cameras installed all over Moscow, the most sophisticated system in the world, not that it would be needed to find an ambulance, even on busy Moscow surface streets. He and Lemore had taken that into account to buy them as much time as possible.

He reached for the nasal spray. He'd have to take the chance. He inserted the nozzle into Ponomayova's nostril, but she pulled her head back sharply. Her eyes fluttered open. Her arms flailed. Jenkins subdued her before she hurt herself.

"Paulina. Paulina," he said softly. "It's okay. It's okay. You're all right." She looked frightened, confused, and uncertain. The pupils of her eyes remained dilated. "It's me. It's Charlie. Charles Jenkins."

She looked at him as if she didn't know him. Tears leaked from the corners of her eyes. She shook her head sadly. "No," she whispered. "No."

"We have to move. Can you walk?"

"You should not have come back," she whispered. "You should not have come back, Charlie."

His heart fluttered and Jenkins thought of what Alex had worried about. Had the Russians leaked news of Paulina surviving to lure him back? He didn't have time to consider it. "Can you walk?"

"Yes, I believe so."

"There are clothes here for you, a wig. Can you see without your glasses?"

"Yes. Well enough."

"Do your best. Hurry. We have a train to catch."

They quickly changed into winter clothing. Paulina pulled on a light-brown, shoulder-length wig. The fur-lined hood of her fashionable jacket would also help to obscure her face. Jenkins knew his disguise was like trying to camouflage a grizzly bear. Given his physical size and his skin color, he would remain an easy target. To try to offset his build he pulled on a bulky, military-green jacket. To reduce his height, he would stoop over a cane. A gray hairpiece beneath a hat would complete his transformation to an old man.

He handed Paulina a passport with train tickets and a small pocketbook. Inside was her Russian identification and an assortment of expected items including rubles, a cell phone, lipstick, hairbrush, and breath mints.

"We'll walk separately to the train station and travel separately on the train, but I'll be close by should anything happen."

"Should anything happen, do not expose yourself," she said.

"Everything is timed. The train schedules have been studied to maximize our chances. Things are in play to help us, but we have to move to make it work." Jenkins explained the scenario in further detail as they stepped from the ambulance. He pointed to a door. "The staircase leads up to Komsomolskaya Square."

"This is my home, Charlie. Once I am above ground, I will know my way. But you must be careful. Moscow has facial-recognition cameras that the FSB will use. Keep your head down."

"I'm aware of that, and we have a plan in place."

Jenkins handed her a duffel bag that she fit over her shoulder. She stumbled, off-kilter, and had to grip the edge of the ambulance to maintain her balance. She took several deep breaths.

"Can you make it?" Jenkins asked. He had considered the possibility that Paulina's weakened physical condition could impact her abilities, but in the end he didn't have much choice or any other options. He was counting on the tough woman he had met in Moscow, and who had resisted Efimov's interrogation, to rise to the occasion.

She took a deep breath, steeling herself. "You named your daughter after me."

"Yes," Jenkins said.

She smiled, and Jenkins saw a glimpse of the woman who'd nearly killed him in a Moscow hotel room. "Then I am eager to meet her. Let's go."

27

Efimov stepped from the elevator onto the third floor of the main Lubyanka building toward the conference room when an administrative assistant intercepted his approach. "The deputy director wishes to speak to you."

Efimov swore under his breath. He didn't have time for what would surely be an administrative beatdown. He needed to get eyes on the ambulance if they were to have any chance of determining where Jenkins and Ponomayova were headed, and how far they were behind.

"Go," he said to Alekseyov and Volkov. "Get me the tape of the ambulance leaving Lefortovo. Find it."

Efimov followed the assistant down the hall and into an anterior office, brushed past her, and pushed open the door, stepping in.

Dmitry Sokalov stood behind his desk, looking angry and uncertain. Without his suit jacket, he also looked six months pregnant, his shirt buttons about to give way from the bulge of his belly. Sokalov had always enjoyed his food and his alcohol, and his position now accorded him ample opportunity to dine at the government's trough.

This office, or the equivalent, should have belonged to Efimov, but Sokalov had political decorum Efimov lacked. He could bullshit, tell others what they wanted to hear, rather than what they needed to hear. More important, he had the ear of both the director and the president, and that meant he had power over Efimov. Power he would no doubt seek to impose.

"Is it true?" Sokalov said. "Has Jenkins gotten Ponomayova out of Lefortovo?"

Word traveled quickly at Lubyanka. Efimov spoke calmly, as if everything remained under control. "That is what I am attempting to determine."

"Do not withhold information, Adam. I am to report to the president in ten minutes. Tell me what happened."

"It appears that Mr. Jenkins is working with Viktor Federov."

"Federov?"

"That is the initial assessment."

"Why?"

"I suspect it relates to the ten million dollars Mr. Jenkins stole from two accounts at the UBS in Moscow."

"But has he successfully removed Ponomayova from Lefortovo?"

"I have confirmed that personally."

Sokalov swore three times, a habit. Then he said, "Tell me what you know."

"With all due respect—"

"Tell me what you know!"

Efimov bit his tongue and let Sokalov have his temper tantrum. "Ponomayova faked a heart attack, a drug most likely. Given her recent willingness to provide information, the prison did not hesitate to rush her to the hospital to keep her alive. It was the right decision, though poorly executed. Federov used the authority of the FSB to travel with her by ambulance. Unfortunately, the ambulance that arrived was not legitimate."

"And Jenkins?"

"He, too, I suspect, was in the ambulance."

"Where is it now?"

Efimov stifled a retort and chose his words carefully. "That is what I was attempting to determine when your assistant summoned me."

"Shit. Shit. Shit." Sokalov put his knuckles on the desk, bracing himself. "And Ponomayova is talking?"

So the deputy director had at least done his homework, or had someone do it for him, and now had his chance to dress down Efimov.

"Nothing of significance. I believe it to have all been part of the plan to get her out of Lefortovo."

"We shall see, Adam, if that is in fact true."

"I can assure you—"

"Of nothing," Sokalov interjected. "She did not speak to you, and so you can assure me of nothing, especially not now." He stepped from behind his desk, checked his watch, and pulled his jacket from the coat-tree, slipping it on while repetitively swearing. "Find that ambulance, Adam, immediately."

"Do not worry, Dmitry—"

"I will not worry," Sokalov said, raising a hand and his voice to speak over Efimov. He pointed a finger, further reducing Efimov's status to a schoolboy being disciplined. Efimov resisted the burning urge to reach out and snap the digit. "Because it will not be my head that rolls if you do not find Ponomayova and Jenkins. It will be yours. I cannot protect you any more than I already have, and the president will not risk the political fallout by stepping in. Not for you. Not for this. This is your last chance. You have burned too many bridges. Fail, and it will fall on your shoulders, whatever punishment the president decides, and we both know his temper can be as bad if not worse than your own."

—

Efimov spoke as he entered the task-force room. Half a dozen analysts sat at computer screens poring through video of Moscow streets and tapping their keyboards. Telephones rang, and sotto voce voices spoke on phones.

"Get the Traffic Management Centre on the line," Efimov said to no one in particular. "And someone provide me an update on the ambulance."

A young woman entered and handed Efimov a mug of tea. He sipped it and set it down.

"The ambulance left Lefortovo and proceeded north on the Third Ring Road," Alekseyov said.

"Bring up the surveillance cameras," Efimov instructed.

He leaned forward, watching the ambulance speed away from Lefortovo and eventually disappear in the Lefortovo Tunnel under the Yauza River. The analyst tapped at his keys and quickly changed camera views to one within the tunnel.

"Two ambulances," Alekseyov said.

Efimov watched a second ambulance enter the tunnel and drive side by side with the first.

"They're identical," Alekseyov said. "Intended to create confusion. I had them both monitored."

When the ambulances exited the tunnel, the analyst switched to cameras on the surface streets. As the lead ambulance neared an intersection, it turned right. The other turned left.

"Third ambulance heading northwest," the first analyst said.

A third ambulance entered the picture frame, heading perpendicular to the first two. A shell game to not just fool anyone following, but also the cameras. Federov would have known of the camera coverage in Moscow, and he had clearly advised Jenkins. This was a well-coordinated plan.

Efimov stepped down the row of computer screens, watching all three ambulances.

"Fourth ambulance," an analyst said.

The first ambulance turned left onto Ol'khovskaya Ulitsa. It again disappeared from the camera's view.

"Find him," Efimov said.

The second analyst, seated beside the first, barked out quickly, "There. Novoryazanskaya Ulitsa, heading west."

"I have another ambulance," an analyst said.

Efimov stepped down the row and watched the second ambulance turn again. The ambulances were being sent all over the city. The first analyst said, "Right turn onto Ryazansky Proyezd." A short street. The ambulance again drove from the camera's view.

"No monitors," the analyst said.

Efimov took a step back, thinking. The ambulances could go anywhere, but Jenkins and Ponomayova could not. Federov would know roadblocks would be set up on the main highways out of Moscow, and airports would be alerted. He and Jenkins would be pragmatic. They would ditch the ambulance as soon as possible. But then what? The analysts called out the various ambulances' locations.

"He's headed to Komsomolskaya," Efimov said. "Get me coverage."

The first analyst typed. In seconds an ambulance reappeared on the screen, heading northeast. Heavily trafficked, the road was congested with cars and delivery trucks. A Moscow trolley car ran down the center of the street and, as it was lunch hour, the sidewalks were also heavily populated, pedestrians wrapped in bulky winter clothing to stave off the cold. Jenkins and Federov would see this as an asset.

"The railway stations are there," Alekseyov said.

"Yes," Efimov said, having already come to that deduction. It was a wise choice by Jenkins or Federov. The Leningradsky railway station, the Kazansky station, and the Yaroslavsky station, three of Moscow's nine main railway stations, were all situated around Komsomolskaya Square, with hundreds of trains departing in every direction to every city in Russia. The subway and light-rail stations were also nearby, providing further options and maximizing the chances of disinformation and confusion. Another shell game. Beyond that, President Putin had made improving Moscow's trains his personal project, modeling them after the Japanese and German railways and their strict adherence to schedules. Efimov had no way to shut down the trains, or to delay them, if Jenkins and Ponomayova were to get on one.

"Follow your ambulances," Efimov said. He leaned over the first analyst's shoulder but spoke to Alekseyov. "Notify Moscow police. I want uniformed and plain-clothed officers at each train station. Tell them we will transmit updated images of the people we are looking for as soon as we have them."

Alekseyov pulled out his cell phone and stepped away to make the call.

On the monitor Efimov watched what he hoped to be the ambulance that had departed Lefortovo turn into a building driveway and disappear down the ramp. "I want access to all cameras within coverage of that building," Efimov said. "Find out if they have cameras in the garage and in the building lobby, all entrances and all exits. Alekseyov!" he yelled. Alekseyov turned to him. "Alert Moscow police that the ambulance is in the garage . . . I need an address. Someone provide me with an address!" A voice barked out the building address and Efimov repeated it to Alekseyov. Then he said, "Tell them to find the ambulance. Make sure it does not leave the garage."

"What of the other ambulances?" an analyst called out.

"Stay on them," Efimov said.

"I have coverage on the side of the building," an analyst called out.

Efimov moved quickly down the row of screens and looked over the man's shoulder. The camera focused on a metal door on the side of the building. "Pull up any footage from closed-circuit cameras in that area with facial-recognition capability."

"The snow will make obtaining a clear picture difficult," an analyst said.

"We don't need to be perfect. Pull up the photograph of the ambulance driver at Lefortovo, as well as known photographs of Jenkins, Federov, and Ponomayova," Efimov said. "We only need a match to those."

The analyst pulled up each of the pictures and kept them at the bottom of his screen. The photograph of the ambulance driver was far from perfect. The man had kept his head down, the bill of his cap and a beard obscuring much of his face. Several people exited the metal door on the side of the building, but Efimov told the analyst to ignore them. He watched the clock in the lower corner of the screen and used the time the ambulance had entered the garage to gauge when the occupants had most likely left the building. Efimov was behind, but he could make up time quickly if he chose wisely and acted with diligence.

A man emerged from the metal door dressed in a dark coat and skullcap. He kept his head down but looked up and to his right to check traffic before crossing the street. The analyst snapped a picture of his face, partially obscured by the swirling snow.

As he did, another analyst called out, "I have a second man . . . He's wearing the exact same clothes."

Efimov shot him a look. "Where?"

"He came out the front of the building."

Efimov swore. They would no doubt also play another shell game with each person in the ambulance. The key was to determine where they would go, not to run around chasing them. "Get a picture of his face. Stay on the first man."

"I have a picture," the first analyst said.

Efimov slid to his console, considering the imperfect photograph on the computer screen. "Compare it to the picture of the ambulance driver," Efimov said. The analyst did so, and within seconds the computer indicated a match.

"That's him," the analyst said.

"Follow him. Stay on him. Forget the other. Do not lose him. I want to know everywhere he goes. If he gets on a train or a bus, alert Moscow police immediately. Transmit his current photograph."

"Another man exiting the building," the analyst called out.

Efimov moved to the screen and watched a man in jeans, boots, and a blue down jacket exit the door to the street. He wore a black baseball cap low on his brow. He, too, kept his head down. Efimov thought he saw portions of a mustache and glasses. The man was not tall enough or broad enough to be Jenkins, but it could be Federov.

"Get an image of his face," Efimov said. "I want it compared to what we have on file for Viktor Federov." Federov may have played Efimov for a fool, but the game was not yet over.

Far from it.

"I can't get a picture of his face," the second analyst said. "Nothing I can use."

As the man passed the entrance of the building, a second man, again in identical clothing and of the same height and build, walked out the entrance. The two crossed paths in the sidewalk crowd, walked together for several feet, then split up.

Efimov turned and spoke to another analyst. "You. Track the second man's movements. I want to know where each goes. Do not lose either of them. Volkov." Volkov stepped forward. "You stay on Federov," Efimov said. "You know him best, where he is most likely to go. Find him."

Efimov returned to the first screen. Waiting. Several minutes passed before the door again opened. A woman stepped out. Fur from the hood of her coat blew in the wind, obscuring much of her face. It also didn't help that the snow flurries had increased. "Can't get a clear shot," the analyst said.

Efimov didn't need one. According to the Lefortovo file he possessed, Paulina Ponomayova walked with a noticeable limp as a result of the injuries sustained in her car accident. Within a few steps he knew it was her. "Someone stay on her."

"I got her," another analyst said from a different computer terminal.

As before, an identically dressed woman emerged from the building entrance onto the street, walking beside her. She, too, walked with a limp.

Efimov was running out of analysts.

"What do we do?"

"Track them both. Try to get a picture of their faces."

"We don't—"

"Do it. No excuses. Do not lose either of them."

"Where are you?" Efimov said to the computer screen. The door opened a fourth time. This time, an old man exited, stooped over with his head down. He shuffled forward. How would a man as big as Charles Jenkins seek to avoid detection? During the previous hunt he'd used a burka.

Efimov turned to Alekseyov. "Get a car and a driver. We are going to Komsomolskaya Square." He then spoke to the room of analysts. "Transmit the most recent photographs of each individual to Moscow police. We are still eleven minutes behind."

28

Jenkins gave Paulina a three-minute head start, and it was difficult to watch her leave. It felt like the time he'd watched her exit the house in Vishnevka, and he again wondered if this would be the last he saw of her. He worried, not about her counterintelligence skills, but her health. She'd been hospitalized for months, and that had likely been the best care she'd received. He doubted they cared about her well-being in Lefortovo, wanting only to keep her alive long enough to interrogate her. Her physical condition certainly supported his theory. As she walked from the van to the stairwell, Jenkins noticed the pronounced limp in her step, and he feared that no matter her disguise, the limp would give her away. He hoped her doubles knew what to do.

He exited onto Krasnoprudnaya Street and immediately dropped his head, though not before feeling the biting cold and wind that gusted, pelting him with snow and the aroma of diesel fuel. Cars flowed past, engines revving and horns honking. In the center of the road a trolley car rumbled down the street. He walked past the building entrance, as scripted, and a man stepped from the building dressed exactly as Jenkins was and nearly as tall. They walked several steps together, then split up, the man headed across the street.

The building garage was three blocks from the Leningradsky train station. It would feel longer, walking into the wind, especially for someone physically compromised, like Paulina. Jenkins shouldered the duffel bag and pulled up the sleeve of his jacket to glance at his watch. 1:03 p.m. He'd have to hurry to catch his train, if he made it that far. Federov described Efimov as practical, pragmatic, and relentless. He also called him ruthless. Efimov would no doubt conclude there was little to gain from finding the ambulances. He would focus his resources on the train stations and the light rail. Even with three train stations and dozens of trains, all within a stone's throw of one another, Jenkins knew this remained primarily a game of disinformation, and his advantage only minutes.

He hoped they still had a precious few to spare.

He kept his head down and his shoulders slumped, proceeding toward the Leningradsky train station. The brutal weather had not stopped seasoned Muscovites; the sidewalks remained congested. A small blessing. Jenkins did his best to blend into the crowd. He saw his doppelganger across the street, doing much the same thing.

He raised his head as a blue Moscow Metro bus rumbled down the center of the road. After the bus passed, he spotted Paulina on the opposite side of the street, in the flow of foot traffic, her limp clearly noticeable. Her mirror image, identically dressed, also walked with a limp, as he had instructed.

Around a bend in the road, Jenkins spotted the Leningradsky pale-yellow train station and recognized it from pictures he'd studied. The building resembled a European town hall, with ground-floor windows and an elegant clock tower rising to a green copper roof, though fog and the steadily increasing snowfall nearly obscured the roof. Though the building was historic, the trains were not. Federov had explained to Jenkins that Russian Railways had spent more than a billion dollars to modernize the system, including adding high-speed electric trains that traveled more than 220 kilometers an hour. Jenkins had decided that if this was to be a shell game, the trains provided the most shells, and there would be no roadblock to stop a high-speed Sapsan train once it left the station, if they could get on it. If the plan worked, they had a chance of getting out of Moscow and, maybe, getting lost.

Across the street, Jenkins watched his and Paulina's doubles break off, moving toward the Yaroslavsky train station. Similar doubles would enter the Kazansky railway station. Paulina climbed the steps to the Leningradsky station entrance. Uniformed police officers stood in their drab gray winter coats and ushankas. He also detected plain-clothed officers considering their phones and watching as commuters ascended the steps and approached the station's glass doors. Federov had been correct about two things: Efimov had been practical and pragmatic. He'd wasted no time getting Moscow police officers in place at Leningradsky and likely the other train stations as well. Jenkins could only hope that Moscow's police would be less than diligent looking for common criminals in a blizzard.

As Paulina approached the building entrance, Jenkins noticed that she no longer limped, and he wondered if she had faked the limp for just such a purpose. To her right, a third woman, similarly dressed, limped up the steps to the entrance.

A Moscow police officer stepped into Paulina's path and Jenkins's nerves spiked, but Paulina, well trained, calmly handed the officer the identification Jenkins had provided. The photograph used Paulina's passport photo and superimposed the brown wig.

The officer quickly studied Paulina's face and handed back her passport, turning to another commuter. Paulina climbed the remaining steps to the door and went inside the building.

Jenkins checked his watch. 1:07. He had eight minutes.

He pulled a collapsible white cane from his coat pocket and slipped on black sunglasses, tapping the cane in front of him as he crossed the street to the building entrance. He stooped his shoulders and lowered his head to further minimize his height. People coming toward him stepped to the side. Rather than avoid the police officers, Jenkins deliberately walked into one.

"Izvinite," he said when the officer turned to him. Behind the officer, his doppelganger entered the train station.

"Where are you going?" the officer asked.

"The train station, of course," Jenkins said.

The officer touched his shoulder, turning Jenkins. "Up the steps," he said. "Straight ahead. Do you need help?"

"Net, spasibo. Ya ne pervyi raz edu na poyezde." No, thank you. I have traveled the train before.

Jenkins tapped the cane as he climbed the steps. A man held the door open for him. Inside, voices echoed in the cavernous terminal, and warm, musty air assaulted him. Jenkins looked for a wall clock and found it across an expansive lobby. It said 1:09. Six minutes.

He did not see Paulina.

He tapped his way to a security line. Commuters stood waiting to send baggage through X-ray machines. Jenkins set his bag on the belt and stepped through a metal detector, grabbing his duffel on the other side. The wall clock ticked forward another minute. 1:10.

Uniformed and plain-clothed officers stood in the cathedral-like main hall. Phones in hand, they studied the faces of the commuters rushing past them. Jenkins noticed his double, tapping a white cane, pass through the terminal. He searched for Paulina, thought he saw her, then realized another identically dressed woman limped through the terminal toward a different train platform.

Jenkins picked up his pace as he crossed the ornate room. Above the cacophony of sounds, a woman's voice spoke Russian, then English, advising commuters of the various platforms for each departing train. Jenkins spotted Paulina across the hall, coming in and out of view as the crowd ebbed and flowed. She walked toward the designated train platform, though still with no discernable limp. To her left, a police officer checked his phone, looked at Paulina, and crossed the marble floor with a determined gait. The photos had likely caught up with their disguises.

Jenkins picked up his pace, intercepting the officer just as he reached out to Paulina, and knocking him off his path. *"Izvinite,"* Jenkins said. *"Ya proshu proshcheniya. Ya opazdyvayu na poyezd. Ne podskazhete, kak proyti na platformu nomer devyat'?"* *Excuse me. I am sorry. I am in a hurry. Can you direct me to platform nine?*

"Where?" The officer looked past Jenkins, to the throng of people into which Paulina had been absorbed.

Jenkins held up his ticket. "I believe it is platform nine?"

The officer checked the ticket. "You're going to be close," he said. "Grab my arm." Jenkins did so, and the officer walked him quickly across the hall to an escalator that descended to a paved platform open to the weather. A police escort. Jenkins smiled.

On the platform, passengers hurried to get on a sleek, white Sapsan train. A crew member in a long gray coat and matching hat with a red brim checked a final passenger's ticket and passport at the door, then turned to go inside the train.

"Wait!" the officer called out. He grabbed Jenkins's ticket and handed it to the man.

"Do you have identification?" the conductor said.

Jenkins looked to the windows on his right. Paulina walked down the car toward the back of the train. Behind him, a low whistle signaled the arrival of another train on the adjacent platform. A crowd awaited it.

"Dayte cheloveku sest' v poyezd, poka on ne uyekhal bez nego," the officer helping Jenkins said. *Let the man on the train before it leaves without him.*

The crew member nodded. "Yes. Yes. Come on then. Do you need help finding your seat?"

"I wish to use the bathroom," Jenkins said.

The conductor moaned. "All right. But be quick about taking your seat. The train leaves in less than three minutes."

"Then I shall have no choice." Jenkins turned to his escort and thanked him. *"Spasibo."*

"Pozhaluysta," the officer said. *"Udachnoy poyezdki." Have a good trip.*

The employee helped Jenkins aboard. A glass door between the cars slid open, and Jenkins stepped to the bathroom.

"Do you wish for me to help you?" the conductor asked.

Jenkins bristled. "Do you wish to hold my dick?"

The young man quickly backtracked. "I meant only—"

"If you'll excuse me," Jenkins said. "I believe you said I do not have much time."

Embarrassed, the man turned and went back into the car.

Across the platform, passengers departed from the train. It would be close.

29

Efimov issued orders from the back seat of the black Mercedes as it sped up Academician Sakharov Avenue toward Leningradsky station, lights flashing and siren wailing. The drive from the Lubyanka building was ordinarily fifteen minutes, but more likely seven given the speed they traveled, despite the persistent poor weather.

Efimov held the roof handle while talking with Alekseyov, who was on the speakerphone to Lubyanka. An analyst was reporting on a number of persons, each dressed similarly to Jenkins and Ponomayova, walking into each of the three train stations, Yaroslavsky, Kazansky, and Leningradsky. Others, similarly dressed, had also entered the Kiyevsky railway station, the Kurskiy Vokzal station, the Belorussky station, and several of the other dozen stations located in the same area.

"Camera footage shows two people . . . Ponomayova and Jenkins going inside the main terminal of Leningradsky station and moving toward platform nine, but officers inside the station are reporting multiple sightings walking in the direction of multiple platforms. Reports from the other stations are the same. Moscow police are overwhelmed," the analyst said.

"Which is exactly what Mr. Jenkins is trying to do," Efimov shot back. "Maintain focus on the people who exited the side of the building."

“We have tried.” The analyst sounded stressed. “But there have been—”

“Do not give me excuses. Tell me where you have tracked them,” Efimov said.

“Leningradsky.”

“Can they be tracked inside the terminal?” Efimov asked.

The analyst said, “Maybe. But one of the women is walking without a limp.”

Efimov shuffled the information in his head. It seemed too easy a mistake to make for someone trying to emulate Ponomayova. “To which platform?”

“Platform nine. The train is scheduled to depart for Pskov at 1:15 p.m.”

Efimov gave that information a moment of thought. It made sense. “Mr. Jenkins is headed for Estonia,” he said. “The border is vast and can be breached by land or by crossing Lake Pihkva. Alert Moscow police to platform nine.”

Alekseyov said, “Yes, but can we be sure?”

Efimov ignored him and checked his watch. 1:11 p.m.

“Do you want me to call the station and have the train delayed?” Alekseyov asked.

“By the time you spoke to the person with such authority, *if* you were able to reach them, it would be too late. It would also not be wise. The railway adheres to strict promptness.”

Efimov had read of trains waiting outside stations to ensure they arrived precisely on schedule. He barked at the analyst, “Do as I said. Alert Moscow police at Leningradsky. Tell them to get to platform nine before the train departs and to remove Ponomayova and Jenkins.”

“But what of all the others similarly dressed?” the analyst said.

“Have Moscow police intercept as many as they can.”

The driver came to Kalanchevskaya Ulitsa, a one-way street in the wrong direction they were traveling.

"Turn right," Efimov ordered.

"It is one way."

Efimov slapped the back of the seat. "Do it."

The driver turned, the car's lights flashing. Its siren wailing. Cars parted and veered quickly to the curb. When the Mercedes reached Leningradsky station, Efimov hurried up the snow-trampled steps, barking out orders. The Moscow police quickly fell in line and escorted him and Alekseyov into the building and past metal detectors. The procession hurried across the crowded main terminal, commuters moving quickly to get out of its way. Those who didn't were bumped and shoved, a few knocked over.

Efimov checked his watch. 1:14. They had one minute.

The group quickly descended a staircase, reaching platform nine just as the white Sapsan train lurched forward, leaving the station precisely at 1:15 p.m.

30

Viktor Federov knew well that Big Brother had returned to Russia, though the method of spying—once Russians reporting on fellow Russians—now employed computer technology, cameras, and cell phones. He utilized every counterintelligence skill he knew to spread misinformation and circumvent the FSB's ability to track him. He had planned for the possibility of this day, when he would have to flee Moscow, though it had come much sooner than he had anticipated.

He got on and off buses and trolley cars, left behind cell phones, and routinely changed clothing and disguises at designated lockers where he had also stashed rubles, euros, and dollars, as well as different forms of identification and passports from multiple countries.

Satisfied he had successfully evaded surveillance, he set to completing two personal tasks before leaving Russia forever, hopefully to live out the remainder of his life in anonymity and wealth—though he knew nothing was guaranteed. Putin's vengefulness was extreme—and patient. Federov would forever need to be on guard.

What bothered Federov more than living the life of an exile was the knowledge that he would not likely see his daughters or grandchildren again, not unless they, too, left Russia. Since being let go by the FSB, he had sought to change his daughters' perception of him, to spend time with them, but they had been understandably distrustful and reluctant. They each held a grudge, and rightfully so.

Still, he would not validate their perception of him by leaving without saying goodbye, and he would not do so in a letter or a text message, as he had done too often when he'd missed their birthday parties and other special occasions. He'd always promised to do better. He never did.

Now, at least, he had the financial ability to do something for each of them, if not the time; something to let them know that while he had not always been present, he had never stopped loving them. Something that, when his daughters thought of him . . . if they thought of him . . . they would do so with fondness. To Renata he would leave his two-bedroom apartment, which was much nicer than her studio apartment and convenient to the theaters at which she plied her trade. To his daughter Tiana he would leave enough money to pay for his grandchildren's education, hopefully ensuring them a good life.

With the wind gusting and the snow swirling, Federov walked to the back of the Vakhtangov Theatre on Arbat Street. Renata had secured a minor role in the cast of the play *Anna Karenina* and would be in rehearsal. The last time they spoke, Renata advised that she had a small singing part and hoped this opportunity would be the one on which to build her career. Federov didn't have the heart to tell her that showcasing her voice could do more to hurt than to help her career.

He sucked down a last breath of nicotine and tossed the cigarette butt into the alley, which gave him a moment to ensure no one else was around. He reached into his coat pocket and retrieved a hotel key card, jimmied the lock of the theater's back door, and stepped inside the building. The hallway beneath the stage smelled of must and body odor. Above him faint voices spoke, and muted musical instruments played. He would need to act quickly, hoping to find Renata in the actors' green room. He would tell her only that he had to leave, and that while he hoped to see her perform again someday, it would not be this night. If she cared enough to ask why not, he would tell her it would be better for her if she did not know where he was going or what he intended.

Then he would hand her the envelope, ask her not to open it until he had departed, and tell her he wanted only for her to know that he loved her, despite his poor performance in the role of her father.

Federov stepped to the staircase just below the rehearsal stage. Above him the muffled sounds of actors became more pronounced, footfalls on the stage floor, instruments playing, voices speaking. When the instruments reached a crescendo, Federov took a step up, thought he heard a noise behind him, and instinctively reached into his black leather coat for his pistol, though not quickly enough. Not this time.

A dull thud impacted the back of his skull.

Efimov and Alekseyov flew above a stark, white Russian Orthodox church, its gold, onion-shaped domes fading in winter's dull-gray light. The wind gusted as the helicopter pilot struggled to touch down in a parking lot behind the church, close to the Tver train station. The station stood in stark contrast to the ornate church: a glass-and-concrete testament to Soviet architecture—functional and without visual appeal. As if to emphasize this, a hideous red stripe adorned the front of the building, advertising a Kentucky Fried Chicken outlet inside the train terminal.

Efimov and Alekseyov had arrived in just under one hour and thirty minutes, a little more than ten minutes ahead of the train's scheduled arrival in Tver, the first stop on the route to Pskov. A dozen Tver police officers, hands raised to deflect the wind generated from the helicopter blades, stood beneath an awning protecting the station's concrete steps from the weather.

"Wait here," Efimov shouted to the pilot through his headset.

The pilot shook his head. "The weather won't allow it. The storm is getting worse. They're grounding flights out of Moscow and Saint Petersburg. If I don't get back to Moscow now, I won't get back at all."

Though unhappy, Efimov realized there was little he could do. He and Alekseyov stepped from the helicopter, ducking beneath the swirling blades, and hurried to the train station. Ilya Vinogradoff introduced himself as the officer in charge. He and Efimov had engaged in an extended telephone conversation during the helicopter ride. Vinogradoff had a head of silver hair, a protruding stomach, and an officious demeanor no doubt intended to impress. It didn't.

They entered the train station, maneuvering around potted palm trees beneath a mosaic mural depicting important sites and events in Tver's history. "The train will be on time," Vinogradoff said, checking his watch. "I have spoken with the president of the Russian Railways and confirmed your instructions. The bathrooms on the train are to be shut down ten minutes before the train's arrival. The passengers will be detained."

Efimov looked about the empty platform. "When the train arrives, I want officers to enter each car—two at the front and two at the rear. They will work their way toward the middle, checking passports and tickets. They have been provided the photographs we forwarded to you?"

Vinogradoff nodded. "They have," he said.

"I want additional officers outside the doors of each car and, also, here, at this exit," Efimov continued. He turned to Alekseyov. "Since you are the most familiar with Mr. Jenkins and Ms. Ponomayova, you will enter the first car and work your way to the back."

Alekseyov nodded but did not speak. He looked uncertain.

Efimov gave him a second look. He did not have time to be second-guessed. "You wish to say something?"

"I am just wondering . . . whether this is too easy?"

"Too easy? We have flown in a storm to get here."

"Viktor Federov and I similarly followed Mr. Jenkins to a hotel in Turkey where we were certain we would apprehend him. We did not."

"The bus of which you speak made multiple stops before it arrived in Bursa, did it not?" Efimov asked, having read the report.

"Yes."

"That is not the situation here."

"No. It is not," Alekseyov said. "But then, we were not trying to decide between multiple targets either."

Efimov did not have time to debate the young agent. In his reports, Federov had written several times that Jenkins had formidable and intuitive counterintelligence skills. Efimov believed that to be part of the problem; Federov had given Jenkins far too much credit and thus he had been far too cautious. Efimov also discredited much of what Federov had written, believing Federov had used this to cover his ass, attempting to provide an excuse for his failure. His most recent actions further put the contents of those reports in doubt.

As for the shell game Jenkins had played, first with the ambulances and then with the disguises, time would tell whether the analyst had kept his eye on the prize or had become confused. During their helicopter ride, Moscow police reported detaining a number of the look-alikes, none of whom had been Jenkins or Ponomayova. As with any shell game, Efimov would not be certain until he had removed the final shell.

"Do as I have instructed," he said to the officers. To Alekseyov he said, "Have you heard from Volkov?"

Alekseyov shook his head.

Efimov would deal with Federov in good time.

31

Federov awoke feeling disoriented and confused, his vision blurred and distorted. The glow of a light emanated from somewhere above him, dull and yellow, and he detected a familiar tobacco smell, sharp and bitter, though he couldn't recall how or from where he knew the smell. He tried to move his hands and realized they had been bound behind his back.

As his senses slowly returned, so, too, did his understanding of his circumstances. He sat in a metal chair, his jacket removed, the holster beneath his left arm empty. He initially surmised from the windowless, bare concrete walls that he was in a cell, perhaps in the basement of Lefortovo, then realized that the room, like the tobacco smell, was familiar.

It was the room beneath the Vakhtangov Theatre—the same room in which he and Arkady Volkov had once interrogated Charles Jenkins.

Across the room someone had placed a briefcase beside a single metal chair. A noise behind him drew Federov's attention, but he could not turn his head sufficiently to see who had made it. A man entered his peripheral vision. Federov had seen that lumbering walk and block-like physique almost every day for nine years. He recognized the bittersweet aroma of Belomorkanal cigarettes.

Arkady.

Arkady sat in the chair, the cigarette in his right hand leaving a smoke stream in the room's stagnant air. Federov didn't know whether to greet him or to remain silent. His perception of their meeting in the elevator had proven accurate. Arkady had known more than he had let on.

"I assume you recognize the room," Arkady said, his voice soft, sounding almost hoarse. Smoke curled from his lips as he spoke each word.

Federov nodded, uncertain. "Yes," he said.

"We didn't have much success," Arkady said, as if reading Federov's mind. "With Mr. Jenkins."

Federov continued to gauge Arkady's actions, the tone of his voice. "We did our best, Arkady."

Arkady nodded but said, "Sometimes I wonder." His face retreated from the circumference of light into the shadows. He raised the cigarette to his lips. The end burned a blood red. A moment later he released another thick cloud of smoke.

"Why am I here, Arkady?"

His former partner did not immediately answer. He leaned forward, but his stoic facial expression revealed little. After a moment, he placed his forearms on his thighs. "I've wondered that myself," he said. "We're here because you got careless, Viktor. Because I suspected you would be careless, though I hoped you would not. I do not know your motive—perhaps guilt. Maybe regret. Maybe a final chance to make peace with your daughter before you left?"

Federov did not respond.

"Guilt, you once told me, Viktor, is a powerful motivator but a poor rationale for one's actions."

"You make me sound more profound than I feel at the moment."

Arkady stood. He crushed the cigarette butt beneath the sole of his black dress shoe. "You had to know that once Efimov suspected your involvement, he would ask me everything I knew of you, including your relationship with your ex-wife and with your two daughters—that he would probe me for any weakness to exploit. You had to know this, Viktor."

"Yes. I suppose I did."

Arkady spoke as if he hadn't heard the response. "I couldn't very well say you had none. We worked together a long time, Viktor, many years. And, of course, every man has a weakness. You also know this." Arkady exhaled and looked to the door. "I told Efimov it was a waste of time, that the Viktor Federov I knew would never make a mistake we could exploit." Arkady shook his head. "Apparently I was wrong. Regrettably. What has happened to you, Viktor?"

Federov shook his head. "I don't know, Arkady. Maybe the months away from Lubyanka have given me time to realize everything I have missed in my life. All that I gave up. The price I paid for my career. My marriage could not be saved, but my daughters . . . I thought maybe." Now he would never know. "They say age and experience bring wisdom. One can hope. I do know failure is easier to live with than regret."

"Yes, but you had to know Efimov would set this trap." Arkady almost sounded as if he were pleading with Federov.

"I suppose I did. But I could not leave this way. Could not disappoint my daughters again and have them believe that their impression of their father, the impression I forged for them, was accurate." He shrugged and offered a thin smile. "And I thought I had evaded surveillance."

"You did," Arkady said, sounding disappointed and a touch angry. "You were free. You could have left with your six million dollars and been free to do as you pleased."

Federov smiled. As always, Arkady knew far more than he let on. "So, you know about the money."

"And of Sergei Vasilyev, of course. I saw you and Mr. Jenkins leaving the M'Istral Hotel."

Federov sighed. He knew what awaited him would be painful. "Efimov also knows then."

Arkady shrugged his massive shoulders and pressed his lips together, a habit. After a pause he said, "No. This he does not know."

The answer surprised Federov. "You didn't tell him?"

"I have told many that what happened with Charles Jenkins was not your fault, that one cannot lose something he never possessed, but the FSB needed a head to put on a stick, and your head was chosen. Maybe mine would also have been, had I not already been in the hospital. No matter. My time, I'm sure, will come."

"What then?" Federov said. "Why am I here, in this room?"

"First, tell me why you would put me in this position."

"I have told you, Arkady. I want to leave without regret, to say goodbye to my daughters. It is as simple as that. Not the man you knew, perhaps, but . . ." He shrugged. "Perhaps, in hindsight it was a poor decision. But I would do it again. I missed too many opportunities to make things right with them. I gave too much to my job and too little to my daughters, and I am paying the price for my years of disinterest. Now they have little interest in me. My grandchildren call me Viktor. *Viktor.* Not *dedulya* or even *dedushka*." He shook his head. "How did it come to this? How did I let it come to this? I do not know."

Federov looked at the floor. The Russian Federation had sold him on an exciting career. He had arrived at Lubyanka thinking his life would be like James Bond. Too often it descended into hours of drudgery and monotony.

"I did not mean to put you in a difficult position, Arkady. You have always had a strong sense of duty and honor, and I respect you for that. I wanted only for my daughters to know that I did not abandon them, again."

Volkov looked to his briefcase at the foot of the chair. "The two envelopes . . . I assume then that those are for Renata and Tiana?"

"To make amends, what amends can be made after a lifetime of neglect."

Volkov lowered his gaze to the floor. "And was it worth it, Viktor? It sounds like it was not."

Federov gave the question some thought. "I guess time will be the arbiter of that question . . . for all of us, Arkady. As for me . . ." He smiled. "I can tell you that for the first time in my life, I am, at least, at peace. For the first time in my life, I sleep at night. Did at least."

Arkady reached down and lifted the briefcase, setting it on his lap. He snapped it open. Federov knew it held the instruments Arkady had been so adept at using to extract information, knives and blowtorches and razor-sharp tile cutters that removed a finger one knuckle at a time. Arkady removed a blade, closed the case with two clicks of the locks, and again set it beside the chair. The light from the single bulb dangling from the ceiling reflected off the metal.

Arkady stood and approached.

"You will give the letters to my daughters?" Federov asked, afraid, but hoping his death would be at least quick and painless, that Arkady would spare him the torture that surely awaited him at Efimov's hands.

"Yes. Of course." Arkady looked down at Federov.

"Do what you must, Arkady. I ask only that you do it quickly."

In one quick motion, Arkady stepped behind Federov and sliced the plastic ties binding Federov's wrists.

Federov looked up at his former partner, uncertain what to think or to say. "I don't understand . . ."

"You were not the only one with time to think, Viktor. I spent many hours and many days in that hospital bed. Yekatarina said you always came. No one came but you, Viktor. *You* kept my Yekatarina company. You gave her hope when I could offer none. The reading material you brought stunk, however. I would have preferred a good book."

Federov laughed, in part at his circumstance, at his nerves, and in part because after nine years he didn't know his partner. "A book? What would you have read, Arkady?"

"*The Count of Monte Cristo*," Arkady said. "You see, Viktor, I, too, have amends to make. And I, too, hope to someday sleep at night."

"But if you intended . . . Why did you hit me?"

Arkady shrugged. "I could think of no other way to be certain you didn't do something stupid."

32

Alekseyov checked his watch when he heard the high-pitched whine of the Sapsan train just before it entered the station precisely on time. The train came to a stop, and the doors pulled apart, but no passengers rushed for the exits.

The police entered the doors to ensure no one left, as Efimov had ordered. Alekseyov entered the first car with Vinogradoff and greeted the head conductor before starting down the aisle. Alekseyov's eyes darted left and right, studying faces, some concerned, some perturbed, others confused. His gaze lingered on the female passengers; Ponomayova would be more easily disguised than Jenkins, whose skin color and size made him readily identifiable.

Alekseyov did not see either seated in the first car. He and Vinogradoff moved to the second car, also without success. They entered and departed the third car, now becoming more deliberate. Alekseyov made men stand. Once or twice he tugged on women's hair, evoking a verbal protest, but again, he did not find either Jenkins or Ponomayova.

When Alekseyov reached the end of the fourth and final car he felt sick to his stomach. *Too easy,* he thought again. *It had been too easy.*

Vinogradoff looked confused. "What?"

Alekseyov did not realize he had spoken his thoughts aloud. "Nothing."

"Do you wish to go back to the beginning?" Vinogradoff asked.

"No one has left the train?" Alekseyov asked the conductor.

"It is not possible," the conductor said. "This was the first stop."

"There is no other way off?"

"Not at two hundred and twenty kilometers an hour."

Alekseyov showed him the pictures of Charles Jenkins and Paulina Ponomayova. "Do you recall seeing either passenger?"

"No."

Alekseyov showed him the pictures of Jenkins and Ponomayova walking through Leningradsky station in disguise. "What about them? Do you recognize them?"

"I do not, but one of my crew mentioned an old, blind man. He said a Moscow police officer helped him to board this train."

"A police officer?"

"Yes."

"I wish to speak to the crewman who remembers the old man."

The conductor led Alekseyov into the third car and motioned a male crew member to join them. Alekseyov showed him the picture of the old man.

"That is the man I helped to board the train," the man confirmed without hesitation.

"Blind?"

"He appeared to be, yes."

"He was escorted by a police officer?"

"Yes. The officer told me not to seek the man's passport for fear he'd miss his train."

"Did you seat him?"

"No. He asked to use the bathroom. I offered to assist him, but he was offended. I have not seen him on the train."

Alekseyov exited the car. The glass doors between the passenger cars opened, and he stepped to the bathroom and tried the door handle. Locked.

"Per instructions," the conductor said.

"Unlock it," Alekseyov said, removing his gun. "Then step aside quickly."

The conductor did so. Alekseyov pulled open the door to the tiny bathroom. Empty. "Have all the bathrooms searched," he said to Vinogradoff. "And the luggage. No one is to leave before the luggage is searched."

The conductor looked confused. "For what are we searching?"

Alekseyov held up the photographs again, suspecting he now knew why Jenkins and Ponomayova had carried duffel bags and why the conductor had not seen the old man on the train. "For the clothes in these pictures, wigs and glasses."

The man checked his watch. "But that could . . ."

Alekseyov, not anxious to speak to Efimov, took out his anger on the conductor. "Would you rather I bring you back to Lubyanka to explain how two passengers seemingly vanished into thin air?"

The conductor shook his head.

Alekseyov reluctantly stepped from the train and approached Efimov, who did not look happy. Alekseyov felt the nerves in his stomach spike. He shook his head. "A member of the crew confirms an old, blind man boarded and asked to use the bathroom. The conductor also ensures there was no way a passenger could have gotten off before Tver. I believe Jenkins and Ponomayova ditched their disguises and left the train before it departed."

Efimov made a noise sucking air between his front teeth and rubbed at the stubble on his chin.

"Do you want me to call Lubyanka and have them go over the tapes of the train station again? Perhaps the analyst was fooled. Perhaps it was the look-alikes who boarded the train. I have ordered the luggage searched."

Efimov checked his watch. His words were terse. "For what purpose?"

"For the disguises."

"I am not interested in finding disguises. I am interested in finding people." He stepped aside, rubbing the back of his neck. "Call Lubyanka," he said to Alekseyov. "Have them pull up the footage of platforms eight and nine at Leningradsky station just before this train departed. I want to know if there was a train on platform eight, and if so, when it departed, and to which cities."

33

Jenkins stood as the train came to a stop at the Moskovsky Rail Terminal in Saint Petersburg. He searched the platform for signs of uniformed police or men standing idly in the freezing temperature. He saw neither. Three rows ahead of him, Paulina stood from her aisle seat. She made brief eye contact and gave Jenkins a small smile, which belied how she otherwise looked. She had slept most of the three-and-a-half-hour train ride to Saint Petersburg. When awake, she'd nibbled on an energy bar and drunk water, telling Jenkins her stomach would not tolerate much food. Jenkins worried about her strength. They still had a long way to travel, *if* they made it off the train. He had no way to be certain the shell game he had arranged with Lemore's help had succeeded, or whether it would buy them sufficient time to slip from the station into Russia's second most populated city.

A duffel bag at the front of the car contained the discarded disguise Jenkins had removed in the Pskov train's bathroom, immediately prior to exiting the last car just seconds before the doors shut and the train pulled from the terminal. He'd moved quickly into the throng of commuters deboarding from and preparing to board the train on platform eight. Paulina had preceded him, after exchanging the light-brown wig for a short, blonde wig and slipping on a different-colored coat.

They'd managed to get on the Saint Petersburg train.

Now they had to get off.

Jenkins's stomach had been in turmoil the entire trip. He'd analyzed and reanalyzed their chances, deciding that it would all depend on how long it took Efimov to realize the ruse and to respond—assuming he had followed the correct pair of travelers. The train to Pskov made an initial stop in Tver. Efimov, if the ruse had worked, would have the train cars searched. When neither Jenkins nor Ponomayova were found, would Efimov have the train cars searched a second time? Would he search the bathrooms? The baggage? Or would he quickly assess that he had been duped and focus on the most likely alternative scenarios Jenkins and Ponomayova took to escape? Would he review the tape of the platform in Moscow, or conclude that a train on platform eight was their logical alternative?

Based on Federov's assessment of Efimov as practical and pragmatic, Jenkins was not confident they would have sufficient time to flee Moskovsky station, but Federov had also said that Efimov's involvement indicated the FSB would distance itself from the investigation and limit the number of FSB officers involved, to reduce the potential for an embarrassing mistake that could draw international attention. That meant that instead of alerting the FSB office in Saint Petersburg, it was far more likely Efimov would again use local police and tell them only that Jenkins and Ponomayova were wanted in Moscow for criminal acts. If his assessment was correct, they had a chance.

The line of passengers funneled toward the exits.

Paulina pulled up the hood of her jacket and stepped onto the platform, keeping her head down as she walked toward the escalators and staircase. No one rushed forward to apprehend her. A good sign. So far.

Jenkins pulled down the bill of the baseball cap to just above the rim of his nonprescription glasses and zipped his jacket closed. He left their duffel bags in the forward luggage rack and stepped onto the platform. Cold air and the smell of tobacco assaulted him as nicotine-starved commuters lit up. He kept his head down and his shoulders hunched and allowed himself to be swept into the sea of commuters.

As Jenkins neared the staircase, he sensed the commuters hesitate and looked up. Half a dozen police officers appeared atop the stairs and escalators. Some descended, shoving and pushing past the flow of people ascending. Additional officers remained on the platform, considering each traveler.

Paulina, already on the escalator, would be quickly made. The new disguise would not be enough.

Jenkins turned and moved quickly down the staircase, against the flow of commuters. The result was as he intended: loud complaints and pushing and shoving as he fought his way down the stairs. He looked back over his shoulder, making eye contact with one of the officers. The man pointed at him and started yelling. The yelling increased in volume, as did the commotion. Officers quickly converged, shoving and pushing their way through the protesting passengers.

When Jenkins reached the platform, he ran, though with nowhere to go. Multiple officers yelled at him to freeze and to get on the ground. He stopped, not wanting to get shot, and raised his arms high over his head.

As he knelt, he glanced back over his shoulder to the top of the escalator.

As the escalator ascended, Paulina heard commotion inside the terminal and noticed the sudden appearance of police officers. Some descended. Others remained at the top of the stairs and escalator, alternately considering the commuters and comparing them with photographs on sheets of paper or cell phones.

Jenkins's ruse to switch trains had been discovered.

She kept her head up, and her body relaxed as the escalator ascended. In her peripheral vision she noted one of the officers staring at her, then at the picture in his hand. It was apparently enough to convince him. He stepped toward her as she stepped from the escalator.

Again, she did not panic. She had identification in her pocket, and she had memorized the Saint Petersburg address and could repeat it fluidly and without hesitation—at least she could do so when she'd practiced on the train. Whether she could repeat the flawless performance now was about to be tested.

As the officer opened his mouth to speak, voices shouted below them. The noise caught the officer's attention and he departed, moving down the escalator with others. Saint Petersburg commuters, familiar with terrorist attacks targeting trains and crowds, including the 2017 attack on a Saint Petersburg Metro bus that had killed more than a dozen people, pushed and shoved and ran up the stairs and escalators.

Paulina watched Jenkins, below her, on the platform, drop to his knees and raise his hands—a sacrifice to draw attention. Tears filled her eyes and rolled down her cheeks and she wished, again, that Jenkins had not come back to Russia. She wished again that she had died in the car accident at Vishnevka, that Federov had not dislodged the cyanide pill.

She briefly contemplated creating a disturbance, but that would only result in both of them being arrested. Jenkins's instructions had been clear. If anything were to happen, she was to keep moving forward. She watched an officer shove Jenkins onto the concrete and jam a knee into his back. Others secured his wrists with zip ties, swarming over him like pigeons above a loaf of bread.

Paulina thought of the photograph Federov had placed on the table in Lefortovo, the one of Jenkins holding his baby girl.

Reluctantly, she stepped into the flow of panicked passengers hurrying across the marbled lobby and past the bronze statue of Peter the Great. She moved deliberately, but did not run, taking advantage of the commotion and the confusion to slide into the mass of people moving toward the main hall and the exits.

She descended three steps and pushed outside with other commuters. A blustering wind carried swirling snow that muted the ornate streetlamps and made it difficult to see more than a few feet. Paulina raised a hand and looked to hail a taxi—Jenkins had provided her rubles and an address. A few cabs remained in the parking lot. She negotiated the steps. The fresh snow compacted beneath the soles of her boots, making walking difficult. Halfway to the parking lot, she raised her arm, but someone grabbed her left elbow, yanking her hard in the opposite direction.

"Vy slishkom toropites', gospozha Ponomayova," the man said. *You are in too big a rush, Ms. Ponomayova.*

34

The side of Charles Jenkins's face burned where the police officers had shoved it against the concrete ground. Voices yelled all around him, too many and too quickly for Jenkins to understand everything being said. After securing his hands behind his back, the officers pulled him to his feet and slid a sack over his head. They gripped each bicep and half dragged, half carried him up the escalator. When they reached the top, Jenkins stumbled and nearly fell, but the officers held him upright, and he got his feet beneath him. They pulled him forward, moving quickly now, a fast jog. He nearly fell a second time when he missed a step he could not see. The misstep caused him to wrench his back, pain flaring down his right leg. He grimaced and collapsed to his knees, but again only momentarily. The officers yanked him to his feet and moved him forward.

Men shouted instructions for doors to be opened. The crowd noise dissipated. The shoving and pulling stopped. A key turned in a door lock. The officers shoved him and he fell forward, landing hard on his shoulder, his head hitting the floor. This time it was carpeted. But this time the officers did not lift him to his feet. The door slammed shut. Keys again in the lock.

Jenkins had not felt the rush of cold air. He had not felt or heard the snow or the wind, which meant he had not been brought outside.

He was still within the rail station, not yet in the custody of the FSB or Adam Efimov.

A good thing.

Enveloped in darkness, locked in a room with his hands zip-tied behind his back and armed officers outside the door, it was a small consolation.

Before Paulina, too weak to do much of anything, had a chance to react, the man forced her down the street and shoved her into the back seat of a car. The door slammed shut and the driver's door quickly pulled open, though the overhead light did not illuminate. The inside of the car was warm, as if it had just been driven, and it smelled of fresh cigarette smoke.

The man started the car and quickly pulled from the curb. He wore a baseball cap seated low on his brow and thick-framed glasses. A street sign she saw out the car window indicated Nevsky Prospekt. Paulina sat up and contemplated reaching over the seat and trying to choke the driver. She also contemplated pushing open the door and rolling into the snow, but where would she go? And how far could she get in her current condition and this weather?

The driver glanced in the rearview mirror and spoke as if reading her mind. "I would suggest you keep to the floor, Ms. Ponomayova. We don't have much time, and neither does Mr. Jenkins."

She recognized the voice, though not the face in the darkened interior. "Federov?"

"Tell me what happened inside the train station," Federov said.

"Why are you here?"

"That is a question for another day, perhaps. Now is not the time. We must act quickly if we are going to act at all. Tell me what happened."

Paulina did so.

"These men were all in uniform?"

"Yes."

"All of them?" he asked again, more insistent.

"Those that I saw, yes."

"Then we still have a chance." Federov made a turn and pulled to a stop at the snow-covered curb. He handed Paulina a street map of Saint Petersburg that looked to have been torn from a tourist pamphlet. It had an X on it. "If I am successful, Mr. Jenkins and I will not get far without a car, but we cannot risk having the car followed from the station. We will meet you here." He pointed to the map.

"Tikhvin Cemetery?" she said.

"The cemetery is just under two kilometers from the train station. Just before it, in the roundabout, you will come to a monument to Alexander Nevsky. To the left of that monument is a narrow road. Park there. You will be well hidden. An hour. Wait no more." Federov pushed out of the car.

"What if you're not there?"

Federov shrugged. "Mr. Jenkins gave you instructions . . . where to go?"

"Yes."

"Then do as you have been told."

When advised that neither Jenkins nor Ponomayova was on the Tver train, Efimov had quickly studied the Leningradsky train schedule and concluded they had exited the train before it left the station and boarded the train leaving platform eight at roughly the same time. That train was traveling nonstop to Saint Petersburg. A subsequent review of videotape streamed from Lubyanka proved Efimov's intuition to have been accurate. Ponomayova, then Jenkins, had entered the train to Pskov, but minutes later, each had emerged at the back of the last car wearing a different disguise, and they blended into commuters rushing to and from the train bound to Saint Petersburg.

Alekseyov had been correct about one thing. It had been too easy.

Perhaps there had been some truth to Federov's reports. Efimov did not have time to analyze it now. With the first mystery solved, their next immediate problem was getting to Saint Petersburg. As the helicopter pilot had warned, the heavy snowfall, darkening cloud cover, and gusting wind had closed the M10 highway into Saint Petersburg and grounded helicopters and commercial and private airplanes. Even if flying were possible, getting to an airport in the current weather, locating a crew, then flying the one hour and thirty minutes of airtime into Saint Petersburg, followed by a commute from the airport to the train station, would take more time than a train to the Moskovsky station. As much as Efimov did not want to sit idly, the train was their best and only real option.

Efimov watched Alekseyov disconnect the call to Lubyanka and make his way down the center aisle of the train car. "Reception is very poor, but from what I could hear, the Saint Petersburg police have arrested Charles Jenkins."

Efimov shot him a look. "What of Ponomayova?"

"She remains at large."

"How?" Efimov asked.

"Again, I had difficulty hearing, but the Saint Petersburg police missed the train's arrival by a minute or two. Passengers had already deboarded. They arrested Mr. Jenkins as he ascended a staircase. Ponomayova was not with him."

"He was alone?"

"So I am told."

"Jenkins would not have left Ponomayova to travel alone. He would be concerned about her health. She is in Saint Petersburg, but with the weather getting worse, she could not have gotten far, even with help," he said. "Blizzards in Saint Petersburg shut down traffic and freeze the bay. Her options of escape will be severely limited. Where is Mr. Jenkins now?"

"The police have him locked in a room at Moskovsky. Do you wish for me to contact the office in Saint Petersburg and have Mr. Jenkins transported to the Big House?" Alekseyov asked, referring to the FSB building on Liteyny Avenue.

"And shall we tell the whole world of our incompetence?" Efimov asked. "That we allowed two spies to escape Moscow?"

"I only meant—"

"I know what you meant." The storm had, at least, provided Efimov an excuse to avoid calling Sokalov and advising him of the latest misstep. "Are you not here only because Viktor Federov was fired for his incompetence? Do you wish for a similar fate?"

"No. I—"

"No, I did not think so. When we arrive at Moskovsky and have Mr. Jenkins in hand, then *we* will escort him to the Big House, where we will await improved weather to return him to Moscow, but not before he tells us where Ms. Ponomayova is going."

35

Federov arrived at the train station sweating and out of breath from the exertion expended trying to run in the heavy snow and gusting wind. For not the first time in his life—and likely not the last—he vowed to give up smoking. He even had a fleeting thought to give up vodka.

Smoking. He'd start with that.

Nevsky Prospekt's sidewalks and the parking lot outside Moskovsky station were all but deserted, buried in snow. The ornate, antique streetlamps offered flickering yellow light. Federov climbed the steps to the station and struggled to open the door against the fierce wind. Inside, he took a moment to straighten his appearance. For what he was about to do, Federov could wear no disguise.

The difference in temperature inside the station was almost as pronounced as the humidity. Federov did not linger. He did not have time.

Arkady Volkov had called Federov and told him that Efimov and Simon Alekseyov were en route to Saint Petersburg by train, and that Efimov was largely using local police to minimize the chances of a public spectacle.

That meant nothing would happen at the train station, at least not until Efimov arrived from Tver, and that gave Federov a chance, though certainly a slim chance, at best. He'd checked the train schedule, then glanced at his watch. He had less than fifteen minutes.

He flashed the FSB badge he had never turned in and utilized his well-honed demeanor on a uniformed officer at the security checkpoint. "I am Viktor Federov with the Federal Security Service. I understand you have detained a man wanted on criminal charges in Moscow."

"Yes. But I do not know where he has been taken." The officer pointed up the stairs. "Ask one of the officers in the main lobby. They should know."

Having now identified himself as law enforcement, Federov removed his pistol and placed it in a tray on the belt without eliciting any questions. It passed through the metal detector and he retrieved it on the other side.

He climbed the marbled steps into the first hall and approached a group of police officers, flipping open his billfold with the same arrogance. "Good evening," he said. The officers' gaze immediately shifted to the identification, and they stood a little taller. Federov flipped the billfold closed. "I am Colonel Viktor Federov with the Federal Security Service. I am told you have arrested a man wanted on criminal charges in Moscow. Tell me who is in charge and how I may find him."

One of the officers pointed Federov to a hallway. "The door to the left," he said. "He's being kept in there."

Federov walked across the hall and pulled open the door. His lungs were assaulted by stale cigarette smoke as he entered a drab reception area. Three officers sat in plastic chairs behind empty desks.

"Who is in charge?" he asked.

"I am," a heavyset man said without enthusiasm.

Federov flipped his billfold in the man's face. "I am Colonel Federov, Viktor Nikolayevich, with the Federal Security Service. I understand you have arrested an American wanted on criminal charges in Moscow?"

The three officers quickly stood. They put on their hats and straightened their uniforms.

"This is true," the man in charge said. He extended a hand. "Ivan Zuyev."

"I am here to bring the prisoner to the Big House before the weather gets any worse and the roads become impassable. Please bring him to me."

Zuyev did not move. "We were told to detain him here, that FSB officers are coming to obtain the prisoner."

Federov smiled, though it was without humor. "Am I not standing here before you?"

"We were told the officers were arriving on a train from Tver—"

"Yes, well, that was before this blizzard. All trains returning to Moscow have been canceled for the evening, and we need to ensure the prisoner is kept in a secure location, not a closet."

"Canceled?"

"The station master will be reporting it soon, I am sure." Federov looked at his watch. "Have you been outside?"

"No—"

"I have. Now, I don't have much time. Have you seen the weather?"

"No, I—"

"Well, I had the pleasure of driving in it. I am to take the prisoner to the Big House until the storm passes, and I don't wish to be delayed any longer. Please bring him to me."

"I was not made aware of a change in plans, Colonel," Zuyev said tentatively. "I am sorry."

Federov gave Zuyev his best withering stare. "Did I not just advise you?"

"Yes, but—"

"But you seek to challenge my authority?" Federov glared. "Perhaps you think I take pleasure in being called out in a storm to pick up a criminal?"

"No, Colonel."

"Would you like to make a phone call to confirm who I am and what I am telling you?" Federov pulled his cell phone from his inner jacket pocket. "Here, let me call for you."

Zuyev spoke quickly. "No, that won't be necessary."

"I insist. If you are going to question my authority, at least allow me the opportunity to gloat when I am proven correct."

"I am sorry, Colonel. It's just that my instructions were very clear, and . . ."

Federov checked his watch. He had nine minutes before the train carrying Efimov arrived. "And what?" Federov asked.

"And I was to keep the prisoner here."

"Was," Federov said. "Past tense. Do you think the FSB can control the weather?"

"No, of course not."

"Exactly. The weather has changed, and we are adapting to that change, upon the order of the deputy director. Or do you question his authority as well?"

"I do not. If I could just call the number that provided my instructions?"

"By all means," Federov said. "Call. But do it quickly."

Zuyev turned his back and removed his phone. When he did, Federov reached beneath his coat, tapping the grip of his pistol.

Efimov sat stoically as the high-speed train sped toward Moskovsky station, reaching speeds of 220 kilometers an hour. Outside, snow whipped past the tinted windows. They would arrive at Moskovsky in less than nine minutes.

Across the aisle, Alekseyov's cell phone buzzed. The young officer answered the call and put a finger to his opposite ear. "Alekseyov. Hello?" He stood and walked to the back of the car, Efimov watching him. "Hello. This is Alekseyov. Yes. Can you . . . Can you hear me? I said, 'Can you hear me?' Yes. Yes, I can hear you. I said, 'I can hear you.' Can you hear me? Hello?"

He walked to the front of the car.

"I'm sorry. Repeat that. I said . . . 'Repeat that.' Hello? Yes, we are . . . We should be arriving in—What? What man . . . Hello? What man? Can you hear me? Do not . . . Do not . . . Hello? Hello?"

Alekseyov lowered the phone. He looked confused. He hit a button, apparently to return the call, then slowly returned to his seat.

"What is it?" Efimov asked.

"That was a police officer at Moskovsky station."

"What did he want?"

"I couldn't hear him. He said something about someone being at the station, about Mr. Jenkins."

"What about him?" Efimov asked, suddenly alarmed.

"I don't know," Alekseyov said again. "I couldn't hear."

Efimov checked his watch. Like it or not, he was stuck for the next eight minutes. "Call him back."

"I tried. The screen freezes then indicates the call failed. The weather, and this train."

"Keep trying," Efimov said. "Tell them no one is to see Jenkins until I arrive."

Zuyev clearly struggled to hear. As Federov had hoped, the storm interfered with his call, though to what extent, Federov could not be certain. He kept his hand on the grip of his pistol. When Zuyev disconnected, he turned and gave Federov an uncertain and perplexed look. It made Federov uneasy, but he slipped his hand from the grip and raised his eyebrows. "Now, may I see the prisoner?"

"I couldn't . . . The storm. I couldn't hear."

"Sukin syn," Federov said. *Son of a bitch.* "What are you going to do?"

"The train should be arriving within minutes, Colonel. Perhaps you can wait?"

"Wait?" Federov raised his voice. "For the storm to get worse? I've told you the prisoner will not be getting on the train. He will not be going back to Moscow, not in this weather. I am to take him to a holding cell at the Big House, or did you think maybe you can hold him here in an unsecure room all evening?" Before Zuyev could respond, Federov tried a different tack. "How have you secured him?"

Zuyev stuttered. "We zip-tied his hands behind his back as well as his ankles."

"That is child's play to this man. Do you have any idea who he is?"

"No. Only that he has committed crimes in Moscow."

"Do you have more ties?"

"Yes, of course." Zuyev turned to one of the other officers. The man opened a desk drawer and drew out a handful of the ties.

"Follow me, all of you, and bring the ties with you." Federov stepped down the hall at the back of the security office.

"For what purpose?" Zuyev said, hurrying around the desk to catch up.

Federov stopped. "I'm going to tell you something that cannot be repeated." He looked to each of the three officers. Then he said, "This man is not a common criminal. He is a highly trained counterintelligence agent. I must speak to him about a second person traveling with him. A woman. It is extremely important that we find her before too much time passes. You were told this, I assume?"

"Of the woman, yes, of course," Zuyev said.

"Good. Lead the way." As Zuyev stepped toward the door, Federov spoke again. "Leave your guns out here, please."

"What? Why?"

"Because I do not wish to be shot by your weapon if Mr. Jenkins has freed himself or if things go poorly."

Zuyev and the two officers removed their weapons, setting them on a desk, then Zuyev led Federov down the hall, stopping just outside the door. Federov instructed the officers where to stand, then nodded to Zuyev to unlock the door. Federov removed his pistol and stepped to the side.

Zuyev paused.

"Open it," Federov said.

Zuyev did so and the three officers braced, as if Charles Jenkins might charge them. Inside the room, Jenkins sat on the floor with his back against the wall. Beside him lay a sack that had apparently once covered his head. Jenkins gave Federov a dull stare.

"Your time seems to be running out, Mr. Jenkins," Federov said.

"Does it?" Jenkins asked.

Federov turned to Zuyev. "What time does the train arrive?"

Zuyev checked his watch. "Seven minutes."

He pointed the gun at Zuyev's temple and spoke to the other guard holding the zip ties. "Bind their hands and ankles."

The officer hesitated.

"Do as I say, and you will all go home to your families when you complete your shift. Fail to do so, and hopefully the alternative is clear to each of you, yes?"

—

Federov closed the door and ensured it was locked. He slipped the key into his pocket and checked his watch. "We have just over five minutes. Maybe less."

Jenkins kept his hands behind his back, though Federov had cut the zip ties. "Do I dare ask what you are doing here, Viktor?"

"Now is not the time, Mr. Jenkins."

Federov picked up the three Makarov pistols left on the desk by the officers, handed two to Jenkins, and shoved the third into his waistband at the small of his back. Jenkins stuffed one in his waistband and covered it with his jacket. He put the other in his coat pocket. Federov tugged on Jenkins's coat sleeve and moved him toward the door.

"What exactly is your plan?" Jenkins asked.

"I wish I knew." Federov moved quickly to the door. "I'm making it up as I go. Keep your hands behind your back."

"Do you know Saint Petersburg?"

"I worked here for a year. Beyond that, I studied Google Maps."

"You're joking?"

"Not so funny, is it?" Federov said. "We must move quickly."

Federov pulled open the door, stepped down the narrow hallway, and pushed through an exit into the nearly deserted main terminal. A loudspeaker announced the impending arrival of the train from Tver. "We are out of time," he said.

Federov walked to the officer who had directed him to Jenkins. "I am taking the prisoner to the Big House. Please take your men to meet the incoming train, platform five, and escort the FSB officers to the holding room, where they can discuss transportation to the Big House."

The police officer nodded and the group moved in unison toward the platforms.

Federov pulled Jenkins to the exit, and they pushed outside into a wicked wind. They started up the sidewalk, the snow pelting them with such force it was difficult to see even a few feet. Jenkins raised his voice over the howling wind. "You have a car, I presume."

"I had a car. I gave it to Ponomayova."

"You what?" Jenkins asked.

"I didn't exactly have a lot of time to find a replacement."

"How did you plan to get away?"

"We walk, Mr. Jenkins. Quickly."

"Walk? Walk where?"

"To the gravesite of Russia's most famous author."

"I hope he has a car."

—

Efimov stepped from the train as it came to a stop, not surprised to find multiple police officers waiting on the platform.

"I am Officer Kotov, Sebastian Nekrasov," the lead officer said. "I am here to escort you."

"Lead the way," Efimov said.

Efimov and Alekseyov followed the officers up the staircase and crossed the deserted main hall to a locked door leading to a hallway and the security office, which was empty.

Efimov looked at Kotov. "Why is there no one here?"

"I do not know."

"Where is the prisoner?"

Kotov motioned with his hand. "Being taken to the Big House to be detained . . . due to the worsening weather."

"On whose authority?" Efimov asked, bells and whistles sounding in his head.

"The FSB."

Efimov looked to Alekseyov, who shook his head. "I specifically told the officer that Jenkins was to remain here."

Efimov hurried to a closed door at the end of the hall and tried the door handle. Locked. He stepped back and raised his leg, striking the knob with the heel of his foot. The doorframe cracked but did not give entirely. Another kick and the door burst open. Efimov entered the room with his gun drawn. Three officers lay on the floor, their hands and feet zip-tied, their faces pale.

Federov, Efimov thought. He turned to Kotov. "How long ago did this FSB officer take the prisoner?"

"Just a few minutes. I spoke to him in the main hall. He instructed me to meet you at the train and arrange—"

"What was his name?" Efimov asked.

"Who?"

"The FSB agent," he said, voice rising. "What was his name?"

"I don't . . . I don't recall."

"Federov," Efimov said. "Viktor Federov?"

"Yes," the officer said. "Yes, that was the name."

"Which way did they leave?" Efimov moved quickly to the door.

"I don't—" Kotov said.

"Bring your men."

"What of the three—"

"Leave them."

Efimov hurried across the main hall, Alekseyov and the officers running to keep up. Viktor Federov remained very much in play and was now also close at hand. Efimov would capture or kill them both. As for Ponomayova, he would deal with her later.

He hit the bar across the exit door, stepped into a gusting wind and blinding snow, and shuffled down the snow-covered steps. He raised his hand to shield his eyes, surveying the deserted parking area, then the streets.

He spotted what appeared to be two men crossing Nevsky Prospekt and disappearing down the block. Efimov's heart rate picked up and he felt an adrenaline rush; he had grown up on the streets of Saint Petersburg, and he had endured many blizzards. They would not outrun him.

He shouted to Alekseyov. "Get as many officers and cars as you can. Radio that we are in pursuit of two men headed north on Vladimirsky, possibly for the subway. Provide their location and their descriptions. In this weather, with the streets empty, they should not be hard to find. Go. Move!"

Then he turned and ran down the sidewalk, into the blizzard.

Federov and Jenkins moved deliberately but did not run, not that they could have in the driving wind and snow. They would be conspicuous enough walking the deserted streets of Saint Petersburg in what amounted to a blizzard, and they weren't exactly dressed for the weather. Both lacked hats and gloves. Jenkins pulled up the collar on his jacket and thrust his hands deep into the pockets, flexing his fingers to keep the blood circulating. His face became numb after just a few blocks.

In the street, cars and buses sat idly, abandoned and covered beneath four to six inches of snow. An eerie silence had enveloped the city, the only sounds the gusting wind and the hum of a snowplow struggling to keep the road clear.

Federov pulled Jenkins behind a building, a respite from the fierce wind. Breathing hard and sounding out of breath, Federov wiped at beads of water rolling down his face.

"The subway is our only option, which means we cannot take it. Efimov will know this. We need to split up," Federov said. "We are too conspicuous together."

Jenkins knew Federov was correct. He blew warm air into his cupped hands, then rubbed them together and shoved them under the armpits of his jacket. "You have a plan?"

"At the end of Nevsky Prospekt is Tikhvin Cemetery, where Dostoevsky is buried. Before the cemetery, in a roundabout, is a monument to Alexander Nevsky. To the left of that monument is an alley. Ponomayova is to meet you there." He quickly checked his watch. "You have less than twenty minutes to get there."

"How far is it?"

"Under two kilometers."

"In this snow? It's not possible."

"It is your only choice. Make it possible."

"What about you?" Jenkins wiped the moisture from beneath his nose.

"I will be fine," Federov said.

"Viktor—"

"Do not thank me, Mr. Jenkins. This is far from over, and we are both far from being safe. Me? Perhaps never again." He turned to leave. Jenkins grabbed his shoulder.

"Tell me why you came back." Jenkins didn't know why, at that moment, this was so important, but he sensed he would not get another opportunity to ask.

"As you said, Mr. Jenkins. I like to win. And I have four million very good reasons to get you back to America." Federov smiled. Then he said, "Karma. I am, how do you say . . . doing this because someone did it for me, and I don't want to get the bad luck. Perhaps someday we will drink that toast in Seattle. Then we shall tell all our secrets."

Federov left the shelter of the alley and turned the street corner, disappearing into the swirling snow.

—

Federov reached the end of the block, about to turn north, when a shadow came around the corner and delivered a blow hard enough to drop him to his knees. The already colorless landscape faded to black and white as Federov pitched forward, the snow softening his fall. Someone shoved a knee into his back, then searched his clothes, removing his weapons.

"Did you think you could betray your country so easily, Colonel Federov?" The voice was gravelly and winded. It was also familiar.

Efimov.

The muzzle of a gun pressed into the flesh of Federov's cheek, making it difficult to speak. Federov grunted, trying to shake the cobwebs from the blow, trying to think. "I did not betray my country."

"Too bad it will not be seen that way," Efimov said.

"No. I doubt that it will."

"Your mistake was underestimating me," Efimov said.

"I don't think I could have thought any less of you," Federov replied.

Efimov yanked Federov to his knees and put the muzzle of the gun to the back of his head. "And that was your mistake, Colonel. It will cost you your life."

The wind gusted, driving the snow into swirling tornados. Everything seemed fuzzy and distant.

"But not here and not now," Federov managed, struggling to think, to stay in the present.

"No? I execute you now and I save the state the trouble of doing so."

"But you won't," Federov said, unable to connect his thoughts.

"Again, you underestimate me."

"And you underestimate me." The thoughts coalesced. "I did not betray my country. I am working for my country."

"You are a liar."

"Am I? I know where Charles Jenkins and Paulina Ponomayova are going, and as much as you want me, I know you want them much more."

"I want you all."

"Yes, but you want me because I embarrassed you—but would that not be a hollow victory?" Federov felt sick. He forced himself not to vomit. "Capture Jenkins and Ponomayova, or capture the entire network seeking to free them? Which is better? Which will bring the greater respect of the deputy director and the president?"

Federov sensed Efimov hesitating, and he hoped it was because his statement hit its mark.

"You've known where they are going, but you said nothing."

"I did not know the extent of their network, and I did not have a gun at my head."

"And now you wish to barter for your life?"

"Is it not obvious from your vantage point? Besides, what do you achieve by killing me?"

"You are a traitor."

Federov shrugged. He blew out a breath. His knees felt weak. "Fine. Let them go. But will not the president reward the man who captures them? I do not mind sharing the credit, Efimov."

Efimov spun Federov and put the muzzle of the gun to his forehead. "A dead man can share nothing."

"And offer even less," Federov replied.

Again, Efimov hesitated. "And you can give me Jenkins and Ponomayova?"

"I give you them both, and there is little reason for you to keep your word and let me live." He began to see shadows. "But I can give you Mr. Jenkins."

Again, Efimov paused. "And if this is another lie?"

"That is obvious, is it not?"

"Where is he?"

Federov smiled. The shadow gained clarity. "He is not far," he said.

Efimov straightened at the touch of the muzzle of a handgun against the base of his skull.

"Bros' pistolet," Jenkins said. *Drop the gun.*

When Efimov did not immediately respond, Jenkins leaned closer and spoke louder. *"Bros' pistolet."*

Efimov released the gun and it fell, silently, in the snow. Then Jenkins hit Efimov in the back of the head with the butt of his pistol, dropping him to his knees. He, too, pitched forward into the snow.

"Time to move, Viktor," Jenkins said.

Federov stepped toward Jenkins, but the nausea and the dizziness intensified and overwhelmed him. He fell sideways, stumbling into a building.

Jenkins grabbed him to keep him from falling to the ground.

"Go, Mr. Jenkins. I will be fine."

"Had that chance. Didn't work out," Jenkins said. "You said something about karma. We can put it on the list of things to discuss in

Seattle." He wrapped Federov's arm around his shoulder and gripped him by the belt.

"We can't outrun the cars," Federov said.

"Not by standing here."

—

Jenkins pulled Federov down the street and turned a corner. A short alley. He turned again, staying off main roads by cutting through the narrow passageways between buildings, hoping he was paralleling Nevsky Prospekt. He struggled to catch his breath; Federov was over six feet and at least two hundred pounds. Jenkins kept talking to keep Federov attentive, but the Russian did not always track the conversation.

One thing Federov had said, however, seemed dead certain.

If they did not reach Paulina in the next twelve minutes, they had little chance of getting away—not in this weather, not on foot, and not with the Saint Petersburg police searching for them.

Jenkins concentrated on taking one step after the next, pulling Federov down another alley, emerging on a deserted street lined by three-story buildings. Cars along the curb lay buried beneath snow, and Jenkins could no longer discern the street from the sidewalk. He was quickly tiring and contemplated how good it would feel to sit, just for a moment, and catch his breath.

He shook the thought. His brain was shutting down, giving in to the cold. Confusion would follow. If he stopped, he would not start again. Hypothermia would follow. He and Federov would both freeze to death. He checked his watch. Less than ten minutes to reach the cemetery.

Headlights appeared on the side of a building, illuminating the falling snow. A car came around the corner. Jenkins pulled Federov back into the alley and pressed against the side of a building. The car slowed.

Someone searching. Federov was right. Jenkins could not outrun them. Not on foot. But maybe if they had a car. If Jenkins could get a car.

He set Federov down and removed the gun.

"What are you doing?" Federov asked.

"Shh," Jenkins said. "They're coming."

Federov, dazed and confused, tried to stand, stumbled, and fell sideways, knocking over a garbage can. The snow muffled the clatter, but the noise still reverberated in the alley.

Time to move.

Jenkins secured the gun and lifted the Russian to his feet, dragging him down the alley. Behind them a door slammed shut, then a second. He heard voices. Jenkins swore under his breath and urged Federov forward. As they neared the end of the alley, additional headlights appeared on the snow-covered road. The police were circling the area, cutting off their escape. Jenkins looked up. Across the street, in the center of a roundabout, stood a snow-covered statue of a man atop a horse.

He hoped it was Alexander Nevsky.

Jenkins checked his watch. Under five minutes.

He was running out of time and alleys. When the wind gusted, causing the snow to swirl, he saw a chance, hoping the poor visibility would allow them to cross the street without being seen and reach the alley beside Tikhvin Cemetery. If not, they might very well be shot.

If so, at least they were headed to the right place.

36

Jenkins reached the monument with just a few minutes to spare and pulled Federov behind the pedestal. He raised a hand to deflect the wind-driven snow, seeing what looked like an alley. "Not much further, Viktor," Jenkins said. The Russian was moving better, getting his legs beneath him, more balanced. He was also tracking their conversation.

They crossed and proceeded down the alley, no wider than the width of two cars, and narrowed by what looked like abandoned vehicles.

"What kind of car?" Jenkins asked.

"A white Lada," Federov said.

Jenkins was not familiar with the car. "What does it look like?"

"A Lada. It looks like a Lada," Federov said.

They reached the end of the block. "It's not here," Jenkins said.

Federov shook his head. "Maybe she's gone already."

To Jenkins's right, headlights glowed. A car edged around the corner, the beams reflecting the swirling snow. No choice now. They needed a car before they froze. He pulled Federov behind one of the abandoned cars and reached for the handgun. Forty years ago, he'd sworn he'd never kill another human being. He hoped he didn't have to do so now.

The car approached slowly, squeezing down the ally. Jenkins crouched behind a car and waited for it to pass. When it had, he rose up and stepped out, reaching for the door handle. He pulled the driver's door open and shoved the muzzle of the gun into the gap.

"Don't shoot," Paulina said. "Don't shoot, Charlie."

Jenkins helped Federov into the back seat and hurried around the car to the passenger seat. Paulina spoke as she backed down the street, unable to turn around and not wanting to drive on Nevsky Prospekt. "There are police everywhere," she said. At an intersection, she straightened and turned down a second narrow alley. "The buildings have blocked much of the snowfall in the alleys," she said. "We can move faster."

Jenkins quickly recognized that having a car this night was both a blessing and a curse. He would not have made it much farther, not lugging Federov beside him. And the snow and heavy cloud cover prevented, or severely limited, the use of police helicopters or satellites to track the car. But with the roads deserted, *any* moving vehicle would be easy to spot by the swarm of Saint Petersburg police searching street by street, and no doubt monitoring traffic cameras deployed throughout the city.

Jenkins looked to Federov in the back seat. "How do you feel?"

"Like someone hit me in the back of the head, twice."

"Twice?" Jenkins said.

"Is long story."

"Is your scalp bleeding?"

"Not much. The cold has helped. How did you know?" Federov asked. "About Efimov."

"I didn't know it was Efimov, not for certain, but I figured anyone out in this weather was either crazy or looking for us."

"In this case, both," Federov said.

"I got that sense." Jenkins turned to Paulina. "You can drive in this snow?" he asked.

Paulina, who had lived her entire life in Moscow, arched one eyebrow and pulled the emergency brake, sending the car into a skid. She released the brake and punched the gas. The car corrected and shot down another alley. Jenkins gripped the handhold to keep upright. He smiled. "I guess that's a yes. We're going to need to ditch this car sooner rather than later."

"Yes," she said. "But the marina is not close, and neither he nor I can walk far in this weather. It is difficult even for you."

Jenkins spoke to Federov. "I assume they have traffic cameras to monitor the streets?"

"Yes, but Saint Petersburg is not Moscow," Federov said. "Most of the cameras in Saint Petersburg are focused on major thoroughfares and tourist sites, for terrorist attacks. If we take back alleys and side streets, we can get far. The snow will help to hide us, especially if we drive without lights."

At the end of each alley, Paulina slowed and turned off the car's headlights. Visibility was not much worse without the headlights, no more than a foot or two beyond the hood of the car. On two occasions she had to retreat when headlights appeared on the intersecting street. Police vehicles drove slowly past. When clear, she crossed the street and continued the game of cat and mouse. They exited an alley to a street running parallel to the Neva River.

"First bridge," Paulina said. Street signs indicated the Blagoveshchenskiy Bridge—with traffic traveling in each direction, though this night the bridge was deserted. "This is the greatest risk, but we have no choice," she said.

Once across the bridge, Paulina quickly found and navigated the alleys and side streets that eventually led to the Betankura Bridge, a shorter span across the Little Neva River. Again, they encountered no traffic. On the other side, however, the Petrovsky District looked largely industrial, with few streets. Paulina had no choice but to drive the deserted main road, Petrovsky Prospekt, increasing their chances of being seen.

Eventually they reached the final bridge, Bolshoy Petrovsky, and crossed to Krestovsky Island. "How much farther to the marina?" Jenkins asked.

"Not much farther. Half a mile," Paulina said.

"I think we've pushed our luck far enough. Let's find a place to ditch the car before we get any closer to our destination," Jenkins said. "Efimov will know we can't walk far in this weather. We need to hide the car to buy us time."

Federov leaned between the seats. "The park." He pointed. "We can hide the car in Primorskiy Park. It is very large."

Paulina drove off the shoulder of the road, the tires bumping over the curb. Jenkins could not distinguish walking paths from the streets. Paulina weaved the car through stands of snow-covered trees until they emerged at a parking lot littered with vehicles covered beneath six inches of snow.

"Drive over the curb," Jenkins said, pointing past the parking lot. "Into those trees."

Paulina kept her speed up so the car wouldn't get stuck and navigated close to the tree trunks. The branches, laden with heavy snow, sagged nearly to the ground, providing a natural canopy.

"Can you walk?" he asked Federov as the Russian stepped from the back seat.

Federov considered the snow-covered landscape. "I think the better question is whether I can ski."

37

Efimov staggered into a room at the police station in Saint Petersburg. He was both embarrassed and angry. The blow to the back of his head had not knocked him out, but it had stunned him long enough for Jenkins and Federov to flee. He had struggled to his feet and followed their shoeprints until the snow obliterated them, then he flagged down a police vehicle.

Efimov assumed Federov and Jenkins had fled by car, since they could not get far on foot, especially not after the blow Efimov had delivered to the back of Federov's skull. Either Jenkins would recognize this and hijack a car, though that seemed unlikely since there were none on the road, or he had reached a previously designated meeting place and had been picked up—most likely by Ponomayova.

Efimov sipped whiskey and flexed his fingers to circulate his blood and warm his limbs. In the police car he had instructed Alekseyov to direct the Saint Petersburg police to scour traffic-camera footage in the general vicinity of Moskovsky station and the surrounding neighborhood, searching for either a moving vehicle or two men walking. Efimov knew traffic cameras were not as prevalent in Saint Petersburg as in Moscow, but then neither were the cars, at least not this night. While he waited, Efimov considered what Federov had said about trying to expose the entire network working to get Jenkins and Ponomayova out of Russia. No doubt these were the ramblings of a desperate man looking down the barrel of a gun, but there was truth in what Federov had told him. Catching Jenkins and

Ponomayova remained the clear objective, but taking down the people assisting them would further elevate Efimov, perhaps enough for the president to consider bringing him back into the fold, a job within the Kremlin.

That, however, was putting the cart before the horse, something his father had warned him to never do. Complete the job. Leave the reward to others.

Alekseyov walked into the room carrying a cold compress and handed it to Efimov. "You should have that looked at by a doctor," he said. Efimov dropped the compress in a waste can. He had no time for doctors. "They could not have gotten far, not in this weather," he said to the officers in the room.

"They could have parked the car. They could be hiding in any of the buildings in that area," Alekseyov said.

Efimov shot him a stern look. "Do not contradict me," he said under his breath.

An analyst monitoring a computer terminal spoke up. "I have located a car on the Blagoveshchenskiy Bridge." Efimov and Alekseyov stepped to the computer screen. The analyst pointed. "This is the bridge approximately twelve minutes ago," he said. "There, you see." He pointed to the moving vehicle. "It is driving without lights." The car disappeared from the screen. The analyst typed. "I picked it up again here, this time crossing the Betankura Bridge to Petrovsky Prospekt."

Efimov watched the vehicle navigate the snowy roundabout at Petrovskaya Square and head north across the Bolshoy Petrovsky Bridge to Krestovsky Island.

"This is where I lose them," the analyst said. "They appear to have driven into Primorskiy Park."

"Get a vehicle, whatever it takes," Efimov instructed Alekseyov as he moved for the door. "Mr. Jenkins likely planned to flee by boat. If so, he has learned that Neva Bay has frozen, as has much of the Gulf of Finland. Have every marina on Krestovsky searched. He is either waiting for the ice to thaw or for an alternative means out."

38

Jenkins took the lead, using his legs to cut a trail through the shin-deep snow, and his body to serve as a wind block for Paulina and Federov, though the wind had eased. Snowflakes now floated softly to the ground, like autumn leaves. Federov had broken off a tree limb to obscure their tracks but discarded it when he saw the depth to which Jenkins's boots sunk, and the trough each step created.

"I'd need a snowplow to obscure our tracks," he'd said.

With the decreased wind came a gray haze and eerie silence—no voices, not the hum of a car engine or a plane flying overhead. Behind Jenkins, Paulina's raspy breaths became more pronounced; she was clearly struggling, though she would not admit it. Air escaped her lips in bursts of white condensation, and her gaunt features and sickly appearance reminded Jenkins of the black-and-white photographs of the faces of Holocaust survivors—men and women horribly undernourished and underdressed. He suggested stopping, but she refused, telling him they were better staying in motion, that stopping would only make starting again more difficult.

When he could, Jenkins kept close to tree trunks, where their natural awnings reduced the snow depth. The burdened limbs also served to hide them and their tracks, were a police car to drive by in search of them.

"How much farther?" Federov asked, keeping his voice low. He complained of a splitting headache, but he had not thrown up or shown further signs of being concussed. He looked and sounded better.

"Not far," Jenkins said. He hoped he was right. He didn't actually know.

The cold burned in his chest with each breath, and he recalled reading, somewhere, that a person could permanently damage their lungs exercising in blistering cold air. Perhaps, but he was more concerned with the amount he was sweating and the possibility of their body temperatures dropping dangerously low and slipping into hypothermia.

Jenkins dropped to a knee at a tree line and considered the intersection ahead—the snow unmarked by tire tracks or shoeprints. A red stop sign and a yellow street sign protruded above the snow, like lollipops. Jenkins shifted his attention to a marina across the intersection, looking for any sign that someone else also watched it.

Federov knelt alongside him. "If the plan was to leave by boat . . ." He shook his head. "The arctic freeze has frozen the bay, Mr. Jenkins, and even if it had not, by now the naval base on Kotlin Island has been alerted to such an attempt."

Federov's concern was something Jenkins had already contemplated, but without his encrypted phone, confiscated at the railway station when he had been arrested, he had no way to transmit to Matt Lemore the success or failure of their efforts, or the weather problems they had encountered. He hoped his contact at the marina had done so and an alternative plan had been formulated.

"We move forward," Jenkins said.

"Yes," Federov said. "But to what?"

Jenkins stood and walked from the trees, trying to stay out of the glow of the streetlamps as he crossed the street. Paulina and Federov followed him past a clubhouse, its windows dark, the flags of various countries fluttering atop flagpoles. As he neared the marina, he could see lights outlining the piers. The bay looked like a block of ice, and the boats in the frozen slips varied in size and purpose—from small fishing boats and sailboats to much larger yachts. The marina, despite the freeze and the snow, emitted a briny smell.

"What are we looking for?" Paulina asked. She coughed, a deep, raspy bark.

Jenkins spoke as he walked. "*Seas the Day.*"

"Clever," Federov said, "but also a dubious sentiment, I am afraid."

Minutes later, Jenkins stopped at a trawler with the words "Seas the Day" across the stern in block letters. The hull was aluminum, painted black, and Jenkins estimated it exceeded forty feet, bow to stern. He walked the pier to the pilothouse, where a hint of light peeked out from between the blinds covering the window. Jenkins stepped down onto the deck and knocked three times on the cabin door.

A woman pulled open the door. Mid-to-late thirties with light-brown hair, she spoke heavily accented English. "It is much too late for a fishing trip."

"But hopefully not too late for a boat ride," Jenkins replied.

"You are very late." She stepped aside so they could enter.

Jenkins ducked down, then helped Paulina inside. Federov followed. The cabin was knotted oak stained with a hint of red, outfitted with a brown leather couch, ottoman, and chair, all atop a throw rug.

"We were delayed," Jenkins said.

The woman shut and locked the door. She had a youthful face but a serious demeanor and a muscular figure evident in navy-blue stretch pants and a white sweater. She stared at Federov. "I was told there would be two."

"Unforeseen change of plans," Jenkins said. "There is also a good chance we have been followed. How far they are behind us, I don't know."

Their contact looked from Federov to Jenkins. "You did not get the information?"

He shook his head. "I had my phone confiscated."

"Neva Bay is frozen. And the Russian Navy has been alerted to the possibility of your fleeing by boat." The woman had the television on, the volume low, a weather channel.

"Again, we made that assumption," Jenkins said. "I'm hoping alternative arrangements have been made."

Paulina coughed. To Jenkins her barking sounded like it was getting worse. The woman directed them to a folding table with sandwiches.

"I have made tea and sandwiches for you while we talk."

"You should try to eat something," Jenkins said to Paulina. "To regain your strength."

When Federov turned to the table, the woman removed a pistol from beneath a seat cushion and pressed the muzzle against the back of his head. "Do not move."

Jenkins raised his hands. "Whoa. Whoa. Take it easy."

Federov didn't flinch, though he raised his hands, half a sandwich in his left hand. "If you are going to shoot me, do so. Just don't hit me in the back of the head. Twice in one night is more than sufficient, I assure you."

"This man is an FSB agent," the woman said.

"Was," Jenkins said.

"That is irrelevant and not yet confirmed."

"He's the only reason we're here," Jenkins said. "The only reason I'm here."

She kept the muzzle to the back of Federov's head. "He cannot be trusted. There is too much at stake. Too many people working to get you out of Russia."

Jenkins considered the woman. "How do you know him?"

"I will say only that I am well familiar with Colonel Viktor Nikolayevich Federov, FSB in Moscow. As well as his colleague, Arkady Volkov."

Federov shrugged. "It seems my reputation precedes me."

"We don't have time for this," Jenkins said to the woman. "Whatever it is we are going to do, we need to do it, now."

"He does not go," the woman said, unrelenting. "Too many lives are at stake."

"Go," Federov said to Jenkins. "I will find my own way."

Jenkins turned to the woman. "He's not armed." Federov had lost his weapons in the confrontation with Efimov. "We bring him with us to keep him from telling anyone where we are going."

"I don't have to bring him with us. I can kill him and leave him here."

"Search him. If he has a transmitter, anything that would give away our location, kill him."

Jenkins looked to Federov, who shrugged.

The woman seemed to consider this, then quickly said, "Check his clothing. But be thorough."

Federov removed his clothing and Jenkins went through the Russian's pockets, the lining of his coat and his pants, then his shoes and socks, even his undergarments. Federov stood naked.

"Nothing," Jenkins said.

"Give me his phone," the woman said.

Jenkins did. The woman set it on the wood counter and smashed it with the butt of her gun. She combed through the pieces. Then she looked to Federov. "If you give me any reason, I will kill you. Are we clear?"

Federov looked to Jenkins. "How do your spies in American movies say it? . . . 'Crystal.' No?"

"Get dressed," the woman said. "We are already behind schedule. And it doesn't sound like we have time to spare." As Federov dressed, the woman said to Jenkins, "What size shoe do you wear?"

"Thirteen. Why?"

"Because we are going to need to walk." She turned to Federov, not about to reveal more. "I suggest we get moving."

—

Saint Petersburg police found the car abandoned beneath tree limbs in a grove in Primorskiy Park. They also found a path leading away from the car. Given the amount of snow that had partially filled the path, Efimov estimated they remained half an hour behind Jenkins, Ponomayova, and Federov. The trail led to a marina of boats moored in slips along three piers. Though the wind had eased, the weather remained numbingly cold. Efimov looked out at the falling snow and the frozen waters of Neva Bay. Further out, the lights in the homes and buildings of the naval base at Kronstadt glistened on Kotlin Island, and streetlights defined the road stretched atop the complex of dams and levees from one side of Neva Bay to the other. Construction of Kronstadt dam and its floodgates had been one of Putin's highest priorities—finally providing the city a defense against flooding, a persistent problem for centuries.

Had Mr. Jenkins intended to get out of Saint Petersburg by boat? Or had he only wanted Efimov to believe that had been his intent? Alekseyov said that during their earlier attempt to capture Jenkins he had provided copious amounts of misinformation, but this time there was a significant difference; this time Jenkins had Ponomayova with him, and her physical health had been compromised—perhaps Federov's as well from the blow Efimov had delivered. Jenkins could not move as quickly as he could alone, and how far he got and by what means would depend to a large extent on Ponomayova's health and the weather.

"Have the ships searched," Efimov instructed Alekseyov. "And the snow on the ice checked for bootprints."

Armed with high-powered flashlights, Alekseyov and a team of officers stepped from the pier onto the frozen water. After just minutes of searching, an officer called to Alekseyov and Efimov.

"Snowshoes." The officer swept the flashlight over the snow. "Someone tried to obscure the prints, but not good enough."

"How many people?" Efimov asked.

"At least three, possibly four," the agent said.

"You can follow the tracks?" Efimov asked.

"I can."

"Do so. We will follow."

39

The woman told Jenkins to call her Nadia, and she led them on snowshoes along frozen Neva Bay. Despite Jenkins's admonition, Nadia set a fast pace and slowed only upon his urging that Paulina had no chance to keep up. Nadia took a circular route, staying away from the marina parking lot and street. She hugged the shoreline before starting up a slope into a grove of trees, then cut a path back the direction they had come. It was important that they keep pace with her; only she knew their destination, and only she wore a headlamp, which she turned on as needed.

Snowflakes fluttered to the ground; sometimes the snowfall grew heavy. Jenkins hoped it would serve to cover their tracks. They walked single file to reduce their imprint, Paulina behind Nadia, then Federov and Jenkins. When instructing Jenkins to go last, Nadia had whispered, "If he gives you any reason, shoot him."

Jenkins shook his head. "If I shoot him on a night this quiet, that bullet will be the death of us all."

With each step his breath exploded in front of his face, and although the exertion warmed him, he knew that to be a double-edged sword. Jenkins already had trouble feeling the tips of his toes and his fingers, despite the woman giving him a pair of wool socks and winter gloves. The chill was wet, as in the winters on Camano Island, and it penetrated deep into his bones.

Paulina's coughing had worsened with exertion, and she looked wearier by the minute. She repeatedly assured Jenkins that she was fine, but Jenkins could see she was not herself. Nadia had given Paulina lozenges to reduce the frequency and severity of her coughing, and, potentially, giving away their position. She'd also provided Paulina with additional winter clothing, including a scarf.

"We don't have far," Nadia had told them when they set out. "Less than two kilometers."

Not far for her, Federov, or Jenkins, perhaps, but for a woman who had spent months in a hospital and then endured the brutality of Lefortovo, two kilometers would feel like a marathon.

In addition to watching Paulina, Jenkins kept his eye on Federov. Nadia had given him reason to doubt the former FSB officer, and Jenkins was unable to completely dismiss her reasoning, though he was here only because of Federov. The former FSB officer had once been dogged in his pursuit of Jenkins, and Jenkins had no doubt Federov would have shot and killed him if the need had arisen. What really had changed in the intervening months? Federov wasn't exactly motivated by altruism. He'd killed Carl Emerson and stole his money. And Jenkins hadn't given Federov much choice. He was holding the man's money and essentially blackmailing him. What if the woman was right? What if Federov still worked for the FSB, or hoped to again someday, and his goal was not to just bring in Jenkins and Paulina, but to use them as bait to take down an entire team of intelligence officers working with the United States? What if Federov had come back to the Moskovsky station to free Jenkins because it was more important for Jenkins to complete his mission and thereby expose the others involved? What if Efimov's blow to the back of Federov's head had been just another part of that ruse?

It did give Jenkins pause, but then he would go back to the chess games, and to the night he had given Federov the code to the Swiss bank account and the password. Federov could have taken the money and walked, but he had not done so. It wasn't about the money. It was about winning. It was about beating Efimov, and the agency that had made him a scapegoat.

At least, that's what Jenkins hoped.

As they started up another slope, Paulina wobbled, and before Jenkins could say anything or get to her, she went down in the snow. He hurried to where she had fallen and whistled once for Nadia, who turned and came back down the hill.

"Are you all right?" Jenkins asked Paulina, as he helped her to her feet.

She coughed, softening the sound by holding the scarf provided by Nadia tight to her lips. "I am all right," she said in between barks.

"We have to keep going," Nadia said. "Already we are behind schedule."

"Can you keep going?" Jenkins asked Paulina.

"There is no alternative." Paulina gave him a resigned smile. "Is there?"

"Get on my back," Federov said.

"What?" Paulina asked.

"You are right, there is no alternative. Not for any of us." He stepped around Jenkins and got in front of Paulina. "Now that I have been inside Lefortovo, I have no desire to go back. I'm sure you would agree. Get on my back."

"I'll carry her," Jenkins said.

"No," Federov said. "You cannot carry her. You need your hands free in case you need to shoot me." He looked to Nadia. Then he looked to Paulina. "Get on my back."

"How far do we have to go?" Jenkins asked Nadia.

"It is not far now. Less than a thousand meters."

"Come," Federov said. "We are wasting time. I used to cross-country ski with my daughters on my back, and you can't weigh much more than they did, I am afraid. Get on."

Jenkins helped Paulina climb onto Federov's back, but as they were about to depart, lights flashed between the trees.

Nadia whispered, "This way." She set out on a path away from the lights, just above the shore, then doubled back to a narrow road, an easement of some sort. She followed a slatted cyclone fence to what looked like an abandoned warehouse and knocked on a metal door next to a rolling bay door. A few seconds passed before a male voice responded and the door opened. They stepped inside to the smell of oil and petrol.

"Ya ozhida chto vy pridyote ran'she," the man said. *I expected you earlier.*

"Ikh zaderzhali," Nadia responded. *They were unavoidably detained.*

"There are four of you?" the man asked, continuing to speak Russian.

"Again, an unforeseen problem," Nadia said.

"Yes, it seems there are many unforeseen problems. There are police in the park. Many of them."

"They will follow their tracks to the marina," she said, "but it will not delay them long."

The man removed a tarp covering two snowmobiles. "You will have to double up," he said.

Jenkins knew that would be a problem, the question being who would ride with Federov.

"What about the noise?" Federov said. "It is quiet outside. The noise from a snowmobile will be heard for kilometers."

The man smiled. "Not these. These are four-stroke machines with the exhaust routed through the back to a muffler. I cannot make them silent, but this is as close as anyone could get."

"I'll put Paulina behind you," Jenkins said to Nadia. "Federov and I will ride together."

"Too much weight," the man said. "Better for you two to split up. The bay and gulf have frozen, but the ice has not been tested."

Federov couldn't very well sit behind Nadia, who had promised to shoot and leave him where he dropped. And Jenkins knew Nadia did not trust Federov to drive Paulina and possibly do something to get them caught.

"We leave him," Nadia said. "This is as far as you go, Colonel."

"We can't leave him here," Jenkins said.

"I'll ride with Colonel Federov," Paulina said.

"Out of the question," Nadia said.

"It is our only option," Paulina said.

"No. Our option is to leave him here."

"I can't drive this machine," Jenkins said, thinking quickly. "I've never even been on one, and I don't think Paulina is in any shape to drive even if she has been. Can you drive one of these?" Jenkins asked Federov.

"I grew up driving them," Federov said. "And fixing them. In the winter in Irkutsk, snowmobiles are a way of life."

Jenkins shrugged. "We need him if we're going to get out of here on two machines."

Nadia appeared to be chewing glass. "Then it looks like you are riding behind me, Mr. Jenkins."

The man went outside to search the area. He came back minutes later. "I did not see the police. For now, they are gone." He pulled on a chain, rolling up the bay door. Together they pushed the machines out of the garage. The man handed each of them a battered helmet with scratched visors. "Hug the shoreline. The ice will be thickest," he said. "I will obscure your tracks before I leave."

—

The officers followed the trail, Efimov pushing them to move faster. Whoever was leading Jenkins, Ponomayova, and Federov knew what he was doing. The footprints had doubled back several times, buying the fugitives precious minutes. Eventually, however, the tracks led down an easement alongside a cyclone fence, stopping well before a metal warehouse, the only building.

Efimov directed the officers to surround the warehouse. He found no windows, only a metal door and a rolling bay door padlocked to an eyelet in the ground. "Get something to break down the door or to cut the lock," Efimov said. While he waited, he stepped away, contemplating Jenkins's move.

"Why would they come here?" he asked, intending the question to be rhetorical. "What do they need most?"

"Transportation," Alekseyov said. "Do you—"

Efimov raised a hand, silencing the junior officer. For once he'd said something productive. Transportation. Efimov closed his eyes, mentally blocking out any familiar noise. He listened. There. A faint mechanical sound, what sounded like the hum of a distant chain saw. He recalled that sound, or something similar. It could have been petrol-powered generators, but there was nothing in the direction from which the noise had come, nothing but the frozen ships and Neva Bay.

A ship? Again, possible but not probable.

Transportation. Jenkins needed transportation.

Over the snow and the ice.

The thought clarified, sharp and clear. No ships could leave or enter the frozen bay. To get out by boat would require that they get farther out onto the Gulf of Finland. Efimov opened his eyes and looked at the frozen bay and the string of lights that linked Kotlin Island to the mainland.

"They're on snowmobiles," he said to Alekseyov. "They're trying to get past the dam. Get me someone from the Saint Petersburg . . . Someone who knows the dam. Then call the coast guard station in Saint Petersburg. Tell them we are in need of Berkuts." He referred to snowmobiles with heated cabins atop two skis and two caterpillar tracks. More importantly, Berkuts were armed with PKP Pecheneg machine guns. "Tell them to get out onto the bay and to patrol the area before the dam. Tell them to shoot anything that approaches."

40

They negotiated their way through the trees, leaving the natural cover only when necessary. Though the machines were quiet, as the man had said, they were not silent. In the stillness of the snowy night, with all other ambient sound absent, every noise was magnified. Each time the machines bogged down in the thick snow and the engines revved to keep them plowing forward, Jenkins feared the noise would be heard and recognized.

Still, what choice did they have?

With the snow continuing to fall and his visor fogging, it was difficult for Jenkins to see much of anything. They left the trees and came back to a field of snow. Neva Bay. Frozen and ringed by lights. Nadia got off the machine and removed a rock from her pocket. She smashed the headlight of her machine, then of the second machine.

"What are you doing?" Jenkins asked.

"We have to make time now, but we cannot run the machines with our headlights on. The lights will be visible for kilometers out on the ice."

"Federov will have no visibility running behind us," Jenkins said.

"Yes" was all Nadia said before she climbed back onto the machine and continued down the slope onto the snow and ice. She hugged the presumed coastline, traveling at roughly fifty kilometers per hour. Though on ice, the ride was far from smooth. The high winds brought by the storm had caused the waves to freeze, creating a rippling effect across the frozen surface. Though Nadia did her best to drive parallel with the ripples, it was not always possible, not while trying to make time. Jenkins felt like he was sitting on a jackhammer, the vibration sending shock waves of pain up his legs and along his lower back. He gripped the seat handholds on each side, but it did little to minimize the jarring. And holding the straps, even with gloves, not only strained his arms but caused blisters that soon burned.

It made Jenkins wonder how Paulina would have the strength to hold on. He didn't have to wonder long. Federov drove alongside them and made a slashing motion across his throat. Nadia slowed and stopped.

Federov flipped up his visor. "We have to slow down," he said, speaking Russian. "She is having trouble hanging on."

Jenkins looked to Paulina, her face hidden by the dark visor. She leaned against Federov's back. From the hunch in her shoulders, Jenkins knew she was weakening.

"We cannot slow down," Nadia said, adamant.

"Then give me your scarf," Federov said. "I will tie her to me. If I do not, she will not stay on."

The woman handed Federov her scarf and he tied it around Paulina's waist and his own.

"Try to stay parallel with the ripples," Jenkins said.

"I am trying, but the ski base is not wide enough."

"Better to endure the pain and make up the time," Nadia said.

They started again, and Jenkins noticed that Nadia reduced her speed, despite her admonition. Though she remained tight-lipped about their plans, likely to keep the details from Federov, Jenkins surmised the goal was to get past the series of levees and dams, though how far past, and for what purpose, he did not know. Snow rushed past his visor, becoming thicker the farther out they drove on the ice. He wasn't sure how Nadia could even see. Jenkins looked behind him, but Federov's snowmobile was almost completely obscured by the swirling snow.

As brutal as the weather made traveling, Jenkins knew it was also their ally. The frozen ice prevented the naval ships at Kronstadt from patrolling the gulf, or the bay, and the snow and the clouds provided cover from satellite technology, much like the heavy fog had protected Jenkins when he had crossed the Black Sea fleeing from Russia the first time. The Russians could not get helicopters in the air to search for them, at least he didn't think so.

Jenkins again looked behind them. He did not see Federov, and he wondered if the Russian had slowed, or stopped, if Paulina had fallen off the seat. He was about to tap Nadia on the shoulder when the front of Federov's machine materialized from the snowfall, like an insect struggling to keep from being swallowed alive.

Roughly forty-five minutes into their ride, with Jenkins's back tortured and his fingers numb and sore from gripping the handles, Nadia slowed. Jenkins used the reprieve to flex his back and his fingers, both painful. Federov drove his machine alongside them. Paulina remained slumped against his back.

Nadia flipped up her visor, unzipped her suit several inches, and pulled out night-vision goggles, holding them to her eyes.

"What are you looking for?" Jenkins asked.

She pulled their strap from around her helmet and pointed. "The sluice. Farthest to the right. The gate remains open. That's our way through to the other side."

Jenkins put the goggles to his eyes and, after a moment for his vision to adjust, he saw the dam and the streetlamps—a green hue—delineating the street across the levee. He scanned the bridge, then beneath it, and saw what appeared to be multiple openings, what he presumed to be the series of sluices of which Nadia spoke. He focused on the sluice farthest to the right. Though it was difficult to see detail, he did see light beneath the dam.

Their opening from the bay to the Gulf of Finland.

Jenkins continued searching, moving his focus to the landmass and following the string of streetlights to additional lights, which he quickly recognized to be something other than streetlamps. These lights were not a single string, but pairs, moving toward the levee.

Car headlights.

Efimov sat beside the engineer in the back seat of the black Mercedes, peppering him with questions as the car moved toward the levee as quickly as the weather allowed. Middle-aged, with thinning gray hair and round, wire-framed glasses, the engineer worked at the Saint Petersburg Flood-Prevention Facility—not that Alekseyov had found him there, not at this early hour. The engineer had been asleep in bed beside his wife at his Saint Petersburg home when the call came, and he still had the look of a man half asleep, and mostly uncertain of his expected function. He held a tablet in his lap, the screen open to a series of blueprints he was using to best answer Efimov's questions.

"The dam is just over twenty-five kilometers," he said. "It consists of eleven embankment dams, six sluices, and two navigation channels, each with floodgates."

"How do the channel floodgates work?" Efimov leaned across the seat to study the engineer's computer screen.

"This one swings closed, like a door. It shuts off the main navigation channels." The man used a simulation on his computer to demonstrate the floodgates swinging shut.

"And the other?" Efimov asked.

"The second channel is closed by a steel barrier that lowers and rises in a concrete slot."

"And what about in weather such as this, when the bay is frozen? Can the barrier still lower and raise?"

“The barrier can punch through the ice, no problem. But there would be no need tonight. The two channels have been closed because of the potential for strong winds blowing waves from the Gulf of Finland over the ice and into the bay, possibly inundating the city. This is a primary reason the dam was built.”

“And those two channels, those are the only ways in or out of the bay?”

“For a ship, yes.”

“Are there other channels?”

“No. Only the two. But there are six sluices that also open and close to control the flow of water into the bay. These are too small for a ship.”

“How do they open and close?”

“They, too, have gates that lower and raise, depending on the water surge.”

“Show me on the map,” Efimov said.

The man typed on his tablet and, a moment later, turned the screen to Efimov, showing him a blown-up detail of the diagram with the sluice gates opening and closing. “Here. You see? They are labeled B1 to B6.”

“And B6 is closest to this side?”

“Yes. The roadway we are on runs over the top.”

“How high above the water?”

“I don’t understand.”

“How high above the water is the roadway? Could a man of average height walk beneath it?”

“I’m not certain of the exact height. Do you want me—”

“No. Are the gates also closed?”

“I don’t know.”

“They don’t automatically close when the channel gates are closed?”

“Not necessarily, no.”

Efimov could not lose them here. If they got through the gates, they were a big step toward getting out of Russia, taking with them any chance he had at redemption.

"Call who you must. If the sluice gates are open, order them closed immediately."

—

Jenkins tapped Nadia's shoulder and handed her the night-vision goggles. He pointed to the road leading to the levee, and she quickly figured out what he had deduced. If there were cars out on a night such as this, it was purposeful.

Nadia stuffed the goggles into her suit. "We go. Now!"

Jenkins had just enough time to grip the seat handles before the woman hit the throttle and their machine shot forward. Behind him, Federov started his machine. Nadia, now intent on making it through the sluice gate, had increased her speed, magnifying the jackhammering. It was all Jenkins could do just to hang on.

As they approached the sluice, Jenkins turned and looked behind him. He did not see Federov's machine. Nadia increased her speed and momentarily took her hand from the handlebar to point at something on the bridge. When she did, they hit a spot where the waves had collided and frozen, leaving an icy speed bump. The left ski hit the bump and lifted from the ice. The machine tilted off balance. The woman quickly gripped the handle again, and Jenkins instinctively leaned to the left. The elevated ski dropped, hit the ice, and bounced. Jenkins was certain they would topple, but Nadia managed to somehow keep the machine upright.

Despite the near miss, Nadia did not decrease her speed. She kept the machine at full throttle, racing for the sluice. Jenkins no longer needed the goggles to see the soft light beneath the darkened solid portion of the bridge. As the machine neared the sluice, the gap beneath it appeared to narrow.

They were lowering the gate.

The woman ducked her head and shoulders to the height of the handlebars, and Jenkins did his best to mimic her movement. He held his breath, half expecting them to strike the closing gate and their bodies to shoot backward. In an instant they had emerged on the other side, the Gulf of Finland. The woman cut her speed and turned, angling the machine to look back to the sluice. Nadia handed Jenkins the goggles and he raised them and focused on the narrowing gap.

He did not see Federov.

The engineer disconnected his call. "The gates were open, but I have ordered them closed."

"How long does it take?" Efimov asked.

"Minutes."

"Are there cameras under the dam?"

"There are cameras, but not specifically under each sluice."

"Have any video in that area sent to you. I want to know if you can detect any snowmobiles approaching or passing under the bridge." Efimov tapped Alekseyov on the shoulder. "What is the status on the Berkuts?"

Alekseyov lowered the cell phone. "Two have left the coast guard base in Saint Petersburg and are en route to the dam."

"How far?"

"I am told thirty minutes."

"Radio the base and have them radio the Berkuts. Tell them to look for snowmobile tracks, specifically near the B6 sluice, but not at the expense of speed. Have they readied a helicopter and a pilot?"

"They say the weather makes it dangerous."

"I don't give a damn what they say. Order them to do it."

41

The sluice faded in and out of view as the snow flurries blew across Jenkins's field of vision. He shifted his focus to the string of lights approaching the dam. The cars neared. He returned his attention to the sluice.

"Come on. Come on," he whispered.

The gap narrowed. *Too small,* Jenkins thought. *It's too small to get under.*

Nadia must have come to the same conclusion. She throttled the machine and it lurched forward. Just as she did, the wind shifted, and Federov's snowmobile shot through the opening. For a brief, terrifying moment, Jenkins saw only the machine and feared Federov and Paulina had been knocked from it.

Then Federov sat up from behind the visor, but Jenkins could not see Paulina.

Nadia flashed her headlamp twice, to ensure Federov did not crash into them. He slowed alongside them. Paulina remained tied to Federov's back.

Nadia did not waste time talking or celebrating. She gunned the throttle, turned the sled north, and shot down the Gulf of Finland. This time, Federov kept the nose of his machine to the right of, and even with, the back of the lead machine. He clearly did not want to lose sight of them again.

Nadia drove for another ten to fifteen minutes before she eased back on the throttle. She removed the headlamp, clicking the beam of light on and off.

Jenkins flipped up his visor, about to speak into her helmet, when a light flashed farther out on the ice. The woman drove toward it. As they neared, a thin strip of land materialized, an island protruding above the ice. The woman slowed and cut through one of the concrete gaps surrounding the island, stopping the machine alongside a white prop plane on three skis, two in the front and one beneath the tail.

Doors on the plane opened beneath the wing, and two men stepped down onto the ice. Jenkins slid off the seat. His back hurt so much he had trouble straightening, and he could feel his gloves sticking to the palms of his hands.

Nadia removed her helmet and handed Jenkins a new encrypted phone, which he slid into his coat pocket. "You have your gun?"

He nodded and touched the grip.

"If Colonel Federov is going to do anything, this would be the time. Watch him closely, Mr. Jenkins, or we may all die." She walked toward the plane and the two approaching men.

Jenkins removed his helmet and placed it on the seat, then turned and looked at Federov, who was untying the scarf that had kept Paulina on the snowmobile. Paulina stood to get off, but her legs wobbled when she stood. Jenkins helped her remove her helmet, then lifted her from the seat. Federov had been correct. She weighed no more than a child.

Federov also looked stiff as he stood and removed his helmet. His facial expression conveyed that he was physically and emotionally spent.

"Weren't sure you were going to make it under that dam," Jenkins said.

Federov shook his head. "I, too, had my doubts. I could feel the gate scrape my back."

Jenkins looked at the two men talking with Nadia.

"No doubt they are discussing the unexpected passenger," Federov said.

Nadia waved them forward. "The pilot is concerned about the additional weight. It will make taking off more challenging, maybe too much."

"I found smooth ice behind the island coming in," the pilot said in unaccented English. "With the additional weight—I'm guessing you're two hundred pounds"—he spoke to Federov but did not wait for an answer—"we might not have a long enough strip of smooth ice, and if we hit those ripples before I can get airborne, it could be hell on those skis."

The pilot was no taller than Nadia—perhaps five foot eight and thin, even wearing a thick leather jacket, but there was something in the way he stood, the cocksure pattern of his speech—not to mention that he must have flown through some hairy shit to get the plane here, and he didn't look fazed. CIA, Jenkins thought, probably of very long standing. He looked older even than Jenkins—late sixties or early seventies. A fur-lined ushanka with earflaps covered his head.

"This is where we part, Mr. Jenkins," Nadia said. "The pilot will take you and Ms. Ponomayova where you need to go. This man and I will take the snowmobiles and draw anyone who may be following away from you. We will hide them further up the coast." She took out a gun and pointed it at Federov. The second man stepped behind Federov. He held zip ties. "Mr. Federov will come with us."

Jenkins shook his head. "You can't take him with you on the back of the snowmobile."

"Then we will leave him here for the FSB, or to freeze to death," she said. "It is your choice, Colonel Federov."

"If the FSB finds him, he will have every reason to disclose everything about our escape, including the help you provided," Jenkins said.

"Alive, that is true," Nadia said.

"He comes with us," Jenkins said.

"He jeopardizes your escape, Mr. Jenkins. My job is to see you and Ms. Ponomayova safely out of Russia, and you are, as of yet, far from out of Russia and far from safe."

"Shoot him or put him on the Goddamn plane," the pilot said. "I don't give a rat's ass which one, but it's got to be done now. I have no way to keep that engine warm, and if we wait any longer, I won't be able to start it, and then none of us is getting out of here."

"Tie his hands behind his back and put him on the plane," Jenkins said. "He can't do anything on the plane unless he has a death wish. When we land, we'll part."

Nadia shook her head. "This is my decision."

"We have to assume Efimov knows we escaped on snowmobiles and that our chances of getting out by ship are nonexistent," Jenkins said. "He will have helicopters and planes in the air as soon as the weather permits, maybe already."

"I agree. We're out of time," the pilot said, definitive. "And I have the type of forty-year background the Russians would dearly love to chat about over a cup of tea in Lubyanka, not to mention a young Finnish woman waiting for me to get home. Each is sufficient incentive for me to get on that plane and get the hell out of here, with or without any of you. If you're coming, I'm leaving. Now." He took Paulina by the arm and led her to the plane.

"Radio whoever you have to," Jenkins said to the woman. "Tell them this is my call. I take full responsibility."

Nadia nodded to the second man.

"Put your hands behind your back," the second man said to Federov, who complied. The man bound Federov's wrists together, then slipped a second zip tie through his belt and bound the tie to Federov's belt.

"I hope for your sake this is not a mistake," Nadia said.

Jenkins grabbed Federov by the bicep and hurried to the plane.

42

Jenkins ducked beneath the wing and looked in the open passenger door. The plane's interior was no larger than a compact car, with two bucket seats side by side—worn orange-and-white leather—and a bench seat across the back. It held a moldy smell, which was perhaps the reason the carpet had been ripped out from the floor, traces of glue and remnants of padding still visible.

Jenkins helped Paulina into the bench seat at the back of the plane.

"Put the man behind me," the pilot said to Jenkins. "You're so damned big you'll never get into the front seat without sliding it all the way back."

Jenkins snapped the buckle at Paulina's waist, much the same way he and Alex buckled Lizzie into her car seat. He adjusted the straps to remove slack, but they remained loose over Paulina's malnourished frame. She smiled as Jenkins cared for her, doing her best to convince him that she was all right, as tough as the woman he had first encountered in a Moscow hotel room. He didn't believe her.

Next, he helped Federov into the bench seat beside Paulina, also buckling him in. He would have cut the ties around Federov's wrists, but he didn't have a blade and, even if he did, he could not do it with the others still present and watching. Federov seemed to understand his circumstance and gave Jenkins a subtle nod, as if reading his mind.

Jenkins set the passenger seat as far back as it would go, then climbed in, ducking his head and pulling in his knees. The U-shaped handles of a yoke protruded between his thighs, and for a moment he thought he was in the wrong seat, then saw the second yoke to his left.

Jenkins felt like a giant on a miniature set. His head brushed the roof, his knees folded on each side of the yoke and pressed against the front panel. He picked up a headset hanging from the yoke and expanded it to fit comfortably on his head, then adjusted the microphone to just below his mouth.

The pilot finished sweeping the snow from the plane with a short broom, stowing it beneath the rear seat before he climbed in. He and Jenkins sat so close their shoulders touched. The man was pure concentration, flipping switches on the dash and going through his preflight routine. He flipped what Jenkins surmised to be the starter switch and slowly advanced the throttle. The propeller whined, made two or three revolutions, then died.

"As I feared," the pilot said, his voice a nasally, distant twang in the headset.

He went through the process a second time. The engine whined, the prop clicked, the blades rotated, and the engine coughed. Then it turned over. The pilot looked over at Jenkins, who felt a rush of relief, and smiled.

"What do I call you?" Jenkins asked.

The pilot continued his preflight check of the various gauges. He pulled the yoke toward him, then pushed it away. Then held out a hand to Jenkins. "Rod Studebaker. Like the car." Jenkins thought it sounded like a fake name. "Most call me Hot Rod."

"Also like the car?"

He grinned. A man who'd successfully set a trap. "Not when it's my girlfriend. She's two decades younger than me and looks it."

Jenkins smiled. "My wife is also."

Studebaker grinned. "Finally, a man who can speak my language."

"I have two kids. My son is nearly eleven, and my daughter is just about a year."

Hot Rod whistled. "You weren't fooling around. Looks like we both have an incentive to get the hell out of here and get back home," he said, which was exactly why Jenkins had brought up his family. "Hang on. It's about to get bumpy."

Studebaker waved to the man and woman on the ground before they hurried to the snowmobiles. The plane's blades rotated, and the noise in the cockpit increased.

"You can fly in this weather?" Jenkins asked over the headset.

"We're about to find out," Studebaker said, then shot Jenkins a mischievous grin. "Relax. I made it here, didn't I?"

Jenkins didn't relax.

Studebaker turned the tail of the plane and faced the propeller into the gusting wind, which caused the plane to shudder.

"Can we get off the ground with these headwinds?" Jenkins asked.

Studebaker quickly explained that the fast air bearing down on the plane's wings generated an upward force that would help to lift it. "And we're going to need all the help we can get with the additional weight. The smooth ice only extends behind the island. Then we hit the ripples."

"What happens when we hit the ripples?"

"We get rattled like the mother of all jackhammers, but hopefully nothing more."

Jenkins could relate after the snowmobile ride.

Studebaker throttled forward and pulled back on the yoke, then pushed it forward. The tail lifted and the plane gained speed, bouncing down the ice and sending additional shivers of pain up Jenkins's already tender spine. Studebaker swore under his breath—the way Jenkins's father used to when working on a project around the house, or on one of the cars.

The wind buffeted the plane, twisting it from side to side. They lifted, momentarily, then dropped back onto the ice. Another second and the plane lifted into the air three or four feet, but again bounced back onto the ice. The rattling changed, dramatically, like steel wheels driving over bumps and threatening to tear the plane apart. Jenkins tucked his chest to keep his head from pounding against the ceiling. Studebaker twisted the yoke left and right and got the plane airborne a third time. This time he did a slow turn to the right.

The plane jolted, as if something had reached up and hooked it, then twisted to the right. The yoke between Jenkins's legs jerked to the left just as the plane slammed back down onto the ice, causing Paulina to let out a scream. The plane kicked free, but with a horrific wrenching of metal. Something whipped past the window and hit just underneath the wing. Something else slammed into the back window, cracking the plastic.

To his right, Jenkins could see the front half of a broken ski dancing on the end of a bungee cord and smashing against the side of the plane and the bottom of the wing. It wrapped under the wing strut but continued to slap the bottom of the plane, making a sound like large rocks being dumped from a truck. When Jenkins turned his head to see what had happened to the back window, he noticed fluid streaming out the bottom of the wing.

This could not be good.

After determining that the gates on the sluice had not been closed quickly enough to prevent the snowmobiles from getting through, Efimov ordered the coast guard officers on the Berkuts to continue to track the snowmobiles. They eventually reported that the tracks led to the downwind side of Fort Totleben, the abandoned concrete fortification constructed on a spit of land once used to protect Russia against invasion. Efimov spoke to them through a dedicated line set up by the coast guard station.

"The snowmobile tracks continue up the coastline," the ranking officer said. "Four people, judging from the bootprints, boarded an airplane and took off into the wind."

Efimov swore under his breath.

"We have also found debris," the officer said.

"What kind of debris?" Efimov asked.

"It is part of a fiberglass ski that likely snapped off on takeoff, judging from where we located it."

Efimov felt suddenly buoyed. "Can you tell anything about the type of plane from the debris?" he asked.

"Not with any specificity. That is a better question for pilots."

"How many ski impressions did you find?"

"Three. Two in the front, likely beneath the wing, and one in the back under the tail. Probably a Cessna, but again that is a guess."

"So you're saying they repaired the ski before the plane took off?"

"Repaired? No. This likely occurred on takeoff, where pressure ridges pushed up the ice."

More good news. "Can the plane land without one of the skis?"

"Again, that's a question best answered by coast guard pilots, but I would think it would be very difficult, especially in these conditions."

"Do you have any estimate how far behind the plane we are?"

"Based on the depth of the snowfall within the tracks, I would estimate less than twenty minutes. I can't be more certain."

"You can still track the snowmobiles?"

"Of course. We've tracked in worse conditions."

"Do so, and radio in your findings." Efimov disconnected the call and turned to Alekseyov. "Call the coast guard station in Saint Petersburg and tell them to ready the helicopter. Tell them I want it armed."

"I think we're leaking fuel," Jenkins said.

Studebaker, still playing with gauges and manhandling the yoke, glanced briefly at the wing. Then he swore. "I'm switching to the right tank."

"That's the side that's leaking."

"And I need every bit of what gas I can get from it if we're going to make it back." Studebaker shrugged. "Fluid blowing in the wind looks a lot worse than it actually is."

Jenkins knew Studebaker was trying to calm him. "Do we have enough to get to wherever we're going?"

"I had about forty gallons when I landed—about two and a half hours of flying. Flying below the radar with the flaps down, I needed two hours to get here."

Jenkins asked again. "So we should have enough?"

This time Studebaker didn't try to appease him. "Maybe," he said. "Pray for a little tailwind."

Jenkins quickly did the math and deduced the problem. "Can we change how we fly?"

"Not if we want to avoid radar. Increased speed will also increase the amount of fuel we use. We're going to be on fumes as it is."

"What was it that shot by my window, a rock?"

"No. What went flying by your head was a portion of the right ski. I hit a pressure ridge with the ski when I banked. What you hear beating the hell out of the bottom of the plane is what remains of the tethered front ski."

Studebaker imparted the information so calmly, Jenkins wasn't sure he'd heard him correctly over the rattle and engine noise, but he'd seen the ski. Jenkins looked out at the strut where the ski used to be—now just a metal stake.

"Hell of a jolt," Studebaker said. "Thank God for the snow. We came down on the left ski and it slid long enough for me to straighten out. We damned near cartwheeled."

"Can you still fly the plane?"

"Flying isn't the problem. Landing is. We have a hunk of steel where the right ski used to be, which rules out landing on solid ground. If we drive that stake into the ground, we'll tear the plane apart."

"So how do we land?"

"I'm going to have to find smooth ice and keep us on the left ski as long as possible. Once I drop that right side that metal stake will dig in. Hopefully it only spins us. If we're lucky."

"And if we're not lucky?"

"We're going to roll over and crash. But at least we won't have any fuel by then."

"You always this positive?"

"You asked. I told you. Besides, no sense worrying about landing. We have enough problems just trying to fly."

Alekseyov's cell phone rang as the Mercedes drove into the Saint Petersburg coast guard detachment facility. He listened for a moment, then disconnected and turned to Efimov. "They have found the snowmobiles along the coastline. Abandoned."

Efimov had figured as much. "How many bootprints?" he asked.

"Two people."

Then the plane had not been intended as misinformation. The footprints indicated that four people boarded the plane—likely Jenkins, Ponomayova, Federov, and the pilot. If the helicopter could catch the plane, he would end this chase here and now.

Efimov stepped from the car and moved quickly through the coast guard facility. He was directed to two men sitting at tables inside a small room at the back of the building sipping bitter coffee, from the smell of it. Windows provided a view of a red-and-white helicopter on a concrete pad. Behind it, the sun peeked over the horizon, but only enough to lighten the dull gray. The men looked relaxed and comfortable. Efimov was about to change that.

"Who is the pilot?" Efimov asked.

"I am." The taller of the two stood. "Captain Yefremov, Nestor Ego." He looked to be early- to mid-forties with close-cropped red hair and freckles.

"You have readied a helicopter."

"Da."

"It is armed?"

"Da," he said again, though looking anything but certain.

"We are searching for a plane, likely headed to Finland. Have you been able to track anything on radar?"

"There is nothing on the radar," the second man said.

"How is that possible?" Efimov asked. "We have confirmation that a plane took off from the ice."

"It doesn't mean the plane is not out there," the man said. "A pilot seeking to avoid radar can skim the surface of the ice to avoid detection. And the falling snow causes radar clutter that can further mask the plane. But to do this, in these winds, would require an extremely skilled pilot. Most would not even attempt to fly. His altimeter would do him little good in these conditions, and one cannot visually detect the horizon in this severe a snowstorm. It would be very dangerous to fly at all, let alone so low to the ground."

"What type of plane could do such flying?"

"Many planes. Not many pilots," Yefremov said.

"I'm trying to understand how fast the pilot might be flying so we can determine how far behind them we are."

"It depends on the plane," Yefremov said, sounding more cautious.

"Then choose one and give me a damn estimate," Efimov snapped.

"In these conditions my choice would be a Cessna 185," the pilot said. "Such a plane can travel up to a hundred and thirty knots, but at the altitude the pilot would have to fly to avoid radar, he would have to do so with the plane flaps lowered to maintain control. That will slow their progress."

"How fast?" Efimov asked, growing impatient.

"A very good pilot could do no more than eighty to eighty-five knots."

"How long would it take for him to reach Finland traveling at that speed?"

The pilot took out a pen, doing some calculations on a notepad on the table. After less than a minute he said, "Two to two and a half hours."

Efimov considered this. They could catch the plane. "If the plane you have proposed snapped off a ski on takeoff, could the pilot still land?"

"Snapped off a ski?" Yefremov said.

"Could the plane land?"

The pilot shook his head. "It would be very difficult even for the most skilled pilot. I would have to say no."

Efimov moved to the window. "And your helicopter. How fast can it fly?"

"One hundred and fifty knots."

"Then we can intercept the plane."

"Theoretically," Yefremov said with a nervous smile, "but it would be crazy to fly in these conditions."

Efimov turned from the window, facing him. "You were instructed to have the helicopter armed and ready, were you not?"

"The helicopter is armed and ready, yes, but . . . the weather is not. It is too dangerous."

"But not for the pilot flying the Cessna?"

"The pilot in the plane . . . He's either crazy or he had no choice."

"Are you crazy?" Efimov asked.

"What? No."

"Then your answer is also clear."

—

Twenty minutes after takeoff, the plane's engine coughed, then sputtered. "That's the right tank burping," Studebaker said. "It's empty. I'm switching to the left tank."

The math doesn't work, Jenkins thought, again doing the numbers in his head. He almost said this, but Studebaker gave him a subtle shrug and headshake, as if to say, *There's nothing we can do about it now. Don't alarm the others.*

Jenkins quickly realized why Studebaker wasn't focused on landing; he had enough problems just staying airborne. Strong crosswinds caused the plane to pitch and bounce like a toy model, and they didn't have a lot of room to spare, flying so low, which Studebaker said was necessary to avoid Russian radar.

Jenkins turned and considered Paulina in the back seat. She looked cold. "Can we get a little heat in here?"

Hot Rod shook his head. "If we heat the windscreen with four of us breathing in here, it will take minutes to coat the inside with frost. And we wouldn't want to screw up this beautiful view any more than it already is."

With each bump and bounce the shoulder straps dug into Jenkins, adding to his growing list of ailments. He'd removed his gloves and noted a strip of red, raw skin across each palm where he'd gripped the straps on the snowmobile seat. Jenkins again looked to the back seat. As badly as he was getting tossed about, it was worse for Federov. With his hands tied behind his back, Federov had no ability to protect himself, and the Russian really couldn't afford a third blow to the head. Unfortunately, the unstable conditions made putting a knife to Federov's back to cut free his ties too dangerous an option. The Russian grimaced with each jolt and otherwise looked miserable.

With the snow whipping past the windscreen, and a white blanket covering the ground, Jenkins couldn't for the life of him figure out how Studebaker was keeping the plane airborne. The pilot kept his focus glued to a four-inch-by-six-inch screen in the center of the console, what Jenkins assumed to be the altimeter, and only occasionally diverted his eyes to what Studebaker called "the artificial horizon," a small plane superimposed on a line he said indicated if the plane was climbing or descending. Beyond that, Studebaker looked out the pilot-side window, his scanning routine relentless. Jenkins asked how Studebaker could even find Finland since he couldn't see three feet. Studebaker tapped on a GPS, explaining that it had tracked his trip into Russia and provided him a line to follow back to Finland.

"How're we doing?" Jenkins asked.

Studebaker checked gauges, while continuing to manhandle the yoke. "We're doing," he said.

"Will flying get any easier when the sun comes up?"

"Eventually, but we are flying west, away from the rising sun. If it doesn't stop snowing, the sun will only make everything a lighter shade of gray, or white. It won't provide me a horizon."

"What about the gas? Can we get to where we need to go?"

"Time will tell, but it's going to be close."

Jenkins looked about the console, for what, exactly, he wasn't sure. "Is there any radar onboard? Will we be able to tell if we're being followed?"

Studebaker shook his head.

"You think the weather might keep the Russians from following us?" Jenkins asked.

"It could, unless they can find a pilot with some brass cojones." Studebaker grinned.

"If they can, what can we expect? Can they catch us?"

"Depends on how much of a head start we got, and what they're flying. The Russian Coast Guard maintains a small detachment in Neva Bay and keeps helicopters on standby. If they're going to give chase, that's their best bet."

"And if they do?"

"They fly the MI-8, probably the highest production helicopter in the world. More recently they made an arctic modification to give it slightly more speed—one hundred and fifty knots. They could push it another ten knots or so, though not likely in this weather. Their advantage is an autopilot to keep them from accidentally losing altitude and slamming into the ice."

"Are those coast guard helicopters armed?"

Again, Studebaker shrugged. "Not normally. Normally they're used for search and rescue. But they can be."

"We don't know for certain."

"Not until they fire on us. Guns, though, not missiles." Studebaker looked over at Jenkins, as if that were good news. "I've been shot at more than once. I really hate holes appearing in my airplane."

"What about the Russian military?"

"The military doesn't keep helicopters on standby. And they wouldn't be able to scramble fast enough to keep us from reaching Finland."

Reading between the lines, Jenkins surmised that if Efimov acted quickly and ordered the coast guard helicopters armed, the plane could take machine-gun fire and never see it coming. Would the Russians risk the political fallout and fire on a Finnish plane? It might not matter—not if the plane didn't have sufficient fuel, and not if they crashed on landing.

"Sometimes you just have to cherish the minutes of safety you're given," Studebaker mumbled into the microphone. It sounded like the final words of a man staring down the barrel of a gun.

Jenkins looked behind him, to Federov, who was not wearing a headset and therefore had not heard any of their conversation. Federov grimaced with the turbulence. His back pain had to be excruciating. With the bindings on, he could only sit with his knees twisted toward

Paulina. Jenkins had left Federov's seat belt loose to accommodate the position.

Paulina had her eyes closed; her body slumped against Federov. She couldn't possibly be asleep, Jenkins thought, but then the alternative—like the plane's damaged ski and lack of sufficient fuel—was not something Jenkins wanted to fully consider. He shifted his gaze to Federov. The Russian tilted his head to look at Paulina, then looked at Jenkins. He'd had the same thought.

43

Simon Alekseyov sat strapped into one of the helicopter's seats, a row behind and to the right of Efimov, who sat directly behind the pilot, Yefremov, and the copilot. Neither looked thrilled to be there.

Nor was Alekseyov.

When Efimov had instructed Alekseyov to call the Russian Coast Guard and tell them to ready a helicopter, the young FSB officer never imagined he'd be on it. Even when they drove onto the base, Alekseyov thought they would wait there, with someone checking radar. But Efimov had never hesitated. He'd walked out the door beside the pilot as if walking to his fate, and not caring whether he lived or died. He stopped only to look back at Alekseyov, who had remained in the doorway.

"This is your case," Efimov had said. "Get on the helicopter."

As Alekseyov listened to the pilot quickly go through preflight checks, Efimov's four words sent shivers up and down his spine. *This is your case.*

Efimov was obsessed now—whether with catching Jenkins and Ponomayova or Viktor Federov, Alekseyov did not know, but like the fictional Captain Ahab and his quest to kill Moby Dick, Efimov's obsession would get them all killed, forcing the pilots to fly in these conditions. Even if Alekseyov lived, his career might not. The fact that Efimov had uttered those four words now, as Jenkins and Ponomayova neared Finland, was a sure sign Alekseyov would be the scapegoat if they failed to apprehend them. Alekseyov knew well what that meant. He'd witnessed it with the firing of Viktor Federov.

This is your case.

A head would roll. This time that head would be his.

If Efimov didn't kill him first.

As the pilot had warned, the weather conditions were abysmal. Crosswinds rattled and shook the helicopter, and the gusting snow had reduced visibility to next to nothing. What made this trip even more absurd was that the helicopter radar's limited range showed no trace of the Cessna. They had no way to even know its current position, where it was headed, or how to cut it off. Efimov had surmised that the plane was headed toward Finland, but he had no real basis for that to be the case. He was guessing, and hoping to get lucky.

Alekseyov had picked a seat a row behind Efimov rather than one directly across the aisle. He wanted to get out of Efimov's line of sight, if only for a few minutes.

"Anything?" Efimov again asked the copilot monitoring the radar.

The copilot turned and looked back at him. "Nothing." Another minute passed before the copilot spoke again. He raised a finger, listening intently. "I have something."

Efimov leaned forward, peering between the seats at the helicopter's instrument panel. The copilot pointed at a tiny screen. "There. You see? Now it is gone again."

"Someone attempting to evade radar?" Efimov asked.

"Possibly."

"Are there any other planes or helicopters in the air?"

"Not this far out. Not in this weather."

"Where did you see it?"

"Roughly one hundred thirty kilometers from the coast of Finland."

"How fast is it traveling?"

"Not fast. Under eighty knots."

Efimov sat back. He looked to be contemplating his strategy. After a moment he said, "Can you radio the plane?"

"We can broadcast over the Finnish emergency frequency," the copilot said. "In this weather, the pilot might be listening. We'll have no way of knowing if they've heard us, however."

"Do it."

Jenkins had likened the ride on the snowmobile to flying. Now he realized how wrong he had been. He'd also wrongly concluded that the snowmobile ride would be the most uncomfortable and terrifying of his life. That ride paled in comparison to flying into turbulent winds just fifty feet above the ice. As Studebaker had warned, the morning light had not tempered Jenkins's fear. It made it worse. The light gave him a better, but not necessarily wanted, perspective. Every so often a dark shape appeared in the windscreen, and Studebaker would jerk the plane up and to the right or to the left, past a ship frozen in the gulf or an island—some just rocks, some with structures. It was a sobering reminder of how small Studebaker's margin for error actually was.

More than once, Jenkins concluded that Paulina had the right idea, closing her eyes and putting her fate in Studebaker's hands, but he and Paulina were in far different positions. She had no family, no one she loved. Each time Jenkins closed his eyes, images of Alex and CJ and his baby girl, Lizzie, filled his mind, and all his fears of never again seeing them rushed back to haunt him.

So, he paid attention. Not that there was anything he could do. More than once he'd asked Studebaker if he could help—hold on to the yoke for a bit to give the man's wiry forearms a break. Each time Studebaker shook his head. "Just sit tight," he'd say. Then he'd burst out singing the Doors song "Light My Fire." Jenkins figured it was Studebaker's way of handling stress, but he could have done without the lyrics about setting the night on fire. He sincerely hoped that would not be the case.

Well past an hour into their flight, the winds remained fierce, though the snow had eased and eventually stopped. Jenkins kept sneaking glances at the fuel gauges, two side-by-side instruments with white needles and the words "Fuel Qty." The needle of the gauge on the right, which Jenkins knew to be empty, rested below the red line. The needle of the gauge on the left had started at just beneath the centerline and had since fallen to one line above the red mark. Jenkins did not know how much gas the tank held, or how much was left, and he didn't know if they had a tailwind or a headwind, or how far they still had to go.

Whenever he asked Studebaker about the gas, the pilot would tap the glass and respond, "We're going to be close," never being more definitive. Maybe he couldn't be. Maybe it was just as Studebaker had said. They'd know when they knew. Jenkins decided he'd just have to take the man at his word. Then Studebaker would start singing again about setting the night on fire.

Another ten minutes and Studebaker removed a hand from the yoke and pressed it to his headset. "We're getting a transmission across the Finnish emergency frequency," he said. "It's in Russian."

"Can you broadcast it so we can all hear it?" Jenkins asked.

Studebaker flipped a switch. Jenkins removed his headset.

"Viktor Federov, ty menya slyshish?" Viktor Federov, can you hear me?

Federov looked to Jenkins. "Efimov," he said over the sound of the plane engine and all the rattling.

"If you are listening, understand that you cannot get away. You will never be free. Your family will pay for your acts of treason. Turn yourself in. Do so and we will spare your family."

Federov paled. It was not like him.

"Sounds like they've given up," Studebaker said.

"Given up?" Jenkins asked.

"I'd say those are the idle threats of a man who has lost. *We'll punish your family.* Screw him," Studebaker said.

Efimov continued. "To the pilot of the Cessna airplane, you are transporting fugitives from the Russian government who are wanted for criminal acts. If you do not turn around immediately, you will be dealt with harshly."

"Like I give a shit," Studebaker said. For the first time since they started flying, he smiled. "Bring it on. Light my fire."

"Are you listening?" Efimov continued. "A Russian Coast Guard helicopter is quickly closing on your location one hundred and thirteen kilometers off the coast of Finland."

Studebaker lost the smile. "Son of a bitch. Maybe he isn't bluffing."

"The helicopter is armed and has received orders to fire upon you unless you immediately decrease your airspeed and turn your aircraft around. I repeat. You have invaded Russian airspace illegally and you are now transporting criminals who are guilty of crimes within Russia. Decrease your airspeed immediately and make a definitive move to return to Saint Petersburg or I will issue the order to fire upon your plane."

Studebaker flipped a switch, ending the communication. "We'll make a definitive move," he said. "Just not the one he's expecting."

"Did he get our location correct?" Jenkins asked.

Studebaker nodded. "Close enough, though we are no longer in Russian airspace."

"That doesn't mean he won't fire on us."

"No, it does not, but it does reduce the likelihood."

"I don't exactly like those odds."

"He might not even be back there. He might have caught a blip on Russian radar and is just trying to scare us."

"Can we find out somehow?" Jenkins asked.

"I was thinking the same thing." Studebaker put his headset back on, flipped a switch, and changed to a different radio channel. He entered a call sign, speaking Finnish. A woman responded, also in Finnish.

"Darling," Studebaker said in English. "Can you check radar and find out if there are any birds in the air near our location? One just threatened to put a load of lead up my ass. I just turned on my transponder."

Nearly a minute passed before the woman hailed him over the speaker.

"I'm still here," Studebaker said.

"On helikopteri, joka sulkeutuu nopeasti."

Studebaker looked to Jenkins. "I'll be damned. He wasn't lying. There's a helicopter, closing fast. *Kuinka kaukana?*" *How far?*

"Viisikymmentä mailia."

"Very good. I'll be home soon. Count on it." He flipped the switch and looked to Jenkins. "We're going to have to get lost for a bit." He spoke over his shoulder, to Federov. "Apparently your boy doesn't make idle threats. We got a helicopter on our butt and closing fast."

"How close?" Jenkins asked.

"Forty-eight kilometers. Time to make time."

"I thought you said that would use up more fuel?"

"Fuel won't matter if the guy flying that chopper can shoot straight. I'm going to gain some altitude so I can raise the flaps and get more speed."

"It could be a bluff. You said the coast guard didn't ordinarily arm its helicopters."

"Yes, but I was wrong once, and I don't plan to stick around and find out if I'm wrong again."

The Russian copilot spoke as he pointed to the screen. "There," he said. "He's back on radar."

Efimov leaned between the seats. "Can you mark his location?" He did not ask whether the plane had made a definitive move, not expecting that it would.

"No need," the man said. "He's gaining altitude to increase his speed."

"How long before we close on him?"

The pilot looked to his instruments. "Roughly twenty minutes. Maybe less."

"How long before he reaches the Finnish shore?"

"Also roughly twenty minutes."

"Do not allow that to happen."

The copilot turned, his look uncertain. "We'll be in Finnish airspace."

"The plane is transporting people who have committed crimes in Russia, has breached Russian airspace illegally, and is a threat to Russian national security. You have your orders. If he does not comply, shoot him down."

The copilot and pilot exchanged a glance.

Alekseyov shot out an arm, touching Efimov's shoulder. "We cannot fire on a Finnish plane in Finnish airspace," he said. "The fallout would be horrific, especially if the plane crashes into an occupied area and kills others."

Efimov glared at the young agent. This was the second time he had publicly questioned Efimov's authority. "It is not my intent for them to reach Finland," Efimov said.

"They are already in Finnish airspace. You heard the pilot. Let me call our resources in Finland and have them track where the plane lands."

Reluctantly, Efimov admitted Alekseyov was partially correct, and the suggestion wise. "If the plane lands, then you may alert our resources to track them down. Until then, I am giving the orders, and my job is to bring in Jenkins and Ponomayova. Barring that, I will kill them both."

"You said this was my case. You said ultimate responsibility falls to me."

"Yes," Efimov said. "And it will. Now remove your hand from my shoulder before I break it."

If the wind and the snow and the constant turbulence hadn't been enough to get Studebaker's blood pumping, the thought of Russian machine-gun fire did the trick. Jenkins watched the pilot transform into combat mode. He increased the plane's altitude and its airspeed to 120 knots, each of his movements quick and decisive. He no longer even considered fuel consumption. Jenkins, however, did. The needle of the fuel gauge had dropped into the red.

"Sweetheart, are you out there?" Studebaker said into the headset.

"Olen vielä täällä."

"You got a bead on the bad guys?"

"Thirty-two kilometers and closing," she said.

"I'm going to leave this frequency on. Keep me posted?"

"Joo," the woman said.

"How close do they need to be to fire?" Jenkins asked.

"Don't know. I told you, I don't like lead in my bird, and I'm not planning to give them the chance to use us as target practice."

For that, Jenkins was thankful. He had no doubt that if the plane had been armed, Studebaker would have made a U-turn and taken on the helicopter head-on. "How far are we from where we need to go?" he asked.

"Not close enough."

"How far?" Efimov asked the pilot, sensing that the plane was close to the Finnish coast and a possible place to attempt a landing.

"Thirty-two kilometers," the copilot said. "We're closing, though not as quickly. He has increased his speed."

"Then increase our speed," Efimov said.

The pilot shook his head. "We are in Finnish airspace."

"I don't care—"

"We are being hailed. They want to know our purpose."

"Ignore them," Efimov said.

"That would not be wise. If anything were to happen—" Alekseyov started.

Efimov cut him off. "If anything happens we will blame the plane, and the Americans. Do not interrupt me again." He spoke again to the pilot. "Respond to the Finnish traffic controllers. Tell them we are searching for two missing snow machines out on the ice," Efimov said. "But stay on the plane. And increase your airspeed."

—

"Kymmenen kilometriä," the woman said over the headset.

"The helicopter is within ten kilometers," Studebaker repeated in English to Jenkins. "Time to get lost again." He pushed the yoke forward and pointed the aircraft's nose at the ice. Jenkins's stomach flipped like when he'd been a kid riding one of the big roller coasters at Coney Island. What had been, a moment before, dark spots through the haze of light quickly became islands. He could see tree branches swaying in the wind, and boat docks and piers extending into the frozen water, even people in the windows of the housing tracts.

"We are passing Pikku Leikosaari," Studebaker said.

"Kahdeksan kilometriä," the woman said.

"Eight kilometers. It's going to be close."

Studebaker flew between the many islands, gaining altitude to fly over a bridge linking a larger island to a smaller one, then dropping again, this time so low Jenkins could almost reach out and touch the water's surface.

"Vissi kilometriä," the woman said.

"Five kilometers," Studebaker repeated. He pulled down his microphone and spoke to Federov in the back seat. "Your guy is a stubborn son of a bitch. What the hell did you do?"

—

The pilot shook his head. "He's dropped altitude again. He's trying to lose us in the islands."

"Stay on him," Efimov said.

"Traffic control is hailing us again."

"Ignore them."

"We are closing on populated islands," Alekseyov said.

"How far are we from shore?" Efimov asked.

"The islands are populated," Alekseyov said. "Did you not hear me?"

"How far?" Efimov asked the copilot again, ignoring Alekseyov.

"Eight kilometers," the copilot said.

"Increase our airspeed."

"I can't safely fly any faster in these winds."

"Increase our speed or I will see that you do not fly again."

The pilot and copilot exchanged another glance, then the pilot increased the helicopter's speed.

Alekseyov spoke again. "We cannot fire over a populated area."

Efimov turned quickly, grabbed Alekseyov by the lapels, and pulled him forward, nearly spitting the words as he spoke. "That is the last time you will question my decisions. Do it again and I will have you sweeping floors at Lubyanka." He shoved Alekseyov away from him. "The pilot cannot fly to a populated area. He cannot land on a solid surface. He is looking for a place to try to land on the ice, if he can find it. It's his only chance."

"Seven kilo—" The copilot abruptly stopped.

"What is it?" Efimov asked.

"He's off radar."

Efimov swore and gripped the back of the seat.

"What should we do?" the pilot asked.

"Stay on the same course and speed. See if we can visually spot him."

When they reached what Jenkins assumed to be the city of Helsinki, Studebaker changed the plane's course, this time to the northwest. Air traffic controllers, now aware of the rogue plane suddenly present on their radar and flying so close over a populated area, were screaming into their microphones, but Studebaker ignored them.

"Where are we headed?" Jenkins asked.

"Home," Studebaker said.

"I thought home was Helsinki?"

"Far too crowded for me. I like my space. Besides, we can't land in Helsinki. We have to land on ice," Studebaker said. Then he said, "Darling? Where are the bad guys?"

"Kahdeksan kilometriä. He ovat vähentäneet nopeuttaan."

"They've decreased their speed," Studebaker said.

"What does that mean?"

"It means we've evaded their radar but not them. They're still searching for us, or for a plane crash."

As Studebaker spoke, the plane shook, then shuddered. Jenkins thought it had been hit. "Relax, that's not machine-gun fire. It's the engine."

The engine coughed and spit, then caught again.

"And that's better?" Jenkins asked.

Studebaker played with the yoke, tilting the plane's wings back and forth, trying to tease as much gas as he could from the tank. "Tighten your straps," he said to all three of them. "This could get interesting."

The copilot held binoculars to his eyes, scanning between the islands. Efimov scanned out the right-side windows with a second set. After several minutes, the pilot said, "They're gone." He did not sound disappointed.

"Look for a plane crash," Efimov said. He lowered the binoculars and stared out the window for a moment, thinking. If the plane crashed, they should be able to see it. If not, then he needed to quickly turn his attention from the plane to the pilot. As the helicopter pilot had confirmed, there weren't many who would or could fly in these conditions, and he hoped Russian assets in Finland could reduce that list to just one or two. He turned to Alekseyov. "You wanted to alert our assets. Do so."

"With all due respect," Alekseyov said, "Finland has a couple hundred thousand lakes on which to land."

"Yes," Efimov said. "But very few pilots who could do so in these conditions and on one ski. Tell our assets we are looking for a pilot, most likely an American, with enough experience, expertise, and guts to do what this pilot has done and, presumably, what he is about to attempt. He is likely ex-military, likely CIA. Tell them I want the name of the pilot or pilots with such a reputation. Tell them to also put their ears to the ground and to advise of any small airplane crashes, and of any fatalities."

Turning back to the pilot, Efimov continued issuing orders. "Tell the Finnish authorities we have some kind of problem and need to land to fix it before resuming our search."

—

Studebaker never changed his demeanor. He flew as if he had a full tank of gas and three functional skis. He even had a small grin on his face, like this was just another challenge, something he had not yet done but was eager to try. Or maybe the pilot was just trying to appear confident, to reassure them things were going to be okay. Then again, what choice did he have? He had to land the plane. He could panic, start cursing a blue streak, but it wouldn't change what he had to do. He reminded Jenkins of a seasoned card player who'd been dealt a bad hand and was taking it as far as he could. He was either going to bluff his way through the hand, or he was going to lay down four aces and live to talk about the time he landed a Cessna with no fuel and missing one ski. People might not believe him. They might think Studebaker had made the story up. Jenkins doubted the man cared what others thought. Studebaker likely had a dozen stories of close calls better than this one.

At least Jenkins hoped he did.

They flew over the tops of houses, barns, industrial buildings, and barren streets. Studebaker again rocked the plane, determined to squeeze the wing for every drop of precious fuel. The engine coughed and sputtered, like a dying man in the final stages of life support.

"What are we looking for?" Jenkins asked.

Studebaker pointed to a clear, flat spot in the distance. "That," he said. "Lake Bodom."

The barren white patch looked no larger than a football field, though Jenkins hoped that was just a matter of distance and perspective. Snow-flocked barren trees and heavy brush surrounded what Jenkins suspected to be the frozen water's edge.

The engine coughed, this time a final gasp. The prop blades slowed, then stopped. So did the engine noise, the tranquility interrupted only by the persistent banging of the broken ski tethered to the bungee cord beneath the plane.

Studebaker pulled off the headset. He flipped switches and adjusted the plane's wing flaps. "When we land, I'm going to try to keep the plane on the left ski for as long as possible. Grab the yoke when I tell you but don't muscle it. Leave that to me. I want your strength to help hold it in place."

Again, Studebaker's voice showed no signs of alarm.

The nose of the plane lifted.

The wind whistled, and Jenkins realized Studebaker was, once again, flying into gusts to keep the plane aloft for as long as possible.

They closed in on the lake, flying over a multilane highway with the first cars of the morning. Jenkins could only imagine what those commuters were thinking, seeing the plane so low. Past the highway loomed the tops of white-flocked trees, then the roof of a red barn, so close Jenkins thought the two remaining skis would scrape it. They dropped lower, approaching the trees at the water's edge. Branches snapped and cracked beneath the plane.

"Everyone brace yourself," Studebaker said. Then he turned to Jenkins. "Grab the yoke."

Jenkins did so, just as the first ski hit the frozen surface. Studebaker tweaked the yoke to the left, and Jenkins let him do it, then held it in position, fighting the weight of the plane on the right side. The plane glided on the ice, bumping and bouncing.

Halfway across, as the plane reduced speed, physics took over and the right side dropped, like someone, or something, had snagged the wing with a grappling hook. The plane spun hard to the right, centrifugal force pushing them all to the left. The yoke yanked from Jenkins's grasp. His shoulder smashed into Studebaker. The plane spun a second time. The wing lifted on the left side. Jenkins pitched to the right, certain the plane was about to roll, but just as suddenly as the wing had lifted, it violently dropped.

The plane came to a jarring stop. So, too, did Jenkins. The force whiplashed him around the interior and he smacked his head against the top of the plane, momentarily seeing stars. His right shoulder ached like he'd smashed it against a concrete wall.

After a moment, Studebaker let out a sigh. Then he turned to Jenkins. The son of a bitch had a grin on his face. His eyes sparkled. "Just like we rehearsed it," he said. "Welcome to Finland, everybody."

Then he pushed open his door and started to sing "Light My Fire."

44

Jenkins briefly contemplated hiding the plane, but the barren lake didn't look to have any place to do so, and with Efimov in a helicopter close by, they didn't have time. Jenkins had no doubt Efimov would land and pursue them. They needed to keep going. They hiked from the plane, all of them moving a little slow, their bodies sore. Jenkins felt as if he'd been put in a blender and spun. Dizzy, he had trouble finding his balance. His back ached and his head throbbed from where he'd struck the ceiling of the Cessna, more than once. He had cut Federov from his bindings, and the man groaned as he stepped out of the plane, clutching his back. Together they helped Paulina. Remarkably, she seemed to be doing better than all of them, still weak, but relatively unscathed by the landing. She walked without assistance to a dirt-and-gravel road.

There, a woman got out of a beat-up, older model Chevy Suburban, greeting Studebaker with a kiss and a hug. She had to be six feet, a good four inches taller than Studebaker, blonde, with unblemished skin and a youthful demeanor that seemed incongruous with the BFR .450 Marlin revolver holstered at her hip. BFR, Jenkins knew, stood for Big Frame Revolver, though gun owners usually used a profanity instead of "Frame."

The gun was that and more.

The woman spoke Finnish. Jenkins couldn't understand a word, but from the grin on Studebaker's face, Jenkins surmised the pilot was telling her their adventure had been no big deal, and he was just fine. They climbed inside the Suburban, and Studebaker picked up another handgun from the passenger seat before he got in, a brushed-chrome Desert Eagle .50 caliber. Jenkins would hate to be the burglar who walked into their house uninvited.

Paulina sat in the back between Jenkins and Federov.

"I'm guessing this car isn't exactly inconspicuous, given its age," Jenkins said.

The woman made a U-turn and sped down the snow-covered road.

"No, but it will drive through just about anything nature has to offer, and trust me, that is the voice of experience," Studebaker said. "Besides, we don't plan to drive for long."

Studebaker rummaged through a black backpack between his feet, then passed it over the seat to Jenkins. "British passports for the two of you, euros, and food." He looked to Federov. "You weren't expected."

"No, I was not. Though I appreciate the ride, terrifying as it was. Drop me in a major city. I can find my way."

"Your FSB will have every asset in every Scandinavian country looking for the three of you."

"Yes," Federov said. "And three people are easier to find than one, which is why I am as anxious to be rid of you as you are of me. No offense, of course. Unlike you, Mr. Jenkins, if I am caught, there will be no trial for betraying my country. The only trial will be how much pain I can take before they shoot me in the head. This I do not wish to find out."

Jenkins handed Paulina a bottle of water and an energy bar. "Is there any place she can rest?" he asked Studebaker. "Even for a day."

"I'm fine," Paulina said. "I'm getting . . . how do you say . . . my wind again."

"Only in the car," Studebaker said. "We don't have time to stop. That helicopter will likely find the plane, and even if it can't, it won't be hard to find me."

"How would they find you?" Jenkins asked.

Federov answered, "They will look for pilots crazy enough to do what he just did. No offense."

"I can't think of anyone else," Studebaker said.

It made sense to Jenkins. "Will you be safe?" Jenkins asked Studebaker.

"As you may have gathered by now, I don't worry about the future or dwell in the past. I live in the here and now, and I never stick around to see what the future holds. Nea and I will get lost in Alaska. That's our second home. We'll come back when this dies down."

"Alaska? Not exactly snowbirds then, are you?" Jenkins said.

"We like the winter. Nea hunts, and she loves to pickle just about anything and everything she kills. Speaking of which, you all should eat and drink something. And when's the last time you slept?"

Jenkins couldn't remember the last time he had slept, but it had been many hours. He was running on empty, his thoughts becoming dull.

Studebaker checked his watch. "You've got a little time to do so now."

Efimov stood outside what amounted to a log cabin, a four-room home on the edge of a lake surrounded by trees, wilderness, and a lot of snow. The home was registered to a fifty-two-year-old woman, a Finnish national, Nea Kuosmanen, but according to FSB assets in Finland, a seventy-two-year-old American pilot, Rod Studebaker, also lived here. Studebaker had once worked for the CIA, and Efimov suspected he still did. The isolated log cabin was a good way to remain anonymous.

It took their Finnish assets little time to target Studebaker as the pilot most likely to have accepted the assignment—and the only pilot with the requisite skill, mental fortitude, and balls to have successfully completed it on one front ski.

FSB assets in Finland described Studebaker as so talented he "could shoe a flea." They also said Studebaker was *"Hullu." Crazy.* As Efimov had suspected, Studebaker had more than forty years of clandestine aviation for and on behalf of the CIA, flying military transport planes in Vietnam, which made Efimov wonder if Jenkins and Studebaker had served together, or at least previously knew one another, since Jenkins, too, had served in that American debacle. After Vietnam, Studebaker flew for Air America, the airline covertly owned and operated by the US government that had been used for CIA operations in Indochina.

Not that any of Studebaker's past mattered now.

Efimov walked through the rooms of the house after officers determined it had not been rigged with explosives or cameras. He didn't have to worry about nosy neighbors because there were none, at least none that could see the cabin. In a central room Efimov found a desk, numerous aviation maps, and equipment. He clicked the keys of a computer, but the screen remained black, likely programmed to wipe clean the drives. Efimov had no doubt that the computer had been open to a high-speed data link to a Finnish radar feed that had allowed Kuosmanen to communicate with Studebaker, which explained the plane's sudden evasive maneuvers as the helicopter closed ground.

The fact that neither Studebaker nor Kuosmanen were at the cabin was a further indication Studebaker had been the pilot, and relatively fresh tire tracks in front of the cabin indicated Kuosmanen had just recently left. Efimov also had assets searching for the downed plane, or for news of a light aircraft crash, which became less likely with each passing minute.

Efimov left the house and descended the porch steps to where Alekseyov talked on his phone. He covered the mouthpiece and spoke to Efimov. "They found the plane," he said.

"Where?"

"Close. It crash-landed on a lake approximately five kilometers southeast of here."

"Any bodies?"

"No. Multiple sets of footprints leading away from the plane to a dirt-and-gravel service road with fresh tire tracks."

Efimov turned and considered the tire tracks at the front of the cabin but spoke to Alekseyov. "Have someone measure the track width—the distance between the center of the left front and right front tires. Also have him measure the wheelbase—he'll have to estimate the center point of the front axle to the center point of the rear axle. I want it compared to the tracks left at the landing site. Also get photographs of the tire tread. I want to know the manufacturer, make, and model." He turned to another officer. "I need a map of the area where the plane landed. If they are driving, they have limited options with the freeze and will seek to move as quickly as possible to a large city with different transportation options."

Minutes later, Efimov analyzed a map on a laptop computer. "They are most likely headed for E18," he said. "Most likely to Turku."

"Why Turku?" Alekseyov asked.

"Turku is close and has multiple ferry crossings. It provides them the most options to flee. They can either drive on and drive off the ferry or walk on and walk off. Find out if the ferries are currently running. If so, provide me with the times of each crossing from each terminal." When Alekseyov made a face, Efimov said, "You have doubts?"

"The ferry seems too obvious a choice," he said.

"Because it is their only choice? If they intended to take another small plane it would have awaited them on the lake, or someplace nearby. It did not, because their original intent had been to leave Saint Petersburg by boat, not by plane. The sudden change in plans was fortuitous for them. It prevented us from scrambling military aircraft out of Kaliningrad." Efimov referred to the military base on the Baltic Sea between Lithuania and Poland established during the years of the Soviet

Union. Russia had steadfastly maintained the base and had recently fortified it to increase its imprint in the Baltic region.

Efimov continued. "Another plane is no longer an option. Mr. Jenkins or the pilot now know we are monitoring radar, and the weather has improved. They will not risk having a second plane diverted or shot down. A commercial flight is also not likely because of Ponomayova's health, and because she and Mr. Jenkins would be too easily identified. They cannot escape by private boat for the same reason they could not leave Neva Bay. Even if they could, the ice would make a crossing too dangerous. Train stations present the same problem as airports." He pointed to the map. "The most direct road from where the plane landed is E18, which travels from east to west to Turku and its ferry ports. I know of at least two departure points, one leaving from Naantali and the other from the Port of Turku."

"They could have driven somewhere to wait for the thaw—a cabin, or a hotel," Alekseyov said.

"You said yourself that Mr. Jenkins will keep moving, that he will not stop until he is safe." Efimov zoomed in on the map and tapped the computer screen. "I want to know how long it takes to drive from where the car picked them up to each ferry terminal. They will travel the speed limit so as not to attract attention."

Minutes later, an officer presented Efimov with a computer screen showing the various Turku ports and sailing times. There were two daily ferry sailings between the Port of Turku and Sweden, one operated by Tallink Silja and the other by Viking. There were also two daily crossings between Naantali and Kapellskär, but one ferry had sailed at 6:15 that morning. The other did not leave until 6:15 in the evening.

The officer continued typing. "The ferry reservation sites require the make and model of the vehicle, if it is to be driven on board, as well as the name of each passenger."

"Get officers to each terminal," Efimov said. "Tell them to book passage on each ferry. Tell them we will provide them with the potential makes and models of the SUV they are looking for, as well as the type of tires."

"They could change cars," Alekseyov said.

"If they believe we can track the car they are driving," Efimov said, "then they will, which is why I also want officers on board each ferry. Call Lubyanka. Have an analyst determine every vehicle that has booked a crossing for each terminal within the past six hours. Tell them to cross-reference each vehicle's track and wheelbase measurements with the measurements we obtain here and at the lake. If we can reduce the potential cars to one or two, we can confirm it by the tire, assuming Jenkins drives on board. If not, we are searching for two passengers, a man and a woman."

"What about Federov?" Alekseyov asked.

"Federov will go his own way. Given Ms. Ponomayova's physical condition, Jenkins will not be so fortunate. If we can detain them in Finland, we shall do so. Otherwise we will detain them on the ship. The crossing is fifteen hours."

45

The drive to Turku on the southwest coast of Finland took just under an hour and a half. They traveled most of that time in silence. Paulina had closed her eyes, and within minutes her head fell to the side, hitting Jenkins halfway up his torso. It reminded him of CJ falling asleep on the couch while they watched television together. Federov, too, slept, or at least he'd closed his eyes and slid down in his seat, putting his head back against the headrest. The driver, Nea, checked her mirrors frequently. Occasionally she glanced over at Studebaker, but the pilot had also given in to fatigue and shut his eyes. Jenkins, too, was exhausted, but he knew sleep would not come, not yet. He did not have the luxury. He needed to figure out a way to get out of Finland.

He typed on Nea's iPad as he considered Efimov's likely next move, and what moves he could make to counter him. It would not be easy. Their possible mode of transportation out of Finland was severely limited by both the weather and geography. The one viable option, the ferry, presented an array of possibilities—a total of about two dozen ferry crossings that would take more than nine different routes to four different ports in Sweden, as well as to the port in Travemünde, Germany. Jenkins was going through those options, determining which routes remained viable, and thinking of diversions and misinformation he could spread to increase their odds of escape.

He quickly decided that it wouldn't be enough.

Nea spoke, drawing Jenkins's attention. Studebaker awoke from his catnap and took a moment to get his bearings. They drove along a frozen river. Studebaker spoke Finnish while pointing to a parking lot. Nea turned into the lot, drove behind an industrial building, and parked at the far end, away from other cars.

Federov awoke as soon as the car slowed. Paulina did not wake until Studebaker spoke. "This is where we say goodbye, Mr. Federov."

Federov squinted at the bright winter sun reflecting on the ice of the frozen river. He cleared his throat, but his voice remained raspy. He had a heavy five-o'clock shadow and bloodshot eyes. "Then I thank you for the rides, interesting as they have been."

"Don't mention it. And I mean that, literally," Studebaker said without humor.

Federov smiled. "Yes. I'm sure you do."

"You going to be okay, Viktor?" Jenkins asked.

"I have many contacts, Mr. Jenkins, and many different ways to disappear. I am like the Hot Rod, here. I don't plan the future. I prefer to live it. Hopefully I will. Don't be surprised if one day I make it to Seattle for that toast we have talked so much about, but for the present, it is best that we do not communicate."

"I'll look forward to it," Jenkins said.

Federov pushed open the back door and stepped from the car. He shoved his hands inside his coat pockets and hunched his shoulders against the cold, leaning down to peer into the back seat. "Do not underestimate Efimov. He is the best for a reason, Mr. Jenkins, and he will not hesitate to kill you both if he cannot capture you alive."

Jenkins smiled. "I thought you were the best, Viktor."

"Yes. But now I am retired." Federov grinned and shut the door.

Paulina slid to Federov's seat as Nea backed from her parking spot and drove off.

"Can he be trusted?" Studebaker asked Jenkins.

Jenkins didn't truly know. Federov was an enigma. There was a time when Jenkins would have said about Federov what the former FSB officer had said about Efimov, that Federov would not have hesitated to shoot Charles Jenkins if he could not capture him alive. Had Federov truly changed? Or did he just want Jenkins to believe he had? Had he just been an FSB officer doing his job to the best of his ability?

One thing was certain. Jenkins had no intention of giving Federov an opportunity to prove him wrong. "Let's assume he can't be," Jenkins said in answer to Studebaker's question.

"I already have," Studebaker said.

Jenkins ran a hand over his face. The whiskers of his beard had grown long enough to be soft to the touch. "Efimov will know our only way out of Finland is by ferry. The ice makes a private boat too risky, even if we could get it out of port, which on first impressions it doesn't appear we can."

"And the temperature is not expected to warm for at least a couple of days," Studebaker confirmed.

"Any other options?"

"Dogsled and skis," Studebaker said, and Jenkins couldn't tell if he was joking or not. He studied the ferry schedules on the laptop.

"At first glance there appear to be five to six different ferry lines leaving from four different ports, but timing limits our options to three or four, at best. And I don't like those odds any more than I like the thought of getting trapped in Turku, somewhere close by, or being stuck at one of those ferry crossings."

"I don't either," Studebaker said. "We need to switch cars."

"Or use this one to our advantage," Jenkins said.

"I had a hunch you might say something like that."

Jenkins couldn't muster a smile. He didn't feel clever or smug. He remained anxious, knowing that Efimov was sitting someplace doing the same analysis, and coming to the same conclusions. Jenkins had one viable option and a handful of choices within that option. None of which he particularly liked. Each choice involved being stuck on a ferry for at least fifteen hours—more than enough time for the FSB to successfully hunt them down.

He needed to find a way to increase his odds by increasing his options. If he didn't, Efimov would surely counter, trapping Jenkins.

End of game.

He pulled out the encrypted phone to call Matt Lemore.

"I need a bottle of Tylenol and about ten hours of sleep. Can you make that happen?" he asked Studebaker.

"Not for a few days, I'm afraid."

46

A Lubyanka analyst provided Efimov with the short list of vehicles matching the track width and wheelbase of the car that had been parked at the cabin and at the lake. The dimensions at the two locations matched, not that the information came as a surprise. The analyst said the track width was 67 inches and the wheelbase 115 inches, which limited the potential vehicle options to an older model Chevy Suburban made between 1961 and 1965, and a Ford F-100 half-ton truck, the latter of which seemed unlikely if there had been four passengers on the plane. He'd also matched the tire tracks to a Nokian Hakkapeliitta studded LT3 225 75R16.

Lubyanka analysts further advised Efimov that within the past six hours, a reservation had been made for a man and a woman driving a Suburban that fit the description for passage on a Viking Line ferry leaving the Port of Turku at 5:10 that evening. Moments later, an analyst advised that a second reservation had also been made for a man and woman of a different name, but also driving a Suburban, seeking passage on a Tallink Silja ferry leaving the Port of Turku at 6:10 that evening. A third reservation had been made for a man and woman driving the same car onto a Finnlines ferry leaving Naantali at 6:20 p.m. During the next ten minutes, analysts determined that similar reservations had also been made on three ferry lines leaving Finland from all three ports early the following morning, as well as the ferry leaving from Vaasa, and two ferries leaving Helsinki.

Mr. Jenkins had thought through his choice of escape, recognized it as limited, and sought to increase his odds by playing another shell game with the SUV, hoping to again spread Efimov's resources as thin as possible. The car had become a prop.

Efimov whittled down the potential ferry options by the time each left port.

"The ferries leaving tomorrow are at present irrelevant," he told Alekseyov. "Based on his past patterns, Mr. Jenkins will seek to leave tonight, which means he has one of three ferry alternatives. I want four agents at each ferry, two to watch the cars boarding and two to watch the passengers walking on board. You and I will focus on the ferry leaving tonight from Naantali."

At 6:15 p.m., Efimov had received word from FSB officers searching the Viking Line ferry leaving the Port of Turku at 5:10 p.m., and from officers watching the Tallink Silja ferry leaving the port at 6:10 p.m. An older Suburban had not driven onto either ferry, nor had Jenkins or Ponomayova been spotted walking on. Efimov left orders that two officers remain on ship for each crossing, in case Jenkins and Ponomayova were again wearing disguises.

With the sun now a fiery red and setting behind Finland's many islands, Efimov directed his binoculars to the tail end of the line of cars loading onto the Finnlines ferry, a line he had dutifully checked since boarding began. This time, however, he watched an older model Chevy Suburban drive to the back of the line. Pale blue with a white hardtop, the vehicle had dents and patches of rust, indicating it to be well used. The windows had also been tinted, clearly not a standard option in the 1960s. Efimov focused his binoculars on the windshield, but the glare of the sun off the glass made it difficult to identify the driver or the passenger with any degree of certainty.

Efimov may have just gotten lucky; Jenkins might not have considered the possibility that they could identify the car from the tracks left in the snow. He lowered his binoculars and quickly moved to the ferry's metal door leading down to the car deck. Alekseyov followed, and their descending footsteps echoed with the footsteps of passengers ascending the staircase. When he reached the lower car deck, Efimov pushed open the ferry door into a cold breeze and stepped onto a deck that smelled of diesel fumes. A crew member in an orange vest directed the Suburban to park at the back of the car deck, then set an orange cone behind the rear bumper.

Efimov moved quickly between the cars, coming up behind the Suburban on the driver's side, keeping his gun low, and watching the car's side mirror as he approached. Alekseyov approached the passenger side doing the same. When Efimov reached the rear bumper, both car doors opened simultaneously. A man stepped down from behind the wheel. Short and fit, he matched the photograph of Rod Studebaker sent to Efimov's phone. Efimov assumed the woman stepping from the passenger side to be Nea Kuosmanen. She walked around the hood of the vehicle to where Studebaker stood smiling, his eyes glancing at the gun at Efimov's side. He looked like an elf, especially next to the much-taller woman.

"Mr. Studebaker, I presume," Efimov said.

"Do we know one another?" Studebaker asked. "I'm detecting a Russian accent."

"Let us not play games and pretend we do not know one another, Mr. Studebaker. You are the pilot who flew Mr. Jenkins and Ms. Ponomayova from Saint Petersburg to the lake in Finland."

"Flew them? First, I'm retired. Second, have you seen the recent weather reports? A pilot would have to be crazy to fly in weather like this."

"Perhaps," Efimov said. He didn't have time to debate it. The ship would depart in minutes. "Where are Mr. Jenkins and Ms. Ponomayova?"

"I'm afraid I don't recognize either name." He turned to Kuosmanen. *"Tunnetko nuo nimet, kultaseni?" Do you recognize those names, darling?*

She shook her head. *"Ei." No.*

"Who are they?" Studebaker asked.

"Would you mind if we searched your car?" Efimov said.

"Ordinarily I would. But I'm feeling cooperative. Have at it. The doors are unlocked."

Efimov motioned for Alekseyov to search the car, though it was now a formality. He was certain Jenkins had considered that the car could be identified and had used it as bait. The young officer pulled open the back door and searched the interior. Efimov stared at Studebaker, who returned his gaze. Alekseyov stepped down and shut the door with a thud. He shook his head.

Efimov directed his attention back to Studebaker. "I ask again. Where are Mr. Jenkins and Ms. Ponomayova?"

"And I'll tell you again. I don't recognize those names. But let's assume, just for the moment, and only to appease you, that I did recognize them. Do you think this Mr. Jenkins fellow would be stupid enough to tell me anything?"

"You violated Russian airspace and illegally transported criminals wanted by the Russian government out of Russia. These are serious offenses, Mr. Studebaker, and carry harsh penalties."

"Prove it."

"Perhaps I will prove it while you wait in Lefortovo."

"Is that a threat?"

"Consider it as you wish. We can place your car and your tire tracks at a road by the lake on which you landed your Cessna 185."

"Can you? Those are studded Nokian Hakkapeliitta tires, which I think you'll find to be quite popular in the winter here in Finland.

And I no longer own a Cessna 185. As I said, I'm retired. Third, I don't like your tone. So I'm going to consider what you said to be a threat. And the way I see it, it's like this: I'm a Finnish citizen on a ferry seeking to vacation in Sweden with my Finnish girlfriend. Oh, and did I say your gun doesn't impress me?" Studebaker pulled back his coat, revealing a large firearm holstered to his side. Kuosmanen did the same. "I've been threatened by people a lot worse than you. So, unless your intent is to start an international incident, and explain to a Finnish court what you're doing on a Finnish ferry making threats to Finnish citizens, I'd get off this ship, while I still could." Studebaker looked at his watch. "In my experience Finnish ferry captains are obsessed with punctuality, which leaves you about two minutes to make up your mind. Otherwise, you have a fifteen-hour ride ahead of you. In which case, I hope you booked a sleeping compartment. Sitting up all night in those chairs can get mighty uncomfortable."

47

Charles Jenkins stepped inside what looked like a college dorm room on the C deck of the large container ship. Immediately to his right was a small bathroom. Chief Mate Martin Bantle pulled open an accordion door on the left, revealing an empty closet, then considered the unkempt appearances of both Jenkins and Paulina. "I'll get you both a change of clothes."

The rest of the room consisted of two beds, a desk and computer screen below a window, a small fridge, and some cabinets. Jenkins looked out the porthole to the deck.

"I'll also get you some toiletries from the store," Bantle said. He checked his watch. "The mess hall is on the A deck, but it won't be open until morning. I'll have some food brought to your room." He looked to Paulina. "There's a medical office on the F deck, but I've asked the doctor to come by your cabin and check on you both."

"Thanks," Jenkins said.

Bantle nodded. "We have three port stops before we head for home. The first is Gdańsk, Poland. The second is Aarhus, Denmark, and the third is Drammen, Norway. That's eight days before we're headed to Virginia." He looked to Jenkins. "If any of the crew members ask, you work for maritime safety and are performing a routine audit. That should be enough to make you radioactive, but don't worry about it too much; the crew are all American citizens, which is mandated to work on a US-flagged ship transporting goods for a government contractor. They've been through this drill before. They'll keep their heads down and won't ask questions."

Jenkins thanked Bantle, who inquired whether they needed anything else before leaving them.

Jenkins knew from his conversation with Matt Lemore that the shipping company was headquartered in Virginia. It provided shipping and transport services for the US government and US government contractors throughout the world. Jenkins would have preferred a ship taking a direct route from the port at Rauma, Finland, to Seattle, but beggars couldn't be choosy. He was just glad to be heading in the right direction and for the chance to recoup and recover. Paulina needed both, as well as medical attention.

The encrypted phone rang. Jenkins fished it from his coat pocket.

"I take it you're not in a Russian prison," Rod Studebaker said.

"I was going to ask you the same question."

"Sitting in our cabin aboard ship enjoying a good bottle of Lakka and the view."

"Any problems?"

Studebaker described his encounter with Efimov. "He doesn't sound like he's ready to give up just yet. Keep your eyes and your ears open."

"You do the same. And thanks again for the help."

"No worries. I'm paid well, and I'm banking it. Nea's hoping I'll retire."

"Yeah. You going to?"

"Let me put it this way . . . I've been on this ship for less than an hour, and I'm already antsy and looking for something to do. It confirms I'm not the cruise ship type."

"I could have told you that."

Studebaker laughed. "I'll see what comes along. Retirement? I don't think I got that in me, though I certainly have a very good reason, and that reason just stepped from the shower in nothing but a small towel."

Jenkins smiled, thinking of Alex. "That's my cue to say goodbye. If you're ever in Seattle, look me up. I owe you."

"Buy me a steak dinner and we'll call it good."

"I'll do that." Jenkins disconnected and set down the phone.

"They are safe?" Paulina sat on her bed across the room.

Jenkins explained what Studebaker had told him of his confrontation with Efimov on the ferryboat.

"He has much at stake if he fails. We will need to be guarded."

Jenkins agreed. "Why don't you use the shower before the food and fresh clothing arrive?"

"I'm not sure I will get out from under the water," she said, smiling. Just a few minutes on the ship, and already Paulina showed glimpses of the tough, defiant woman he had first encountered in Moscow. "I can't recall the last time I took a warm shower."

"Take as long as you need," Jenkins said. "I'm going to get on the computer for a bit, then call home."

Paulina stood from the bed and started for the bathroom. She stopped after a few steps. "Your daughter's name?"

Jenkins nodded. "Elizabeth Paulina. Elizabeth was my mother's name."

"I feel it is a great honor."

"So did I," Jenkins said. "Naming my daughter after you was a way to remember the sacrifice you made so I could see her birth."

"I did so willingly."

"That's what made it a sacrifice," he said.

She gave him a thin smile. "I should like to meet your daughter, and your wife and son."

"You will."

"For years I was a woman without a family, without a home, without even a country. All I had was my routine each day to keep me busy. Now no longer that."

Paulina looked worried, and Jenkins knew what she was going through. When he left the CIA those many years ago and returned to Camano Island, he got up every day wondering how he'd keep himself busy. "I understand," Jenkins said. "I know it can be overwhelming to think about, but I can provide you with the first three, and we'll find you a new routine to keep you busy."

Paulina wiped at tears. "Why would you do this, Charlie? This I do not understand."

Jenkins thought of Studebaker's comment that he'd go stir-crazy standing on the deck of a cruise ship waiting to die. He wondered if that was the reason for Nea Kuosmanen, because she made an old man feel young. He knew people thought the same thing about him and Alex. Studebaker had also said he didn't like to think about the future too much—not because he feared it; Jenkins doubted there was much that struck fear in "Hot Rod" Studebaker. The pilot had served in Vietnam and that meant Studebaker knew, as did Jenkins, what it was like to get up each morning and wonder if it would be his last day on earth. After a while you stopped wondering. Then you stopped caring. You figured what was to be was already written, already a part of God's plan, and there wasn't much reason to worry since there wasn't a damn thing you or anyone else could do to change it.

So you learned to live in the present, much like the Buddhists.

"It's the right thing to do," he said.

48

Alekseyov sat in Efimov's office in Lubyanka listening to Efimov's telephone conversation with the deputy director. Though only privy to Efimov's side of the conversation, Alekseyov could tell it was not going well. Dmitry Sokalov was not happy, and Efimov was taking the brunt of that anger. But Alekseyov knew he, not Efimov, would ultimately be deemed responsible for losing Jenkins and Ponomayova, and it was his head that would roll.

This is your case.

Efimov had elected to return to Lubyanka rather than remain in Finland. He had analysts searching for other options Jenkins could have taken out of Finland, and scouring what camera footage they could obtain to detect where Jenkins and Ponomayova had parted company with Studebaker. Efimov was clearly trying to convince the deputy director that the chase was not yet over.

"An analyst has confirmed that a United States cargo ship sailed under a US flag from the Port of Rauma at roughly the same time as the last of the car and passenger ferries," Efimov said. "Satellite footage of the Port of Rauma showed the Suburban arriving at the shipyard and two persons exiting the vehicle and boarding the ship."

Alekseyov had obtained the ship's European ports-of-call schedule, and Efimov now provided Sokalov with that information, though for what purpose Alekseyov did not yet know.

"I believe the best option is to get someone on board when the ship is in port in Gdańsk to load and offload cargo," Efimov said. He looked tired, frustrated, and angry. He listened for another moment, then said, "I do." Another pause. Alekseyov could hear Sokalov's voice coming through the speaker, though not well enough to understand anything being said.

Efimov's free hand flexed repeatedly. "No, of course not." Efimov sat back. "Because Mr. Jenkins and Ms. Ponomayova need to remain alive until the ship reaches Aarhus. This man will disembark and be gone before they show signs of illness."

Signs of illness?

Again, Efimov listened to the deputy director. "No. He has no connection to any agency or any person. Very dependable. *Da*," he said. After several more seconds, Efimov hung up, though it was clear the deputy director had done so first.

"You are talking about a poison?" Alekseyov said.

Efimov did not respond.

Alekseyov sat forward. "If what you are suggesting is a radioactive poison, as in London, do we not risk potentially contaminating the entire ship and putting all of the crew at risk?"

"You said it was a US-flagged ship operating on behalf of the US government. Did you not?"

"All the more reason—"

"And this ship has allowed two individuals guilty of criminal acts in Russia to board their vessel? Do you think they boarded without the crew's knowledge?"

"No, but . . . There are innocent men and women on board. This could create an international incident that would reflect poorly on the Kremlin, and President Putin."

"It seems, Simon, that you have lost your nerve," Efimov said.

"And it seems that you have become desperate, and potentially careless." Alekseyov realized that what he had just said could be career threatening, but he no longer cared. He was convinced that Efimov had become obsessed, and his obsession was leading to more and more irrational decisions. But it was Alekseyov who wore the large bull's-eye on his chest. "You have said this matter was to be handled discreetly, so as not to attract unnecessary attention . . . or blame."

"This is your case, Simon."

"If it is my case, then why is this not my decision?" Alekseyov shot back.

Efimov sat back in his chair. "Please. Do you have an alternative?"

No words came to him.

"Please. Enlighten me," Efimov said. "I will call back the deputy director . . . or perhaps I should call the president, and you can tell him of your plans?"

Alekseyov sat back in the chair, lightheaded and sick to his stomach and uncertain what he might do, but certain he would not be held responsible for what Efimov had just proposed, for the deaths of innocent crew members.

—

Arkady Volkov stopped chewing in midbite, a highly unusual occurrence, especially when eating his wife's golubsti. Yekatarina mixed lean pork with cabbage, then covered the roll with a light sauce of white wine and tomatoes. When his wife made golubsti, Volkov could smell the cabbage as soon as he stepped from the elevator, which only teased his hunger. Volkov looked across the table. Yekatarina, too, looked to have frozen, her fork in one hand, knife in the other. She, too, had heard the knock on the door. Visitors were rare in the Volkov home, but nonexistent during the dinner hour, which remained sacrosanct in Russia, often the only time families sat down together to discuss their day.

Volkov looked at his watch, then set down his utensils. He wiped the corners of his mouth with the napkin in his lap and set it on the table.

"Are you expecting anyone?" Yekatarina asked.

He shook his head. "*Nyet.* Are you?"

"*Nyet.*"

"Let me get rid of whoever it is."

At the front door Volkov looked through the peephole. Simon Alekseyov stood in the hallway looking left and right, like a cat expecting a dog to come around the corner at any moment. The young FSB officer had never been to Volkov's home. In fact, in all the years that Volkov and Viktor Federov had worked together, Federov had never been to Volkov's home.

Volkov pulled open the door. Alekseyov turned at the sound. "Arkady."

"Simon?"

Alekseyov looked flushed. Beads of perspiration glistened on his forehead and above his upper lip. He'd pulled down the knot of his tie and unbuttoned the collar of his shirt. His winter coat looked as if it weighed on him. "I'm sorry to disturb you at your home, Arkady, but may we talk?" He spoke in a hushed tone. His breath reeked of alcohol but he did not look drunk. He looked scared.

"*Da.*" Volkov stepped aside and the young officer quickly ducked inside. Volkov shut the door and followed Alekseyov down the hall. Alekseyov greeted Yekatarina, who stood in the doorframe between the living room and dining room.

"Good evening, Mrs. Volkov. I am sorry for disturbing your dinner. Cabbage rolls," he said, smelling the air. "My mother used to make them. Forgive me. We have not met. I am Simon Alekseyov. I work with your husband."

"Would you care for a plate? Have you eaten?"

"No, thank you. It is very kind of you to offer, but I don't wish to be long. I just need a moment of Arkady's time."

Yekatarina looked at Volkov with the same expression as when Volkov told her he could not discuss the details of his day—her mouth pinched and eyebrows raised. Sensing what Alekseyov wished to discuss to be sensitive, Volkov told Yekatarina he would be just a minute and gently eased her into the dining room, then slid closed the dining room doors. The two men moved into the living room of the two-bedroom apartment. At the radio, Volkov switched on music, a classical station. When he turned to face Alekseyov, the young officer held up a piece of paper. On it he had scribbled:

Is it safe to talk here?

Volkov nodded but increased the radio volume and lowered his voice. "What is it, Simon?"

"Do you have a way to get in contact with Viktor Federov?" Alekseyov asked in a hushed whisper.

Uncertain of the reason for Alekseyov's question, Volkov displayed no reaction. Inside, however, his stomach and his mind churned. "No," he said. "Why do you ask?"

"Something is going to happen . . . Something wrong."

Volkov gestured. "Why don't you sit down and tell me what is going to happen. Can I get you something to drink?"

Alekseyov shook his head and collapsed onto the floral sofa. Volkov sat in the chair his wife had reupholstered and pulled it close. For the next ten minutes Alekseyov leaned over his knees, speaking in a hoarse whisper and occasionally glancing at the closed dining room doors. Then he said, "I realize that I am taking a chance coming to you, Arkady. But I have a sense that you would agree with me, that Efimov is obsessed and he is using a sledgehammer to crack a nut. When it goes wrong, I will be the next Viktor Federov. Perhaps you as well."

Volkov sat back, trying to assess Alekseyov. The young officer looked spooked, but was he sincere? Or was it an act to trip up Volkov and get him to admit that he had known all along that Viktor Federov was Sergei Vasilyev, and that he had not just allowed Federov to escape, but that he had divulged to Federov information on Jenkins and Paulina's escape to Saint Petersburg and the agency's knowledge of their subterfuge and the trap they had set there?

"What is it that you want from me, Simon?"

Alekseyov sat back. He now looked worried, as if he were no longer certain he had read this situation correctly. His voice took on a more cautious tone. "I don't know, Arkady, I thought that, perhaps, if you had a way to get in touch with Federov . . . perhaps you could . . . that he might . . ." Alekseyov shook his head and sighed, a deep exhale he looked to have been holding. "I don't know anything anymore. I thought I wanted this job, but now . . . After what happened to Viktor, after this . . ." He shook his head and gave Volkov a tired and resigned smile. "I'm going to leave, Arkady, before I can be blamed. Before I am fired. Before this incident becomes public."

"Leave?"

"The FSB. Moscow."

"What will you do, Simon?"

"I'm going to go back home to my father's farm. He needs the help and I wish to do something meaningful again. Something that I can feel with my hands and see progress in with my eyes." He paused before continuing. "Something I am not ashamed of when I go home at night."

Volkov had similar thoughts, but unlike Alekseyov, he had nothing to run to. He'd been KGB, then FSB, all his adult life. "It sounds as if you have given this much thought, Simon."

Alekseyov stood. "I am sorry to have disturbed you, Arkady, to have interrupted your dinner. Please, apologize to your wife for me and forget that I have bothered you." He stuck out his hand. Volkov shook it.

"It is not a problem, Simon. I wish you the very best in whatever you decide to do."

"I'm sorry we did not work together longer. I feel there is much I could have learned from you."

Volkov walked Alekseyov to the door. *"Dobroy nochi,"* he said. *Good night.*

"*Proshchay*, Arkady."

Volkov shut the door and leaned his forehead against the wood. His scar burned.

"Arkady?" Yekatarina said from behind him. "Is everything all right?"

"Are you ashamed of me, Yekatarina?" he asked, still facing the door.

Her hand rubbed his back. "Ashamed? Arkady, why would you ask me that?"

Volkov did not answer. He had never brought his work home with him, never shared the gruesome details of his job, what he had to do to extract information, all in defense of the Russian Federation. He turned and gave his wife a closed-lip smile. "Nothing. It is nothing."

"What did that young man want? You work together?"

"Just a little career advice."

She smiled. "You see? The young officers now look up to you. They come to you with their questions. That is a sign of respect, Arkady. It is a sign that you have nothing to be ashamed of, that others think so highly of you."

"Yes, of course," he said. A thought came to him, and he walked to the apartment windows and looked down at the street. Alekseyov departed the building, now wearing a hat and gloves. He walked north. Volkov searched the sidewalk in each direction, as well as across the street. No one followed the young FSB officer on foot or by car.

"Come and finish your dinner before it gets cold," Yekatarina said.

Volkov turned from the window. "I am full." He walked to the hall closet, opening it. "I am going to go out for a cigarette. A walk in the cold weather will clear my head."

His wife eyed him with suspicion.

He pulled on his coat and scarf and retrieved his gloves and cap from the pockets. He held his wife by her shoulders. "Do not look so worried. I won't be long. I promise. Only a short walk this night."

—

Viktor Federov walked the streets of London in a drizzle that had painted the night nearly black and elongated the lights from the many taxicabs, double-decker buses, and cars. He carried a plastic bag of Chinese takeout. With each block, Federov glanced to his left and to his right. He studied the faces of others walking the street, looking for anyone he had already seen that night, or those who appeared purposefully disinterested and disengaged. He hoped that, with time, he would become less paranoid, but he wondered if that would only make him more vulnerable. He sighed. Had he made the right choice? It was a question he would surely ask himself often. He had long been a man without a family. Now he did not have a country. A man without a country, eating takeout food from Styrofoam containers because he did not trust that his food would not be poisoned if he ordered room service. He would change restaurants each night as well as hotels, always living under one false passport or another.

What a way to live.

But what option did he have?

The FSB had been the only life he had ever known. He had no pension to show for his service, and supporting his wife and his daughters had not allowed him to save any money. What he had was the six million he'd stolen from Carl Emerson, with a promise of more to come. He had done what he had to do to survive. Sometimes you didn't have the luxury to make the right choice. Sometimes you only had one choice.

When the traffic light changed, Federov crossed the street and walked up Buckingham Palace Road to the Grosvenor Hotel. The doorman pulled open the door for him, and Federov crossed the enormous throw rug atop the marbled entrance, stepping past an elaborate floral centerpiece. The hotel bar tempted him, but even after two days of downtime, after having slept nearly sixteen hours, he remained mentally and physically exhausted.

He took the elevator to his room, pausing when the elevator car's doors pulled apart, his hand beneath his coat, on the grip of his handgun. He searched the hallway in both directions before stepping into the hall and making his way to his room. As he walked, he pulled his phone from his pocket and activated a recently installed app that connected to the iPad he'd also purchased, which now sat on his desk. The cameras on the iPad provided a live feed to the app on his phone, which allowed him to view the inside of his hotel room.

No one. He reversed the video to the moment he had departed the room, and fast-forwarded to confirm no one had entered his room while he was out. Satisfied, he slid the plastic takeout bag up his forearm to free his hand to grip the gun, if necessary. The "Do Not Disturb" sign hung from the door handle. He swiped the card key, waited a beat, then pushed the door open, pausing before he stepped inside. He checked the threads he'd torn from the pillowcase and placed atop the bathroom door and the bedroom closet. The threads remained. Neither had been disturbed.

He deadbolted the door and put his gun on the desk along with his dinner. Then he removed his coat and hat and draped the coat over the back of the chair. He looked about the single room. He had the money to rent a suite, but a single room was easier to secure. Besides, who was he trying to impress?

He walked to the bathroom, unzipped his fly, and relieved himself. A phone rang, a low muffled sound Federov initially thought to be coming from the room next door. He washed his hands at the sink and walked back into his room. The phone rang again, but the sound was not from next door, nor was it the burner phone on the desk, or the room phone. It came from his iPad. The call was being made to a virtual phone number, a number Federov had opened through the cloud when he worked for the FSB; he had not wanted the FSB to monitor his calls, especially those of a sensitive or personal nature.

Only three people knew the virtual number. His two daughters—neither had ever used it—and his former partner, Arkady Volkov.

Worried the FSB could be harassing his daughters, as Efimov had threatened, he answered the call, speaking Russian. *"Privet?"*

"Viktor?"

The male voice surprised him. "Arkady?"

"I was uncertain you kept this number."

"So was I," Federov said. The pit in his stomach lessened somewhat. "Is something wrong?"

"I do not know, Viktor, but Simon Alekseyov just visited me at my home."

"Your home? What did he want?"

"I am not certain. A trick perhaps."

"For what purpose?"

"Perhaps to test my loyalty."

"What did he say?"

"He wanted to know if I had a way to get in touch with you."

"What did you tell him?"

"I told him no, of course."

"Did he say why he asked?"

Volkov relayed what Alekseyov had told him. When he finished, Federov said, "Do you believe him?"

"I don't easily trust anyone but my wife, Viktor. This you know."

"Yes, I do. I've often wondered: Why do you trust me, Arkady?"

"Next to my wife, I have spent more time with you than anyone. But I am not telling you this for you, Viktor, or for Mr. Jenkins or Ms. Ponomayova."

"Why then?"

"I do this for Simon, and for the FSB that I still believe in. If Simon is telling the truth, Efimov is allowing his obsession to influence his decisions, and this will surely get Simon fired, possibly me also, and reflect poorly on all the FSB and, I am sure, the Kremlin, though they will deny any knowledge."

"I understand, Arkady."

"*Do svidaniya,* Viktor. I doubt we will talk again."

"One never knows, Arkady. Anything can happen."

"For you, maybe. For me, not so likely," he said.

Federov disconnected the call, then pulled out his desk chair and sat, considering what Volkov had told him. If it was true, and he had no reason to believe it was not, then Charles Jenkins and Paulina Ponomayova were about to suffer a horrible death.

Federov sat back, thinking of what Volkov had told him and what he might do. Could this be a trap?

He did not put anything past Efimov.

49

After two days of catching up on his usual daily calories and sleep, Jenkins felt almost like himself again. Paulina, too, looked better, and she said she felt better. The doctor had put her on a round of antibiotics and provided her with protein shakes, which Jenkins ensured she drank, until her appetite returned. She remained painfully thin. A red hue had returned to her cheeks, and her skin was no longer sallow.

More noticeable than her physical appearance was Paulina's old demeanor. The woman who had intended to die and who had spent months suffering without giving up any information had slowly receded, replaced by the woman Jenkins had first encountered. Paulina even sounded excited about the prospects of living in the United States and starting her life over.

They had spent most of the two days in their cabin, reading books Bantle provided and watching movies streamed through the computer. Paulina had become a big fan of *The Godfather* and *The Godfather Part II*, which she had never before seen. She wanted to watch the third movie in the series, but Jenkins dissuaded her, telling her it would ruin the first two. They settled instead on a comedy, *My Cousin Vinny*. Paulina's pronunciation of certain English words had now taken on a Brooklyn accent.

At night, with fewer crew members on duty, Jenkins and Paulina walked the deck in the cold breeze to build Paulina's strength and to clear their minds before going to sleep.

After leaving the port in Gdańsk, Poland, they were eager to get outside after staying in their cabin all day. They pulled on crew-member uniforms—light-blue jumpsuits and dark knit caps—and went up top to walk the deck. The weather was changing, not nearly as cold, and the sky had cleared. They watched the sun set, painting the horizon a mixture of rich colors, and they saw the emergence of the first stars and planets.

The cold air invigorated and refreshed him, and Jenkins breathed it in deeply. Something about being out on the water, with the wind on their faces, made them both feel free, though Jenkins knew they were not yet out of danger. They talked about Jenkins's family, and about life in the United States. Paulina worried about what she might do for a living, but Jenkins assured her that she would be given a new identity and that she would be in demand, with her degrees from Moscow State University in computer science and systems hardware, as well as mathematics.

"You're coming to the right place," he said. "The United States is home to Microsoft, Amazon, Google, and hundreds of other computer and software companies. You won't have a problem. It's good pay; you can make a good living with your background."

Paulina smiled but looked pensive.

"What's wrong?"

"I wish Ivan had this kind of a chance." She spoke of her brother, whose dream to dance for the Bolshoi had ended in suicide. "He would have been a great dancer."

"I'm sure he would have."

They returned to the metal door they used to enter and exit the deck. "I will go back to the cabin so you can call your family," Paulina said.

It had become their routine to circle the stacked cargo containers four times. Jenkins used the time alone on deck to call Alex on a secure phone and update her on their progress. She would tell him about the kids, whom he missed. He'd also talk to CJ about school, but mostly about soccer, and anything else the boy wanted to discuss.

Jenkins pulled the encrypted phone from his pocket and dialed Alex's burner phone. It was early morning in Seattle. She answered on the third ring.

"Hey. Where are you?" she asked. "I've been worried."

"Leaving Poland and heading to Denmark. After that it's Norway. Then home."

"How many more days until you get to Norway?"

"Three."

"Anything going on?"

"Nothing so far. I'm looking forward to steaming for home."

"Don't drop your guard. Not just yet."

The cell phone buzzed in his hand and Jenkins read the screen, though the caller could only be one other person. "Hang on. I'm getting a call from Matt Lemore."

"You need to take it?"

"I'd better. I'll call you back."

Jenkins answered the call but didn't get out a word after "Hello." He listened, quickly becoming sick to his stomach. He shoved the phone in his pocket and rushed to the metal door, yanked it open, and stepped into the inner lock. He opened the interior door and hurried down the metal steps, the sound of each footfall echoing.

Paulina passed the diagram of the C deck floor plan hanging on the hallway wall. It identified the multitude of rooms off the narrow corridors. Fluorescent lights illuminated pale walls and the linoleum floor. The walk in the cold was something she now looked forward to. The pain in her ankle, which she had swallowed boarding the train in Moscow, had improved, her limp no longer so pronounced. So, too, had her stamina. She turned a corner, nearly walking into a crew member traveling in the opposite direction. He wore a white helmet and kept his head down, his hands stuffed in the pockets of his light-blue jumpsuit.

Out of politeness, Paulina apologized, but the man ignored her. Bantle had told her the crew members might be reluctant to engage them; that they knew enough not to ask questions and to keep to themselves.

She stepped to her cabin door and looked down the hall. The man glanced back over his shoulder at her before he turned the corner. She punched in the room access code and pushed open the door. When she stepped inside, she detected the smell of mint. A metal teapot and two cups rested on a brown food tray on the computer desk. On the tray was a small note.

Thought tea might help you sleep more soundly. 😊

Paulina smiled. Martin Bantle had gone out of his way to make them feel welcome. He had provided meals, medical attention, and medicine. Tea would remove the chill from the nightly walk. She reached for the pot but then decided to first change out of her coveralls. In the process of doing so, she caught sight of the picture of Charles Jenkins with his daughter that she had taped above her bed, and she smiled at the thought of a little girl sharing her name. Maybe, in some small way, it was a chance for her to live on. With her parents and her brother gone, it gave her hope for the future. Far too often she had considered her life not worth living, but now, having just been out on the deck of a ship that would carry her one step closer to a new home and to new opportunities, she realized she had an obligation to her parents, who had lived under the oppressive communist regime, and to her brother, who had taken his life when his dreams were stolen from him.

She let the coveralls drop to her waist, then sat on her bed and slid out of her shoes to pull off the coveralls. Underneath she wore borrowed pants, the cuffs rolled, a white T-shirt, and a gray wool sweater, the sleeves also rolled. She stood and hung her coveralls on one of the hooks by the door, then looked again to the tea. Charlie would be at least half an hour.

Cold tea was never as good as hot. She decided to drink the first cup without him.

—

Jenkins swung around the bright-yellow painted handrail, feeling it rattle from his weight and momentum. He dropped onto the B deck landing, the noise resonating in the stairwell. Below him a door opened, then slammed shut. He peered over the railing, hoping to see Paulina. A crew member in a white hard hat descended the staircase, likely headed to the engine room or the main control room. The man looked up at Jenkins, then ducked his head and quickly continued down the stairs.

Jenkins gripped the handrail and descended to the C deck. If someone stepped from their cabin at that moment, there was going to be one hell of a collision. He turned a corner, his momentum carrying him into the wall, pushed off, and rushed to their door at the far end. He banged on it as he fingered the numbers on the keypad and pushed the door open.

Paulina reached for a metal teapot. A cup on the table in front of her.

"Don't!" Jenkins yelled, startling her. She pulled back her hand. "Did you drink any of the tea?"

"No. I was just about to—"

"Step away from the desk."

"What is wrong?"

"Step back."

Paulina did so. Jenkins pulled her out into the hall, telling her in a hushed voice the gist of his conversation with Matt Lemore. Then he said, "Come with me."

They hurried down the hall and climbed the stairs to the A deck, entering the large mess hall with the ship's kitchen. Jenkins rummaged in the cabinets and drawers, then pushed through a door at the back of the kitchen to a storage room.

"What are you looking for?"

"Rubber gloves. And a mask."

He found them on a shelf and pulled out two sets, handing one to Paulina. They put on the protection and hurried back to their cabin. He told Paulina to hold the door for him.

Jenkins did not know what was in the tea. Lemore had mentioned polonium-210, the poison used in the attack on a former KGB and FSB agent living in London. The man had ingested the polonium-210 after it had been poured in his tea. Jenkins did not know whether the poison could be absorbed by touch or by smell, but he was taking no chances.

He walked to the desk and opened the top drawer, finding paper clips, pens, and pencils, but no tape. He looked through the other drawers, also without success, and eventually used toilet paper to fashion a cork and stuff it in the spout. It would have to do.

He picked up the tray and slowly walked to the open door. Stepping through, he said, "Get the stairwell doors for me."

Paulina did so, and Jenkins carefully ascended three flights of stairs, Paulina in front of him to ensure no one got in his way. About to open the inner lock leading to the door to the deck, Paulina stepped back suddenly when the door pushed in. She nearly collided with the tray behind her, which caused Jenkins to step back. He lost his balance, stumbled, but managed to keep the tray, and the teapot, upright.

The crew member gave them an odd look but otherwise did not ask questions.

Paulina held the door open for Jenkins, looking in both directions, then nodded for him to proceed. He carefully stepped over the lip at the bottom of the door into a gusting wind. He turned his back to serve as a wind block and walked backward to the deck railing.

Beneath him, the boat churned, the engines emitting a loud humming noise and vibration. Whitecaps rolled atop gray waves. Jenkins did not want to throw the tray for fear the lid would pop off the pot and the wind would blow the tea back in his face.

He reached over the railing as far as his arms would extend and let the tray drop, stepping back and crouching behind the boat's steel edge. After a moment he stood and looked over the side at the churning water illuminated in the boat's lights.

If poison had been put into the tea, it was now gone.

But there was a more imminent problem. The person who had planted it remained on ship, and that meant Jenkins and Paulina were no longer one step ahead of Efimov. They were one step behind.

50

Jenkins waited in the hallway outside their cabin with Paulina and Chief Mate Martin Bantle. Bantle confirmed that neither he nor any other officer had sent tea to their room.

Inside their cabin, a ship engineer in a decontamination suit analyzed the room inch by inch with a Geiger counter. With increased terrorist threats, the equipment had become standard on US-flagged ships carrying sensitive cargo. Bantle had confined all nonessential crew to their quarters, and he dispatched ship security officers to search for the man Ponomayova had seen walking down the hall just before she found the tea. Jenkins told Bantle he had seen a man descending the staircase from the C deck.

After forty-five minutes, the engineer emerged from the cabin and removed his protective headgear, his hair damp with perspiration. "I'm not getting any readings, but that doesn't mean the cabin is safe."

"I don't understand," Jenkins said.

"It has to do with the different forms of radiation," the engineer said. "Beta radiation consists of both electrons and gamma radiation—which are a form of high-energy electromagnetic radiation detectable on a Geiger counter. The fact that I'm not getting any hits is a good thing for the two of you, because beta and gamma radiation can penetrate skin tissue and be absorbed into the body."

"What's the alternative?" Jenkins asked.

"Alpha particles, radiation given off by chemical elements like polonium-210. They produce no signs of radioactivity when tested with a Geiger counter. That's the bad news. The good news is alpha particles don't travel far before losing all their energy, centimeters at most, which limits contamination to drinking the tea or inhalation at a close distance. It cannot penetrate the skin unless there is an open wound."

"But it can be inhaled?" Jenkins asked, worried about Paulina.

"We all have low levels of polonium in our systems, especially those who smoke cigarettes or eat a lot of fish. So long as polonium, or any other element giving off alpha particles, is not ingested or inhaled in sufficient amounts, it poses little danger."

"What amount needs to be ingested?" Jenkins asked.

"No way for me to know that. All I can tell you is if it is ingested or inhaled in a sufficient amount, the damage to internal organs is extensive and death is certain." The engineer looked to Bantle. "We're going to need to watch the crew for nausea and vomiting, hair loss, diarrhea. Since we can't be one hundred percent certain if this room is contaminated, given the equipment available, we need to seal it, probably this deck as well, and deal with this when we arrive in Norway. Tell the crew to pee into vials and seal them. We can have their urine analyzed when we dock. I'm going to check the kitchen since we can assume that's where he made the tea."

"We're fortunate the kitchen was closed," Bantle said. "And I assume this guy would avoid being seen by any of the crew for fear of being confronted."

"Just the same, you might want to seal the kitchen as well, at least until we get to Norway and can get hazmat in here to go over the ship and have medical personnel check out the crew."

"How did you find out about this?" Bantle asked Jenkins.

Jenkins gave that question some thought. "I'm not really sure. Maybe a couple of people who still have a conscience."

"Well, whoever it was, they likely saved your lives," the engineer said. "If it was polonium-210, you were looking at a long and very painful death."

Bantle told the engineer to do what was necessary, and the man left. "I'll find you another room on another deck," he said to Jenkins and Paulina. "And until this individual is located, I'm confining everyone to their rooms. That includes you."

"If he's not caught, he'll sneak off at the next port," Jenkins said.

"We'll find him," Bantle said.

"I doubt he'll be armed or will give you any problems. But don't expect him to admit anything either."

"There is something else to consider as well," Paulina said. Jenkins knew what she was about to say, and that it was far more problematic. "The FSB has clearly figured out we left Finland on this container ship."

"I know," Jenkins said. "They needed days to plan this attack and get their man on ship at the last port. We no longer have a head start. We might even be a step behind."

Nearly two hours later, Bantle stepped inside their new room and exhaled a held breath. "We got him. He was hiding on one of the storage decks."

Bantle looked spent. Jenkins suspected his and Paulina's presence on board was more than Bantle had bargained for, and the stress had caught up with him.

"Was anyone hurt?" Jenkins asked.

"No. You were right; he wasn't armed and he isn't talking. He's acting like a stowaway. I've locked him in a secure room. The question now is: What do we do with him?"

"If we take him to the Port of Aarhus and hand him over to Danish authorities, the wheels in the Kremlin will start turning to get him back," Jenkins said. "And I don't like the idea of watching him walk away with a slap on the wrist for something as minor as stowing away."

"He tried to poison us," Paulina said.

"I know, but we have no evidence to prove that, do we? We tossed the tea overboard and the engineer didn't find any Geiger counter readings. Since neither of us drank the tea, there's no physical evidence we were poisoned. Thank God for that." He looked to Bantle. "Even if we did have evidence, you saw how the Russians handled the London incident."

"They denied it."

"They'll do the same here. They'll claim they know nothing and demand that the man be returned to Russia, or that proof be provided that he did what we claim. If we publicly accuse him, the Russians will use the opportunity to point out that you are smuggling two people wanted in Russia for crimes."

"You have any suggestions?" Bantle asked Jenkins. "'Cause I'm all ears."

Jenkins did. He'd already spoken to Matt Lemore, and they had come up with an alternative game plan. "Play the same game as the Russians. Play dumb. If they ask, and it's unlikely they will, deny you have the man on board. Flip it. Tell them to prove that you do."

"The FSB will not claim him as one of their own," Paulina said.

To Bantle, Jenkins said, "And you said, your crew knows enough to keep their heads down and their mouths shut. This would be a good time for them to practice that. Don't acknowledge him and don't release him at Aarhus or while in port in Norway. Take him back to the United States, to Virginia."

"I suppose we could do that," Bantle said.

"There's still another problem," Jenkins said. "When the man fails to disembark in Aarhus, the Russians will know he didn't succeed in killing us, or at least will suspect something has gone wrong."

"They could still be waiting for you when we reach port at Drammen in Norway."

"But we will not get off the ship there either," Paulina said, looking concerned.

Bantle rubbed a hand across the stubble on his chin. "That might not matter. The Russians could have international authorities waiting to arrest you."

Jenkins nodded. "They've had time to get things in place and gin up charges against us for crimes we allegedly committed."

"They could even put out a diffusion to Interpol."

"What's a diffusion?" Jenkins asked.

"You've heard of a red notice?" Bantle asked.

Jenkins had. A red notice was a request to international law enforcement to arrest a person pending extradition to stand trial for his crimes in the country where the crimes were allegedly committed.

"A diffusion is similar, but it isn't vetted by Interpol before it's issued," Bantle said. "You're guilty until proven innocent, and you'll never be innocent if you're sent back to Russia."

Jenkins gave that some thought. "It would be a risky move by the Russians to make a public claim, not one I'm sure they'd take, but also not a risk I'm willing to take."

"Nor am I. An arrest could put this entire crew, and this ship, at risk of seizure. The Russians would love to tell the world that a United States–flagged ship was helping a Russian and American to escape punishment for crimes committed," Bantle said. "And our government wouldn't be happy about it either."

"So Paulina and I need to get off the ship before we reach Norway," Jenkins said.

Bantle shook his head. "Easier said than done. No good options in port, and we can't stop the ship once we're underway."

"Is there any other way you get people off? What do you do if someone is seriously injured or becomes ill?"

"We can airlift them, but if we do that you might as well just send up fireworks to draw attention to yourself. Russian fighter jets would escort the helicopter right back to Saint Petersburg—or the military base at Kaliningrad." Bantle sighed. He looked at Jenkins but not with confidence. "There might be another way. It's been used once or twice to get a pilot on board when ships have needed help navigating dangerous waters, like the ice in the Baltic. But I don't know that it has ever been tried to get someone off the ship the same way."

"What do you need?"

"Another boat, preferably with a portable ramp to bridge the gap."

"What gap?"

"The gap between the boat and where you will be hanging off the side of this ship."

"What am I doing hanging off the side of this ship?"

"Holding on to a rope ladder . . . hopefully."

"I don't like this idea already."

51

Efimov sat in Dmitry Sokalov's office. The chair to his left was vacant. Alekseyov was not there, and Efimov had not been able to reach him by phone.

"Where is Alekseyov?" Efimov asked.

"He has resigned," Sokalov said.

The news caught Efimov by surprise, and he wondered if Alekseyov's resignation had been strategic, and if Alekseyov had had anything to do with the failed attempt to poison Jenkins and Ponomayova, though he could not immediately think of any way he could have warned them. "Resigned?"

Sokalov adjusted his considerable weight in his chair and looked to be taking pleasure in delivering this news. "You did not know this?"

"No. But it makes me wonder."

"About?" Sokalov asked, though Efimov was certain the deputy director knew the answer to his own question.

"Our man did not get off the ship at the Port of Aarhus," Efimov said. "He was to disembark before Jenkins or Ponomayova showed signs of illness."

"When did you last hear from him?" Sokalov asked, and Efimov again sensed the deputy director already knew the answer. He was toying with him, trying to determine to what extent Efimov had control over this investigation.

"He provided confirmation that the tea had been delivered to their room on ship."

"Nothing since?"

"No. Nothing."

Sokalov leaned forward and rested his forearms on his desk. "Did we pick up anything on the ship's communications?"

The FSB had been monitoring the ship's communications since learning Jenkins and Ponomayova were on board but reported no transmission regarding the man attempting to poison them.

"There has been nothing of interest," Efimov said.

"No unexpected stops?"

"None."

Sokalov sat back. "Then we have to assume *your man* has been caught."

Efimov picked up the deputy director's subtlety. "There is no connection between this man and the FSB, or any other agency."

"Not yet," Sokalov said. "But make no mistake, Adam. There is a definite connection to you."

Efimov did not respond.

"Assuming he was caught," Sokalov said, "why would they not turn him over to Danish authorities when the ship arrived in port?"

Again, Efimov suspected Sokalov was asking a question to which he already knew the answer, treating Efimov like a pupil hauled before the teacher. He bit back his anger. Exploding on Sokalov would only justify whatever the deputy director intended.

"Mr. Jenkins would know that the man would be handled much less severely in Denmark than in the United States. He would possibly even be released, if Danish police had no evidence to bring charges."

"Which is a problem you assured me we would not face," Sokalov said, throwing Efimov's assurances at him.

Efimov said, "The Americans will have no choice but to remain silent, or risk the embarrassment that they are aiding fugitives. Political pressure can be applied to gain his return."

"Yes, but after he has been questioned."

"He will reveal nothing."

"Is that another promise, Adam?"

Efimov did not respond. He would not allow Sokalov to bait him. At the moment, something else continued to bother him. "What did Alekseyov say when he resigned?"

Sokalov waved it off. "I'm told that he had to return home to care for the family farm. His father is sick."

Sokalov's tone indicated he did not believe the excuse but it served his purpose, which was to place blame for this matter directly on Efimov.

"The timing is suspicious," Efimov said.

"I believe you have more pressing problems," Sokalov said. "Jenkins and Ponomayova remain alive. That is your immediate problem. And this is your case."

"They won't remain on ship and risk the possibility of being arrested at the Port of Drammen," Efimov said. "They will seek to get off before then."

"You said there were no other port stops before Drammen."

"There are none, but Jenkins will find a way. We need to alert our assets in Norway."

Sokalov looked around his office, then to the empty chair beside Efimov. "Do you see anyone else in this office, Adam?"

Efimov bristled but kept his mouth shut.

"If this were my case, I would get to Norway and personally handle this matter. I would get eyes and ears on that ship and on every marina along the Oslo Fjord. I would see this as a final chance to end this. Once and for all. But it is not my case. It is yours."

Efimov stood and started for the door.

"And Adam."

Efimov turned back around.

"I would not expect your friendship with the president to somehow protect you," Sokalov said. "Should you fail."

52

Late at night, a day after leaving the Port of Aarhus, Charles Jenkins and Paulina Ponomayova stood on the lower cargo deck, near a ten-foot-by-five-foot hull hatch ordinarily used to load and offload cargo by crew members in port. The opening stood about twenty feet above the water, and the scenery outside it reminded Jenkins of the San Juan Islands in the Pacific Northwest—many islands of all shapes and sizes, some inhabited, some with lights sparkling in dwellings, some covered in trees, others barren rock. Though the scenery was not his focus or his concern. His concern was hanging from the rope ladder dangling out the side of the ship above the foaming water.

Martin Bantle and two other crew members stood with them, peering out the hatch and waiting for Jenkins and Paulina's transport. Bantle looked as though he had a headache at the back of his eyes. Jenkins had no doubt the chief mate would be glad when this was finished.

Bantle had explained to Jenkins in private that, to his knowledge, what they were about to do had never been done before. He explained that when ships boarded a pilot, the pilot stood on the end of a portable ramp on the ice. As the ship passed, the ramp was extended and the pilot grabbed the rope ladder on the side of the ship and climbed up into the hull hatch. Bantle had even shown Jenkins a video clip of the pickup being performed. It looked simple enough, but they both knew that it didn't minimize the dire consequences of a mistake. Slip from the ramp, or from the ladder, and you could be pulled under the ship and crushed.

Bantle also told Jenkins that getting off the ship would be a lot trickier than getting on. For one, getting off required stepping from the rope ladder onto a moving ramp. As Bantle explained it, a boat would approach the cargo ship and match the ship's speed but keep a safe distance from the hull. The boat would then extend a ramp from its bow to the rope ladder. Paulina, then Jenkins, would climb down the rope ladder and, when the ramp reached them, step on it and walk across onto the boat. Simple in theory, but practice was another ball game.

To complicate things, a breeze had stirred up the fjord, creating rolling waves—nothing that the massive container ship couldn't churn through, but Jenkins wondered how the waves would impact a smaller boat, and the stability of the ramp.

The ship had slowed to fifteen knots when it entered the Oslo Fjord, but cold air blew through the opening. Jenkins and Paulina had dressed in lightweight clothing—insufficient to stave off the cold, but necessary for them to remain nimble for the task at hand. They each wore life jackets, not that a jacket would do either of them much good if they slipped from the rope ladder.

Minutes into their wait, a green light on the water indicated an approaching boat. A second later, a white light flashed three times.

"There's your ride," Bantle said.

Jenkins shook Bantle's hand. "Thanks for the lift. Sorry to have caused you any trouble."

Bantle smiled. "I spent a career finding interesting things to do with my life, and I've lived several lifetimes as a result. I can add this to the list."

Jenkins helped Paulina climb down the first rungs of the rope ladder. Though the ladder had wooden steps to help stabilize it, the rope swayed with each of her movements. Given that Jenkins outweighed Paulina by 125 pounds, he wondered how much more the ladder would sway with him on it.

"Be sure of your steps," he called down to her.

She looked up at him and gave him a cocksure smile. It could have been bravado, or it could have been her way to keep him from worrying. It could have been the old Paulina he'd first encountered—defiant and confident.

Jenkins dropped to his belly as the boat approached. He estimated the craft to be forty feet in length, with an enclosed pilothouse, but it looked like a miniature next to the cargo ship. Two men dressed in dark clothing stood on the bow as the boat slowly closed the distance to the hatch hole. After another minute of maneuvering, when the boat appeared to have matched the ship's speed, the two men swung open a section of the railing on the bow and extended the platform, which rolled out in sections, roughly eight feet in length with a handrailing. The gap from the rope ladder to the platform was approximately two feet, but the platform also rose and fell anywhere from six to eighteen inches with each cresting wave.

On board, one of the crew members used his hands to signal to the boat the distance of the ramp to the rope ladder. The platform inched closer. When the platform was within less than a foot, and relatively stable, the crew member shouted down to Paulina, "Grab the railing."

Paulina did so, then extended her left leg. The crew member had told them to commit at this point, not to delay. He didn't want them to get caught in between, with one leg on the platform and the other on the rope ladder.

Paulina did not delay. She let go of the rope with her right hand, grabbed the handrail, and stepped onto the platform. Once on, she quickly and safely crossed to the boat, where the two men grabbed her and helped her step down onto the bow. She turned and looked back to the ship, smiling. Piece of cake.

Once Paulina boarded the boat, Jenkins descended the rope ladder, feeling it sway with each movement. The wind gusted in his face and he could feel the cold on his exposed skin. He had to be certain of his footing before he removed a gloved hand from the rope, what the crew member had called maintaining three points of contact with the ladder. On the bottom step, Jenkins turned, waiting for the boat captain to maneuver the platform closer to the ladder. As the captain did, the ship passed to the far side of an island, which Jenkins quickly realized had served as a windbreak during Paulina's transfer. Without the island and trees, the wind picked up, and so, too, did the size of the waves. The rise and fall of the platform became much more severe.

The platform inched closer. Jenkins timed his step, reached out, grabbed the handrail with his right hand, and stepped with his right foot. In that split second, however, the platform dropped into a trough, and his foot dangled above it. The platform rose on the crest of the next wave. Jenkins planted his foot and committed. He let go of the rope with his left hand, grabbed the platform railing, and stepped with his left foot, but as he turned, one of the snaps on his life vest caught on the rope ladder. In that split-second delay, the wave fell and the platform dropped in the trough. Jenkins's feet, momentarily suspended, dropped off the front of the platform, though he managed to hang onto the railing with both hands, now dangling beneath the ramp.

The boat captain slowed to keep Jenkins from getting sucked under the ship and crushed by the hull, should he fall into the water. Voices shouted to him, but he could not understand them. Jenkins tried to pull himself onto the ramp, but the railing, not built to take the full weight of a 225-pound man, bent and threatened to collapse.

Jenkins swung his legs up, trying to get the heels of his boots over the platform's sides to take the weight off the handrail. He missed, however, and his leg fell, hitting the water. His weight caused the handrail to bend more severely. Jenkins sensed it was about to snap. He kicked again. The heel of his boot found the platform, and he swung his left leg up onto the other side just before the handrailing snapped. Jenkins's upper body dropped, but he grabbed the platform with both hands, now firmly beneath it. He turned his head, looking forward, and watched a large wave hurl toward him. The front of the boat dipped, and he held his breath. The wave hit him, the water freezing cold.

The ramp popped back up. The boat slowed, then stopped, bobbing like a cork in the waves. One of the men crawled out onto the platform on his belly and grabbed Jenkins's arm and his boot. Another wave crashed over them. With the man's help, Jenkins managed to drag himself onto the ramp and crawl backward onto the bow of the boat.

Jenkins rolled onto his back, breathing heavily from the adrenaline rush. He looked at the two men, who stared at him shell-shocked and uncertain. When Jenkins got to his feet, Paulina stepped forward and hugged him. Jenkins thought of Hot Rod Studebaker and his bravado landing the airplane.

He smiled. "Piece of cake."

—

Efimov sat in a car in Oslo, Norway, monitoring the frequency being used by the FSB's assets he had dispersed throughout the piers and marinas along the fjord. His cell phone rang and he picked it up from the seat.

"Two people were just removed from the container ship by boat," the caller said. "The ship is proceeding to Drammen, but the boat is headed to Oslo."

"Describe the boat."

"White, approximately forty feet in length, with a pilothouse. The boat's name is *Suicide Blonde*."

"You are following it?"

"At a distance. Without running lights."

"Let me know when and where it docks. Do not intercept it. Do not let them know you are following."

"You don't want us to intercept it?"

"No," Efimov said.

"We have four armed men on board."

"Do as I have ordered," Efimov said, disconnecting. He stared out the windshield, thinking again of his meeting in Sokalov's office. He would not give the fat bastard the pleasure of having others capture Jenkins and Ponomayova, would not give Sokalov an excuse to demean and denigrate him ever again. Efimov would end this personally. He'd kill Jenkins, but he would return to Russia with Ponomayova and bring her not to the deputy director, but to the president's office. Vladimir could not ignore him, not if Efimov stood outside his office with the one person who they now knew could provide the president with answers to questions that had existed for decades—the names of the remaining four sisters.

He contemplated Sokalov's final words to him. An ultimatum. So be it. His father had issued many. Efimov had survived him. He would survive the deputy director as well.

53

The container ship continued toward the Port of Drammen, a deepwater harbor forty-five kilometers to the southwest of Oslo. Jenkins and Bantle hoped it would draw anyone following the ship with it.

Jenkins and Paulina sat in the pilothouse, warmed by a propane heater and mugs of coffee. Jenkins thanked the captain, a woman with a thick, dishwater-blonde braid running down the center of her back.

"I feared for a moment we had lost you," she said in a Norwegian accent.

"So did I," Jenkins said.

"We have fresh clothes for you to change into. And weapons."

A radio mounted over her head crackled. Jenkins nodded to it as he removed his vest and his shirt. "Have you heard anything?"

"There has been some chatter," she said. "Nothing out of the usual, but we are listening carefully. If the Russians suspect you will seek to get off the cargo ship they will watch the marinas closely. We will avoid those. My instructions are to bring you to the pier just beneath the Akershus Fortress. You will cross the street to a cobblestone ramp. Walk up the ramp to the fortress. Someone will make themselves known to you."

"How?" Jenkins asked, slipping off his pants and handing them to a crew member, who handed him another pair.

"Look for the church. When the person makes himself known to you, ask 'Is it too late for a tour of the church?' This person will answer 'Yes, but not too late for confession.'"

"And from there?"

"I know nothing more," she said. "We are thirty minutes away. There is more coffee."

Half an hour later the boat turned off its running lights and docked in front of the bow of a massive cruise ship moored across the street from a brick-and-stone fortress high on the hill. The Akershus Fortress looked orange in color from the glow of spotlights, and its mirror image reflected on the surface of the fjord's dark water. The two crewmen on board helped Jenkins and Paulina climb from the bow of the boat up onto the concrete pier, above the ship.

"Cross the street," one said in a hushed voice. "Look for the cobblestone ramp." Then he jumped down onto the bow, and the boat pulled away.

In Oslo's inner harbor, the wind was mild and the evening quiet. A full moon, partially obscured by passing clouds, illuminated the night, rendering everything an indigo blue. Jenkins was dressed in a black turtleneck and warm knit hat. He searched the street, looking for anyone who appeared to be loitering or homeless, or for people sitting in parked cars. Seeing no one, he nodded to Paulina, and they crossed the street.

Fifty feet down the block, following the stone wall of the fortress, they found the cobblestone ramp. Jenkins pulled the gun from his waistband; Paulina did the same. They pointed the muzzles at the ground as they walked up the cobblestone ramp, passing beneath a brick arch, a church on their right. They walked into a courtyard at the top of the ramp and looked about, seeing no one. Jenkins didn't like being out in the open, with nothing to hide them, and he quickly made his way toward an inner stone courtyard.

A match flared. Jenkins glimpsed someone leaning against a stone wall on the other side of the courtyard. Jenkins and Paulina approached.

The man had one leg bent, the sole of his boot braced against the archway. He looked like a sailor in a dark peacoat and knit cap. Strands of blond hair—nearly white—peeked out from beneath the cap. His cigarette glowed a bright red when he inhaled. A camera hung by a strap around his neck.

"Is it too late for a tour of the church?" Jenkins asked.

"Yes. But not too late for confession." The man dropped his cigarette and crushed it with the toe of his boot. "I am André. Come."

André led them through the arch into an inner courtyard with antique cannons on wooden wheels. Maple trees lined cobblestone walkways. The wind rustled the leaves and circled the courtyard, emitting a soft, ghostly howl. André climbed a stone step and pressed down on an iron door handle to a wood door. Jenkins and Paulina followed him inside.

The church smelled of incense and burnt candles. Ambient light streamed through a round, stained-glass window at the rear of the nave, and below the window rose the pipes of an organ. The church was empty. André led them quickly down a side aisle to a confession box and pulled open the door. Inside the small confessional he touched something on the back wall and the edge popped free. Inserting his fingers into the gap, he slid back the wall, revealing a hidden passage. He switched on a penlight and handed a second one to Jenkins, then directed the beam of light onto steep descending steps carved into rock. André started down, Paulina following. He looked up at Jenkins, speaking softly. "Close the confessional door behind you."

Jenkins shut the door, eliminating what little ambient light had helped him to see. Shining his penlight into the gap, he stepped down the first stone step, turning his foot sideways because the stairs were too narrow to accommodate his size 13 shoe.

"Slide the wall closed until you hear it click," André said from the tunnel at the bottom of the stairs. Again, Jenkins did so. Then he descended into darkness.

Efimov emerged from behind the stone wall, watching Jenkins and Ponomayova ascend a cobblestone ramp to the Akershus Fortress. His initial instinct was to shoot Jenkins immediately, but he had to assume there were others waiting for Jenkins and Ponomayova, or in position to provide them security. He needed to find a situation in which he could act quickly and slip away, making Jenkins's death look like a criminal act.

After Jenkins had turned the corner at the top of the ramp, Efimov stepped forward, walking briskly but remaining on high alert. He slid behind the trunk of a tree and waited a beat before proceeding to an archway, where he stopped again behind the stone wall. He leaned out and caught sight of Jenkins and Ponomayova talking to a man beneath an archway. The three stepped beneath the arch, out of sight. Efimov gave them a few seconds before he followed. He removed his gun and screwed on a silencer.

At the archway he braced his back against the wall and then peered around it, looking into an inner courtyard. He did not see them, but he did see a wooden door on the side of the church. He stepped into the courtyard, again deserted, and crossed to the door. He pressed down on the handle until he heard it click. Carefully, quietly, he opened the door, waiting a second to ensure it was not an ambush. He slid inside a dark interior, holding the door until it closed, silently. He took a moment to listen for voices.

Hearing none, he stepped into a church with rows of wood chairs aligned from an altar to the back of the nave. The altar sat beneath a chandelier, with a raised pulpit extending from the wall. Near the back of the nave, another door swung shut. Efimov slid down the aisle past statues and ducked beneath a Norwegian flag hanging from a pole set into the wall.

As he stepped to the door, he heard a faint whisper, a man's voice. He gripped the door handle, raised the muzzle of his gun, and pulled the door open, aiming inside. The room was no larger than a few square feet. But no one was inside.

Efimov removed a light from his pocket and turned it on, shining the narrow beam along the edge where the walls met, but not seeing a seam. He pressed on the wood, and on the carved features. Nothing. He stepped closer. A faint, cool breeze blew on his face. He pulled a hair from his head and held it along the wall edge. Up high, the hair fluttered. He moved it closer to the gap and the flutter increased. A passageway.

He pressed and pulled on anything protruding from the wall. Nothing. He kept at it, lifting up onto his toes to press on a carved rose near the ceiling. It depressed and the wall snapped open a few inches. Efimov waited a beat, gripped the edge, and slid the wall back, revealing a descending staircase.

—

At the bottom of the steps Jenkins encountered a narrow passageway with an arched ceiling cut into rock but clearly not intended for a man his height. He had to duck his head to keep from hitting it. The tunnel was cold and damp, and the stone walls looked slickened by water, but the dirt floor remained dry. He directed the light down to his feet and noticed that they were leaving shoeprints. As André and Paulina went down the tunnel, Jenkins looked about the passage and saw some stones on the ground. He gathered a handful and climbed halfway back up the steps, dropping the stones and pebbles on two of the stairs. Then he hurried to catch up, though his size prevented him from moving quickly.

"What is this place?" he asked in a hushed voice when he reached the back of the line.

"The Akershus Fortress has existed for more than seven hundred years," André said, his voice a near whisper. "Many have tried to rule it because of its proximity to the sea. These tunnels were dug for those in power to flee when the fortress was besieged. In World War II the Nazis expanded the tunnels, as did the Norwegian resistance, who used them to move around much of Oslo undetected to commit sabotage. Few know of the tunnels' existence. You will not find them on any map, and the military does not acknowledge they exist. Some remain escape routes, others security rooms for government officials in the event of a nuclear attack."

Jenkins turned and stopped walking at the sound of the stones being displaced and bouncing down the staircase in the otherwise silent passageway. He looked for a light, but didn't see any. André and Paulina continued on, but Jenkins remained still, listening, certain he had heard the rocks. He directed the beam of light to the floor and picked up additional stones, then hurried down the tunnel.

André turned right at the first fork, leading them down another passageway. Jenkins stopped at the fork and strategically dropped the rocks across the dirt floor. He went another few feet and planted more rocks across the ground.

"Where are we headed?" Paulina asked.

"Where I lead you," André said. "It is not far. A kilometer."

They pressed on.

A minute later, Jenkins heard another sound behind them, someone stepping awkwardly on the rocks he'd dropped. "Shh," he said. Paulina and André stopped and turned back. Jenkins directed the light to his face, put his finger to his lips, then pointed to his ear. Paulina and André shook their heads to indicate they had not heard anything.

About to continue, Jenkins heard the sound a second time. This time, when he looked to Paulina and André, their eyes confirmed they, too, had heard it.

Someone was coming.

Efimov's foot slipped on one of the stairs, and he fell on his ass, but managed to keep from tumbling down the remainder of the staircase.

Stones, however, pinged as they hit the steps. He directed the light to the stairs, illuminating pebbles on several steps.

He wondered if they had been deliberately placed.

He descended to the floor and used the penlight to illuminate a narrow, arched tunnel cut into the rock. He shone light on the ground, seeing faint footprints, and followed them, keeping the beam of the light low—just a foot or two ahead of him so as not to unexpectedly give himself away. After several minutes he came to the first fork in the road. The footprints continued to the right. Efimov stopped, listening, not wanting to unwittingly come upon Jenkins or to step into a trap.

He stepped forward and stumbled on uneven ground, more rocks. His ankle twisted and he fell into the wall, the gun scraping the rock with a metallic *tink*. He listened for a moment, waiting, but heard nothing. Cautiously, he stepped forward, the muzzle of the gun raised. Several more steps and again he stepped on uneven ground. This time he stumbled but regained his balance before he hit the wall.

No doubt now. The rocks had been placed in his path.

Jenkins knew, or suspected, they were being followed.

Efimov picked up his pace.

At the second fork, André took a right. Jenkins motioned for them to go forward without him. "Stay straight," André said, looking back at him in the dim light. "It is not far."

Jenkins stepped down the opposite fork and dropped to his knees. He lowered his mouth just inches above the ground, which he illuminated with the light, and blew the dust and dirt until the footprints were no longer detectable.

Then he stood and placed his back against the wall.

Soft footfalls approached the fork. Jenkins peeked around the wall and saw a dim beam of light directed at the ground. He pulled back, struggling to control the adrenaline rush and the rapid breathing.

Surprise was his ally, one he would no doubt need.

Efimov came to a second fork in the tunnel and used the light to study the ground. The shoeprints continued to the left but not the right.

He stepped to the left. The blow caught him by surprise, flush in the face. It drove him backward. Though stunned, he managed to remain upright, back braced against the rock wall. He'd dropped the penlight, but not his gun. His assailant grabbed the hand holding the gun and delivered a second blow, an elbow across Efimov's jaw, but in the narrow passageway it was without momentum.

Short and compact, Efimov sensed he had an advantage. He held the man while struggling to clear his head. He sprung from the balls of his feet and launched his body. The top of his head struck just beneath the man's chin and drove him backward into the stone wall on the other side. Efimov heard the man's gun clatter against the rock and land in the dirt.

They bounced off the rock walls, each fighting to gain leverage. Efimov drove a hand up and delivered another blow to the chin, again knocking his opponent's head against the stone wall. The grip on Efimov's gun weakened, the man's strength fading. Efimov felt another elbow strike his jaw, and the two men pinballed down the tunnel walls until the tunnel came to an end and Efimov saw ambient light.

Efimov spun, broke the man's hold, and shoved him, hearing his head strike the stone arch just before he stumbled and fell backward into the dimly lit room. Charles Jenkins's knees buckled and he landed hard on his back.

Efimov aimed the gun.

For once Sokalov had been right. Efimov would personally end this matter.

—

Jenkins's head smashed the top of the tunnel a second time. Stars clouded his vision. He stumbled backward, felt the gun wrenched from his hand, and lost his balance, his back striking the ground. He looked up into the muted light and saw Efimov step from the tunnel, the muzzle of the gun pointed at him.

Efimov took aim but turned his head, likely searching for Paulina, or perhaps others who had helped them. Jenkins, however, could not take advantage. He'd lost his gun in the tunnel and he could not shake the cobwebs, could not get his limbs to move quickly enough. In his blurred vision he saw Paulina ten feet to his left, her gun in hand and aimed directly at Efimov.

"Bros' pistolet, ili ya yego ub'yu," Efimov shouted. *Drop the gun or I will kill him.*

"Pozdno," Paulina said. *Too late.*

She squeezed the trigger and advanced, each bullet hitting its mark. The gunshots echoed like cannon blasts inside the stone room.

Efimov's pistol flew from his hand with the impact of the first bullet. The second and third drove him backward. His arms and legs flailed, much like a marionette dropped from his strings by his puppeteer. He struck the ground, bounced, and struck it a second time.

Paulina stood over him for the briefest moment. Then she fired one last bullet, finishing it.

She turned her steel-eyed gaze to Jenkins.

"This time," she said, "there is no doubt about who lives and who dies."

Epilogue

Months after Jenkins had returned to his Camano Island farm, he walked into his backyard, Max plodding along at his side. Jenkins pulled off the black plastic to prepare his vegetable garden for the spring. He'd purchased seeds in Stanwood and planned to plant squash, lettuce, tomatoes, green beans, zucchini, even some corn. There was nothing quite like homegrown, fresh vegetables.

As he pulled on the tarp, he flexed his hand, feeling a dull pain in his ring and pinky fingers, remnants of his fight in the tunnel with Efimov. He'd fractured two small bones in his right hand and had only recently had the cast removed. His doctor said arthritis was possible in the knuckles. Jenkins laughed. The hand would not be the only place for arthritis. But at the moment, he felt physically strong and mentally fresh. He'd maintained his weight and even increased his conditioning, taking up sparring at a gym in Stanwood and doing more than holding his own. The younger fighters refused to believe Jenkins was in his sixties. His mother, who Jenkins most resembled, hadn't turned gray until her late seventies, and she had lived by herself into her late nineties. She'd told Charlie the family had good genes, if he took care of himself.

He'd had stitches to close the wounds on the top of his head where he'd struck the tunnel ceiling multiple times, as well as along his chin. And he'd had his nose straightened, a hellacious experience he hoped never again to experience. He'd also suffered a concussion, and remembered very little about his battle with Efimov or the plane ride home from Oslo. Paulina had filled him in while he recuperated in Virginia.

Matt Lemore had them both flown to Virginia on a private jet. After a few days recovering, Jenkins spent a week at Langley being debriefed at CIA headquarters. Anxious to get back to Camano Island, he told Lemore they could talk further by phone, and Lemore made arrangements to fly Jenkins back to Seattle and then to Camano. Paulina's stay in Virginia had been longer by several weeks. She had given years of her life spying for the CIA, and she had learned much and still had more to provide. After debriefing her, the agency supplied her with a new name and a new identity, and otherwise helped her to get situated in America. She told Jenkins she was uncertain where she would settle, but she promised she would see him and meet his family.

More than his physical well-being, Jenkins felt mentally recharged. He hadn't felt so good in years, and while he gave some credit to a better diet and to his increased workout regime, he knew much of his rejuvenation was because he once again felt useful. The investigative work he'd performed, the lip balm and beeswax and the cords of wood he had sold were all well and good, but he'd always felt as though he was just living out his years on the farm, each day getting one step closer to the grave. Even after meeting Alex, and CJ's and Lizzie's births, he'd never felt personally fulfilled. He'd walked away from the only job he'd ever truly loved, the only job that made his blood rush and his adrenaline spike and gave him a strong sense of purpose. It was one of the reasons why he had agreed to start CJ Security. Sure, he had needed the money, but getting up each morning and going to work had also fulfilled his desire to do something with his life. It made him feel young again. It made him feel needed. It made him feel important. No, CJ Security hadn't worked out, but he couldn't deny the feeling of accomplishment he felt running his own company.

That rush of intoxicating and addictive excitement had never faded, nor had his need to once again feel that his professional life had a purpose, and that he was useful.

"Charlie?" Alex stepped down from the back porch and approached. "Someone here to see you."

Jenkins dropped the plastic covering and met her halfway across the pasture. He sensed she had something to tell him. "Who is it?" he asked.

"Better for you to see for yourself." She put a hand on his chest. "Before you do, I wanted to ask you something."

"Sure. Everything okay?"

"Are you happy?"

"What? Of course I'm happy. How could I not be happy with you and CJ and Lizzie?"

"No. Are *you* happy? I know you love me and the kids, and you're a great husband and father. A great lover. You're everything I ever wanted and more. Which is why it's important to me."

"What?"

"That you're happy. That you feel fulfilled."

He smiled, glanced away, then back to her. "You always could read my mind," he said.

She nodded. "It isn't that hard. And it isn't wrong to want more," she said. "It's human nature. I've watched you the past couple months, and I've never seen you this alive."

"I'm getting older," he said. "I need to be realistic about what I can and can't do."

"Maybe. But maybe you should let others be realistic. You know what you can and can't do. Seems to me you can still do more than most men, some half your age."

"Why are you telling me this?"

"I just wanted you to know that it's okay if you want to . . . be happy. I'll never stop worrying about you, but I realize I can't hold you so close that I crush your spirit. That would be selfish, I know. Okay?"

"Okay," he said. "But now I'm a little scared to find out who's in the house."

She smiled and kissed him. "You may be a tough guy, but you're still a big chicken. Come on. See for yourself."

Jenkins followed Alex in through the sliding door. CJ sat on the couch watching television. "Is this how you're going to spend your weekend?" Jenkins said as he passed through the room.

"I need to unwind from school."

Jenkins stifled a laugh and walked through the kitchen to the front entry. Alex stood beside Matt Lemore and Paulina Ponomayova. Lemore held a bottle of wine. Paulina held Lizzie, and his little girl, currently going through stranger anxiety, didn't look the least bit scared or uncertain. Maybe there was more of the steely-eyed woman Jenkins first met in Moscow, and saw again in the Oslo tunnels, in Lizzie than Jenkins knew.

Paulina looked to Jenkins, beaming. She had tears in her eyes and a broad smile. "She is beautiful," she said.

"She looks like your wife," Lemore said.

Jenkins smiled. "That she does."

"You've healed up nicely," Lemore said. "You were a bit of a mess last time I saw you. How do you feel?"

Jenkins looked to Alex. "Twenty years younger," he said.

Lemore nodded.

Paulina had put on weight, and it looked good on her. Her hair had grown and now looked like a pixie cut. Lizzie clutched at it. "You look good also," Jenkins said. "Healthy."

"I am doing the physical therapy and getting stronger," she said, not taking her eyes off Lizzie.

"How long can you stay?" Jenkins asked. "Can you have dinner at least?"

"Yes," she said. "I can stay for dinner."

"I'm hoping it's lasagna again," Lemore said. "I brought an Italian red. The guy at the store in Stanwood recommended it."

Alex smiled. "We'll see."

"You found a job?" Jenkins asked Paulina.

"I am told that is classified," she said, smiling and looking to Lemore.

"She'll be in another city under an assumed name, at least for the time being," Lemore said. "It's for the best if you two don't have any direct communication, at least for a while. At least until we're sure you're not being watched. Have you noticed anything?"

Jenkins shook his head. "No."

Lemore had offered to move Jenkins with Alex and the kids, to provide them with new identities, but Jenkins wasn't going to run, and he wasn't going to hide.

"I'm glad it has worked out for you," Jenkins said to Paulina, but she ignored him in favor of Lizzie.

"Why don't we open the wine and see what we can put together," Alex said.

"I don't think Paulina is going to let Lizzie go." Jenkins smiled at the pair.

"I'm happy to give you a hand," Lemore said to Alex. "Just give me a second to talk to your husband."

Alex looked to Jenkins and smiled. "You do that," she said.

Jenkins grabbed two beers from the fridge, and he and Lemore stepped out the back door onto the porch. Jenkins closed the door behind them and handed one of the beers to Lemore. They stood looking out at his pasture and the boarded horses.

"You've got a nice place here," Lemore said.

"It's home," Jenkins said. "Used to be just a place to hide, but it's home now." He sipped his beer, assuming Lemore didn't come to talk about the farm. "Paulina looks good. Strong again," he said.

"She's doing well," Lemore said. "We're keeping a close eye on her. Physically everything is healing, but I suspect the emotional aspects of what she experienced will take some time. She's set up with a psychiatrist. The issue with her brother is still pretty raw. So is Lefortovo. She's been through a lot."

Jenkins nodded. "Judging by the number of bullets she emptied into Efimov, I assumed that was the case. You can keep her safe?"

"I'm not sure the Russians will try anything on US soil, but if they were planning something, they'll have a hell of a time finding her. We wiped clean her background. She never existed. She has a whole new identity and history. You don't have that luxury."

"I know."

"We're going to keep some officers around town, have them keep their eyes and ears open. It's a good training exercise. We might even throw in a couple of decoys just to see how they react. And don't argue with me about it."

Jenkins smiled. "No, I won't."

"How are you doing? You all healed?"

"For the most part. A little stiff, but that comes with age. Still, I've never felt better."

"Have you heard from Federov?"

"I received a postcard in the mail from Africa. It didn't say anything, and it wasn't signed, but it was from him."

"How do you know?"

"It came shortly after you released the rest of the money. I think it was Federov's way of acknowledging he received it and thanking me for keeping my word."

Lemore drank from the bottle, then said, "You gave up a lot of money."

"It was never mine. It was blood money. I didn't like the karma. Federov . . . I don't think he cares."

"Makes what I pay you pale in comparison."

"It was still a lot more than I expected. Besides, I told you I didn't do it for the money."

"I know you didn't," Lemore said. "But now that I have a kid on the way, I know what they cost."

"Wait until they get to college. Our knees are already buckling, and CJ hasn't even started high school." He took another sip of beer. Then he asked, "Any blowback from the Kremlin?"

Lemore shook his head. "And we don't expect any. The Kremlin doesn't like to be embarrassed. They'll let this go, deny they had any involvement." Lemore gave Jenkins that charm-school smile. "Besides, you don't exist. You're not on our books and haven't been for forty years."

He thought of his conversation with Federov. "I'm a ghost," Jenkins said. He smiled. "Sometimes I feel like it."

"It's an advantage, in some instances. So are your human-intelligence skills." Lemore sipped his beer. Then he said, "Which brings me to why we're out here on the porch."

Jenkins looked over his shoulder, at Alex in the kitchen. "I guess we're both big chickens."

Lemore chuckled. "She made it pretty clear the last time that she'd string me up by my balls if I let anything happen to you."

"What's going on?"

"Something I learned from Paulina about the remaining four of the original seven sisters."

"She knows who they are?"

"She does."

Jenkins couldn't believe it. Federov said Efimov was a brutal interrogator, one of Russia's best. Paulina had to have endured hours of agony. Perhaps wanting to die, having nothing left to live for, had been a blessing but . . . still. He couldn't imagine what she'd been through, and she'd never said a word. "My God," he said.

"Amen to that," Lemore agreed. "She said back when Emerson was around that the danger to the four remaining sisters was more imminent than we understood at that time. Putin isn't wallowing in pity. Our assets in Russia tell us he's ramped up his efforts to find the remaining four sisters." Lemore paused. "Listen, this is nothing—"

"You need to get them out."

Lemore nodded. "We're going to need someone to get them out sooner rather than later. Someone who knows the language, the terrain, and what's at stake. Someone who can convince them of a clear and present danger. Someone who they'll trust."

Jenkins nodded. He sensed what was coming, and he felt both intrigued and concerned.

"But we don't have to decide this tonight," Lemore said.

"That's good," Jenkins said. "Because if you told Alex tonight, you might be wearing that lasagna instead of eating it."

ACKNOWLEDGMENTS

As always, it takes a village to write a novel, especially one such as this. I will try to thank all who helped me. Some I can name. Others I cannot. I am grateful to all. As always, any mistakes are my own.

Much of my knowledge of Russia comes from a visit that I detailed in the acknowledgments to *The Eighth Sister*. Though I have traveled extensively, that trip to Moscow and Saint Petersburg remains a highlight for the sights I saw and for the people I met. I experienced the paranoia and the concern—I was searched at the airport and followed around Red Square and other sights for days—but also the generosity of the people, who did not hesitate to provide directions, even if those directions were out of their way. When I got past their stoic façade, I found a warmth and kindness, as I have found most everywhere I travel.

Special thanks to those who helped me with the spycraft. We didn't agree on everything, and at times I asked, "Is it beyond the realm of fiction?" Getting out of Lefortovo was particularly difficult, but we finally came up with a plan that might work, at least within the pages of a novel. I am grateful for their generous help.

Special thanks to John Black and others who helped with the Russian language. Again, I'm sure I made mistakes, but hopefully not too many, and none that butchered the language too much.

Getting Charles Jenkins and the other characters out of Saint Petersburg was another problem, especially after I froze Neva Bay and the Gulf of Finland, which does happen. We experienced a partially frozen Saint Petersburg on our visit. I came to the conclusion that a small aircraft would be one of my few options, but I've never flown an airplane and I sensed to do so would be harrowing in the conditions I had created. Ah, tension! Luckily, I have a good friend, Rodger Davis, who flew for the navy and has flown his Cessna in Alaska for decades, sometimes in similar harrowing conditions. Rodger, always willing to help, answered dozens of questions, corrected many mistakes, and offered insightful suggestions to bring the scenes alive. He even gave me the name of a pilot who could fly in such conditions and did so, usually while singing the Doors. Rod Studebaker was particularly fond of "Light My Fire." Rodger is also a talented and gifted writer, and I've been mesmerized by several of his novels.

Special thanks also to my sister Bonnie, who is a clinical pharmacist and helped me with the drug to make it look like Paulina suffered a heart attack. Again, I had to improvise a bit and to ask whether it was "beyond the realm of fiction." The improvisation was mine.

Special thanks also to my good friend and law school roommate, Charles Jenkins. In law school I used to tell Chaz that he was larger than life. In many ways he is. I told him I would someday put him in a novel, and did so in my first, *The Jury Master*. He was kind enough to let me continue the character in *The Eighth Sister* and *The Last Agent*. Chaz has never been in the CIA, or to Russia, at least not that I know of. He is a good man with a good heart, and I consider him a blessed friend.

Thank you to Maureen Harlan of La Conner, Washington, who helped to raise funds to build a library in that city by purchasing a character in this novel. Maureen is a lovely lady nothing like the cantankerous waitress in my novel. I'm always pleased when my novels can be used for such worthwhile projects as a new library.

Thank you to Meg Ruley, Rebecca Scherer, and the entire Jane Rotrosen Agency. Talk about a one-stop shop! They negotiate my contracts, read and comment on the drafts of my novels, analyze my royalties, and handle just about everything else book related. Recently Meg and Rebecca traveled from New York to Seattle for a single night—to celebrate a milestone at a party thrown by Amazon Publishing in my honor. Talk about dedication and kindness. I am so very grateful to you both.

Thank you to agent Angela Cheng Caplan, who has been nothing short of spectacular. Angela negotiated the sale of *The Eighth Sister* and *The Last Agent* to Roadside Productions for development into a major television series. I'm excited to see Charles Jenkins and the crew come to life on the screen.

Special thanks also to the team at Amazon Publishing. From the moment I first met the team at APub, they have treated me as a professional writer. They go to great lengths to ensure that I am treated with respect and dignity, and that everything that can be done is done to ensure the success of my novels. Thank you to my developmental editor, Charlotte Herscher. We've collaborated now on a dozen novels, and Charlotte is remarkable for making sure everything makes sense, and that the tension and suspense remain a priority throughout the pages.

Thank you to my copyeditor, Scott Calamar, who has also worked with me on many of my novels and no doubt has scratched his head at some of my punctuation. I'm always happy to thank those who make me look smart.

Thank you to publisher Mikyla Bruder; Jeff Belle, vice president of Amazon Publishing; associate publishers Hai-Yen Mura and Galen Maynard; and everyone on the Amazon Publishing team. I'm grateful to call Amazon Publishing my home, and it was kind of each of you to put busy lives on hold to help me celebrate the recent milestone. I've enjoyed getting to know each of you.

Thank you to Dennelle Catlett, publicist, for the tireless promotion of me and my work. Special thanks for handling the many requests for the use of my novels for charitable purposes.

Thank you to Laura Constantino, Lindsey Bragg, and Kyla Pigoni, the marketing team that works to keep me and my novels relevant. And a special thanks to Sarah Shaw for all the fabulous parties and fabulous gifts that bring my family wonderful surprises and memories.

Thank you to Sean Baker, head of production; Laura Barrett, production manager; and Oisin O'Malley, art director, who oversees the design of the amazing covers, including those for *The Eighth Sister* and *The Last Agent*. Each time I get to see the cover, I'm stunned at the depth to which he understands the novel and can make it come to life. This cover was simply amazing.

Most importantly, thank you to Gracie Doyle, my editor at Thomas & Mercer. Writing can be a lonely profession, but I'm blessed to have an editor who keeps me on the move for signings and events, and who has become a dear friend. Thanks for everything you do, from the initial editing of my novels to responding to each of my many questions, not to mention making this about as fun a job as anyone could ever hope for. I look forward to placing many more books in your capable hands, and to our Christmas celebrations.

Thank you to Tami Taylor, who runs my website, creates my newsletters, and keeps me alive on the Internet. Thank you to Pam Binder, president of the Pacific Northwest Writers Association, for her support of my work.

I dedicated this novel to my friend Martin Bantle. Like me, Martin was a San Francisco Bay Area kid with a lot of friends, but he moved to Seattle to be with the woman he loved. In the 1980s, Martin and I spent a memorable week in Hawaii with two other friends. We traveled the same month that the movie *The Dream Team* came out, and youthful hubris being at a peak, we immediately dubbed ourselves "The Dream Team." It remains one of the best trips I have ever taken. I will fondly remember Martin's classic smile and sharp wit. Though busy with family in Seattle, including his lovely wife and two supremely athletic and intelligent children, Martin always found the time to include me and my family in celebrations. I only wish there were many more such celebrations.

Martin's sudden passing is another reminder that none of us is promised a tomorrow. So, I say yes to today, even when the yes is inconvenient or impractical or I just don't have the time. Saying yes has taken me to China, Cuba, Cabo, Africa, and many other places. It has helped me to make friends with people I would have never otherwise met. It has given me the courage to golf with strangers, and to finally break 100 on my scorecard—and no, that is not nine holes! I go to lunch with friends when I don't think I have the time, and I spend a moment with others just to be present, because I know I will need their presence someday. Most importantly, saying yes has taught me to cherish each moment, and to treat getting old—and the inevitable difficulties that come with aging—as a gift, and never as a burden. Thank you for that gift, Martin.

My mother, who gave me my love of reading and writing, is eighty-seven years old. She can no longer read this print, but she can hear the narration. I should be so blessed to reach the same milestone. You remain an inspiration to me.

I'm blessed to share today with a wife I love, a truly remarkable woman in so many ways it would be impossible to list them all here. She gave me two children who have grown to be two of the finest people I know. I'm proud to be their father. I love you all. Thanks for putting up with my imaginary friends, my mood swings, the long hours I spend at the computer, and the times when I've been away to promote my novels.

No man could be any richer or more blessed.

Until our next adventure, faithful readers, wherever it takes us, thank you for making my todays.

ABOUT THE AUTHOR

Photo © 2018 Douglas Sonderss

Robert Dugoni is the *New York Times*, *Wall Street Journal*, *Washington Post*, and Amazon Charts bestselling author of the Tracy Crosswhite series, which has sold more than five million books worldwide; the David Sloane series; *The Eighth Sister*, the first book in the Charles Jenkins series; the stand-alone novels *The 7th Canon*, *Damage Control*, and *The Extraordinary Life of Sam Hell*, for which he won an AudioFile Earphones Award for the narration; and the nonfiction exposé *The Cyanide Canary*, a *Washington Post* Best Book of the Year. He is the recipient of the Nancy Pearl Book Award for fiction and the Friends of Mystery Spotted Owl Award. He is a two-time finalist for the International Thriller Award, the Harper Lee Prize for legal fiction, the Silver Falchion Award for mystery, and the Mystery Writers of America Edgar Award. His books are sold in more than twenty-five countries and have been translated into more than two dozen languages. Visit his website at www.robertdugoni.com.